Books by Eugene FitzMaurice

CIRCUMSTANTIAL EVIDENCE

THE HAWKELAND CACHE

THE HAWKELAND CACHE

Eugene FitzMaurice

WYNDHAM BOOKS • NEW YORK

Designed by Eve Kirch
Manufactured in the United States of America

1 2 3 4 5 6 7 8 9 10

Library of Congress Cataloging in Publication Data

FitzMaurice, Eugene.
The Hawkeland Cache.
I.   Title.
PZ4.F58H65Haw   [PS3556.187]   813'.54
80-162

ISBN 0-671-25345-X

The author is grateful for permission to reprint the following:

Excerpts from *Sunflower Splendor,* edited by Wu-chi Liu and Irving Lo. Copyright ©
1975 by Wu-Chi Liu and Irving Lo. Reprinted by permission of Doubleday & Company,
Inc.

Four lines of Wallace Stevens poetry from *Souvenirs and Prophecies* by Holly Stevens.
Copyright © 1966, 1976, by Holly Stevens. Reprinted by permission of Alfred A. Knopf,
Inc.

For my children, David and Hillary,
with deepest love
And for my niece, Sara Abigail Quinn,
who will know forever
the joy of being a child

AUTHOR'S NOTE

This is a novel about the Jesuits. It is about other things as well, but it is primarily about the Jesuits. Many readers will believe that the story of *The Hawkeland Cache* is a libel on the Society of Jesus, the Jesuits' real name. To them, the Jesuits are only kindly clerics conducting colleges and preparatory schools. In fact, however, ample historical evidence exists to support every aspect of the novel, although the book *is* a novel.

Most source material on the Society is either irrationally hostile or slavishly forgiving. I was fortunate enough to be given access to various collections of Jesuit material which transcend both of these categories. The individuals who made the books available to me wish to remain anonymous. They know who they are and I thank them.

I have used all Jesuit source material only as a starting point, carefully comparing it with the works of historians who have no prejudice for or against the Jesuits. Rather than simply name these sources, I will here relate them to the episodes in the novel which they supported.

The Jesuits did have an Indian army in Paraguay. The story is told by contemporaneous authors *(The History of Paraguay,* Pierre Charlevois, London: L. Davis, 1796), and confirmed by later writers *(A Vanished Arcadia in a Jesuit Land,* Robert Gredon, New York: The Dial Press, 1924).

A Jesuit did perfect both the camellia and strychnine. *(The Jesuits in the Philippines,* H. de la Costa, Cambridge, Massachusetts: Harvard University Press, 1967). Another did give his life in the slave trade *(Peter Claver,* Angel Vattierra, Westminster, Maryland: The Newman Press). And the Society maintained successful espionage rings in England for many decades *(The English Jesuits—From Campion to Martindale,* Bernard Bosset, New York: Herder & Herder, 1968).

If the concept of a fleet under Jesuit command seems outrageous, consider the life of Alexis Clerc, a career French naval officer who sailed to Shanghai, became a Jesuit, and was martyred in 1871, only a few years before the start of the Hawkeland mission *(Alexis Clerc, Sailor and Martyr,* New York: C. & J. Sodbir, 1879).

Similarly, the fact of an anti-Nazi Jesuit underground is told from both a religious point of view *(The Prison Meditations of Father Delp,* New York: Herder & Herder, 1953) and by a section chief of the Gestapo *(Hitler's Secret Service,* Walter Schellenberg, New York: Harper & Row, 1956).

Jesuit operations in Russia are detailed in Clarkson's *History of Russia* and James H. Billington's *The Icon and the Axe.* The latter was also a primary source for information on religion in Russia and the administration of Pobedonostsev. The espionage activities in Poland were the subject of the Lothian Essay at Jesus College Oxford in 1892 *(The Jesuits in Poland,* A. F. Pollard, reprinted by Haskell House, New York, 1971).

The priests connected with Peter the Painter and the McHenry mission, and their exploits, are fictional. All of the other Jesuits named in the book lived, and the deeds I ascribe to them were actually performed by them.

For some of the Wall Street material, I relied on John Brooks' *Once in Golconda,* as well as my own observations. The principal reference sources on anarchists and their philosophy were Barbara Tuchman's *The Proud Tower,* and *The Russian Anarchists,* by Paul Avrich.

I consulted many sources on Russia. Principal among them was *The Shadow of the Winter Palace,* by Edward Crankshaw, whose descriptions of the Decembrists, the Alexander Ravelin, and the social life of Tsarist Russia were invaluable.

For the history of opium, the story of the Jesuit church of Saint Paul's, and much of the geography of Peter's mission, I relied on *The Opium War,* by Peter Ward Fay. Although Hugh Trevor-Roper has shown, in *The Hermit of Peking,* that Edmund Backhouse was generally a liar, I have consulted the latter's *Annals and Memoirs of the Court of Peking,* not for facts, but for social commentary. A number of additional books were helpful for historical and cultural information, particularly *Myths and Legends of China,* by E.T. Chalmers Werner. The organization and history of Chinese intelligence operations is based on *The Chinese Secret Service,* by Richard Deacon.

For the Antarctic section, I relied on *Shackleton's Incredible Journey,* and his two-volume *The Heart of the Antarctic*; Amundsen's *The South Pole*; Elizabeth Huxley's *Scott of the Antarctic*; and two photo journals, *Scott's Last Voyage,* edited by Ann Savours, and *Captain Scott and the Antarctic Tragedy,* by Peter Brent. The mechanics for the repair of the *Python* are outlined in *Supership* by Noel Mostert.

Whatever I did with the material derived from these sources is my responsibility, and cannot be considered the fault of others.

Special thanks go to both my agent, Theron Raines, for suggesting that I write about the Jesuits, and encouraging me after I began to do so; and my publisher, Lawrence Freundlich, whose suggestions added immeasurably to whatever strengths the book may have.

Finally, and first, I thank my wife, Ann, for reasons which only we can share.

From the Associated Press, March 20, 1979

"The Peoples Republic of China has requested that the Jesuits return to our country to teach in Aurora University in Shanghai."

> DENG XIAOPING
> Deputy Premier of China

"The Jesuits would be happy and wish to serve China as they used to during the last 400 years. Today there are more and greater opportunities than before, and it is our responsibility to take advantage of them."

> REV. PEDRO ARRUPE
> Superior General of the
> Society of Jesus

"The end justifies the means."

> ST. IGNATIUS LOYOLA
> Founder of the Jesuits

PROLOGUE

On the first shop morning of 1911, shortly after Winston Churchill became Home Secretary, the London Metropolitan Police surrounded the Sidney Street hideout of three suspected bank robbers. Because they were believed to be responsible for the murder of two constables several days earlier, a call was placed to the Home Office requesting the issuance of arms to the police. The telephone was answered by Churchill's Parliamentary Under-Secretary, Charles Masterman, who listened for a moment and said, "Sir, it's the police."

Churchill, who had been reading *Emma,* lifted his slippered feet from an ottoman, placed the book on his desk, and walked to the boxed telephone grinning. He removed the Jamaica corona from his mouth and said, "This is going to be an exciting job." Taking the receiver, he said, "Home Secretary."

"Sir, this is Principal Superintendent Escott. We have three gentlemen in a building. Anarchists we believes them to be, sir. May be the boys from the Houndsditch job. Armed, if we're right. I'd like my men to meet 'em equal-like."

"Arm the constables as you see fit, Principal Superintendent. And bring up field pieces. I want no chances taken on their escape."

Field pieces, Escott thought. The papers is right. He is crazy. "Yes, sir. And thank you, sir."

"Do you believe the Painter to be among them?"

"Yes, sir."

"Then there will be a book in the building. Take the men or kill them. But bring me the book."

"Yes, sir. As soon as it's done."

"Oh no!" Churchill had no intention of relying on others to bring him the prize which the Jesuits had dangled before him. He would personally supervise its recovery, or its destruction. "I'll be down," he told Escott. The Home Secretary hung up, turned to his aide, and said, "Ah, I think the search is nearly at an end."

The search for Peter the Painter, the artist assassin who once terrorized Russia, began thirteen years before in Moscow. It was there that he had been imprisoned in the Peter and Paul Fortress by Melikov's Third Section Police before being transported to the Imperial retreat at Tsarskoye Selo for execution. The fortress, long and low to the ground, was built by Peter the Great, who christened its official use by torturing his son to death there. It is, ironically, dominated by the airy, slender spire of the cathedral built into it as a joke by Peter's favorite architect, Rastrelli. The original dungeon block, the Alexander Ravelin, is an entryway to hell: wholly surrounded by water within the fortress, which is itself behind a moat, the Ravelin is a single piece of stone. Every cell is a cave carved from the block, connected to reality only by the steel rings which hang from the walls and keep clamped the necks, hands, and feet of prisoners. It was there that Radischev was kept by Catherine; that Dostoevsky and Bakunin awaited death; and Peter the Painter was prepared for transport in the Death Box.

So important was his delivery to the Tsar, dead or alive, that neither the Master of the Fortress nor his warders were permitted any contact with the Painter. His chains permitted him enough play to reach, lying on his belly, a slot through which were passed bowls of rainwater and chunks of maggot-ridden bread. So great was the fear that he would escape, he was permitted no visitors, no priests, no mail. The only break in his absolute detention was by personal order of His Imperial Majesty Nicholas II.

The Painter's mother had asked the mitered priest of her department to draft a petition to the Tsar. (Most priests of lower rank were illiterate.) The petition was received by Nicholas at his Crimean resort at Livordia, and begged that he grant her the mercy of a brief, guarded meeting with her son, who, she admitted, should die for his crime. The letter concluded: "You, descendant of the great Nicholas I, who showed clemency to the families of the Decembrists, are begged to perpetuate the glorious mercy of your dynasty. As they died for their crimes after seeing their loved ones, may my son be condemned after kissing his mother one last time."

Nicholas was a shallow, stolid man who hated even the slightest contact with his people. Like all in his line, however, he was dim-witted enough to believe himself a great ruler. And great rulers showed mercy. The petition was granted.

One week before Nicholas left for Tsarskoye Selo, where he planned to watch Peter hang, the assassin's mother met her son in the fortress master's office. She had been warned that her son's appearance would be shocking: he would be clothed only in ropes of chains.

The master asked if she, a Christian woman, could endure her son's nakedness. "Before there were Christians," she said, "there were mothers." A typical enough response, the master thought, for an anarchist's mother. The Painter was brought in under guard. The meeting was brief and conducted at a distance of three feet. At the end the Painter said, "I must go now, Mother, to my death." Unable to control herself, the woman leaped forward, screaming, and embraced her son. Guards pulled her back and led the Painter out. In the hall he was subjected to a thorough body search which took several minutes. Traditionally, the final, most distasteful part of the search, inserting three fingers up the prisoner's forcibly spread buttocks, was performed by the most junior guard. When he had finished, the senior guards began to laugh and pulled on the prisoner's neck chain. Then he was dragged down the hall to his cage.

On the day of transportation Peter was once again brought naked to the master's office. The search was repeated and he was dressed in a thin shroud which draped over his shoulders. A four-by-one-inch steel collar was placed around his neck and locked at the back. Hanging from the lock were two chains, the pinion. The prisoner's hands were secured at shoulder level by the pinion, and leg irons were fastened around his ankles. A long chain was threaded through the leg irons and run up through the pinion, then dropped again and fastened to a leather belt. He was hooded and led hopping to the courtyard.

The master proudly led the procession of guards, warders, curious noblemen, and the Painter. While he had had nothing to do with the capture, the master was of a sufficient rank to be able to claim a share in the credit of the Third Section Police. He had, after all, held the young assassin for delivery. And the Tsar very much wanted to receive this package.

As the group moved along the only above-ground corridor in the prison, the master's contemplation of the rewards certain to come from the Tsar was interrupted by the mutterings of a mitered priest assigned to say the Office of the Dead over the prisoner. The master smiled. No one could survive the lengthy journey to Nicholas' retreat at Tsarskoye Selo. If, by some extraordinary chance, the assassin lived to the moment of delivery, he would be hanged in the grand court of the Emperor's favorite home. If, as expected, he froze to death, his corpse would receive six thousand lashes and then be transported from village to village for the edification of those once called, but now only treated as, serfs.

In the courtyard, the master ordered Peter's hood removed. The burly, red-faced, semiliterate jailer smiled, drew back his head and let fly a wad of phlegm into the prisoner's face.

The Painter did not flinch. He took the abuse and returned the insult. The master jumped back, struck the prisoner twice across the face with his riding crop, and ordered the hood replaced. Then Peter the Painter was thrown into the Death Box.

This security transport, a rolling coffin, appeared to be a wooden wagon. The exterior was a ten-foot-square wall of bundles of hay, tightly interwoven and splashed regularly with water to keep each straw frozen to the others. Anyone foolish enough to storm the wagon would have found, if they survived the Gatling guns mounted on top, that the baled straw was a deceptive cover. Beneath the exterior was a sheet of steel two inches thick. The only breaks in the design were a small window behind the driver's seat which double-bolted and was used to verify the prisoner's presence when the guards were changed; and a small door in the bottom, through which a plate of water was passed every second morning. The rear door was triple-locked and a bar secured over it. The keys were given to a Cossack guard who was to carry them in a sealed pouch to the Emperor.

As the van left the prison, it passed the first of thousands who would come out to see it carry the Painter to his doom. They did as all Russians did when it moved before them, and said prayers for the dead. Common priests, if not abed with their concubines, muttered a few words of exhortation to any peasant standing nearby. Mitered priests waved an absent blessing and cast holy water. Rabbis wondered if they would be next and called on God to remember that He was all merciful.

When the transport was three days out, the guards checked the front-mounted window. The driver looked down into the box and saw nothing. He lifted himself slightly and turned for a better view. When he still saw nothing, he jostled the guard who knelt on the boarded seat. It took him only an instant to realize that either the Painter was in a dark corner or they would soon take his place on the gallows.

The two men jumped down, ran to the back of the transport, and hurriedly unlocked the rear door. Moving locks and steel bar to the ground, they tore open the compartment and saw only a hole. Peter had somehow cut an opening around the bottom door, pushed it out, and escaped, leaving behind his chains.

Desperate to avoid the death that would face them when they made their report, the guards ripped their fingers pulling out the straw floor, hoping foolishly that it was all a grand joke. After a few moments they knew that it was not. They cried for an hour, then walked into the snow, preferring the gentle sleep of winter to the gallows.

The search for the anarchist spread through all of Muscovy, west to the Urals, out of Russia and into Eastern Europe, through the Continent and the northern tip of Africa.

The government announced that Peter had frozen to death and been buried in the tundra.

The peasants rejoiced.

In the years which followed, the search went on in spurts, revived when a new police prefect would recirculate drawings of the Painter to his fellow officers. There was little response. Even then, Russia was viewed as a black country behind a curtain of torture, and European police departments had enough to do controlling native anarchists without wasting time and men searching for an escaped Russian prisoner.

At the end of 1910, a series of robberies startled London. Three men robbed a number of private banks. Witnesses were able to give police artists enough random facts for sketches to be drawn which each witness agreed bore some similarity to the robbers. But the police could not find them.

Then as now, the London police maintained almost a gamesman's relationship with their opponents. Neither side ever armed itself; each respected the other; and, when pressed, a felon could be turned to good use against his fellows. Despite the accommodations the two sides had made, British prisons were as vile as any on the Continent. It was not difficult to develop informers and use them to solve crimes. The bigger the offense, the greater the pressure on the underworld to turn on one of its own members. Armed robberies of merchant banks were very great, very unusual crimes, yet no informer could be developed.

As part of his first dispatch box, Churchill, as commander of police, a duty of the Home Secretary, reviewed the composite sketches and remembered the old file on the Painter which he had inherited. And the current description given him by the Jesuits. One of the robbers, he knew, was Peter.

The chartered bank of Joyce and Sons was robbed by three armed men on Christmas Eve, 1910. They entered through the swinging front doors, and, while one shouted for silence, two vaulted the counter onto the tellers' side. Three bags were filled with money and more than two dozen customers were relieved of their personal effects.

17

"No time for the safe today, gentlemen," the gunman at the door said as the other two ran out. "We'll be back." He placed his rifle under his overcoat and followed his associates to an alley beside the bank. They ran thirty yards along the alley, turned right into another alley, then took two quick lefts and a right through a series of lanes boarded on both sides by the green wooden fences which blocked the outdoor privies of the City's many banking institutions. The final turn took them onto a small square fronting on the Fire Monument. Walking slowly to the base of the pillar, they pulled back police barricades which they had earlier set around a small grate. The man with the gun opened the grate in a businesslike manner, held it up for his companions, and turned to go down the ladder. A costermonger pushed his cart to the grate and studied the robber, who smiled and said, "Sanitary Commission. Care to join us?"

"Coor."

The gunman smiled again and followed his friends down into the London sewers. Once underground they followed the slime-covered walkways to a ramp by the river. The gunmen opened a screen, stepped out onto the embankment, and disappeared.

The police circulars drawn up after the robbery were circulated throughout the financial district and all adjoining areas of metropolitan London. When three men entered a jeweler's shop in Houndsditch, they were immediately recognized as the robbers on the poster by a diamond cutter on the way to his own establishment. He went for a constable, who ran toward the shop, collecting another officer on the way. The P.C.'s clutched their mackintoshes and entered the shop. The tightly rolled oilskins, sufficient in the right hands to kill a man, were the only weapon carried by the London police. Nothing more had ever been needed.

Upon entering the shop, the policemen heard the clanging of a brass bell hooked to the door latch. Then they heard the clatter of pistols, and, finally, the constables heard their own muted death rattles.

By evening the jeweler's statement had been taken and his version of the men's appearances circulated. The most important new fact supplied by him was that one man carried what appeared to be a physician's bag.

This piece of information registered in the mind of a shopgirl in a chemist's on Sidney Street. For several days she had observed the furtive comings and goings of three bearded men. One of them frequently carried a doctor's bag. When, on the first shop morning of 1911, she saw one of the men clean shaven, she became alarmed at who they might be and thought to call the police. Before going to the Mile End Station, however, she followed the man she suspected to an abandoned building being refinished for use as a tenancy. She watched him walk down an alley, go to the rear of the building, and enter it. Then she went for a constable.

The station commander called Principal Superintendent Escott, who called Churchill, and then led his men into position and waited for the Home Secretary's arrival.

Winston Churchill was pleased with the appearance he made. The first Cabinet member to motor to all functions, he had ordered an open landau for the trip to Sidney Street. Protected against the cold by a Chesterfield, tall beaverskin hat, and a flask of Spanish brandy, he knew how striking he was as he arrived at the police barricades. Standing in the car, he lit another Jamaican corona, puffed it for a moment, then watched as Principal Superintendent Escott opened the landau's door for him.

"Will you take personal command, sir?" Escott asked.

Churchill did not wish to appear too anxious; he had already been attacked in Parliament for his immaturity. "I'd like to, Principal Superintendent. But I shall leave it all to you."

"Thank you, sir." Escott turned to go to his men when Churchill called him back.

"There is one thing," the Home Secretary said.

"Sir?"

"If it is the Painter, and I believe it is, there will be a book."

"You mentioned it, sir." Escott was anxious to begin, to lead his men and protect them. He wondered if Churchill was losing his memory, if the young politician could be losing his mind to the syphilis which had killed his father.

"Did I? Well, now." Churchill drew on his cigar. "Well, now. I want it."

"Yes, sir." Escott walked to the barricade which had been set up in the alleyway, took a megaphone from a constable, and yelled through it. "You in there. Peter the Painter. This is the metropolitan police."

A wooden slat covering a window was kicked out and a pistol splattered the alley with bullets.

"Now, now," Escott said into the funnel. "That will get you nowhere. Come out now and let's have an end to this."

A hand snaked through the opening and a metal canister fell near the barricade, exploding short of Escott.

"Very well," he said quietly. "Now, boys. Open fire."

The first volley of police bullets ignited buckets of paint and cleaning fluid left behind by workmen. The flames quickly climbed the wooden walls and arced over the roof. A fire brigade was brought up from a reserve position. The brigade's first officer gave the command for a hose to be run from the police barricade to a horse-drawn pumper.

Churchill walked up behind Escott and the fireman. "Let it burn," he said. The two men turned, but before they could speak, Churchill said, "Let it burn."

Escott motioned to the Home Secretary and led him away from the brigade officer. "Beggin' your pardon, sir, but the book."

"Thank you, Principal Superintendent. But while I want it greatly, I will not risk the life of one Englishman to obtain it. Instruct the brigade only to splash down adjoining buildings. You will receive my signed confirmation of these orders tomorrow."

Escott saluted and ran back to his post. As he crossed the alley several men pointed toward the building. A black curtain of smoke completely covered the upper stories, except for a small hole which was quickly being enlarged. A pair of hands ripped timber from the hole, which then exposed a face, trunk, and legs. The carbon smoke was burned away by the torched manhood of a robber who waved wildly, as if to command the inferno's withdrawal. He raised his hands toward heaven and fell forward, his body's flames crackling like an exploding log as he crashed into the alley. The brigade played a hose over him, knowing that it was an act of decency only, the man having died before he fell.

The hand which had tossed the grenade appeared again, extending a pistol through the same small window. Escott waved once and a Gatling gun team, mounted on a wagon, shot away the wood and exposed the man. He stood a moment, studying his bleeding arms, then fell face forward onto the cobblestone.

A single shot sounded within the building and Escott looked to Churchill, who nodded. The Principal Superintendent ordered the fire brigade forward. In fifteen minutes the blaze was controlled, and in thirty it was dead. Escott led his men into the building. They found a trail of blood leading from the second floor to a thin wall which had been kicked apart. Behind the wall a stairway, and the stream of blood, led the police to a manhole in a boarded-up section of the cellar. Removing the cover, Escott found yet another stairway and descended it into a sewer, telling his men to remain behind. The blood stopped at the water's edge.

Overcome by the smell, Escott could stand there for only a moment, watching with horror as London's garbage, its citizens' feces, and thousands of rats which rode on one another's backs, were carried toward the Thames.

The thunder of the water played bass to the shrill screams of the rats, each sound cascading up against the walls and back into the water, increasing in density and horror as it was tossed about the tunnel.

On a small footpath used by sanitary workers was a square oilskin-wrapped package. Escott crouched, took the handkerchief which he had been holding over his mouth and used it to wipe away the blood which covered the book. He lifted it, placed it beneath his greatcoat and went back up the stairs. Only after he had secured the area did he bother to give the package to Churchill.

"There was only the package, sir," Escott said. "The others were found dead, so we'll never know if we got the Painter, or if he drowned. Or perhaps got away."

"As it should be, Principal Superintendent. As it should be."

Returning to his office that evening, Churchill hung up his Chesterfield and hat, lit another cigar, poured a brandy, and sat by the fire. He carefully unwrapped the package, tossed the oilskin and string into the fire, and sniffed his brandy while the flames filled the room with the acrid odor of the wrappings. Only then did he begin to read: "I became an anarchist on my sixth birthday. My philosophy was a gift from the Tsar . . ."

At that moment Masterman entered the room. "What are you reading, sir?" he asked.

"Nothing that would interest you," Churchill said, "Nothing that would interest you."

THE MISSION

Late in This Century

Chapter One

The firm of Ingersoll & Constance is located at 21 Wall Street. Its closest neighbor to the west is the New York Stock Exchange, of which George Ingersoll has twice been president. The first time he sought the position. Several years later the Board of Governors made him a gift of it after he saved the Exchange with a loan of one hundred million dollars during the panic of 1981. To the east is J. P. Morgan & Co., of which an Ingersoll has always been a board member. South of the building is New York Harbor, where the Statue of Liberty, a gift to America from France, sits on Bedloe's Island, a gift to America from Bedloe Ingersoll, given in memory of his mother. From his corner office on the thirty-seventh floor, George Ingersoll had an unobstructed view of the statue. The floor was reserved for the partners of the firm, the youngest of whom was Simon McHenry.

The two men became acquainted when McHenry received the Ingersoll Family Fund scholarship to Yale for the class of 1966, wrote the standard letter of thanks to his benefactor, and was invited to lunch at 21 Wall. The luncheons were a custom of Ingersoll's, a bachelor who viewed the scholarships as a method of enjoying some of the pride of fatherhood without incurring any of the obligations. As he always did, Ingersoll invited several of his partners to join him at the luncheon, including Viscount Ernest Bowen, his visiting London representative.

Ingersoll used the luncheons to hold forth in a parental way, traditionally ending with a suggestion that the youth study economics, that there might be a place for him at the firm after graduation. It was usually a safe offer. He had learned that the brilliant poor seldom wanted riches; they desired only to change the world.

"I will major in languages," McHenry said. "Economics doesn't interest me."

"Don't you think that's disrespectful?" asked Viscount Bowen, who was unfamiliar with Ingersoll's empty gesture.

"I think," McHenry said, "that there is a difference between respect and servility."

Ingersoll studied the young man. The banker was unlike the fictional portraits of his class: he did not enjoy having the irreverent poor stand up to him. It wasted time and, more, went against the orderly functioning of his life. But neither did he tolerate the subservient. He could not have built his empire without the knowledge of men who had known enough to disagree with him. McHenry had been given the scholarship to study what he wanted. More importantly, he suspected that the offer of possible employment was a hollow one. The youth had been right to speak up, Ingersoll knew. And McHenry knew that he knew.

They did not meet again for seven years. Ingersoll had gone to Oxford to be honored for donating the American Indian Room to the Ashmolean. He invited McHenry, then a Rhodes Scholar about to receive a first in Oriental studies, to join him at the reception. This time the mention of a place with the firm was made in the form of an offer. His friends on the Yale faculty had assured him that the youth's ability with languages would make him useful to the firm's international operations.

"Perhaps later," McHenry said. "I owe the army four years from my reserve officer course. One in Special Forces training, then three in the field." He took a glass from a passing waiter's tray and toasted Ingersoll. "After all, what better training is there for Wall Street than service as a jungle fighter?"

"Don't assume too much about my work, Simon. Occasionally, perhaps even intentionally, some good comes out of what we do."

"I believe that."

Ingersoll knew from McHenry's voice that he did believe it. "Other than preparing for a life in finance, Simon, why do you want to join Special Forces? There's no draft."

"To test myself. To see if I'm the best."

Ingersoll understood and this time promised that he would be the one to keep in touch. Years later, when he was intelligence adviser to the President, Ingersoll put into operation a plan known as S.O.G.-South. The plan, for reasons which will become clear, ended the public careers of both the banker and the youth and brought them together at 21 Wall Street. Ingersoll was in his office there when McHenry entered.

"Ernest Bowen has sent us a deal," Ingersoll said. "I want you to go to London tonight and handle it."

McHenry nodded. Viscount Bowen was a business getter, a taker to lunch, a professional board member. He did not do deals; he only originated them. Someone from 21 Wall always did the due diligence, always put together the syndicate and sold the paper. "What's it all about?"

"I don't really know. Ernest said only that it was to settle an old debt of H.M.'s broke Britannic government."

"He usually fills us in."

"I know. But Ernest apparently wants to feel that he's doing something besides having people in for cocktails. The proposal came from an old wartime chum who's now with the British Secret Service. It seems that M.I. Six wants to do a favor for an old operative."

"A forty-year-old debt?"

"We pay off on long-term paper."

"Of course. It just seems a bit strange. Any conflict with our friends in Washington?" He paused. "Or Langley?"

"Langley is not in this. And Treasury has promised to implement a very helpful tax ruling to go with the deal. If it flies, all well and good. If not, the investor will have a secure shelter. A charming inducement for our clientele to consider a unique venture."

"Drilling?"

"Manufacturing. Somewhere on the Continent. As I said, Ernest wants to feel important, so he's personally going to give you all the details. You'll need to conduct the due diligence investigation so that our friends at the S.E.C."—he grimaced—"will believe that we believe in the deal. Other than that, I can say only bon voyage."

That evening, McHenry seated himself in the first-class cabin of the Concorde IV three-hour shuttle to London. He watched a startlingly beautiful black stewardess named Nicole work the non-smoking rows, greeting the passengers and taking their drink orders. The second flight attendant, an equally striking woman of almost Circassian coloring, was standing in the aisle speaking to the second officer. Her name plate read Elspeth, which puzzled McHenry as he was certain that the word patterns were Finno-Ugric. He strained to catch the pacing and idiom, and decided that the language was Hungarian. An English mother, perhaps. Or father. All crew members in the Tri-National Concorde fleet spoke several languages. He would learn about the woman first, then her parentage.

She turned and began to work the aisle. It seemed to him that she was either a superb actress or her amiability and intelligence far surpassed the level of a college-educated waitress, which was how he viewed flight attendants.

McHenry glanced at the copy of *L'Expansion* open on his lap, turning his head only when the unmistakable scent of Joy filled his nostrils. He watched Elspeth lower her extraordinary figure into aisle space beside his seat and consult her clipboard.

"Good evening, sir. Is it Mr. McHenry?"

"It is. Good evening."

"I am Elspeth and I will be in the first-class cabin with Nicole. Would you care for a cocktail before we take off?"

"*Badacsonyi Szurk e Barat,* please."

"How could you *know*?"

"An educated man should know everything that is important."

"And are the wines of Hungary important?"

"Not as important as its women."

She smiled. "About which you know everything that is important."

"About which I know nothing."

"It is said in Hungary that a wise man is always available for learning."

"I will be available in my suite at Claridge's at midnight."

"A poor teacher could starve by then."

"Not if she called room service. Ask for Victor, the executive chef. Tell him whose guest you are. He prepares an excellent *halkocsonta.*"

"And cherry soup?"

"Served in a bowl of cracked ice."

"Can't you join me?"

McHenry studied her long, carefully sculptured face but did not look further. He knew what beauty she carried so easily, and that she would appreciate his knowing, his not subjecting her to the crude undressing stares of the sexually inadequate. He said, "Regrettably, I have a dinner meeting. And then I have a weekend."

"As have I." She smiled again, less professionally, knowing that he would satisfy her. She stood, allowing passengers to pass, took his order for a tall glass of The Glenlivet with one ice cube placed in the glass after the Scotch had been poured, then moved down the aisle.

Once in the air, McHenry declined dinner. He thought how fortunate it was that the trip was now so brief that no meal was necessary. It relieved him of the duty of consuming food that was at best tiresome and would be a sin this night, when he was expected at the home of Viscount Ernest Bowen, a poor excuse for a banker, but master of the best table in England. Then he smiled. There had been a time when he was grateful for any food at all.

What little Simon McHenry knew about his own background was

ludicrous. Nearly four decades before, he had been taken to a Catholic orphanage in Baltimore and left there, an infant, to be raised by the nuns.

The Home of Saint Simon Stock was staffed by Carmelite nuns from five East European countries. They had fled to America as the Russians moved west. The order's American mother house had arranged for their collective shipment to Baltimore, where the archbishop gave them a home in many senses of the word. In its latter meaning, the nuns were entrusted with the upbringing of seventy children provided by unwed mothers in the years before the Supreme Court reversed a millennium of common law and ruled that the unborn living are without rights. The nuns named Simon for the founder of their order and the fort located a mile away.

He was a strangely handsome child, with blond hair and Aryan features dominated by pale blue eyes set in a mildly Oriental cast. Because of the eyes, he was never adopted. Parents, he soon learned, wanted a provenance for a child, as a collector does for any treasure; and the orphanage did not have even the usual scraps of information to provide. More importantly, parents wanted physical perfection. They would look at his eyes and wonder if he suffered from some strange malady. Or, far worse, if he was of mixed blood. "Sorry," the adults would say as they turned away. "We can't take the chance."

Neither would he. With the sullen maturity that necessity visits upon the orphan, the abandoned child, and the offspring of the divorced, he resolved that if he could not be loved he would not love in return. In place of the traditional emotion which sustains children he practiced the trait which made him closest to his family of nuns and orphans: loyalty. McHenry rewarded the Carmelites for their affection by quickly mastering each of their European and Slavic tongues. It was a task which was easily accomplished. Other children, whether through heredity or necessity, became skilled with their hands or engines or shop tools. He learned languages.

Another talent was Simon's ability to see into people. He could quickly discern a man's motives and anticipate why he had acted and what he wanted. It was a natural defense mechanism for him to develop. Unlike most in his position, however, he had the intellectual skills necessary to do so. He rarely let people know of his gift; it frightened them too much. He learned that fact quickly, and took care to conceal the skill while at the orphanage.

He also learned to care for the other children. Strong and tall, he became the protector of the orphans. Whether in street fights, the dor-

29

mitory, or the classroom, he protected them. This fierce loyalty to friends became the overriding passion of his life and remained with him always. And the children responded: they made him their leader in all things.

It was a position he first accepted, then enjoyed, and eventually came to expect from life. He recognized that all positions of leadership required loyalty to one's followers and fierceness in their defense. These things, and all material possessions, he gave willingly. It was, he often thought, why women responded to him. They sensed that he recognized the obligation that came with having them. They expected that he would give them pleasure with his hard, demanding body. He never failed his women.

At the orphanage school his work was not merely exceptional; it was brilliant. As he began the eighth grade, Simon was called to the mother superior's office, where he was introduced to a Jesuit priest named Quinn. The priest explained that he had heard of the boy's academic accomplishments, and that he was invited to compete for a scholarship to Loyola, the private Jesuit academy in the Baltimore suburbs. Simon accepted and passed the test. Each day for four years he spent two hours on city buses and twenty minutes on the academy's bus, then repeated the trip each night. Neither the wearying travel nor the taunts of his wealthy classmates prevented him from taking honors in every course. He endured because the Jesuits offered him a superb education. Unfortunately, what the Jesuits consider the greatest strength of their seminarians' program is also its greatest weakness. The Society requires most of its young men to spend three years between college and theological studies as teachers, while the gifted seminarians go on to graduate school. These ordinary youths, sheltered in the seminary from the age of eighteen, have no idea of how to teach. As a result, many of them rely on physical force to impart knowledge. McHenry accepted their training and their beatings, graduated an atheist, and left for Yale.

To understand McHenry's disciplined and subtle mind—a mind which could give and demand excellence, honesty, and loyalty without emotional commitment—it is necessary to understand the Jesuits.

The Society of Jesus was founded in 1541 by Saint Ignatius Loyola, a former soldier and onetime prisoner of the Inquisition. Today he would be called charismatic. To his contemporaries he was a man afire with a mission from God. The mission can be stated simply enough: to change the concept of the priesthood. All prior religious orders were designed to live in a cloister under a Rule of Life drawn up by the founder, to dress in his robes, to perform his favorite ministry, and to report to a mother abbey. All of the orders conformed to this pattern, and silently watched the Reformation take the people from Catholicism.

Loyola ordered his men to dress as local priests, to maintain no mother house, and to serve at the pleasure of the papacy. The Pope's first commands were to win Europe back from the Protestants and convert the heathen. To do these things, Loyola ordered his men to give up prayer. Not all prayer, to be certain, but the most important prayer after the Mass. The Divine Office is a series of readings that consume an hour of each priest's day. The obligation to say the Office begins two years before ordination, when a man becomes a subdeacon. Loyola decreed that his men would achieve this rank not two years, but two days before their ordination. This would provide seven hundred additional hours for study and preparation. The Church was scandalized. The Pope was delighted. At last he had priests who valued the intellect: troops with mobility, not men tied to monastic rules laid down by a fourth-century hermit. At last he had thinkers, not clerics who solicited lands and concubines from kings. He had men to do his work.

In order to do this work, the Jesuits acted differently. Where the Church was established, they went among the peasantry, treated them as the monks had treated royalty, and slowly began to win them back. In mission lands, they reversed the process. The Jesuits did not build isolated huts and harangue nomadic tribesmen over the evil of their customs. They went to the crown. In India they lived as Brahmins and worked downward. In China they became advisers to the emperors, then to their astrologers and physicians, built the Emperor's summer palace, and worked outward from the Forbidden City. And in America, where the people and their rulers were supposed to be one, they built a seat of power: education.

Ironically, this temporal power base began to grow in 1773, when the Vatican, under great political pressure, disbanded the order. Until then, the Jesuits in America had worked among the Indians as a society. Now, forbidden to do so, they built schools and academies where, as ordinary priests, they trained the children of the Catholic elite. One of these men was John Carroll of Baltimore, the first archbishop of America, whose cousin Charles signed not only his name to the Declaration of Independence, but also his address, "so that if the King wants to hang me, he'll know where to find me." By the time the Society was restored in 1814, the Jesuits were themselves part of America's elite.

31

Every Catholic justice of the Supreme Court—and there has been one since Roger Brooke Taney in 1837—has had some Jesuit connection. Among the Catholics, only the Jesuits have placed priests in Congress and on the White House staff. America's School of Foreign Service, at Georgetown, is staffed by Jesuits.

There is one final way in which the Jesuits are different. They all take the traditional priestly vows of poverty, chastity, and obedience. But a few of them, those chosen to lead the Society, take a fourth vow: absolute obedience to the Pope. Kings and emperors, prime ministers and presidents know of this vow, and of the fact that those who take it will carry messages to and from the Vatican. They will transmit intelligence which realpolitik dictates must pass through no other source. These chosen Jesuits once served as the Pope's spymasters and now are his intelligence corps to the world's leaders.

Most of these world leaders, both in and out of government, are not Catholics. Realizing this, and knowing that priests can only do so much, the Jesuits prepare their best young men to live in a pluralistic world, indebted to the Society which advanced them. One such man was Simon McHenry. When he was graduated from Loyola School, the Jesuits arranged his scholarship to Yale through George Ingersoll. To do so was simplicity itself, because the debt of Ingersoll & Constance to the Jesuits was far greater than anyone could imagine.

Twenty-one Wall Street is a century old, less than one-half the age of the firm that built it. Ingersoll & Constance constructed the building after the extraordinary profits generated by the Civil War, the Gold Corner and bear market of the next decades, and the firm's private trading treaties with the Orient forced it out of smaller quarters.

Only twice has its name been in the papers against its wishes. The first occurred when anarchists exploded a bomb outside J. P. Morgan & Company in 1919. The dynamite-powered bag of nails ripped chunks of marble from 21 Wall Street as well, placing the building's picture on the front page of almost every daily in America. Duncan Ingersoll, then the chairman, ordered the workmen who replaced the windows and doors to leave the scars as a constant reminder of the danger to capitalism which existed even in America.

The second time was the occasion of the same Mr. Ingersoll's testifying before Congress on the cause of the crash of 1929. A moment before he was sworn, a circus publicity agent pushed a lady dwarf named Claudia Kinder onto his lap. Again, the firm was front-page news. Ingersoll was not without a sense of humor, and admired the girl's spunk in climbing onto his great and powerful hulk. In the years that followed, he spoke of her often, corresponded with her, and reminded her that he was her friend should she ever need him. Tragically, the press also remembered her. Reporters constantly visited her at the circus where she had made a home, where her abnormality was normal. The quiet life which she had constructed in the circus's residence wagons was destroyed, and she went home to Germany for a rest. Because she was a dwarf, she was shipped to a concentration camp and executed. Duncan Ingersoll never mentioned her again.

In the decades which followed World War II, the partners resisted the pressure to move uptown, razed the old building, and built a skyscraper at 21 Wall. Professional decorators filled its corridors and employees' offices with priceless artworks. Only the partners were permitted to decorate their own offices. Most of these rooms were hung with old prints of the financial district, sporting scenes and tombstones, the framed notices of the firm's underwritings. Simon McHenry, an amateur ornithologist, decorated his office with paintings of waterfowl. A glassed-in bookcase in George Ingersoll's office was filled with early American Indian carvings, including several of men in robes, each caught in the act of dying. These were statues done by the Iroquois and Mohawk Indians to commemorate Jesuit missionaries they had killed under orders of the Earl of Bellomont, the colonial governor who had offered one hundred pieces-of-eight for every Jesuit scalp brought to him. The bookcase also contained a diary prepared by the Jesuit Marquette, whose exploration of the Mississippi is commemorated by a statue of the man in the Capitol. Beside the diary, to amuse himself, Ingersoll had placed two framed letters. The first, from President John Adams, complained of the Jesuit presence in America. The reply, from Jefferson, called the restoration of the Society, "a step backwards into darkness." On the wall hung only two paintings, portraits of the firm's founders, and a framed document too faded to be read. It was the certificate of indenture which had brought Josiah Ingersoll to America as a slave.

Only Ingersoll's condition, not his title, marked him as a slave. Officially he was an articled apprentice to an accountant, Ian McCandlish. His status, however, was worse than that of any other indentured servant of the day. While the hundreds of other young men sent to New York in the middle of the eighteenth century—bound to serve seven years each for gunsmiths, farmers, teamsters, and tradesmen—were assured of freedom at the end of their term, Ingersoll was not. Mc-

Candlish had added to his apprentice's bond the condition that he repay the cost of his transport, seven pounds, plus interest and keep. As the cost of gruel rose, so too did the amount of Ingersoll's debt. McCandlish knew that his clerk was brilliant and would take no chance on losing him. As for Ingersoll, he resolved to use the time to plan and learn. If the cost of his freedom was to be high, his time as a clerk would one day repay that cost.

While the other apprentices learned how to record the earnings of the rich, Josiah Ingersoll studied how they came to have those earnings. He learned which type of vessel was best suited for each kind of cargo, which plantation owners could cover New York paper when their crops failed, and how to buy up a man's notes without his learning that his ruination had passed into a competitor's hands.

The man from whom he learned much of this was Anthony Constance, his master's most important client. The firm of Anthony Constance Ltd. had prospered as sole New York shipping agent for the family of Lord Baltimore, Catholic proprietors of the Maryland colony, whose dealings required agents in many cities. Every item shipped in or out of Maryland by way of New York was brokered by Constance. Slaves, tobacco, cotton, and rum all added to the wealth of this wizened, crook-backed little man who lived alone in a dismal home which housed the only Crown-licensed Catholic chapel in New York. Any priest who unavoidably found himself in the city was given two days' grace before official expulsion. This time was always spent at Constance's home, where the priest rewarded his host with a privately celebrated Mass and confession. The only exception to the rule was if the man was a Jesuit. So feared and reviled were the members of the order that the mere fact of being a Jesuit was punishable by death.

During the seven years of Ingersoll's bond, Constance came to rely on him as the brightest, most creative of McCandlish's clerks. Every question which Constance answered was repaid with not only the extra effort needed to keep his vast sets of records in order, but a lucid series of documents which could reveal in a moment the location, cost, and projected return and risk of each of Constance's ventures. It was a type of effort which he had never previously expected or received. It helped to make easier the growth of friendship between the ugly old man and the articled orphan.

Constance was neither surprised nor offended when Ingersoll asked for a private meeting at the merchant's home. He had already learned from McCandlish that the accountant would never release the gifted youth. By constantly adding interest charges to Ingersoll's bond, Mc-Candlish could bind him forever. At the end of Ingersoll's seventh year, McCandlish gleefully admitted to Constance that he planned to do just that. Ingersoll knew that he could run or he could plan. If he ran, he would be caught, as bondsmen always were, branded on the cheek, and imprisoned for twice the length of his period of service. And so he planned, with Constance.

He proposed that Constance buy his bond, employ him as his personal accountant, and be repaid both out of Ingersoll's earnings and the savings he would realize by not having to pay McCandlish. Ingersoll was certain the accountant would sell the bond for a short-term profit and rely on Constance to use his firm when the workload overpowered Ingersoll.

Constance agreed, as did McCandlish. All went according to Ingersoll's plan until Constance called for him.

"I do not propose to retain you as my accountant," Constance said. Before the startled Ingersoll could speak, he held up his hand. "For me to chain you to an accountant's stool would be far worse than anything Ian McCandlish ever did. I know your worth. He only guessed at it." He handed Ingersoll the bond and a fifty-pound note. "There is no place in New York for a poor man," he said. "Go on the road. Become a peddler. When you have learned how to buy and sell, I will make you my agent. When you are wealthy enough, I will bring you back. Then the debt will be paid."

Ingersoll embraced his benefactor and left without a word. Silently, however, he vowed to repay the debt in a manner more fitting than simply tendering money. Unlike his former bondmaster, Ingersoll swore that he would always honor his obligations, no matter how long it took, and without regard to whether the form of repayment was vengeance or riches.

As some men and women are born to write music or paint, to build a house or sow a field, each with a master's grace, Josiah Ingersoll was put on earth to make money. His agile mind could juggle a dozen deals at once, with all the financial permutations of the twelve worked out simultaneously as he chatted with his competitors. He could recall the rates for slaves, cotton futures, and bright-leaf tobacco in each colony on a given day and trade one against the other. He was the first to realize the advantage of employing riders to carry word of adverse weather, shipping conditions, and civil unrest; and he used the advantage to buy, sell, and speculate before others knew of the problem. Like all truly successful businessmen, he was ruthless but honest, recognizing that fairness and sympathy had no part in the equation. The only element missing from his makeup was the affection for an investment which can destroy a man. This enabled him to gamble intelligently and take his winnings, or cut his losses at the most prudent point. When he returned to New York eleven years later, he had added 117,000 pounds to the assets of Anthony Constance Ltd., and he became a partner.

In the years which followed, he continued to add to the firm's wealth, made a successful marriage, and was vaguely dissatisfied. This was because the ledgers of his conscience carried two open debts. Every moment not spent on the partnership's business was devoted to finding a way to settling the two accounts.

The first required three years to resolve. Through a series of agents and employees, Ingersoll bought up all of McCandlish's outstanding debts. Due bills, store accounts, futures investments, mortgages, all were collected and paid. Ingersoll then confronted McCandlish with the notes and demanded repayment. When the accountant could not meet the huge demand, Ingersoll had him prosecuted for debt. Quickly convicted, McCandlish was sentenced to seven years transportation and led, chained, out of New York.

The second debt was to Anthony Constance. Both men had prospered beyond their fondest hopes, but to Ingersoll, his contributions were only what he was obliged to make. He sought some grand gesture but could think of none. Constance the Catholic would have been thrilled if the publicly Anglican, privately atheistic Ingersoll had embraced his faith. Neither man, however, would have been happy with a lie. Constance the miser, who lived on prayer, work, boiled beef, and water, needed nothing from Ingersoll, who enjoyed the fruits of his wealth. Constance the celibate did not even have an ugly daughter to marry off to his friend.

The only kindness which Ingersoll paid Constance beyond the requirements of their friendship was his silence when Constance entertained Jesuits. More than two dozen priests and brothers stopped in New York on their way north from Maryland to the Indian missions. They were given shelter in the priest hole cut beneath Constance's stairwell, food and money to be used to purchase supplies from a friendly trader in Fort Ticonderoga, and horses to take them there. All met Ingersoll, thanked him for his silence, and mentioned his name in their dispatches to the Vatican.

Fourteen years after their partnership began, Constance died, leaving a will which provided that his share of the business go to Ingersoll if he would place his name first on their accounts, and asking that he be remembered in an occasional Mass.

At last, Ingersoll thought, he had a way to repay his friend. Ingersoll had never thought small. He had staked seven years of his life against a career in the New World. He had gambled on a prolonged indenture against the day when he would be wealthy. He had amassed great riches by taking great chances. Now his friend would have his Masses.

Like any astute businessman, Ingersoll knew that one of the best possible investments was a public servant. Weaker than an ass, but marginally brighter; more anxious than a whore to please the moneyed, but with fewer scruples; more profitable than an annuity, but more difficult to choose—a well-bought elected official is profitable for life. Ingersoll spent a year buying every member of the New York House of Delegates. Some required money; some favors; some threats; and a few needed to be confronted with a due bill for all their indebtedness. But each one eventually was seduced. The bill itself was easy enough to pass once properly worded. The colonies were all aglow with cries for equality. Surely no one would object too long or too loudly if the delegates unanimously repealed the death penalty for Jesuits and accorded them the same limited rights given to other priests. No one did. Ingersoll considered the debt paid.

The Vatican did not. The White Pope, who governs the Church, and the Black Pope, the Superior General of the Jesuits, recognized that America would one day offer an entire continent of souls for saving. It would be up to them to connect the Spanish missions on the Pacific with the burgeoning colonies across the land. Josiah Ingersoll had given them a base from which they could begin to do God's work. He would have to be rewarded.

Over the next forty-four years, Ingersoll came to expect the unannounced calls of travelers who began each conversation by stating that they brought a message from a friend on the Continent. Through these messengers Josiah Ingersoll learned that it would be advisable to buy several thousand acres on Manhattan Island, a tract which ran from river to river, and from Wall Street to what the Dutch had called Haarlem. From these men he also learned of foreign treaties before news of them had spread to the New World; of crop failures on the Continent, and the concomitant need for imported grain; and of new ventures for the Americas, ventures which needed the financing of private houses.

Ingersoll, and later his sons and their partners, also performed services for the Church. The firm arranged a secret loan of one million pounds to the Continental Congress, a debt which was settled by the ratification of the First Amendment. Investments were made in several ventures, including those of Robert Fulton and Eli Whitney. In exchange for the first loans, priests were permitted free access to the Western lands opened by steamships and barges, the first step in connecting the California missions with those in the East. As for the second, government officers and wealthy planters in the South were more difficult to move; but the Jesuits sent alumni throughout the country, including Atlanta. Those alumni helped found a law firm, King and Spaulding, which prospered. A century later, two of the firm's partners, Charles Kirbo and Griffin Bell, became President Carter's closest advisers.

During the Civil War, Ingersoll & Constance, at the Vatican's request, financed five regiments of New York Irish, veterans of which later took over Tammany Hall. For its own account, the firm underwrote the construction of the Confederacy's ironclad fleet.

In the late 1800s American industry was racked by labor unrest. Carnegie's steel works were struck by laborers. The Pennsylvania coal mines exploded into open warfare between the Molly Maguires and Pinkertons. The Pullman works was the scene of savage battling between workers and troops. An Irish immigrant named Terence Powderly attempted to bring peace to his fellow workers and progress to their cause while he was a member of the Knights of Labor. The industrialists turned to their financial advisers, Ingersoll & Constance. The firm's European representative approached the Vatican. Immediately thereafter, Pope Leo XIII condemned the Knights and forbade membership in the union. It would take two decades and World War I for the Church to lend its limited support to the cause of organized labor in America.

Ingersoll & Constance was rewarded by being named manager of a new consortium. This special syndicate underwrote the sale of Carnegie's interests for $250 million, guaranteed that all coal burned in the Pittsburgh steel works for fifty years would be supplied by the Pennsylvania mines, and shipped on gondola cars manufactured by the Pullman works. Its fee, paid before there was an income tax, was twenty-five million dollars.

By the turn of the century, Irish-Americans, not yet aware that they would always be hyphenated citizens, were numerically strong enough

38

to assume control of most big-city political organizations. Cities need services, and these can be funded only by taxes and bonds. The Catholics who controlled the cities resolved that the money would be disbursed by the politicians' own kind. The firm of Ingersoll & Constance, whose Vatican connection had always been a secret, was not one of the firms utilized by the politicians. The partners fully expected that their friend on the Continent would consider its debt long since paid, as they did. Instead, in 1905, the Vatican declared that America was no longer a mission country. From that time forward, it was expected to finance and staff its own foreign missions. The American church built its schools and hospitals, convents and seminaries, with bonds floated by their own kind. The Vatican financed many of its missions through Ingersoll & Constance.

During World War I, the firm did not repeat its Civil War practice of supporting both sides. It gave interest-free loans and gifts of equipment to the Allies only. One of these gifts was two million dollars in medical equipment for the Italian army. The money was disbursed by Eugenio Pacelli, a member of the Vatican's Secretariat of State, later to become Pius XII. One soldier whose life was saved by the supplies was a priest drafted to serve as a common soldier, a fat peasant named Angelo Roncalli, later known as John XXIII.

These gifts, and the overall private American contribution to the war's financing, were managed by Duncan Ingersoll. Like all in his family, he was tall and heavy, bald and forbidding. And, most importantly, he had inherited the rare gene of ruthlessness. Beginning with the crushing and imprisonment of Josiah Ingersoll's bondmaster, the firm had observed its founder's personal code: Ingersoll & Constance honored its debts and destroyed its enemies. That was why it had survived.

One reason why the Ingersolls had been able to concentrate their complete intelligence on business was their habit of ridding themselves of the desire for pleasure by indulging it before they entered the firm. Service to charities, government duty, collecting objets d'art, fishing and boating, these were the legitimate outlets of a man of finance, the time fillers which consumed the hours between new issues. They were the pursuits of leaders, of men happily, safely, and profitably married. Women obtained for pleasure, and the women's profit, however, had no place in a private banker's life. Such things were best attended to as a youth.

It was for this reason that Duncan Ingersoll journeyed to New Haven in the spring of 1941, when his son George was graduated from Yale. His graduation gift to the boy was two hundred thousand dollars and whatever time it took him to spend it.

"This will buy you three fine years," Duncan Ingersoll said. "Or two superb years. Or one year of such incredible pleasure that it will last you through a lifetime in this sewer where we make our fortune.

"Remember always that the world of men's affairs *is* a sewer, not a jungle as outsiders say. Jungle animals kill only in self-defense and for food. Sewer rats kill for sport. So do our competitors. And so must you.

"Nothing must divert you from the tasks which will be set before you. Not women, not a longing for a newly discovered pleasure, if any are still secret, not a hobby which becomes an obsession. Nothing. Take this money and enjoy every delight, every perversion, every woman available in every corner of the globe. Sate yourself in ways you have until now only imagined. Then come home, get married, and kill whomever you must. But never abandon the firm. Never fail it or dishonor its debts. If you do, I will destroy you.

"Now leave.

"I'll expect you when I see you."

He saw him ten months later. George Ingersoll was in a brothel in Rio where he had paid one thousand dollars for three nights with a giant black woman known as Chat Noir. The madame had guaranteed that she was a Nubian, and Ingersoll believed her. Nearly seven feet tall, with skin like a desert night and strangely pale eyes that seemed to swim in sperm, each moment that she gave to Ingersoll buried him in a dark growth from which he had no desire to cut free.

Ingersoll was interrupted on the third morning. He was seated in a whirlpool bath while Chat worked him with her breasts. Around his penis was a silken cord which the girl had tied there to keep him from coming until she was ready.

The man who dragged him out of the bath barely noticed the cord. He had come to deliver a message. George Ingersoll was needed at home. General William Donovan, his father's lawyer, was organizing the Office of Strategic Services. He had often stated publicly that "Wall Street types made good second-story men." George Ingersoll was one of the types he wanted.

He was taken to his room, where he removed the cord, came in a splat, and left the girl a five-hundred-dollar tip. Two days later he was in Washington.

George Ingersoll requested a combat assignment so often that Donovan had his typed refusal run off on a mimeograph machine. The master spy knew that Ingersoll was too valuable—planning the economic ruin of Il Duce's Italy and commuting secretly to the Vatican to implement those plans—to be wasted in the field. Ingersoll knew it too, and eventually settled into a pattern of doing his work. It was work which required him to establish close liaison with other young men, bankers, and economists who would one day administer their countries' central banks. Men who, with George Ingersoll, would control finance in the postwar world. As America prospered in those years, so did Ingersoll & Constance. Its Green Book, an annual list of services performed for clients, grew to include private banking (minimum checking account balance required: $250,000); domestic and international placement of equity and debt financing; arbitrage; corporate real estate construction; and investment management for corporations and any individual with a personal portfolio in excess of ten million dollars.

The final entry on the list was entitled "Services to Governments." Under this benign heading were three categories. The first, "Domestic Placements," included a representative sampling of the local debt financings which provided everything from sewers to schools in each of the fifty states. The second, "International," listed all offerings managed for the World Bank and the International Bank for Reconstruction and Development. The last category consisted of only one line: "Other." The total beside it exceeded all of the preceding entries combined. This was the extraordinary sum of money placed by the firm for secret projects set in motion by the United States and its allies.

Every American president learns soon after assuming office, if he does not already know it, that he needs the great private banks for the expertise and mobility which they alone possess. The arcane world of transnational finance is as complex as the politics of a Byzantine court, its struggles as ruthless as those of competing eunuchs in a harem. The financing of private military missions, the bribing of heads of state, the construction of governmentally desired projects which the government cannot afford financially or politically: all of these require the quick, legitimate international raising and placing of capital. These loans, deals, and settlements of old debts are always listed as "Other."

One of the ways in which such business is obtained is the constant shuttling of men back and forth between Wall Street and Washington. The great New York banking houses have placed men in every administration. The name of the party in power is unimportant. Only the connection counts. These men never steal, nor do they ever give their private employers preferential treatment while they serve the government. That would be corrupt. Waiting until they return to Wall Street is simply good business.

George Ingersoll followed this pattern. He served in every Cabinet or advised each President from 1956 onward. During each tenure in Washington he put his holdings in a blind trust. When he returned to 21 Wall Street he always brought several new assignments.

During one of these sabbaticals, Ingersoll served as chairman of the Committee of Estimate, a senior intelligence advisory group maintained by each President. It serves to provide the Oval Office with a unique perspective on world affairs, that view which is held by America's leading financiers and industrialists. It was there that Ingersoll conceived the plan for S.O.G.-South.

Special Forces-staffed, C.I.A.-financed, Special Operations Groups were first used in Vietnam, where they operated intelligence networks in the north, led the raid on the Son Tay prison camp, carried out assassinations, and engaged in psychological warfare. After the fall of Vietnam, they were employed around the world to establish, maintain, and destabilize governments which the United States wished to either support or destroy.

Every government which America wanted to influence needed men for one of these operations at some time. S.O.G. teams often equipped, trained, and led insurgent elements against governments which they had earlier established out of other insurgent elements. The only constant was that every government established with American help was rightist and every government destabilized had started to move left.

The Committee of Estimate, and Ingersoll, had long agreed that wars of national liberation would sweep the third world, driven by a force stronger than great-power allegiances. The American government was urged to accept the fact that people suffered as much under repressive fascists as they did under repressive communists. Ingersoll the financier knew that American capitalism could not be transplanted to third world nations, but it could be adapted to them. If for no other reason, he argued, aid should be given as freely to leftist insurgents as to right-wing statists.

No one listened. This was because the highest levels of government are made up of nonprofessionals, academics, and planners who are always new to power. The liberal observer who studies government is always shocked by the transformation which overtakes him when he

42

becomes the government. Having achieved his advisory power by arguing that politics must be liberalized, he fears that if he puts his plans into effect his own patriotism will be questioned. And so these men become even more rigid in the exercise of power, in the maintenance of rightist countries, than the professional politician who appreciates the beauty of opportunism.

An occasional exception to this is the man who shuttles between government and business. These lawyers (who are, after all, businessmen), bankers, and brokers are schooled only in the exercise of power. They have no constituency except their own ego and the partners who let them go in the hope that they will one day return with new business. The advice of such men is both valued and suspect. It takes a catastrophe for them to be heeded.

By 1970, the year that Lieutenant McHenry completed Special Forces training, it was clear that such a catastrophe was at hand. Ingersoll argued that Vietnam would soon fall, and with it much if not all of Southeast Asia. It was too late then to do anything but minimize losses. In the rest of the world, however, there was still a chance to win the support of prospective governments.

Ingersoll insisted that there were only two choices: ignore ideology and support insurgents who offered a form of third world freedom; or oppose them, and have them as enemies when they eventually prevailed. What he suggested was one of the countless missions which the C.I.A. ran under an appropriate cloak of secrecy. It was carried out in the early and mid-1970s, when America was concerned with pulling out of Vietnam. The target country was Paraguay, where refugee Nazis and a native dictator ruled barbarically. The people were skirmishing, preparing for revolution under a great guerrilla leader. Send men, Ingersoll argued, to aid the insurgents. He insisted that one of those chosen be the disrespectful, brilliant linguist Simon McHenry. The man he was to contact was named Chechoweo. Chechoweo, like McHenry, had been prepared by the Jesuits.

The Society had gone to Paraguay in the early seventeenth century. In exchange for payments to the financially troubled Philip III of Spain, the Jesuits were given a patent to establish a "Kingdom of Christ upon Earth," a sanctuary free of Spanish prospectors, planters, and slavers.

The first name of the Jesuits' territory was the "Musical Kingdom." This odd title arose from the fact that the priests knew that the principal tribe, the peaceful Guaranis, loved music. As a result, the missionaries entered the jungle by canoe, constantly singing the more cheerful religious melodies. The Indians, intrigued, came out of the bush and lined up along the riverbank. The Jesuits paddled ashore, then shocked the Indians by explaining the music in their own dialect. When they had finished, the shock was repaid as the Guarani sang back much of what they had heard. Sharing both music and language, the Jesuits were soon able to begin constructing the "reductions," villages of three to six thousand Indians each.

It had long been a Jesuit dream to remove the various tribes from the constant danger of slavery. While most priests of the era quoted Saint Paul and Aquinas to support the popular belief that the white man could enslave all others, the Jesuits relied on Augustine to condemn it. "Man should not have dominion over man," the great sinner-saint had declared, "but only over the animal world."

The Jesuit concern with slavery had begun with a priest named Peter Claver. Traveling to the slave port of Cartagena after his ordination, he delivered a series of sermons which persuaded the local authorities to issue an order that no newly imported slave could be sold until he had received instructions leading to baptism. Thus, armed with the authority to visit the slaves, Claver boarded every newly arrived slaver, went below deck, and persuaded the captives to ask for instructions. He then had them taken to clean huts he had built and kept them for lengthy sessions of teaching. At the height of his success, he prevented thousands of blacks from being shipped out to sale. When the merchants realized the loss of profit resulting from these delays, they obtained new orders banning Claver's work. Undaunted, he returned to the ships, bringing food and water, tending to the sick, cleaning their waste, and carrying ashore the bodies of those fortunate enough to have died in transit.

While still a young man, Claver succumbed to weariness and tropical disease, dying below the decks of a slaver. For his heroic sanctity, Peter Claver was canonized a saint.

Other Jesuits resolved to carry on his work. They believed that the reduction, with religious protection, shared labor, and land consecrated to God and man, might serve as a sanctuary for the Indians. They did not realize that the Guarani would soon prove themselves valuable as more than farmers, and so of particular interest to slavers.

The Guarani gift for mimicry was capable of extending beyond music. They had only to be shown the latest Spanish fashions in metal, lace, and waxwork, given the materials, and set to work. Their cleverness soon made the reductions self-supporting. Their skills, however, also made them particularly valuable to slavers, who were certain that the Indians would bring a high price if sold to artisans. Whenever the colonial government attempted to enter the reductions and carry off the tribespeople, the Jesuits confronted them with the royal patent and the anti-slavery injunction of the Gospels. Prohibited by political and religious scruples from proceeding, the Spanish obtained helpers who would not be so restrained. These men were mestizos, descendants of transported European criminals who had married Indian women. Forced by social restrictions to live on the edge of the law, these men had no chance to obtain land or enter commerce.

The colonial governor proposed to the mestizo leaders that they capture and transport as slaves as many of the 140,000 tribespeople as could be taken. In return, the mestizos were offered the Indians' private fields, the *abamba*, and a share of the sale value of the Jesuits' communal land, known as the "God Fields." Correspondence between colonial officials corrupted the name of the mestizos, and they were sent into battle as "Mamelukes."

The Jesuits, meanwhile, had used their friends in Europe to obtain guns for the Indians. While awaiting the arrival of the arms, the priests drilled the Indians. The guns were delivered at the very time that the Mamelukes were called back from the field and pressed into a colonial war against the Portuguese. Marching independently, the Jesuits led their Indian troops to the Fortress of San Sacramento. The Society fielded 3300 cavalry and 200 sharpshooters, who turned the battle for Spain. As the priests had hoped, Philip V rewarded the Indians by declaring them free forever and bestowing the title "Military Bulwark of Spain."

These royal emoluments, however, were forgotten in 1750, when Spain settled several border claims with Portugal by awarding to the latter several of the reductions and title to the Indians. When the priests refused to surrender the people to bondage, Lisbon and Madrid formed an alliance against the power of the reductions, which the Society now called the Jesuit Republic. The combined European troops required six months to overcome their first reduction. After that, the Portuguese brought in a fresh army, and the Jesuits fell back to the eastern bank of the Uruguay River with an Indian force of fourteen thousand.

The Jesuits, as they had so often done before, invited their own ruin. When priests outside the Republic refused to follow lawful civilian orders, Lisbon and Madrid pressured the Vatican to allow the expulsion of the Society from Spain first and then Portugal. Once this was completed, in 1767, the Jesuits were cut off from all sources of protection, and the Republic was destroyed.

The Jesuits went underground, establishing a network of traveling priests, men secretly sent to the jungles to keep the work of the Society alive. As in so many other countries, these men looked for promising youths, developed them, and brought them into the Jesuits. In 1848, the Paraguayan dictator Carlos Lopez decreed that all Indian reduction property was sequestrated by the state. Ironically, the work of the Society in finding and educating young Indians of promise had restored the priests to popularity on the Continent, where pro-slavery attitudes had been replaced by a desire to help the tribespeople. By the end of the twentieth century, the Society was entrenched again in Portugal. In 1910, however, with the fall of their protector, the dictator Manuel II of the house of Braganza, the Jesuits were again dispersed. Many of the priests returned to Paraguay, where they built on their underground network and the patronage of other Portuguese exiles to set up schools and churches. Once again the Society of Jesus sought out brilliant young men.

One of these was Diego Ramon Cabala y Monsurat, who was to become Chechoweo. He was plucked from a parish school in the *barrio negro* by an observant Jesuit. Diego went to one of the Society's preparatory schools, then was given a scholarship to the Jesuit-run Georgetown University. He took part in the beginnings of the civil rights movement in the 1950s, became convinced that America would always be racist, and loudly denounced his host country before leaving for the Soviet Union to study medicine.

In Russia he acquired his medical degree, an expatriate American wife, and the realization that racism is a universally acquired character trait. Publicly the Russians applauded his marriage to a white woman as proof of the success of their classless, non-racist state. Privately they made life so difficult for the couple that Chechoweo again angrily denounced a host nation and returned to Paraguay.

There he quickly established himself as a major agitator for social reform. He escaped the swift injustice of the Stroessner government only because the strongman was afraid to act against a man with such close ties to the United States.

In the late 1960s, several years before President Carter came to power and announced that he supported the rights of all men, where politically convenient, the Paraguayan government, realizing how quickly the secret war was escalating, ordered the arrest of Cabala.

He went underground, taking the name of Cetewayo, the Zulu chieftain of the nineteenth century who had done so much to rid his land of oppressors. But Cabala, always attuned to the subtleties of modern politics, spelled the chieftain's name as Chechoweo so the American media could more easily discuss him. Without the media, he would have no support.

The Jesuits did not concern themselves with Chechoweo's politics. They knew that their best products did not count their beads, attend daily Mass, join the Knights of Columbus or the Altar Society. Their proudest products made their way in the world. Such a man was Chechoweo. The priests knew that he, like any man of disciplined intellect, would rebel against the political and social structure of his environment. They were convinced from the beginning that his romance with communism would die, that his world travels would eventually end at home, and that he would turn to the Society for assistance.

Chechoweo knew that the organizational structure of the Church in Latin America favored not only stable government but had allowed itself to be co-opted into serving the state. Alternatively, the majority of younger priests had chosen Marx over Jesus, a choice equally repugnant to Chechoweo. He was a patriot and a nationalist. He would take financing from any source and worry about repayment—in dollars or concessions—when he had won his war. The Jesuits had made many mistakes in politics, but only a few in choosing men. They were confident that their belief in Chechoweo would be repaid. They succeeded, after all, by choosing men wisely, and seeking repayment only when necessary.

Chapter Two

Chechoweo followed the traditional method of building his army. Beginning with a few devoted followers, he relied on the misplaced confidence of the first government troops sent against him, easily killed them and took their weapons. His raids on villages were carefully controlled, his men taking food only from those opposed to him, with no looting or molesting of women.

The government began sending more and larger detachments to find him. He wore them down and used his victories to develop his reputation in the media. With the increasing scale of his operations, he knew, would come increasing offers of aid, both financial and of men and matériel. The Americans and Russians, the Cubans and Chinese, each sent representatives to tell Chechoweo what he could have and what he would be required to do to obtain their assistance. Governments both disregard and live by the theory that one who will not learn by his mistakes is condemned to repeat them. Each political commissar, *jefe*, people's officer, and S.O.G. soldier put conditions on his country's offer. Chechoweo believed that he should set the conditions. As a result, he fought on without aid. He did have, however, a sense of amusement at the flounderings of his would-be friends. Because of this spark of humor, he agreed to meet with the newest American representative.

McHenry entered Paraguay as Alfredo Aleman, a Portuguese businessman. He introduced himself to the passport control officer in unaccented German and stood quietly while the inspector took in his blue eyes, blond hair, and squarely cut suit. The minor official smiled and stamped the passport. He had survived in his comfortable job by not becoming greedy with his demands for bribes and knowing enough not to question the Aryan young men who still delivered money to the aging Nazis hiding in the country. A Portuguese passport, he knew, was as good as any.

McHenry nodded and took back his stamped papers. He was pleased with how well S.O.G. planning had done its homework. A Portuguese businessman might have been questioned, if only routinely. A Nazi never was.

He rented a car, drove to his hotel, registered, and turned in his papers. From his room he called the state tourist service, and a guide was arranged. In fact, it had been prearranged, and McHenry waited for her.

The girl's name was Wylda. When she entered his room, McHenry studied her with respect. He saw her as lush, long, and dark, like the recesses of the jungle, with the same beautifully inviting approaches. She was Chechoweo's daughter by his now dead wife. Six feet tall, with hair the color of a December night and skin like beige velvet, she was, like the jungle, something which could be penetrated but never conquered.

She absorbed McHenry with as practiced and direct an eye as he had. She smiled at him and said, "I'm sorry that this is all business."

He returned her warmth and felt a true affection for her. It was so rarely that one met an honest woman. "When the war is over."

Wylda shaded her face. "We will win the war. Your assistance will be considered."

"Agreed."

"Leave everything here except what you will wear."

He turned for his jacket and she said, "No. Change into something comfortable. We are going into the jungle."

McHenry dropped the jacket, unlocked his suitcase, and took out a change of linen, a bush suit, and combat boots. When he turned to walk to the bathroom, Wylda said, "No. You will undress here. In front of me."

The idea amused McHenry. It was like being displayed at the orphanage, but here he would be wanted. He stripped and stood before the girl. She crossed to him and ran her fingers through the golden curls which covered his body. Then she hefted his penis and said, "Black men are bigger. Some whites, too."

"It's not the size. It's what you do with it."

"After the war is over."

He lifted her by the buttocks and she held her arms around his neck. Their tongues played, moving back and forth between lips that quickly coupled and parted, then clenched together. He began to stroke the roof of her mouth and felt her tongue go limp as he kissed her beautiful, moist lips. She dropped one hand to his erect penis and began to stroke it and then grasped it fiercely, moaning. Both of their bodies strained as he held her. Then she shrieked quietly as she felt him lowering her. McHenry smiled. "After the war is over."

"Bastard."

"Bitch."

He gently stood her on the floor, then worked behind and undid the ribbon which held her blouse. He withdrew the bottom of the shirt from her pants, lifted it over her head and stepped forward to kiss her. As he did so, his practiced hand unsnapped her bra. He stepped back, removing it and allowing her breasts to fall free.

Her black nipples stood erect against her cocoa-colored skin. He fondled them while continuing to explore her mouth, her face, her ears, and hair with his tongue. When her nipples were fully engorged, he lifted her onto the bed, slid down her pants, and placed two pillows under her buttocks. He knelt between her legs and entered her immediately, willing himself into restraint in order to assure her pleasure. When he could contain himself no longer, he brought her to climax and joined her in the long and falling sensation of delight.

Twenty miles into the interior they pulled the state tourist car into the bush and were met by two men. McHenry and the girl walked to waiting horses and held them while the two men riddled the car with machine-gun fire and sprinkled goat's blood over the passenger side. Wylda was struck in the face, smeared with dirt and goat's blood, and began the long walk back to deliver a note.

> We have Alfredo Aleman, the profit-
> monger who would destroy our country.
> He is wounded but will be kept alive
> for one week, at which time he will
> be executed for economic crimes
> unless the Portuguese government
> delivers one million United States
> dollars to this place by parachute.
>   The People of Chechoweo

Then they rode off into the jungle.

The note was delivered a day later. The car was picked up, driven back to the city, cleaned, repaired, and returned to government service. The note was sent by the Paraguayan government to the Portuguese foreign office, where it was routed to the Paraguayan desk, to that desk officer's American control, and then to Langley, where it was burned.

None of the wire services carried the story.

Chechoweo had been carved from evening. He was taller than his daughter, well-muscled but lean. Years in the jungle had bleached his hair and skin gray and pallid. He was not well: a city man, a physician who had chosen the bush as his home but had never fully adjusted to it. He knew that there was no going back and so survived in his adopted element; but he was not comfortable there, no matter how thoroughly he had mastered the wilds.

McHenry greeted him in the dialect of the Indian tribe which made up a large part of his forces. "It is an honor to meet Chechoweo. Victory to his people and long life to the government he will bring to them."

The guerrilla chieftain stopped his hand in mid-passage to

McHenry's own, then clasped the American's hand firmly. In English he said, "You do not bring us Coca-Cola and Zippo lighters?"

"I bring you the respect of my government and its commitment to serve you."

"In exchange for . . . ?"

"In exchange for your promise to remember us in your days of glory as friends from the old times. And, when you remember us, to let us be among those you will choose from as allies."

"And if I do not choose you?"

"That is the right of a free man and a free man's government."

Chechoweo smiled. "You will do."

McHenry would do, but he could not act. The American plan had been for him to teach advanced tactics and techniques to the guerrillas. Chechoweo's policy of bleeding the enemy could work, but it would take years. McHenry could prepare the men for more aggressive warfare, leading to the destruction of government outposts. As each outlying area was weakened, village chieftains in the pay of the government could be turned or executed without fear of reprisal from either federal troops or the villagers. Regional officers could be bought, local government neutralized, and the people converted by spreading Chechoweo's influence ever farther inward, toward the capital. To do this, equipment more advanced than anything Chechoweo could capture was needed. McHenry was to call in night drops of the equipment at villages designated by Chechoweo. This was not to be done, however, until McHenry was certain that Chechoweo would follow the American plan to carry the war to the government. After the slow blood-letting process of Vietnam, the American government would not finance, could not endure, another long war, no matter how limited its involvement.

Chechoweo would not agree. He had run too long in the jungle as a hare to now rest comfortably with a large fox. He liked McHenry and respected the fact that the Americans had sent a man like him to serve in the field. But he did not yet trust him. As time passed, only the liking grew. Perhaps because McHenry had no heritage of his own, he was fascinated by the customs of others. He had been brilliant in languages because he did not merely study grammar and vocabulary: from the beginning, with the nuns, he had studied culture and learned the words only to advance that study. So it was in his dealings with Chechoweo, the Indians, and villagers. He spoke their languages. He knew their ways. He would talk of their legends. He respected their life, and they responded. But they did not trust him.

They moved him from village to village. Every third morning

Chechoweo and his men left one compound for another. To have remained in one place too long would have risked exposure to the Lobos: the wolves, headhunters and mercenaries sent by the government to kill Chechoweo.

The villages that they traveled in a circuit were not worthy of the name. Huts on yellow dirt roads that were really only tracks. Clusterings of emaciated people offering monkey meat and cups of water with a scummy gray cast; peasants begging Chechoweo, the headman, to share rice from bowls that smelled as foul as the children who urinated in their rags and walked around for days, crying with the rash.

The only constant was fear. The villagers were afraid of McHenry, the men and women each for their own reasons. The men had seen foreign officers before. They knew how they worked. A few days on tour, some cigarettes, toys for the children. If the men did not smile at the foreigner, he might not help the headman. If they were friendly, it could be reported by an unsuspected spy, and the Lobos would be certain that the men never smiled again.

The women were afraid that if they were kind to Chechoweo and he did not win quickly, the Lobos would come and take their daughters, only for a night, but take them, and split them, screaming and bleeding, right up the front.

McHenry's fear was of the children. He relied on Chechoweo to root out spies, and counted on his own training when he accompanied the guerrillas on minor missions. But he could do nothing about the children that the Lobos used so well. A girl with a swollen belly might have grenades fastened beneath her coverlet. Lift the rag to see if she could be helped, and steel springs would rip out the face. A child crying in the middle of the road might be strapped to a mine, waiting to be picked up. A youth whose father was with the federal troops might say how ashamed he was of his parent, how much he admired Chechoweo. And, an evening or two later, he might slip away and tell the *federales,* "They are all asleep now." McHenry feared the children, and there was no defense against them.

He feared too the delay in assuming tactical command of some of the troops. Each wireless report was answered with a demand for action. Only the fact that McHenry had been allowed to remain on circuit with Chechoweo, and Ingersoll's sponsorship of his methods, kept the mission from being aborted.

By the end of the second circuit, McHenry realized that there was one other constant. The last village visited was always the same. Fortified

52

like some of the others, it was obviously being prepared as a command post. Set behind log walls which surmounted a catwalk, its huts were clustered near a hidden escape door built into the rear wall. Redoubts had been set up for machine-gun emplacements. A large stack of building materials changed in size with each visit as the fortification of the camp continued. There were two others like it. What made McHenry realize that it was different, that it was the constant, was that when they visited it Chechoweo did not sleep alone in his hut. A boy, about eight, shared the headman's quarters. On the first visit McHenry thought that Chechoweo was simply a man who needed a diversion. On the second stop at the camp he watched the headman leave his hut as they prepared to go back into the jungle. The boy was at his side. Chechoweo kissed his forehead and McHenry knew. He said nothing until they were again on the road. After an hour a break was called in the march, and he spoke of his knowledge to Chechoweo.

"I apologize," McHenry said. "I thought we had good intelligence to offer you."

"Don't you?"

"No. We never knew that you had a son."

Chechoweo started, then smiled. "You are an observant young man."

"It's my job."

"Do not be too anxious to do your job."

"I have no choice. If we do not act soon, support for the mission may be withdrawn."

"Do not pressure me."

"I'm not. You know better. I received a radio transmission last night. They're dropping in another officer. He wants a progress report. Then he'll recommend whether or not we go ahead."

Chechoweo turned angrily. "I will not give you control of my revolution."

"You must know by now that we don't want it. But Langley will not tolerate a drawn-out war."

"Then let them withdraw. We will still win. We are a patient people."

"Perhaps too patient."

"There is no such fault when the stakes are so great."

"If the new officer—"

"Let me speak." McHenry nodded. "We have a custom among the Indians. When a man does good to you, if you do not repay him instantly, you have lost dignity forever. But when a man does you evil, you do not take vengeance immediately. To act quickly is to lose half the enjoyment of your revenge. Like any sensual act, getting even must have foreplay, a sense of inhaling your victim's fear before you enter him. And, if you act too quickly, you will not choose an appropriate revenge. If a man rapes your wife, you do not kill him. You do not even cut off his balls. You bide your time and, when you can, you slowly hack off his penis. In that way his desire for sex remains strong, which it does not in a eunuch. But he can do nothing but suffer. The same way with a traitor, whose tongue must be cut out. And so on."

"I do not disagree. There is a saying in my country: 'Don't get mad. Get even.'"

"Your country may not be so barbarous after all."

McHenry smiled. "But if one waits too long . . ."

"There is always tomorrow." Chechoweo raised his arm and they moved on. "Tomorrow," he said as they started. "Tomorrow."

Major Gordon was parachuted in that night. McHenry instantly disliked him. A short bug-eyed man, he swaggered and preened, making it clear from the beginning that he disliked his assignment and the people he had been sent to serve. He was in combat only to have his ticket punched. He would be happy again only when he was back in a secure office, treacherously working his way to the top by betraying those around him, playing the bureaucratic game which required only bootlicking, not skill and courage.

"Langley is very disturbed," Gordon told McHenry. "They want action. Either this jungle messiah grows a set of balls or we replace him."

"Listen, you malignant dwarf . . ."

Gordon drew himself up to the limited extent possible. "You listen, *Lieutenant.*"

"No, Major, you listen. And don't get into a pissing contest on protocol. Your cock's not big enough. I'm trying to move Chechoweo, but it's his war. He was out here years before we offered him a pitcher of warm spit. He doesn't trust us. He's beginning to trust *me,* but he can't be certain I can commit the government. He wants to fight this war his way. Keep it his war. He doesn't plan to establish our government here and then be destabilized. He's coming around. Don't you fuck it up!"

"You're the one fucking it up. Your orders were to build up Chechoweo's forces with major equipment, then fight a standing war. If you or your nigger buddy don't have the balls, we'll get someone who does."

54

"You touch Chechoweo and the entire system will turn on us. Not that you'll be alive to see it."

"Chechoweo won't be touched. He'll be neutralized."

McHenry bent low to reach Gordon's mental and moral level. The little man drew back in fear and McHenry grinned. "Talk about having a set of balls," he said.

Gordon marched with them for three weeks. In small engagements with the enemy, Gordon hung back, telling McHenry that he was under orders to observe and report, and that he could not do that if he was killed in an inconsequential engagement.

Chechoweo found it all amusing.

They completed the cycle of camp visits and returned to the base. As he always was when he was there, McHenry was most alert. On the trail, everyone was on guard. The possibility of ambush or booby trap was ever present, and an awareness of the danger heightened everyone's powers of observation. But at the home camp, weary men assumed that they were safe. Guards were always posted, and the usual precautions taken. There was, however, a relaxation.

McHenry was bothered by what he considered the foolhardly belief that they were secure. It was, he believed, only a matter of time before the government found a camp which was used so regularly. For that reason he expected an attack whenever they were at their base. He expected it, but he was afraid of its inevitability. He had never killed a man, or even seen his enemy's face. He did not know how he would react.

It came, as McHenry had always believed it would, at dawn, when the gray and purple sky masked the jungle, and all movement seemed naturally soft and furtive. McHenry was drinking coffee and eating strips of roasted monkey. He was standing on the catwalk that ringed the walls, surveying the interior of the village. At the far side of the small square, beyond a pile of construction materials, he saw a man move. Then another. A third. Each was crouched and hard to make out in the violet morning. It was not until a fourth moved from the redoubt to the supply pile that McHenry was able to move his line of vision backward, past the cluster of huts to the escape door which was hidden in the wall. It was open.

Chechoweo had heard them. Small arms fire spread dust across his boot tops as he ran. Within seconds his men were moving out of their huts. He looked to McHenry, who pointed to the far side of the village. The terrain beyond was scrub and weeds, not enough cover for a probe.

McHenry crossed his arms before his face, then pointed to the nearer, left side. His arm cut forward toward the escape door. Chechoweo nodded and ran to deploy his men.

Then the Lobos broke. A few to the right, feinting. The big push came on the left, where Chechoweo's men took up positions to hold them back.

A team of Lobos ran behind the bags of sand and piles of wood and hid there. McHenry ran down the catwalk. He was above them, to their right. If they looked over the clutter to see him, he was dead. Instead they waited for the battle to spread so they could move to the main gate and let in the rest of the force.

McHenry crouched on the wooden walk and pulled a grenade from his shirt clip. Sweat poured from his face and neck. He wiped his eyes with his sleeve, but they only stung more.

He was stalling for time. He didn't want to act. He wanted to stay crouched there. He didn't want to throw the grenade. But then he pulled the pin and tossed the grenade underhand into the bags of building materials. The Lobos began to run out from behind the boards and mortar. When they were going over the front of the sacks, Chechoweo saw them and took aim. A boy about twenty looked amazed as a third eye opened wide above his nose, then he lay dead on the bags. Another one going out the front suddenly turned and ran back into the breach. McHenry shot him, the black top of his head imploding as the hole became wider going through and took out the whole groin on the underside.

The dozen or more remaining Lobos broke cover and ran to the back, where they were stopped by the field of fire that Chechoweo's waiting men put down. The Lobos were backed up, not knowing which way to run. They were blocked. They knew only not to run back into the square, except for one that Chechoweo shot in the stomach. As he fell backward, his glasses flew off and landed beside his arm. He sat in the dust, playing with the blood as it came out of his belly. Then Chechoweo shot him again, a little above the first wound. The man reached for his glasses, put them on, and studied the sun as he died.

The Lobos kept moving toward the rear, then turned and started out to the center of the village. McHenry opened up on them from the catwalk, and five went down in the village square. They didn't yell or clutch at anything or even look surprised. They simply fell down, just as they had so often done when they were children playing war.

The ones remaining began to yell, then ran toward the breach. There was no other way for them to go. They ran and hid behind the sandbags and then opened spot firing on the catwalk. The first two who rose up to fire at McHenry were cut down by Chechoweo's men. McHenry lay face down on the catwalk, waiting for the firing to stop. Then he got up and ran to the corner of the walk, crouched, and opened fire with his pistol. There was no room to crouch and fire with his rifle, and he wanted to crouch, so he had to use the pistol. He looked down at the men he was killing, swallowed, but not very hard, then went back to firing on them after he had wiped his brow.

They kept falling. One of them went over the top of the sandbags, firing as he climbed. He hit the steps to the catwalk and closed. McHenry let him run almost to within touching distance. They were standing across a living-room floor. It was any warm morning at home, and the guest kept coming closer and closer across the room, knowing that no one would make him unwelcome at this close range. Then McHenry just shut his eyes and went squeeze, squeeze, squeeze, and the body fell at his feet, unwelcome at last, blood running out the back of his head where the hair was held in place by a white kerchief.

I used to date a girl who always wore a kerchief, McHenry thought. One for every outfit. Even when we played tennis she used to wear her hair in a little ring with a scarf around it. It always kept it in place. She could play tennis better than anyone I ever knew. Boy, she was some swell girl.

McHenry looked around the village. Silence. There had never been a move to the main gate. It had all been diversionary, keeping them in front. For no reason that he could imagine.

Jesus, he thought, it's all over. Just like that. He started down the steps. Gordon was walking across the square, a martinet on his way to conduct a white-glove inspection on Saturday morning.

"What about the villagers?" McHenry asked.

"Scared is all maybe."

"Maybe!" He looked at Gordon. "Fuck *maybe.*" He shook his head and said, "You ever know a girl who played tennis?"

"Yeah. Why?"

"Just wondered is all." He walked to the rear of the village, where Chechoweo was standing in a knot of tribesmen. "Are you all right?"

The headman looked at him and said, "No. They have taken my son." There was no emotion on his face. Only resignation.

McHenry turned and walked to his hut. He had killed his first man, and now knew that he could do it. There was no exhilaration or remorse, no moral outrage or anguish; only the satisfying realization that he was alive, and that he would kill as often as necessary to stay alive.

There was one other feeling, a heightened awareness of Chechoweo's relationship to his son. The Lobos had hurt the guerrilla chieftain in the only way possible: he was not afraid to suffer or to die, but he was vulnerable through his love for his children. McHenry the orphan had caused that vulnerability to be exploited. He respected, perhaps loved, Chechoweo, and now he had caused him to be hurt. That would have to be set right.

McHenry felt as though he would vomit. His sphincter contracted and relaxed in fear. He knew what he would have to do, and it terrified him. He put on his utility belt, cleared his AR-16, inserted a fresh clip, and hung two more on the belt. He cleaned and reloaded his pistol, dropped his sunglasses on his bedroll, pulled out a can of Kiwi shoe wax, opened it, and drew a black stripe of polish under each eye to cut down on glare. Then he went outside and walked to the gate.

"Young one." Chechoweo's voice cut into him. He turned to face the chieftain. "Why do you go? If you bring him back, it will change nothing between us."

"I know that." He turned to leave but was stopped by Chechoweo's voice.

"One life means that much to you?"

"Yes." He walked forward.

"Young one." McHenry turned again and Chechoweo said, "He is not your people."

"He is your son. They took him because of me. He will return because of me."

Chechoweo thought a moment, then walked back to the center of the village. As McHenry turned to go out into the clearing and the woods beyond, the people looked after him as the village gate swung shut. Chechoweo turned to watch him leave. Gordon ran up to the catwalk and was the last to see him as he walked into the woods, but the old man kept the image stronger than any of the others.

McHenry moved into the woods. It was not difficult to see which directions they had gone. They were very good; after Special Forces they were the best in the world. He never let himself forget this. That was why he did not bother to follow the easier trail to the right, the one that ran downhill, the one spotted with drops of blood trailing off into the jungle.

He stayed with the harder one to see, with branches, newly broken off, at a level nearly half a foot below his own shoulder. The head-hunters were shorter than he was and he had to keep bent over to follow them. The ground depressions were as difficult to see, but the need to keep low to follow the ragged tree edges made it easier for him to keep his mind on the gray-bottom clay beneath. Their bare feet had hardly dented the ground; his boots would make easier tracking, but they were not behind him. They were moving quickly, too, that much he knew. That meant that the boy was unconscious.

There was a good wind blowing toward him, but the stench of bodies living in the jungle was not on it, so they were not close enough for the smell to reach him. There was no blood on the track. The wounded had made the easier-to-follow trail at the mouth of the jungle, not to lure him, but in their fleeing.

The Lobos could not expect him to come after them, but their trail was becoming more and more difficult; long years of leaving an unseen path had become habit with them.

The ground was depressed more clearly than before; the grass was pressed down harder, in a wider circle than it had been. They had stopped here and made their plans. The larger group had branched off to the right, probably to rejoin the wounded, certainly to move toward their staging area farther down the great valley.

The smaller group definitely had the boy: where before the carrier's footprints had been heavier than the others', now one set of tracks was light on the left and heavy on the right. A Lobo was carrying the boy—who had probably awakened, and whom they feared to strike again—under his right arm. They were taking the longer, safer way around. That was why the others had split off: this group had nothing to fear and would not now need their protection. But they would be careful with the boy. They needed him. With him they could control Chechoweo, and the Americans could not replace the leader. They would take the safe way around.

McHenry checked over the entire area. They were at least ten minutes ahead of him. He knew that from the cold feel of the American cigarette butts that he found in the clearing. They were not afraid of being followed, but they were afraid, from habit, of stopping too long in an open area. If they had not been, the cigarettes would have been smoked all the way down and field-stripped. Calm men did not leave one-inch butts.

It sometimes seemed that they could go on as long as they wished, but

McHenry knew that in fact they tired easily and could not make the long treks that American soldiers could. They traveled light, which gave them an advantage over a regular infantry counterpart, but McHenry was traveling as light as they, and had no difficulty matching their pace. They would need to stop again before he would.

He followed the trail uphill. Six or eight figures, with the one carrying the boy somewhere in the back of the column. Not last, because that would not have been safe, but nearer to the end, so that the lead man could set a quick pace.

The woods were so thick that he could see only the green stalks protruding before his eyes. He could have cut through the underbrush, but that would have taken time, energy, silence from him, and he needed them all.

The sky was very blue, and the sun not at all blinding if he looked up, just a stream of yolk that had filtered across the green table of the treetops. He crossed a small creek, stepping very softly on his toes, leaning slightly into each step. He put his foot down very gently. The mud bubbled up onto his boots. He made no noise. He did not let his feet become slippery. On the banks he patted dust on the boots so they would not slide. He knew that they were very close, around the bend of the creek where the rocks cleaned the water. If he can, even a man accustomed to drinking slime will choose water without trails of liquid filth to run down his throat.

McHenry moved very quietly, one giant step softly falling after another, and then listened to the silence as he crouched at the base of the little rise. It was the silence that had been so well orchestrated for him at Fort Bragg. The too quiet silence of the forest when the animals are frightened by the presence of men. The silence that comes in droves of seconds, assaulting the eardrums with the hollow beating: here, here, here. The Lobos would not notice the silence. They had caused it.

He moved, slinking up to the top of the rise, then looked down. There were packs below him, with five guards, and the boy sitting in their midst. There were signs of others, though. The men looked around occasionally, but they were not expecting him, and so were not looking for him. It was their friends that they expected, the men out of sight through the brush, down by the small beach he could see from the rise. It was around a bend where the creek was wider. Fifty yards away. Time to get down there, but not up again.

All right for that, he thought. Meet them when they come back.

He took off his beret; at the crest of the rise his silver bar would flash in the sun and warn the ones by the river. He folded it with the bar inside, slipped it under his belt, then leaned over his weapon as he put it at the ready.

He inched forward without moving a twig, knelt down, and brought his rifle to just above the top of the rise. Pop, pop, through the tops of their heads. Forty yards away. Pop, pop, through their chests. Pop, through the last man's stomach. Thirty yards away. He vaulted over the top. His pistol fell from its holster as he tore down the vine-tangled black dirt slope.

McHenry crouched and squeezed one round for each man coming from the beach. They fell instantly. He looked closely at them all and found them all to be the same. He walked to the boy, who sat looking at him, wondering with his eyes, *Is it you?*

McHenry smiled but could think of nothing to say.

The boy smiled at him through tears, not understanding a word of the conversation that neither one bothered to begin.

"I'll take you back now," McHenry said, holding the boy against his chest and gently rocking him.

"Aiyeee!" On the left! Through the break. You bastard, McHenry thought. Hiding on me! The Lobo charged, machete held high. McHenry pushed the boy away, and fell on his stomach. Squeeze. Squeeze. Fire. Fire. Nothing. The weapon had jammed. He tossed the rifle away, then kicked out, catching the Lobo in the stomach, and saw the blade fall by his shoulder, cutting it slightly. Then he felt the man fall forward over his back.

McHenry was afraid, terribly afraid. This was worse than before. It wasn't the closeness that frightened him so.

But not with a knife, he thought. Please God, no. Not this way.

He jumped up and ran toward the break in the woods. The Lobo followed him. He swung, whoosh, by McHenry's chest. McHenry danced away, trying to get to one of their weapons, but he couldn't reach it. Rrrip, very slowly, the blade caught in his fatigue jacket and quietly cut him open. He reached up and began to rub the green cloth under the gash; it was already beginning to burn. Blood ran out onto his fingers. He rubbed them quickly on his pants, then backed around the clearing.

This is preposterous, he thought. You don't even have shoes on. How can you kill me?

A knife from one of their packs was all that he could hope for. "Swing again, you slimy bastard," McHenry shouted as he balanced himself. The Lobo swung and McHenry stepped back from it, then moved forward, under the enemy's arms before he could get the backswing up.

Now, you bastard, he thought. I'll beat you at your own game. He ran by the Lobo, punching him in the stomach as he ran, throwing the man off balance. McHenry fell on a pack and grabbed at the nearest weapon, a machete. He pulled the blade handle with him as he rolled over onto his back and came up in one motion, crouched, his back to the Lobo. McHenry spun and faced the other man.

They circled once around the clearing, feinted, moved one step in, then out again.

The Lobo nodded. The American knows the weapon, he thought. He holds it right. But he is afraid of me. It will not be easy, but I will kill him.

McHenry's chest burned, but he knew that if he looked down at the wound he would die. His eyes never left the Lobo as the other man lunged, swinging the blade straight down, the blow meant to split McHenry from top to bottom. McHenry turned to the left and the blade came down in the dirt. But he was off balance then, unable to turn and rip open the Lobo's back. McHenry skipped two steps, regained his balance, then turned to face his enemy.

The Lobo moved on McHenry, feinting with his foot and shoulders to the right. McHenry leaned down to block the blow, then knew that it would not come, and stepped back quickly, his shoulders pulling him out of the way. He kicked his left leg around, into the Lobo's kidneys, knocking him down. The Lobo moved quickly, rolling away, but McHenry had what he wanted, a moment to prepare.

The enemy lay on his back, wondering when McHenry would charge him, so that he could cut through his bowels and lay him out on the forest floor. But McHenry stood waiting for him to rise, so that he could rush him and catch him with his greatest weight. He still waited, hoping to get to a gun. He wanted to avoid the knife if he could. The Lobo scrambled to his feet. McHenry charged him, but the Lobo dropped back onto the ground, and McHenry's momentum carried him forward and down onto his own stomach.

McHenry rolled over onto his back as his enemy rose and came toward him, then he kicked up into the man's chest with both feet and the other soldier dropped onto his back. McHenry sprang up and ran for a rifle, but the other man was after him, and he ducked as he heard the blade break through the air. He felt it go over his head as he stumbled forward, turned, and looked for an opening. The Lobo's charge carried him away.

McHenry sank down for an instant as his enemy circled the outside of the clearing. McHenry grasped the machete and shook his head. He sucked in air, climbed slowly to his feet and screamed, "I don't want to use the knife."

But they both knew it would have to be the knife. They both knew and they circled again. Once, twice, and again the *whoosh* as they traded lunges at the air, each hoping to catch the other leaning one way one instant too long. But it did not happen. Then, for the first time, they threw steel against steel: *clang,* over McHenry's head, *ring,* through his wrists and arms. His chest shook with the strength of this thin soldier's blow.

McHenry backed off, holding his weapon like a baseball bat, and swung once, connecting in mid-air. He moved again and threw another swing into the air. The blades met above his head, McHenry's machete beneath the other's. They slowly let their weapons come to each other's tips, and then the enemy moved off first, swinging low onto McHenry's weapon, catching it almost at the hilt. McHenry moved back again, by the side of a large tree. He swung from the shoulders, from the legs, from the waist.

Drive him back, McHenry thought. Now that way, back across the clearing. The Lobo fell.

McHenry looked at him now but did not swing. The Lobo rolled away.

You didn't swing, McHenry thought. Why didn't you swing? You didn't swing. Swing! That's all there is to it. Just swing!

The Lobo was up and coming back across the clearing, throwing a wild overhead blow that McHenry caught on the point of his machete, knocking him off balance.

McHenry moved backward, stopping by a tree, then leaning up against it. He moved around the tree, then followed the Lobo as he turned and danced around him, back to where McHenry had begun. The Lobo swung again, while turning, from off-balance. McHenry ducked, more from exhaustion than skill. The Lobo's blade crashed into the tree. McHenry backed off before he saw that the blade was stuck there.

The Lobo panicked. He twisted horribly, trying to work the blade loose. He was suddenly so terror-stricken that he forgot to run.

McHenry swung his blade, feeling the soft entrance, then the crunch of steel against bone going through the neck, and the soft exit, the blood coming out, spurting onto him. The Lobo's head simply sat on his shoulders. McHenry's blade was stuck in the edge of the tree's bark. He couldn't pull it out, his strength spent in looking at the Lobo. Then the man's head rolled back away from the trunk and fell on the ground, bounced, and looked up at McHenry. The body fell forward, all over McHenry, and bumped down his chest, his crotch, his legs. It just fell, its trunk without a head resting on his boot, the boot soaked red, and immovable.

McHenry fell off to the side. He vomited. It came up warm and vile in his throat, out through his mouth. It poured onto his shirt front. He coughed, and his body lifted itself with the coughing. Monkey meat was coming up through his nostrils. He looked at it lying there on the ground, all that vomit; he saw it after it passed through his mouth and nose. He was breathing it, bubbling it in his nostrils. It was on the leaves. It came again, pieces of everything inside him. A last time, then he sat on his hands, vomit all over them, his clothes soaked with vomit and waste. He choked out hot, weak breaths, though his skin was cold to the touch. He began to wet his pants, but stopped himself after only a second.

He got up and staggered through the brush to the river and washed his face delicately, almost dabbing at the skin. He wanted to be rid of the awful smell, but it would not leave him. He could not close his eyes, because then the head would look up at him, an American in a strange land. He could not keep them open, because they burned from the vomiting.

He brushed his face with his sleeve, got up from his waist, then on all fours, and finally rested on his knees. He coughed again, then sat down for a moment. He finally struggled up, looked across the river, lowered his head to the water, and forced a handful down his throat. Then he turned into the brush. He came out and found the little boy still kneeling with his face in his hands as he must have been throughout the fight.

McHenry gently touched him. The boy cried, "Uuh! Nuh!" He pulled away, fell onto his side, then saw that it was McHenry. He began to cry as he held his arms out to McHenry. He picked the boy up, sat him down, and checked him over for injuries. He seemed to be all right. McHenry found his weapon, cleared and reloaded it, then put on his beret. He held the boy against him, and the child broke down and sobbed. When he had finished, McHenry said, "Come on, son, I'll take you home." Then he lifted the boy onto his back. As the child's arms closed about McHenry's neck, he reached back and grasped the boy's shoulder, then climbed up out of the clearing without looking back.

McHenry came out of the jungle and stood before the village. One of Chechoweo's men saw him and gave the command to open the gates. He said nothing about the child. That would be wrong, he thought. It is the American's moment.

As he came through the gate, the citizens and soldiers clustered around McHenry, then stood back to form a guard of honor for him. The boy rode high on his shoulders.

Chechoweo came out of his hut and stumbled, alone, toward McHenry, who let the boy down. The child looked up at him, then ran to his father. The headman took the boy in his arms, held him for a moment, then allowed his son to lead him to where McHenry stood. "Today" was all that he said.

McHenry nodded. "First," he said, "there is vengeance to be done. Not after waiting, but still according to the custom of your people."

"What vengeance?"

"The Lobos knew where you would be. They knew about the escape door and used it. It can only be opened from inside. Someone let them in, not to kill you but to steal your son and neutralize you.

"I was wrong. I told you that we did not know that you had a son. I didn't. My government did."

McHenry turned and walked toward Gordon, who was standing outside his hut. The little man ran, but was blocked by villagers who had heard. They moved forward, tightening a circle until McHenry and Gordon were inches apart. Without a word, McHenry backflipped the major, struck him in the face, and inserted his hand in Gordon's mouth. Gordon struggled desperately, twisting and begging until his animal screams were cut off by McHenry's hand forcing his jaws apart. Just before he shut his eyes, Gordon saw McHenry's knife flash once. He tried desperately to faint, but was fully awake when McHenry cut out his tongue.

George Ingersoll would not let the army imprison McHenry during the investigation. Instead, he was sent to the Arctic Warfare School while the facts were collected. Gordon, and others in S.O.G.-South, had kept important facts from both McHenry in the field and the Committee of Estimate in Washington. Soldiers had decided to control a civilian operation, and they had failed. The little martinet was pensioned off; Ingersoll resigned; and McHenry was permitted to leave the army with a promise of non-prosecution.

Chechoweo withdrew into the hills, vowing to fight his war of attrition without any man's aid.

Ingersoll, who had arranged for McHenry's quick exit from the army, again offered the younger man a position with his firm. He accepted and, seven years later, Simon McHenry was made a partner of Ingersoll & Constance.

Chapter Three

Viscount Ernest Bowen was perfectly equipped for each of the few duties which life had assigned to him. Sturdy enough to shake hands, sociable enough to be an eligible extra man when needed by a hostess, immoral enough to pimp for a prospective client, wealthy enough to retain a French chef and discreet house staff, he was the perfect London manager for Ingersoll & Constance.

Of the two caricatures of British aristocrat—the lean semi-schooled, condescending old boy, and the wine-faced, dog-loving, good-shoot country cousin—he was decidedly the former. Educated at Gordonstoun, he had been sent down from Cambridge, the first male in his line to win neither a degree—which was acceptable—nor a blue—which was not. A series of cordial letters between tutors and his father put a patina on the truth: Ernest Bowen was no student and something less of a human being.

Publicly his father called it youthful academic indolence, no handicap to his class in the 1930s. Privately, he recognized that the indolence was almost a physical necessity, a rest cure taken during academic hours and required by the young man's inordinate squandering of his physical and financial resources on gambling, drinking, and the importation of Chinese whores from Soho.

While Cambridge today offers three honors degrees, it was once rumored that a fourth degree diploma was available. It was said that this was the most difficult to obtain, as it required the student to gauge exactly the minimum amount of effort required to avoid failure. The university would have tolerated Ernest Bowen enough to award such a diploma if he had not been caught by the local police establishing a brothel of Oriental women in an off-grounds house.

His father, Viscount Michael Bowen, K.G., D.S.O., M.C., could have tolerated even more than Cambridge had his son only exercised the slightest amount of discretion and shown the smallest amount of humanity to others. Instead, young Ernest worked diligently to get his exploits into the tabloids, going to great lengths to insure the presence in every article of his father's name and position as chairman of United British Steel. In his dealings with all not of his class, he also relied prominently, almost cruelly, on his father. Professors, tradesmen, the police, other students, all suffered the social arrogance of the youth.

To Viscount Bowen, this was all the result of some failing on his son's part. He could not admit that he had been too busy as High Commissioner of Hong Kong, too driven as director of the Empire's largest steel works, to impart any love to his son. Viscount Bowen viewed his heritage as a trust. His son viewed trust, like other emotional responsibilities, as a burden he could not bear. When the elder Bowen cut his son off from every part of the Bowen estate under his control, the youth was almost grateful.

Ernest returned from Cambridge in time to be recruited by Lord Logan, a family friend, for his Special Commando Section. Presented with a legitimate, indeed honorable, outlet for his cruelty, young Bowen performed well at Dieppe and Normandy and emerged from the war with what his class termed decent decorations.

Although he would not admit it for decades, even to himself, the war had done something strange and wonderful for his character: he had learned that shared combat forges an intimacy more intense, less understandable, and at least as enduring as that between lovers. He had been shocked to find himself dashing blindly across a field to save a commando of the Free Polish Forces, crying as he cradled a dying private of His Majesty's Loyal Jewish Brigade, feeling personally diminished as a limb of one of the exiles in the Special Commandoes was buried while the barely living body was carried away.

Lord Logan took an interest in the young soldier, first because of his father, and then because of Ernest's performance. Experienced enough in combat to be pleased but not surprised by the youth's emotional response, he had passed the information on to one of his junior officers, a man on leave from counterintelligence, M.I.6. The knowledge of Ernest's potential was filed away to be used, if necessary, in the years, or decades, to come.

Unable to remain in the reduced army as a private soldier, Bowen returned to civilian life and began to recoup the lost pleasures of the war years. Once again forced to live in a world where his father was a man of power, he quickly reverted to the Ernest Bowen of Cambridge. When his separation pay and forced military savings were gone, he knew that he had to work. The British public, remembering that Churchill's mother had been an American, turned their wartime leader out of office. His replacements set about doing what the Axis had been unable to achieve, and had soon dismembered England's economy. The Labour party boasted enough ironmongers and common seamen and assembly-line workers to believe that industry could safely be turned over to the shop stewards. But even to the social-reforming politician who believes he has been sent to abolish economic Darwinism, banking remains a mystery.

And so, because he had no skill except that inherited trait which can only be acquired—good instincts—and because banking welcomed that skill and repelled the new social order, Ernest Bowen chose finance.

In honor of the democratic spirit which prevailed after the war, and because his father refused to endorse him, Ernest entered banking entirely without requests for favoritism. Bowen joined Barclay's. He soon learned that even if the government did not staff the industry directly, its adherents were entering it and rising. Out of resentment, he worked the minimum number of hours necessary, treated everyone with a studied contempt sustained by both a belief in his inherent superiority and his fear of failure, and was tolerated by Barclay's only because a succession of branch managers enjoyed having an inchoate member of the peerage as a subordinate. Fortunately for the creditors created by his non-clerk's life style, certain trust funds were beyond his remote father's reach.

In 1960, Viscount Bowen died in an auto accident. Ernest succeeded to all of the family's titles and estates. Being only an unlearned man and not a moron, he placed his new holdings in the hands of professional managers and went to New York, where, then as now, a good title guaranteed a good round of parties. And, he thought, there might be an offer of a job more to his liking.

As capable of scheming as any game warden, he arranged to meet

George Ingersoll, telling his go-between that he had often done business with Ingersoll & Constance's London representative, Sir John Catch. The lie earned him an invitation to Ingersoll's town house. After greetings were exchanged, his host led Bowen to a billiard room overlooking the East River.

The visitor studied the gray night, which shaded the water and steamers into a scene of fog flecked with the running lights of commerce. He was startled to realize that this great home, this seat of international power, sat overlooking a river which ran down to a great port. It was the first of the evening's surprises.

He turned to see Ingersoll smiling and knew the older man appreciated his surprise. "I will never move to the country," his host said. "Not when I can survey the entry to the seas from my home."

"England once relied on the seas and time has passed her by."

"England stood still. The sea will soon be our major conduit of oil, and . . ." He smiled. "But no business. Not now." He gestured to the billiard table. "Do you play?"

"Oh, a bit."

"Actually more than that. You've been your club's champion for nine years."

Bowen smiled. "I suppose I was a bit modest."

"No, you were very stupid. You thought I'd play you for money while you played me for a fool."

"Now see here."

"Don't put on a scene or I'll stuff your grinning face with a billiard ball. Sit down." Ingersoll waited as Bowen decided whether or not he was bluffing. When he realized that he was not, Bowen's expression turned to fear as he attempted to anticipate what might happen next. He slowly settled into a seat and reached for his cigarette case.

"Don't smoke," Ingersoll said. "Particularly not those Blue Macedonians you have blended at Burlington Arcade. It will ruin the palate for dinner." Ingersoll allowed himself to laugh as Bowen shuddered. "You see, Ernest, I knew your father. As a result, I would have invited you here when I heard you were in the city. But then you lied about knowing John Catch and I realized it would be necessary to learn more about you than the well-known fact that you are a fop.

"How do I know that you have never met Catch? It wouldn't have been through business because your father was quite open about the fact that he considered you a dunce. The only way you could have met Catch on business was if you were delivering bonds and he brushed into

69

you while going through the cashier's cage on his way to the men's room.

"If you find this insulting, you may of course leave. It's probably not too early for you to buy a woman from the bell captain. For the right commission he could probably find you an Oriental girl." Ingersoll smiled. "Or you may bear up under it for another moment and listen to the business proposition you came here to receive."

The banker watched Bowen hold up his hands, and he smiled a gracious assent to the surrender. "Since the end of the war, Ingersoll and Constance has done only a general commission business in London. A little arbitrage, some commercial credit, and some small services rendered to clients passing through. For sound business reasons we have not attempted to take clients from the good merchant bankers there, even those headquartered on the Continent. In accord with our nonexistent agreement, they have not attempted to buy into syndicates here or offer European services to my clients.

"All of that is changing. London bankers no longer do ship financing, because your government has taken over the maritime industry and destroyed it. They are no longer asked to manage syndicates, because your businesses are owned by Europeans who lost the war that you won.

"A major failing of your people is their willingness to allow power to pass by descent. Your father's disgust with you was only a small step in the right direction. Now I am going to reverse it. I believe that you do have a role to play in my business. Your family title, after all, was established only a few decades after my ancestors founded the firm which bears my name.

"You distinguished yourself in a horrible war. I am, therefore, required to believe that you are capable of much more than you have shown until now. I can always buy someone with a title. I much prefer someone who has never had an outlet for the skill and ruthlessness which I need, and you possess. Your salary will be fifty thousand pounds annually, with an equal amount, unaudited, for entertaining.

"You want the job. Is there any reason I should not want you?"

Bowen thought briefly of making a sharp or humorous remark, then realized how stupid it would be. Instead he said only, "I do not buy my women, *generally*; have no interest in boys; and am not addicted to any drug. Is there anything else you need to know?"

The only thing that Ingersoll wanted to know was the bottom line at the end of each month. He was never disappointed. Syndicate fees grew annually as Bowen was invited to join more and better boards. Private offerings were first discussed with members of old family alliances and, when officially tendered, were fully subscribed. The same alliances made public placements easier. All of the corporations underwritten by Ingersoll & Constance transferred their banking business to the firm. Bowen's European horse-breeding friends sent ship financing from the Continent. The need for arbitrage grew and was satisfied.

After a point, Ingersoll knew, it was all circular. Business had come to the firm because of Bowen; it stayed because of the excellence of the services rendered. At what point Bowen might be considered superfluous, Ingersoll did not know. Nor did he care. He had struck a bargain with the man and would not break it now that he had what he wanted. The agreement had been without a fixed term, and the house of Ingersoll always kept its agreements.

And, Ingersoll was forced to admit, Bowen had become more tolerable. He had learned how to treat people better.

Ingersoll attributed this new attitude to delayed maturity; but Bowen knew that he was coming near the end and needed to keep contact with the only humans who had ever touched him. He used some of his expense funds to subscribe to public charities, and he spent part of his personal estate to support veterans' causes decades after the war, when the sacrifices that would always be remembered were forgotten. Bowen would often stop on a business visit to chat about the service ribbons worn by British doormen. He inquired about a gimping worker's regiment. These forgotten men remembered the kindness and mentioned it to their shopmates.

To Ingersoll, who knew that industrial excellence in Britain was both rare and despised, such kindness could lead to extra effort, a larger profit, the financing of the expansion such profits could bring.

To an unremembered former member of the Logan Commandoes, such kindness meant that Bowen might be the man to call on in certain circumstances. The information was put to use.

The man at M.I.6 knew that if Bowen had changed, his responsibilities had not. In the beginning the rule at Ingersoll & Constance had been that matters of substance were not to be discussed with him. He was a business getter, useful but not essential. By the time George Ingersoll was ready to relax the rule, it was too late. Bowen was popular and well paid, but not respected by his partners. He made the contacts but other men did the deals. It was a weakness, and the man at M.I.6 relied on weaknesses as well as strengths.

71

His approach was simple enough. It was a financing for a nominally neutral government. The deal would enable Ingersoll & Constance to expand even further into Europe. But, the man from M.I.6 emphasized, it was a British deal. Bowen was the contact. All information was to be routed through him. Ingersoll agreed; and it was for that reason that Simon McHenry was being sent blind to his London meeting.

Cabelend—the name came from the 1802 battleground where Joshua Bowen had established his family in the aristocracy—was perhaps the most famous private home in England. (To Bowen, Buckingham Palace was a public building, and, in any event, the residents were of German descent.) Its great hall, hung with portraits of the fourteen men who had preceded Bowen in his title, was the scene of two major charity balls each year. The main dining room seated two hundred guests and was used every September to host the dinner of the Military Relief Society. The pantries and kitchen were larger than those at Claridge's and provided extraordinary baskets for the semi-annual picnics given on the grounds. Somber from without, funereal within, an invitation to breach its oaken doors was London's most sought-after bid.

The third floor contained Bowen's private apartment. Furnished in the style of a men's club, with leather and mahogany appointments, it was not warm to women. He did not need it to be. Only close male business and social acquaintances ever entered its rooms. Except for a uniquely furnished, concealed extra bedroom, which was visited only by Oriental prostitutes. All that was publicly known about the floor was that Bowen presided there over the best table in London.

On this autumn evening the table was being prepared for Bowen's only guest, Simon McHenry.

As good a host as Bowen was, McHenry was an equally competent guest. He knew the Londoner was a man of no depth and a negative position in intellectual reserves. As a guest, he always prepared himself for these meetings by reading up on subjects that fascinated Bowen and bored himself: horses, golf, racing cars and photographic equipment. Each man knew his own and the other's position in the firm, and each knew what the other knew. Bowen was grateful for McHenry's preparations because they allowed him to take the lead without feeling patronized. McHenry did what he did out of sympathy for one he viewed as a man with little of life left before him, and nothing of value to be left behind.

During the meal, the firm's rule against business discussions at table was scrupulously observed. Despite McHenry's social preparations, little conversation was necessary, as it would only have detracted from the dinner. They began with fresh duck liver in aspic, a salad of endive and raw mushrooms, a cassoulet of Belon oysters in champagne sauce, each accompanied by one glass of an appropriately chosen wine. They cleared the palate by sipping a pear sorbet, then had duck with green peppercorns, served without vegetables, and port with Stilton.

When they had finished, Bowen led the younger man into his library, seated him, and served a privately bottled cognac. Snipped Romeo y Julieta coronas had already been removed from a humidor and placed beside each man's chair to allow the tobacco time to breathe. Bowen seated himself and asked, "How much did George tell you?"

"Not a great deal. It was all rather rushed. Apparently the Yugoslavians' resident German economists have asked that Britain's German economists arrange for our resident German economists to settle an old debt."

Bowen smiled. "Yes, it would be foolish of your government to be rude to the fascisti when it so desires to remain popular in South America."

"It must be a very old debt."

"It is. As you know, the firm has a long history of honoring obligations. Sometimes these are incurred by the house or its partners. Sometimes by clients. Occasionally by a nation. In these latter instances we are usually asked to pay a country's private debt to another state. These transactions usually cost us money in the short term, but pay handsomely in later years. This is how we survive. How countries, as well as men, can continue to do business with one another.

"This particular debt accrued more than forty years ago, in what we were fond of calling democracy's darkest hour. The Allies knew that Hitler was about to invade Russia and wanted to delay his start so that his arrival would coincide with winter. The Yugoslavians, who we had hoped would offer a bit of resistance, decided instead to allow Prince Paul to capitulate. A group of officers, however, saw to it that the Prince-Regent was overthrown; and, in retaliation, the Luftwaffe began to raze Belgrade. A man carrying a British passport in the cover name of Spiridon Mekas was smuggled into the country. With Allied arms, this man bogged Hitler down for six weeks, just enough time to delay the German offensive so that when it began it moved quickly into the Russian winter. In addition, tens of thousands of German troops which might have made a difference in Russia, or elsewhere, were instead hopelessly mired down in four years of guerrilla warfare against the Yugoslavians.

"After the war, this Mekas was rewarded in various ways by both the

Allies and the Russians. But the rewards were sought, and given, for the internal political goals of the donor nations, not because Mekas relied upon his wartime contributions.

"Shortly before his death some years ago, Mekas, correct name Josip Broz, known to you as Tito, brought this debt to the attention of younger men, told them what officers to contact here to obtain repayment, and put the former Allies on notice of the fact that at some future date he or one of his delegates would seek satisfaction for a campaign which had cost one of every nine Yugoslavs his life.

"That debt has now been called. The Yugoslavian government desperately needs to pump money into its economy. The first group after Tito maintained some semblance of his balancing act between East and West. The Russians would tolerate that from the old boy because they couldn't remove him without provoking a full-sized war. But they pinched the economy to discipline his successors. This latest group, however, is a bit more adventuresome; wants to start importing a bit of true capitalism, which shouldn't surprise us. Lord knows they've got a nation no more communistic than Great Britain." He drew on his cigar. "Perhaps that was not the best comparison."

McHenry smiled. "Might not the Soviets intervene?"

"Apparently the locals don't think so. They'll be using our money and so needing less of Mother Russia's rubles. Anyway, they have no intention of letting us get too deeply entrenched politically."

"How did they come to us?"

"The proposal was made to the British Secret Service, for the reasons I've just given you. Obviously this country cannot be of financial assistance to anyone. But M.I. Six has ties to me; I'm tied to Ingersoll and Constance; the firm is tied to your government, which would like to be tied to the Yugoslavians. Isn't that marvelously incestuous?" He rose and walked to the liquor cabinet. "More cognac?" McHenry shook his head. When Bowen had poured another five fingers, he resumed his chair.

"We have been asked," he said, "to arrange financing for the Yugoslavian government to build an automobile plant. What do you know about the technical side of automobiles?"

"They don't float."

"Quite so. For that reason, the locals are going to arrange for you to tour their presently existing plant. It makes a line called, not surprisingly, the Tito. I believe the grille piece is an ugly little man. I've explained to them that you will need a complete knowledge of their operation in

74

order to do your due diligence report before drawing up an offering circular. You're to place sixty percent in the States, half the remainder here, half on the Continent.''

"No problem. If it flies, we have a new market for financings. If not, there will be tax write-offs.''

"Does your government allow them for Central European investments that go bad?''

"It is being arranged.''

Bowen smiled humorlessly. "George can be wonderful.'' He pinged his index finger against the side of the snifter. "You said that you were told nothing. Were you told who is doing the deal?''

"It's all your show. I'm here because the Securities and Exchange Commission will require information that I can develop. But it is all to start and end with you.''

"Splendid. Before you leave, I'll provide you with a packet containing all that we now know, as well as your flight time, hotels, whatever. I trust that you are willing to rely on my arrangements.''

"Of course.''

"Good. Speaking of which, will you want a woman?''

"I've scheduled my free time, thank you.''

"Of course.''

McHenry left within the hour. Bowen watched his driver pull away. The man knew enough to stay in his quarters when he returned. Any unexpected calls would be handled by the houseman. There would be no interruption.

Bowen walked into his private office and studied a portrait of his father which he kept as a private joke. He pulled the picture back, unlocked a safe and withdrew five fifty-pound notes. Then he locked the safe, swung the painting back, and walked toward his secret bedroom. It was one of the regular girls tonight, a splendid Hunanese. She would know enough to repeat over and over, "I am Hai Yin.'' It pleased him to hear the name of the Oriental woman who had raised him so cruelly while his father had attended to the King's business and so totally ignored him.

Chapter Four

When McHenry returned to the hotel, Elspeth was in his room. She was wearing a floor-length pink negligee which perfectly framed her cream and gold beauty. A room-service cart sat in the corner.

"Was the poor teacher satisfied?"

"Put the tray in the hall."

McHenry did so, locked the door, turned, and crossed the room. He took Elspeth's gown, lowered it from her shoulders, admired her quietly and completely, then began to undress. They did not engage in any of the coyness or game playing which can ruin any lovemaking, whether the random coupling of strangers or an act as truly erotic as a love affair between husband and wife. She was a beautiful woman and he was an attractive man. There was nothing else between them. Or so McHenry thought.

They made love four times that night. After the first time they rested. After the others they talked. The hours were consumed with gentle probing, the asking and admitting by words and silences of much that was important. It had rarely been a part of either's lovemaking, yet it had become an essential aspect of their being together. Beyond her supple body (horseback riding, some tennis) and knowledge of languages (English father, Hungarian mother), he sensed a fragility which instinctively drew the strongest boy in the orphanage to her. He realized that he was perhaps confusing fragility with decency and reserve; she had not pursued questions about his childhood or the scar that the Lobo's machete had left on his chest and stomach. She seemed saddened by his life, and he was grateful that she cared.

His first reaction was that he should remember her as a good lay and otherwise forget her. But as their night passed, he realized that that was unworthy of her; and he did have a sense of justice. Elspeth was sharing with him some openness of caring that he had rarely bothered to elicit. It put him in her debt, and he always paid his debts.

"Why didn't you speak to me during the flight?" she asked after he had made her come without entering her.

"I didn't want to ruin it." Then, fearing that he was becoming too serious, he added, "Besides, you seemed quite occupied with those Indian gentlemen."

She made a face. "'Miz Elspeth is a mobes byoodifull woman. Is berry dezirobble to be pinching huh ahs.'"

He laughed. "How'd you stop him?"

"I pulled off his little red dot. Where do you go from here?"

"The Continent."

"How mysterious."

"I'm sorry. I suppose that I just think of it as one mass of land for the business traveler."

"One deal is pretty much like another?"

"In some ways."

"Then I won't inquire. It sounds too dull."

"In some ways."

"Do you want to sleep?"

"I did, but I don't."

"Good." She mounted him and took him inside. "Just be still and you'll come soon."

He remained almost motionless, then was drawn up into her truth. They slept for nine hours.

Over breakfast he asked the question that should have ended their relationship: Why was a woman so attractive, so intelligent, a waitress on an airplane? The answer was one which he could accept: Her parents had provided her with an appreciation of what was good in life, but not the money to enjoy it at will. The Concorde service took her where she wanted to go. Once she arrived, there was rarely an expense.

"That's an intriguing comment," he said.

"If you mean, do I want anything from you, no. Only to be treated well while I do what you do. And no matter what you were doing, if I didn't like you and want you, I wouldn't be here."

"That's fair enough."

"I'm a *Hausfrau* in the air. It serves its purposes. On the ground I do as I like."

"As long as you like me."

"I'm afraid I do."

"Yes." He stood up from the table. "It has become rather intense rather quickly, hasn't it?"

"Yes." With her spoon, Elspeth traced riverbeds in the linen. At last she said, "I can just go now. It was a good night for both of us. Nicely remembered, easily forgotten."

"Do that." He walked to the window and stood looking out while she dressed. As she crossed to the door, he said, "I'll call you when I get back."

McHenry hoped that she had nodded her head before leaving.

Chapter Five

Brian Gourley was an economist. It is a discipline traditionally known as the dismal science; and since Gourley was a dismal man, he often thought how appropriately he had chosen his career. (An exception, of course, was the glamorous Galbraith of the 1960s and '70s, remembered now, if at all, only as the intellectual sparring partner of the former American Secretary of State William Buckley.)

If the science was dismal (if it was a science at all), it was also essential. Economists determined how much money would enter the world, what it would cost the powerful to borrow from the solvent, and how fast the gap between income and costs (traditionally known as a healthy amount of inflation) would spread. The financial numerologist who occupied the right position could wield enormous power over a public which did not know that he existed.

Brian Gourley occupied no such position. A product of redbrick schools, perpetually disheveled, meek to the point of caricature, he could have earned a living playing slum-area schoolmasters on BBC. Most tragically, his accumulated failures had prevented any acquisition of self-confidence, the only true requirement for success with women.

As a result, he approached age forty as a virgin: a man who would always be vaguely uncomfortable with life. Acutely aware of his non-Oxbridge background, he had intentionally chosen the field of Central European economics because he thought it would offer the fewest competitors as he struggled for advancement in the elitist world of M.I.6. It mattered not at all. Some men never fit, and Gourley could honestly claim all the perks of membership in this body.

Gourley's work was difficult and tedious, precisely what he was suited to do. On those occasions when an agent in Zone Three, Central Europe, forwarded information or requested interpretation of an economic problem, Gourley wrote up the analysis. Because he was also a brilliant mathematician, he was responsible for the cipher grouping. A language clerk received flashes in Polish, Yugoslavian, Croatian, or any of the innumerable other tongues which Middle Europeans persisted in wagging. Gourley would then convert the jumbled English letters into statistical groups, enter a numeral for each letter, then convert the digits to words. Interpretations and instructions returned to the field were processed in reverse fashion, with the agent receiving his flash in the local dialect. He then converted it to understandable English using an E Code. This was so named because *E* is the most often used letter in the English language. M.I.6 believed that an intercepting agent could only assume that no English-speaking network would use an E Code and so be left to wonder what the next translation should read after he had reduced the code to a perfectly understandable message.

Brian Gourley's life consisted of work. There was no White's or Boodles, no trips to the West End, no fittings at Huntsman's.

There was only work and the London Library. This most famous of all publicly private libraries was his only recreation, his solace, his club, his tailor, his place to go when he could not face the prospect of a lonely night in his flat. For a bit more than twenty pounds a year he enjoyed the classics, books on sciences less demanding than his own, every periodical of note, the easiest chairs in the U.K., and twenty miles of stacks for his desiccated soul to roam in quiet.

On the evening that Simon McHenry left for London, Gourley was at the library. He was reading, as he always did when tired, Thackeray. It was his treat to himself, something that only his type of mind could have conceived of as an enjoyment. This questionable pleasure was first detracted from, then destroyed, by the violent autumn rain. Gourley put down his book and walked to a smoking area.

As he left the reading room, he pulled an oil- and finger-smudged tobacco pouch from his shapeless blue woolen Burton's suit. Unzipping the bottom section of the case, he withdrew a gnarled Dunhill briar, bought at discount through a friend in the store's accounts office. He packed the bowl, lit it, allowed the ember to die, then tamped down the string-cut tobacco and relit it. Satisfied that the bowl was properly fired, he walked down the corridor.

"Balkan Sobranie," a woman said as he turned to walk through the catalogue area.

"I beg your pardon."

"Balkan Sobranie. That's what you're smoking. My father always smoked it."

Gourley blushed. He could no more recall speaking to a woman not of his acquaintance than he could recall ever having thought that any woman would sleep with him. "Yes," he finally managed. "Yes." Gourley knew as much about casual conversation as he did about making a wheel of Stilton.

"I like it," she said. "It's a strong tobacco. Takes getting used to."

Gourley made another short inane response as he studied the woman. She was as tall as he, which made her tall for a woman, with expensively cropped black hair, bright violet eyes, and what foreigners called an English complexion. He could see that the body beneath the severe brown district-check suit was voluptuous. Gourley was suddenly embarrassed by his own cheap clothing, tufted ears, and wire spectacles. He nodded and turned to go.

"As long as I've interrupted you," she said, "would you be good enough to assist me. I'm only a new member and can't make any sense out of the catalogues. You see I'm researching a paper on Korea and —"

Gourley laughed. "I do apologize. This old place. Hates change, you know. Korea still goes under *C*. Israel goes under Palestine. So on. I've a friend, a Jewish merchant, belongs here but doesn't care much for that kind of filing, I can tell you."

She smiled, showing not mirth but a genuine interest in Gourley, his friends, his library.

"Let me see if I can do it now," she said. The woman walked to a row of filing cabinets, drew out a drawer, and quickly rifled the entries. Her fingers backed up from the rear center, moved forward and spread two cards. "Pickwell's *Life of Early Korean Martyrs*," she muttered, then turned to Gourley, obviously puzzled as to what to do next.

"Religion is upstairs," he said.

"I was afraid you were going to say that. These stack floors are atrocious. I've twisted off two heels in three weeks' membership. I usually only wear flats here now, but I had to come over unexpectedly and —"

80

"Please," Gourley said, looking at the card. He noted the book's location and turned to go to the stairs. Remembering the lit pipe, he turned back to the woman and handed it to her.

"I shan't break it," she said. "And thank you."

"Of course."

She smiled, then looked down at the pipe. "Oh, a Dunhill. I learned that from my father too."

Gourley stopped again, embarrassed that she might think him vain for smoking such an expensive pipe. He considered telling her that it was only an investment, bought at discount, when he heard himself say, "Hagberg Wright."

"Sylvia Bloom."

"Oh, no. No. Hagberg Wright designed the library and put in those awful grate walkways that are always nipping your shoes."

"I'm so glad that he did."

Gourley blushed and went for the book. Although he had spent a dry life in stacks such as these, the volume was one of the few he had ever handled that actually needed to be blown clean of dust. He snorted. Religion was such an imprecise study.

Sylvia Bloom was standing by a window turning the pipe, bowl to stem to bowl, rhythmically against the rain. The storm was so severe that now the water collapsed like sheets of cellophane against the building. When he cleared his throat, she turned and offered him the smile that he was beginning, at last, to think might be more than automatic.

"Thank you," she said softly. "You might tell me your name."

"Brian Gourley. Are you leaving?"

"Yes."

"They don't like books going out without a cover. Have you a brief-case?"

"No. Have you?"

He walked her to the counter, where she signed out the book while he fetched their coats and his plastic bookbag. On the steps he said, "We'll never get a taxi."

"We could wait. Or walk."

"We can't wait. It'll never stop."

"It'll stop," she said. "The fire next time."

"I don't understand."

"The Lord promised Noah that when he finally destroyed the world it would not be by flood but by fire." She leaned closer and caught him

81

in the scents of face powder and wet wool, perfume and the pleasing late afternoon musk of a statuesque woman's long day. "Let's go to my flat. We can warm up with our own fire."

An hour later, after they had undressed, he took her in his arms and bent his face to her breasts. His tongue flicked each nipple, which instantly rose to await his pleasure.

Good God, he thought, you are a good, good God.

Chapter Six

Sylvia Bloom had promised to be at his flat when Gourley returned from the office. She was not. He was so anxious to see her, touch her, have her again, that he ran through each room before he smelled cigarette smoke and turned in fear. She did not smoke.

Across the sitting room from Gourley was a young man dressed in a blazer jacket, striped pants, wing collar, and blue tie. He was a Pinewood Studios imitation of the British civil servant. On his lap was a bowler.

"Who the bloody hell are you?" Gourley demanded.

"A friend of Sylvia's. Sit down please, Mr. Gourley. I have a gun beneath my hat and am prepared to use it if you do not listen closely to what I have to say." The young man lifted the bowler and brought into firing position a small black automatic. With a nudge of his free hand he removed the safety. Gourley sat down.

"Good. I am here only to present you with a gift from Sylvia. A small packet of what are called, I believe, candids. Truly candid, in fact." He tossed the envelope to Gourley. It hit his chest and began to slide down beneath his legs. The economist slowly brought his knees together, stopped the envelope, and lifted it. The pictures were indeed candid.

"How much?" Gourley asked.

The visitor laughed. "Mr. Gourley, please. You know better. They're not for sale. You may keep them. As they say in the movies, we have the negatives."

"Then what?"

"Among the ciphers which you translate for the British Secret Service are several dealing with international financing in Eastern Bloc countries.

"We wish merely to learn of the internal financial plans of such countries. We are not asking for any information vital to Great Britain. We know that you wouldn't give it to us. We want to know only about Western investment plans in certain countries, particularly Yugoslavia."

"You're mad."

"Probably. But not compromised. If you do not help us, our employer, who knows your employer, will send him those photographs. And because you are compromised, you will be liquidated.

"Please think about it. We'll be in touch."

Chapter Seven

In the morning Brian Gourley went down to the City.

To the brokers and bankers around him in the underground carriage he must have seemed the embodiment of all that was unpleasant in modern financial London: ill-fitting cheap tweeds, soft hat, redbrick, theoretical, and invading. An economist perhaps. Or an *emigré arbitrageur* come to profit off the pound. For his part, Gourley felt that he adequately showed his contempt for the dozens of bowler-hatted, *Financial Times*-carrying, bumbershoot-straight bankers. He was, Gourley knew, smarter than these men. But without their self-confidence. And today he needed confidence desperately, for today he was to meet the managing director, and he was afraid.

It was, of course, not unheard of for a low-grade staffer to call outside his station and request a meeting with the managing director. It was simply that such things were done only in circumstances of the most appalling nature. Sir Fraser Dole, the managing director, had told Gourley to save the circumstances for their meeting.

The Fund for the Preservation of Land Trusts occupied the top three floors of a skyscraper which adjoined Saint Helen's, Bishopsgate—the Westminster Abbey of the City of London. On the church grounds there is a marble monument to Sir Andrew Judde. By prearrangement, Gourley was to stand at the stone and pretend to read of Sir Andrew's accomplishments, some of which may have taken place, and which begin in this fashion:

> To Russia and MUSCOVA
> To SPAYNE gynny without fable
> Traveld he by Land and Sea
> Bothe Mayor of London and Staple
> The commonwealth he norished
> So worthelie in all his dayes
> That ech state full well him loved
> To his perpetval prayes.

A white rose was propped against the monument, touching the next line of the inscription. The flower was open. It was Gourley's signal to come ahead.

Sir Fraser Dole—forty-eight, erect, perfectly tailored in blue flannels, white shirt, and Winchester school tie—sat behind a double-sized oak desk rocking gently in a red leather chair. The Civil Service regulations as to allowed furnishings were not followed here in headquarters section as they were in Gourley's department. It would not have mattered. It was obvious that Sir Fraser had spent a great deal of his own funds on the Oriental porcelains, maroon carpeting with royal Sharoz overlay, and Chinese watercolors. It was Gourley's first visit to the managing director's office, and he was more than impressed with objects that Dole never noticed but occasionally took the time to see.

"Would you like some coffee?" Dole asked. "I have tea, of course, but I prefer coffee. It keeps me awake. Actually, tea is said to contain more caffeine, but I like the taste of coffee."

"Coffee would be fine, sir, thank you."

"Do you take cream and sugar? It's not good for you, but I take cream and sugar."

"Black would be fine, sir."

Dole frowned, hit a button on his desk console, and ordered coffee and biscuits. He held up a hand for Gourley to hold his emergency until after the tray was served, and filled the time with a discussion of the biscuits they were about to eat. "They're McVittie's 'Morning

Coffee,'" he said. "So common they're actually amusing. I find that one or two at this time of day carries me over until half-twelve. I don't like to eat before then, you see."

"Yes, sir."

"My secretary offered to bring in something fresh to go with the morning coffee, but I can't help thinking that carrying pastries to work, even by secretary, is so much more common than eating common cookies packaged by McVittie's. Don't you agree?"

"Oh, yes, sir."

"Good." Dole smiled as the girl put a tray on a small serving board by his desk and left the room. "Help yourself," he said, transferring the smile to Gourley, "and then tell me what the bloody fuck you want."

Gourley closed his eyes and slowly lowered his head. For a moment Dole was afraid that the man was about to cry. Instead he said very softly, "I am so sorry."

"Why?"

"Sir, well, sir, I think I've been compromised."

The managing director very quietly asked, "You're not a homosexual, are you, Gourley? I thought that was restricted to Cambridge graduates."

"This is not the first time, sir, that my lack of establishment credentials—"

"For God's sake, man."

"Yes, sir." Gourley watched Dole light a cigarette. Desperate to change the subject, he said, "You're smoking Sweet Aftons, sir. Our studies indicate they're very popular in Ireland. Have you been there, sir?"

"Really, Gourley. This is beyond endurance. You go outside channels for an appointment, tell me you've been compromised, then ask if I've been to Belfast fomenting rebellion. Would you like my itinerary to pass on to your compromiser?"

"No, sir. I'm sorry, sir."

"Then tell me what it is that brings you to this contrite state."

At last Gourley was able to recite his pathetic tale. No matter how he tried to retain the tone of the statistician, he could not do so. In broken, sobbing phrases, he told how he, a middle-aged virgin, had lapsed not into another spinster's love, but into the arms of an agent who was trying to turn him around.

Dole betrayed no emotion, not even his great contempt. Very calmly he told Gourley, "All right. You were a fool to get into this, but you've at least handled the back end well."

"Then I'm not to be liquidated, sir?"

Dole laughed violently. "No, Gourley, no cinema ending."

"Then do I go back to my flat, sir, and wait for their contact?"

"No, you were almost certainly followed here. I'll arrange for you to go down to the garage in my private lift. We'll take you to a safe house in the country. Your concubine's friends will assume that you slipped away. We'll have a man go back to your flat and wait for their visit. Let's see if we can't switch things about on them."

Gourley rose and stammered out his thanks. When his rambling ended, Dole said, "Not at all. Not at all. You're much too good a man to lose. Now be kind enough to wait outside, will you. I have to make the arrangements."

As the door shut behind Gourley, the managing director pressed a button which sounded in an adjoining room. He was immediately joined by a man whose build and bearing suggested a fireplug: squat, strong, ugly, functional in a crisis but otherwise repugnant.

This man was Dick Sharp, a native of Manchester who had escaped that city's slums at age fourteen by lying his way into the Royal Marines. He had gone from there on special posting to VI Commandoes in Palestine. There he quickly rose to the rank of sergeant, bestowed by the protectorate force in grateful recognition of his love of killing. He spent several months as an interrogator, waiting patiently for the Royal Navy to intercept Jews attempting to come ashore to join the Haganah. His sole function was to wait until they were broken, then torture them to death and arrange for the bodies to be shipped to Zionist enclaves as a warning. After partition, he happily taught those he had not butchered how to kill Arabs.

After a few unpleasant years of base duty, his unique skills were employed in the Philippines, where he was given a brevet commission in the war against the Huks. At the campaign's end he was assured of the permanence of both his commission and his reputation for unparalleled savagery.

Over the next fifteen years he slaughtered Eoka fighters on Cyprus, castrated tribesmen in Aden, and tortured captured Catholics and Protestants alike in Northern Ireland. It was only in this last assignment that he felt truly at ease with his surroundings. By then a lieutenant colonel, he was accustomed to being shunned by his fellow officers, not because of his reputation but because of his often stated belief that all men were animals, and that those who believed such conduct unique to wogs were naive. In Northern Ireland he found the perfect proof of his belief: an English-speaking land of Anglo-Saxons who were prepared to destroy their nation rather than resolve their differences with logic.

By the early 1980s he was nearing fifty and already once passed over for promotion. His youthful fear that one day the wars would run out had been allayed by observation of the Irish. That fear was replaced by the realization that a second passing over would mean discharge. He could tolerate months, even a few years, of base duty if he knew that another outlet for his skills was being prepared by his fellow man. He could not tolerate the prospect of a life spent in what was jokingly referred to as civilization.

He need not have been concerned. When his skills became too dazzling for even the two sides in Ireland to tolerate, he was discharged. Sharp was told that he was to be sent back to England by private transport for his own safety. As he packed, he secreted both a .357 magnum and a bowie knife beneath his civilian suit. He had no doubt that he was about to be liquidated. He welcomed the challenge. His death would resolve his fears of retirement while offering his first chance to officially kill his countrymen in hand-to-hand combat.

He was both disappointed and relieved to find that he was being gazetted to Sir Fraser Dole's private staff as the managing director's personal assistant. His services consisted entirely of assassination. His only discontent was the occasional period when he sat for weeks on end without assignment. Dole then usually found something to amuse him. As he entered his superior's office on the morning of Gourley's visit, he knew that his special talents were once again to be put to use.

"Gourley has been compromised," Dole said. "Arrange for his final severance."

Dole watched Sharp's face betray a hint of pleasure. It was becoming more and more difficult to arrange such matters for the assassin. And without them he was even more dangerous, a cancerous pustule that could not be lanced.

"Am I to . . . ?" Sharp asked.

Dole looked amused. "No. So sorry to disappoint you, but he can't be marked up. The necessary evidence of homosexual conduct will be arranged at the far end." He smiled. "Not that that part of it would interest you."

Sharp stiffened.

"See to it all, will you?" Dole said. "Let's give Gourley a real cinema ending."

Chapter Eight

McHenry returned to his room at Claridge's with a book of Yugoslavian history and a volume of the poems of Goran Kovacic. What he would read before leaving, and what he would force himself to remember from his days with the nuns, would enable him to be as pleasing a guest in business as he was in society. Of such small points were large deals constructed. When he turned on the light, he saw a tall, elegantly dressed man seated with one leg draped over the arm of a chair. He appeared to be Foreign Office. The other, however, was clearly an enforcer. That made the first man M.I.5 or—6.

"Forgive the intrusion, Mr. McHenry. I am Sir Fraser Dole. And this is my associate, Colonel Sharp."

The enforcer closed the door as McHenry moved toward a writing desk. He wanted some buffer if he had to move.

"Why are you here?" McHenry asked.

"Sit down, please."

"Again: why?"

"Not yet."

McHenry sprang forward, his hands propelling him over the desk, aligning his body as his left leg became bolt straight, catching Dole in the chest, throwing him over his chair and onto the floor. McHenry's right leg came down in a kneeling position by Dole's head, giving him perfect balance as he slipped his left knee into Dole's throat. His left hand was poised just beneath the Englishman's nose. "Leash your dog," he said.

"Sharp." Dole choked out the name as the enforcer came up behind them. McHenry heard the footsteps clump into stillness, then repeated, "Why?" He heard the safety fall on Sharp's automatic.

"Kill me," Dole wheezed, "and you die."

McHenry smiled and shook his head. "If his gun doesn't hit the floor *now,* I'll drive your nose into your brain. Wherever he sends me, you'll be waiting." He pushed up on Dole's nose.

In a louder voice he said, "And you won't be far behind, goon. Not after you explain to Whitehall how you let an unarmed prisoner kill your master while you stood there."

McHenry eased his knee back an inch, and Dole moved his head slightly. "Down," he gasped. "Gun. Now." McHenry heard Sharp engage the safety and bend down, as a professional would, to place the gun on the floor. "Over here," he said. Sharp gently moved the weapon forward with his foot. McHenry picked it up without moving his other hand from Dole's nose, slipped the safety off, and rose slowly, lifting Dole with the undeniable invitation of the Walther PPK at the Englishman's head. McHenry stepped to the far side of the desk, motioned both men to the wall, ordered them to assume the position, and searched them. He found a Colt .38 police special strapped to the small of Sharp's back, and a bowie knife sheathed on his right leg. Dole was unarmed, except for a Dupont butane lighter which could be calibrated to shoot a jet of flame twenty feet. He ordered the men into the seats facing a desk, then backed behind it and sat down with the Colt and knife before him. He trained the Walther on Dole's stomach.

McHenry said, "I believe I asked you why."

"We are here on a matter of interest to your government," Dole said.

"Why didn't they contact me directly?"

"First, what you will be going after technically belongs to us. Because of financial considerations, we cannot properly staff the mission." McHenry smiled at Sharp and said, "Obviously." Dole cleared his throat. The gun had not moved from his heart. "I was about to say that your government can finance it, and has agreed to do so.

"Second, it was believed that you would not be amenable to any proposal from Langley. Something about a loose tongue."

"Go on."

"Langley's computers picked you. That's why we're here."

"There are other people."

"You have combat experience, a facility for languages, and Arctic training."

"The Arctic?"

"Antarctica, actually, but the weather is similar enough. And, most importantly, you spent several years studying under the Jesuits. They have advanced you. You know how they think, and yet you are not their friend. We require someone who can view those men dispassionately and understand them. As I said, Langley's computer picked you."

"Not that I will help you, or the Jesuits, but what have they to do with this?"

"Ah, but Mr. McHenry, you are going." Dole reached for his inside pocket, then smiled. "May I?" McHenry nodded. Dole slowly withdrew an envelope and tossed it onto the desk. Without looking down, McHenry turned it over and opened it, then spread the photographs on the desk. He glanced down quickly and asked, "Who is it?"

"A security risk named Brian Gourley."

"Whatever his failings, I am certain that you arranged them."

"Brav-o!"

"What has he to do with me?"

"If necessary, he will find eternal peace in your bed. The pathologist will understand."

"The frame is too weak for the picture. It would seem more likely that you found a convenient excuse to feed your animal fresh meat. I imagine that Gourley was weak and you arranged the whole thing, just to guarantee that he would go docilely to the block."

Dole, for once, was stunned. "The computers were right, Mr. McHenry. You possess a shocking ability to read people."

"A necessary defense of the orphan. In any event, the ability could be sharper: I believed Keith's story."

"It was true enough. The deal needs to be done. The financing fee is merely a bonus to George Ingersoll for not complaining too loudly about your absence."

"I won't be absent. Even for someone with the narrow morality of your calling, you are loathsome. And I owe the Jesuits nothing. Whatever they have to do with this."

"We've chatted, Mr. McHenry. That makes you a risk. You're very young to die so needlessly."

"I'm still the one with the gun. If I'm to die anyway—and I hope that your next wave is more professional—I'll dispatch you first. But I will listen."

"That's better. That's much better." Dole smiled. "May I smoke?"

"No. I'm really much too tired for parlor games."

"Mr. McHenry. Do you think me so unprofessional?"

"In a sense." He looked at Sharp. "I thought the professionals had weeded out their perverts and sadists. Now tell me about it."

90

Dole's eyes hardened. "Are you familiar with Sir Basil Hawkeland?"

"British explorer. Late 1800s. Died on an Antarctic expedition."

"Precisely. In the final years of the nineteenth century he undertook a mission to China.

"At that time, England was in the throes of what today would be called a sexual revolution. Brothels were kept openly. Young women were sold by their families to provide food for those who stayed on the farms or lived in factory-owned villages. The term "Victorian" applied only to public life. In private, every type of sexual service imaginable was available to those who could pay. Unfortunately, such amorous license has certain unpleasant side effects, as I am certain you can imagine.

"Medicine being what it was in those days, a bare step above butchery, there was no cure for syphilis except a 'fresh.' A virgin. It was widely believed that syphilis resulted only from excessive sexual success. It was thought that a man who enjoyed such success could be cured if he slept with a virgin. The cure was not effective.

"The British ambassador to Peking sent word that some Jesuits at the Chinese court had found a remedy for syphilis. This research had been made necessary by the conduct of the Empress Tzu Hsi."

"I'm familiar with the lady," McHenry said. Without yielding in his intense study of the two men, McHenry the Orientalist scanned in his memory the woman who had come to the Emperor's harem as a concubine of the third class, risen to become his favorite, then his wife, and then arranged for his death. She had installed her former lover and personal eunuch as, respectively, chief of security and head of intelligence. When she was thirty-seven, her son reached adulthood and became Emperor. Although she ruled the youth, she did not formally rule China. Unhappy with this separation of powers, she arranged for one Chou, a body eunuch, to lead her dim-witted son on excursions to the Imperial City's most disreputable brothels. Within two years he was dead of syphilis, and Tzu Hsi was again on the throne.

"In any event," Dole was saying, "one of the Jesuits that Tzu Hsi's husband had brought to court as his personal physician had diagnosed the boy's ailment and attempted to find a cure. It was necessary to work in absolute secrecy. The Empress and her retainers obviously had no wish to see the boy cured. The priest-physician suffered from the double burden of wishing to bring release to the moron's body and soul. To achieve these presumably worthwhile goals the priest arranged a system for getting any test results out of the palace and to another priest.

"At that time, what scientific thought there was considered arsenic the best cure for syphilis. The Jesuit was learned enough to reject that course of treatment. For obvious reasons, the good father would not provide the Emperor with a virgin. The youth died, but the priest continued working for several years.

"The Jesuit knew enough to recognize that what we would laugh at as folk medicine was not without value. He considered a number of herbal treatments and rejected them. His next step was to grow mold for poultices. His notes indicate that if he had stayed with that line of inquiry he might have saved Sir Alexander Fleming a great deal of trouble."

"But he didn't get that far."

"No. In the process of combining certain natural elements, he placed the composition over a heater, where it literally exploded, burned down, and left a scummy film. Intrigued, he repeated the experiment. After the second fire, he placed the residue under a microscope. Even with the primitive equipment he had at his disposal, he was able to separate out certain elements of the residue."

"Go on."

"Hydrocarbons and nitrogenous compounds."

"*Oil,*" McHenry whispered. Then he became silent, stunned by the enormity of what he had been told.

Dole smiled. "Yes, Mr. McHenry, the ancient alchemists' trick. Only, instead of base matter to gold, base matter to oil."

"Is there . . . ?"

"Don't bother with questions. For once I will be truthful and admit that we know nothing. Not the nature of the materials, their quantities, or how they were prepared. Nothing. Except that the priest passed a message out of the Forbidden City to the Imperial City, whence it was smuggled to another Jesuit. As the Society was having one of its periodic spats with the Chinese government, it was deemed wise to give the information to the English ambassador. His fleet stood an excellent chance of getting the message out, and did so. Naturally, despite political differences with Rome, Her Britannic Majesty's government obeyed its moral obligation to turn the message over to the papal nuncio in England. He, ahh, then obtained the key to the Jesuit code from Rome."

"In exchange for getting either the priest or the formula, England was to split the proceeds?"

"Something like that. Politics makes strange bedfellows, eh." Dole smiled. "Forgive me. I had no right to ascribe the sexual failings of the

English public school system to a dead Jesuit.''

"Hawkeland was sent to get the formula?''

"Yes. The priest wouldn't commit it to writing, even in the Jesuit code. In fact, we believe that the formula is in an entirely different code, one which you may be able to break.''

"I have no training in the field.''

"No, but you are reported by our computer to have an even greater skill. One which I have seen demonstrated. You can make connections that others fail to see. You called it a gift of the orphan. We call it a gift which will enable you to understand what the Jesuit said and why. You are the only man with the necessary physical training who can get inside their thought processes.''

"What happened next?''

"It had taken eight weeks for the message to reach London. Another four for decoding, translation, and negotiations between England and the Vatican. Four more to establish the expedition. Eight back. The Jesuit was safe as long as Yien Ling, the eunuch, thought that he was still floundering after a cure. The expedition was safe as long as it had a cover.''

"Which was?''

"Trade negotiations. You fella gimme gold statue. I give you fella pretty mirror.''

"Some things never change.''

"Of course. I'd forgotten that you're a broker. In any event, something happened at the Forbidden City. Hawkeland and his crew had to get quickly out of China. In making their escape by sea, they suffered a grievous loss of men and severe damage to the ship. Blown off course, running in fog for days on end, they beached up in Antarctica. After suffering God knows what horrors there, Hawkeland was lost with the formula.

"One of the crew members kept a diary. He was a Russian who has come down through history as Peter the Painter.''

"The Sidney Street shootout.''

"You *did* learn something at Oxford. That diary was eventually delivered to Winston Churchill, in a manner which will become clear to you. Unfortunately, the diary was stored with some random papers. Its existence, and value, only recently became known to us.''

"And to others.''

"And to others.''

"What about a cooperative effort?''

93

"Don't disappoint me. No alignment is perfect, or perpetual. Iran, after all, supplied the West with endless barrels of crude, until the Shah increased the price, throwing the world into an incredible economic imbalance. Then the people's demands increased on the Shah, and he went into something worse than imbalance. The Cambodians helped the Viet Cong win their war, hoping for some of that offshore crude. Only the Vietnamese turned around and conquered Cambodia. Do you need other examples?"

"No."

"Good, because no matter how friendly we may be with any country, including China, we cannot rely on their good offices in a matter of this sort. They are, after all, communists, with different goals. Where petroleum is concerned, we must learn self-reliance."

"And what of the Vatican? What reliance can it place on the mission?"

"Your concern is not unexpected, Jesuit school and all that."

"The Church is far behind me. I am a partner of Ingersoll and Constance. We pay our debts. You will pay yours."

"Do not dictate to me."

"I will dictate these terms, and you will accept them or do another computer scan for someone with my identical capabilities."

"It isn't worth the time. Very well, we will honor our debt to the Vatican."

"Your country's history of dealings with the Church does not reassure me. I want some guarantee that you will discharge your debt."

"The computer said that you were a very complex man, Mr. McHenry. As always, it was right. Are you familiar with the Lake District?"

"I am."

"We will arrange for you to meet a man there. He is an Englishman and a Catholic. He will satisfy your demands. After that, we will expect you to proceed immediately."

"And, based on one Arctic training course twenty years ago, you think I'm going to find the formula by going right to what is obviously an unknown spot near the South Pole."

"Worse than unknown. Totally lost. I can assure you that we exhausted all the easy alternatives before setting you up. But no, we do not expect it to be simple. For that reason we have arranged for you to have the very best equipment and scientific aides we could borrow from your government.

"More importantly, we have obtained the finest guide in the world. You are going with Vultan."

Chapter Nine

Vultan stood alone.

In an age when courage was defined as an astronaut in a controlled capsule uttering banalities while earthbound scientists pushed buttons, Vultan was unique: the private adventurer with a public following. He had not only lived in an underwater atmosphere longer than any other man, he had built the inner-space station from his own design. His first three trips to the South Pole had charted new land-to-water routes for the scientists who were to follow. The fourth exploration had been the only one begun by parachute and concluded by a man alone, on snowshoes. Vultan's exploration of New Guinea had actually culminated in the discovery of a previously unknown tribe. And, more than any other explorer of his era, he had become a hero to the public, owing to the work of his wife.

Most of Vultan's major expeditions had been recorded for the public by Katherine Bates Vultan, writer, photographer, artist, and spouse. Her books detailed their searches and discoveries in a style marked by grace and clarity. Her photographs and drawings caught the mystery of each tribe, each ruin, each civilization, in images impossible to dispel.

The books that they created out of their shared adventures were prepared in their famous study. Occupying the entire second floor of their Manhattan town house, the study housed rollaway walls, behind which were screens, projectors, and maps. There was a library of dialect tapes and language-teaching machines. Eight thousand volumes dealt with every aspect of anthropology, ethnicity, geography, and weapons. Over the years the room had become almost as famous as the Vultans.

It was in this room that Vultan had sat for months on end following the announcement that he was retiring. And it was in this room that he had later considered Sir Fraser Dole's proposal. The British intelligence chief hoped that his retirement was not permanent. As did the Central Intelligence Agency.

The only aspect of his work in which Katherine Vultan had not shared, by her own choice, was Vultan's missions for the Central Intelligence Agency. Vultan performed in the world of observation the type of high-level task reserved to George Ingersoll in the world of finance. He was the highly visible, universally welcome, totally unsuspected expert observer. Unlike Ingersoll, Vultan did not do what he did out of a sense of hereditary obligation. Nor did he do it for adventure or money. His sole motivation was patriotism to a country other than America. And the C.I.A. approved.

It had, in fact, been with C.I.A. approval that the British had invited him to join McHenry on the ice. There was no mention of Langley's approval, but Vultan knew that M.I.5 would not have contacted him without American consent. That meant that the British had a prior claim to something the Americans wanted. And, he knew, it must have been a claim of strange intensity. In the world of the two agencies, title meant nothing. So whatever it was, it was England's due; and America would not interfere. And it was in Antarctica.

Vultan raced through possible British interests there. It was nothing scientific; the English could not afford to join even one of the research teams which worked the ice. Nor was it anything strategic. H.M. government did not have even the money to repair the weapons it issued to the Home Guard.

Which left history. Scott was buried in the ice—the "grave which kings must envy," his men had called it. Shackleton was forgotten. Amundsen had done nothing for the British. As for Basil Hawkeland, why, the simple bastard hadn't even meant to go to Antarctica. He had been blown off course on his way back from China.

"Judas priest!" Vultan shouted in his den. The Americans did not want an incident, but they *did* want whatever the British wanted; and the British wanted whatever it was that Hawkeland had been bringing back from China.

"Judas priest," he said again, much more quietly. In five seconds he reasoned out all that would be asked of him and why. It would take slightly longer for him to learn if he could go. He was certain that he knew what the answer would be.

Vultan rang for Cartier and Bresnau, his principal aides. He told them only that he might be going to the South Pole, and that if he went they would accompany him. They were delighted with the prospect. They too had feared that his retirement might be permanent. But now there was to be a new expedition. They were more excited than at any time since they had gone to work for the Albanian.

Viator Vultan had been raised by his father to love Albania. It was said among the people of his mountain village that only an Albanian could care for the country, because, according to legend, it was the land that even Satan had refused.

The story, as passed along from one generation of mountain farmers to another, was quite simple. It held that God took Lucifer to a high peak and caused the earth to spin beneath them. After the fallen angel had seen all of the beauty that God was about to give man, he was told that, because of his unpardonable pride, he would have nothing good from the earth. Instead he was forced to choose from two scraps of land which God had not yet assigned. The first patch was a desolate landscape of parched and broken dirt, rivers of brackish water, stones that burned like coal, plants that never bloomed, and animals that were all barren. The second plot was worse. The devil claimed the first parcel for hell. What was left God called Albania.

As World War II ended, it seemed to the young Vultan, orphaned and made hard by the conflict, that Satan had made an understandable choice. With one agony ending, another was about to begin. Almost immediately after the war, the country was split into factions, with both Chinese and Russian commissars attempting to influence the direction Albanian communism would take. Arrayed against them were monarchists, republicans, and even the beginnings of a neo-Nazi group. Vultan knew that whichever faction prevailed in the long and bloody struggle to come, the winner would be able to rule only by imposing absolute dictatorship.

He left Albania and made his way to Greece and United States Army Intelligence. The army sent him to the C.I.A., which heard him out. He told the debriefing officer that he would not remain in a country where his only choices were to submit to totalitarianism or make a futile stand against it. He loved his country too much to stay, he said. By escaping, he offered himself an opportunity to live as a free man and perhaps one day return.

If a place could be found for him with the Americans . . .

The debriefing officer said that they would let him know. For now, there was a holding cell.

It took American intelligence two months to learn enough about the youth's background to realize that he was telling the truth about both his life and his country. Then, as now, Albania allowed little information to pass beyond its borders. What was obtained was expensive and dangerously derived. Once they came to believe him, the Americans knew that Vultan could be helpful, and so found a place for him. With it went the promise that five years of intelligence service in Europe would be recommended to the Immigration and Naturalization Service as an acceptable substitute for the landed immigrant status required before citizenship could be conferred.

During those five years, Vultan performed a number of functions for the Americans, primarily translator, occasionally assassin, always ostensibly a clerk. At the end of the agreed-upon time, the Americans kept their word. Vultan was sent to America, naturalized, and, by choice, became a regular agent for Langley.

It soon became apparent to his control that the time Vultan had spent working out of European offices had been wasted. His control believed that he should be assigned to the Adversity Group. The Adversity Group was so named because its members worked exclusively in hostile elements—jungles, mountains, the desert—wherever regular agents could not function. Even among the men of the Adversity Group, Vultan stood out. In the Iranian desert, helping to overthrow Mossadegh; in Honduras, establishing a junta; in Guatemala, wiping out revolutionaries, Vultan was a leader. And because he was a leader, Vultan was not content to spend his life following orders. He wanted his independence. To obtain it, he offered Langley an opportunity to use him in ways his control had never considered.

With Langley's financing, he organized Vultan Ventures. His company stood ready to outfit, train, and guide the wealthy, the corporate explorer, the restless, to any place on or beneath the earth, no matter how remote or inhospitable. The service offered opportunities for true exploration and the sort of luxurious camping trip favored by the wealthy. Those in the second group enjoyed everything but Vultan's presence. The true explorer enjoyed the pleasure of adventure under his personal command. It was the perfect cover for his work as an agent.

In the years to come, a Chilean mountaineering expedition under Vultan's command came down to the cities immediately before the fall of the Allende government. Vultan's privately constructed midget submarine was tested for commercial use in the very waters where, weeks later, the *Glomar Explorer* recovered a submerged Russian naval vessel. Vultan Ventures' archeological expeditions always seemed to open in the desert immediately before each major Arab-Israeli conflict. Each of the employees spoke Hebrew. And while all of this was happening, dozens of tours, trips, and mild adventures were being arranged for paying guests around the world, making Vultan very legitimate indeed.

After each mission, Vultan would submit a detailed report to Langley, attempting to show how what he had learned on the venture could be used against Albania. It was well known to his control that it ripped at Vultan's soul that Albania's Radio Tirana could broadcast into America. The broadcasts were made over radio teleprinter links which the Chinese communists had provided to their only non-Asian ally. Vultan constantly argued that a surgical strike against Tirana could be efficiently executed. Langley always refused, and his missions always continued. Then something happened to Vultan which affected him more deeply than Albania or Langley ever could.

In 1970, Vultan broke his first rule for the successful administration of a Venture and became involved with a lady guest. Katherine Bates was a twenty-two-year-old product of Bryn Mawr who had chosen a Vultan Venture up the Orinoco as a graduation present.

He knew too many unpleasant stories about hunters and guides who had bedded down a guest. The story always followed a similar path. If the husband was on the journey, he accepted his disgrace until safely back on his own turf. Then he set about destroying the guide's business. That could not happen to Vultan, of course, but he saw no reason to create a problem. If there was no husband present (or in existence), the possibilities for long-term complications made the effort self-defeating. He had bedded many women, but always in a private life that he kept private. Katherine Bates was different.

Vultan would never know what caused him to fall hopelessly, childishly in love. Whether it was the loneliness of his life, the emptiness caused by his family's early death, or merely an aging man's desire to touch again the softness of youth, what began as an interesting affair ended with his marriage to Katherine Bates.

Katherine Bates Vultan knew from the beginning of their marriage that she could never persuade her husband to give up his work for the Central Intelligence Agency. She was, however, able to persuade him to change its nature. She saw in him a man who was wasted as a planner of tours, no matter how important they seemed to be. Katherine Vultan recognized in her husband the ability to function alone, as an explorer and anthropologist. She possessed the power to record what he saw and did. Together, she argued, their contribution could be a great one. Her joy in his agreement was marred only slightly when he passed the matter through his control. Control approved. Langley recognized how valuable his independent travels would be.

As the years passed, his ventures provided income, his daring provided material, and her intelligence created a valuable contribution to the study of man. Their one regret—that they could not have a child—they put behind them. Their lives were full of their love for one another. The life together did not survive. The love did.

In the second decade of their marriage, Katherine Bates Vultan visited her physician, Ronald Wellers Deville, holder of the Chair of Endocrinological Medicine at the Manhattan Medical Center, professor of gynecology at two medical schools, and a leading expert on fertility experimentation. On the day of Katherine Bates Vultan's visit, he was dictating an application for a government grant, reviewing the results of fertility tests conducted on a hundred Rhesus monkeys, and thinking about the three hysterectomies he had scheduled for that afternoon. He was also listening, vaguely, to Katherine Bates Vultan complain of lower right quadrant pain, nausea, diarrhea, and headaches. When a laboratory assistant telephoned to report that three of the Rhesus monkeys had died as a result of a reaction to a form of synthetic progesterone, Dr. Deville told Katherine Vultan that she had a summer cold and sent her home.

When her condition worsened that night, she returned to the hospital. The resident on duty ordered a blood work-up and cultures. He also left instructions that the results were to be sent to Dr. Deville. Vultan took his wife home. The next afternoon she attempted to call Dr. Deville, who was frantically running around his laboratory attempting to learn why his monkeys were dying.

Like many women, Katherine Vultan had a misplaced trust in her physician. Like most physicians, Deville, when confronted with a potential loss of income, was unconcerned with a potential loss of life. He took her call and told her angrily that he had made his diagnosis, that she was creating problems where none existed, and that she should not call him again. Vultan, who had listened to the conversation on an extension, demanded that his wife allow him to take her to another physician. With the blind trust in a gynecologist which has killed so many women, she refused. With the realization that he could prevail against any force but his wife, Vultan acquiesced.

Twenty-four hours later, Katherine Vultan, now entirely without pain, again spoke to her physician. She wanted to know the results of her tests. Deville, who had not even known of the tests, flipped absently through the reports on his desk. When he found the right one, he saw the name of the resident who had been on duty, remembered that he was a good man, and assumed that he would have called Deville if there had been a problem. Deville told Mrs. Vultan that all was well and that she was not to disturb him again.

That night she died. A review of her test results would have disclosed to Dr. Deville a white count which almost guaranteed the presence of an infected appendix. He should have recognized the condition from Mrs. Vultan's office recital, but he had not been listening. Deville should have remembered that the sudden cessation of pain meant that the appendix had ruptured, but as a scientist he had been trained not to care. He closed her file and sent a bill for the visit, tests, and telephone consultation. He was paid promptly.

Vultan buried his wife privately. He then announced his retirement from active exploration and the business of Vultan Ventures. His control had been contacted and said that he understood. He also offered certain services, which Vultan declined. What he would do, he would do in his own way.

Would he want the use of a safe house? Control wanted to know. And a drop when it was done?

Vultan would.

Everything was arranged.

Vultan waited three months. Then he sent Cartier and Bresnau to the basement garage of Dr. Deville's apartment building. They parked behind his Mercedes and waited. When Deville emerged from the elevator and crossed the floor, Cartier and Bresnau left their vehicle, walked toward the Mercedes, and intercepted Deville. In a moment he was chloroformed and on his way to meet his dead patient's husband.

When Deville awoke in the safe house, Vultan was the first object to come into focus. As the physician's eyes locked on Vultan, his face became contorted with fear. "Mr. Vultan," he said.

"Yes, Doctor. Good evening."

"What is this all about?" Deville was not successful in his attempt to hide his terror.

"It's about you, Doctor. And my wife. My *dead* wife."

"Mr. Vultan, surely you must understand—"

Vultan pressed his right thumb and index finger down on the doctor's lips. When the doctor shook his head, indicating that he would be silent, Vultan nodded and said, "Everything which you could possibly wish to say, Doctor, has been anticipated. Please spare us both the embarrassment of begging." Vultan smiled. "Now let me tell you what I am going to do. Or rather what I am not going to do. I am not going to kill you. Although by my code the life you took makes your own forfeit. But no, I am merely going to make you even with me. I must live in a void now. Not touching, or walking to, or seeing, or hearing, or speaking with the one person I have ever loved. I will make my condition your condition."

Vultan's years as an agent had taught him to do professionally what he had planned. His love for his wife enabled him to do it without regret. His friends at Langley enabled him to do it at his leisure. The New York police had been told that the eminent doctor was away on government business. Word was discreetly spread through the medical community.

On the first night, Vultan amputated the doctor's hands. Deville did not awaken for two days. When he did so, he saw that the stumps of his arms were perfectly taped. He raised the useless pegs toward Vultan and began to cry. "Please," he begged. *"Please."*

Vultan smiled and said, "Tonight the feet."

Four days later, when he was strong enough, Dr. Deville was shown the needles that were to be used to blind him. His eardrums were pierced and his tongue removed. Then he was picked up by control and placed in a safe hospital for the insane.

The New York police were told that Deville had suffered an accident while doing secret research. For that reason, they did nothing when the doctor's medical colleagues contacted them. In a short time there were no further inquiries. The only one who ever thought about Deville was Vultan. Control complimented him on the excellence of his work; Langley's doctors thought that Deville should live for decades, during which time he would slowly waste into insanity.

Control did not contact Vultan for several months. He could think of no mission that would tempt him out of retirement. When he saw the British proposal, however, he was pleased. He thought that there was an excellent chance that Vultan would take it.

He did. Now Vultan had only to meet McHenry.

Chapter Ten

The Vatican was still. Along its corridors an occasional priest scurried to a chapel for evening prayer. The kitchen nuns silently reviewed the menus for the next day's luncheon meetings. Swiss Guards walked their posts, their garishly striped and stiffly collared uniforms and outsize halberds and visored helmets Michelangelo's eternal vengeance for being forced to design their costumes when he wanted to finish the Sistine Chapel. There was peace in the Holy See.

The Church itself, however, was in anguish. In the Soviet Union, negotiations to restore some public function to the Church had broken down. In Eastern Europe, all concessions had been withdrawn. Throughout the remainder of the world, the institutional Church was almost irreparably divided against itself. The traditionalists had established separate seminaries and dioceses, conducted the Latin Mass, and had drawn off nearly every Catholic over the age of fifty. Those under fifty had simply stopped attending church. To them, the sight of ancient Italian cardinals fighting change had been at first worrisome, then ludicrous, and finally irrelevant. Where there was still an active Church, its moral hold was frail: Mass was unattended; the sacraments unreceived. Worst of all, America, once the great jewel in the triple tiara of the papacy, was a desert home to the Church. Few young men studied for the priesthood; few schools were financially solvent; few Catholics cared. And, greatest of all moral tragedies, for every child born, two were aborted.

At that thought, Pope Xavier sighed wearily as a small clock chimed ten times. He tapped a soup spoon against his untouched bowl of broth and lentils. When the clock stopped, he continued to tap, then realized what he was doing and put the spoon on his tray. Beside it sat a bottle of Perrier, bread, and melon. Like most of his meals, this one would be consumed by one of the kitchen cats.

Father Agnelli, the Pope's secretary, silently entered the room

103

and inclined his head. "Your Holiness has not eaten."

"No. No." He smiled. "Before our elevation, we enjoyed a cigarette after dinner. Now we do not even care to eat dinner."

"If you eat, Papa, perhaps a cigarette can be found."

Xavier laughed. "No, dear Father. There shall be no dessert for the Pope tonight." He shook his head. "We cannot eat."

"There are still cigarettes in my desk."

"No. We may one day start again, but we will never have the strength to stop again."

"A cognac?"

"No, Father, thank you. Is there any word from Father Halloran?"

"He left twenty minutes ago. I will tell Your Holiness when he is at the gate."

"Thank you, Father."

"Holiness?" Xavier looked at the young priest. "There is time yet before Father Halloran arrives. Would you be kind enough to hear my confession, Your Holiness?"

The Pope nodded. He had been flattered when Agnelli had asked him to be his confessor. The young man was pure and holy, and Xavier felt that he had profited more than the penitent. They crossed to the small room where only Xavier and his secretary had their confessions heard. The younger priest knelt behind a thin screen. The Church had long since given the penitent the option of talking casually, without the screen, but Agnelli said that he preferred the old ways of his youth, and Pope Xavier understood.

Agnelli knelt beneath a crucifix which had been a gift from a Russian Orthodox bishop. Unlike the Roman crucifix, this had a small resting pad beneath the feet of Jesus, signifying the different description of the cross which is accepted by the Russians. The two men spoke for only a few minutes.

After the sacrament had been administered, Xavier told Agnelli, "Go to bed. Charles Halloran is too good a friend to be announced."

Father Agnelli nodded. He knew that Xavier was not rebuking him. It was his job to announce all who passed the outer perimeters of the Pope's apartment. Even Father Halloran. Father Agnelli would be back at his post in a matter of minutes.

Watching Father Agnelli, strong and refreshed, anxious to serve God and the Pope without question, Xavier remembered himself as a young priest. He had always been assigned to someone's staff, but he had always volunteered to work weekends in an understaffed parish. He needed to be with the people, to feel that he was helping them. There were always sinners in need of confession. But most people in the confessional were sad and repetitive: young women who thought that their softly, slowly, sensuously whispered fantasies would shock him; the scrupulous confessing to sins that were not sins; the very young and the very old confessing to the torment of sexual desires that could not be satisfied.

He had never reprimanded them. He did not believe that it was his place to do so. It was his duty to instruct, to impart forgiveness, and to impose a light penance. He never lectured or became angry, as so many foolish priests did. He did not believe himself good enough to admonish others. For that reason, he asked every penitent to pray for him, after he had absolved their sins.

The sins. Adultery, buggery, robbery, murder, arson, treason, kidnapping, theft, fornication, sodomy, sacrilege. No matter what the offense, he was under God's injunction to forgive the truly sorrowful.

But not when the sin was abortion. So singularly evil was the murder of a fetus that no priest could forgive it without the consent of his bishop. "Come back in one week," the priest would whisper through his fingers, fingers which were pressed against the grille of anonymity.

"Do you believe this person to be truly sorrowful?" the bishop would later ask.

"Yes, Your Excellency."

"Then you may forgive. And hope that God does."

Now, Xavier realized, no one bothered to confess abortion at all. Ex-priests married ex-nuns on church steps, then supported themselves by running abortion centers.

Let them. And let them be damned. He had his duty.

Internally he was locked in a death struggle with the Curia, the collection of bishops and bureaucrats who administered the Church as ruthlessly as the Imperial eunuchs had once run the Manchu court. The curialists were diplomats all, attenuated to every subtlety and immune to every emotion. To them the world was evil, and it would either repent or be condemned. To the curialists the essence of truth was contained within the Vatican; any reaching out was contrary to God's wishes. Xavier's own well-known desire to reach out was the reason the Curia's representatives in the College of Cardinals had opposed his election. The Curia's medieval insularity and intellectual pride required them always to seek another man like the foremost of their ranks to have attained the papacy.

That man was Eugenio Pacelli. Pacelli the scholar, who thought in Latin. Pacelli the aristocrat, who shunned audiences with the poor. Pacelli the diplomat, who, as Pius XII, secured the safety of Church property during World War II. It was arranged in exchange for his silence. He could have excommunicated the Catholic Hitler, but did not. Instead, he appointed bishops friendly to fascism, warned against the creation of a Jewish homeland, and gave his benediction to the contemporary crucifixion of six million men, women, and children whose only offense was to share the heritage of Jesus, Mary, and Joseph.

Xavier had no doubt that whatever views theologians held of the nature of hell, Pius XII's torment was unique in all of history.

Between the death of Pius and the election of Xavier, there were six popes. The first, in the spirit of *aggiornamento,* the opening, attempted to admit light and human feeling into the Church's deliberations. Instead, he unleashed a revolution of expectations which could not be satisfied. An educated, articulate laity was no longer willing to blindly memorize the catechism. People wanted to know why. The first of the popes to follow Pius told the faithful that it was no sin to ask. The next one attempted to reverse that stand. Two did not reach the question. Two ignored it. As a result, when Xavier came to the papacy, the Church was more grievously wounded than at any time in its history. The process had taken only a few decades, no measurable time at all to the Church. Yet it could not be stopped once it had begun.

When Pius died, Church law required the College of Cardinals to elect his successor. Alone among the ranks of priests the office of cardinal has no justification in the words of Jesus or the writings of the great theologians. The title comes from the Latin root *cardo:* hinge. The election of a Pope hinges on their deliberations. In all other things they are superfluous. Theirs is the title of an office once given to the second sons and first ministers of ambitious kings. Theirs is the honor now given to men who can lift mortgages and clear debts and, on occasion, save souls. Most often, it is the title given to the bishops who administer the various offices of the Curia.

The Curia, with its hundreds of departments and holy offices and sacred commissions, is an endless web of desiccated priests who surround the Church and study questions ranging from the sanctity of candidates for sainthood to whether or not rosaries may be made of plastic.

In much the manner of the Victorian army, where barracks soldiers looked down upon those who had served in the field, the curialists detested the priests who worked in parishes, rode jungle trails, cared for the sick, and comforted the survivor. The field priests could not understand that a life in the Curia meant a life concerned with the essence of Catholicism: obedience to one's superiors and reverence for tradition. Everything else was a form of human contact which could infect and destroy the Church. For that reason, everything else was to be excluded and the new Pope drawn from the ranks of the Curia. Pius had made it clear that he was to be succeeded by Archbishop Giovanni Montini, a longtime intimate of the Curia, only recently assigned a diocese so that he could develop his administrative skills prior to his elevation to the papacy. Pius had planned to elevate Montini to the red hat, but delayed doing so because of a minor squabble. Both were Italian aristocrats, and easily incurred wounds to their vanity. As punishment for a slight disagreement, Montini saw his name deleted from a proposed list of new cardinals. Pius planned to forgive and forget, accept Montini's apology (although the nature of the offense had slipped his mind), and create him cardinal at a forthcoming consistory. Pius died before the red hat could be bestowed; but the other members of the Sacred College knew of the dead Pope's plans for Montini. It was not impossible for the cardinals to reach outside their ranks for a new Pope. As they arrived in Rome, they knew that they were expected to choose Montini. Montini, the cardinals knew, would do all the right things in the right way, which was to say that nothing would change. And, as for the Jews, Montini had had nothing to do with Pius's conduct. In any case, the Curia reasoned, the Jews had killed Christ.

The various members of the Sacred College of Cardinals entered the Sistine Chapel and stood before their individual thrones that were covered by silken canopies. When one of their number was elected, all of the canopies but his would be dropped. As they seated themselves, each saw at his side a small table with his coat of arms and name in Latin.

Above the altar hung a tapestry of the Holy Spirit descending upon the Apostles, giving them guidance. On the altar was a chalice and a small golden plate called a paten.

To the side was a potbellied stove with its flue projecting out a window onto Saint Peter's Square. At each ballot the cardinals would write the name of their choice on a slip of paper, lay it on the paten, then place it in the chalice to signify the completion of a sacred act. The master of ceremonies would collect and count the ballots. If no one was elected, he would place the ballots in the stove and burn them with wet straw. The flue would pour black smoke out over the heads of the faithful. The process would continue. The master of ceremonies would circle the chapel and hand each cardinal one sheet of paper, then leave them with each other and, hopefully, the guiding presence of the Holy Spirit. When the choice was finally made, the ballots were burned without straw, white smoke would issue, and the greatest dynasty in the history of man would continue.

Certain things are understood before the election begins. The new Pope must be Italian, to avoid beginning a cycle of nationalism. (This rule, violated in 1978, is again intact.) The new Pope must not be elected on the first ballot, to avoid exposing him to the sin of pride. The first ballot must be used to recognize the loyal service of those who will never be Pope.

At the election following the death of Pius, the first ballot went according to tradition. The growth of the American Church was recognized by a few votes for Spellman, the diplomat, and Cushing, the ward leader. Worthies of the Curia, too hated to be elected, voted for one another, causing many smiles and some polite applause. Jean Cardinal Tisserant, Dean of the College of Cardinals, received ten votes in honor of his diligence and piety. With the aid of his cane, the venerable Frenchman rose and said, "*Je ne suis pas ici* [I am not here]."

After the ballots were burned, several cardinals spoke of the great work of Pius, carefully avoiding all mention of his complicity in the slaughter of the Jews. Each spoke of Pius's final wish, that Montini succeed him. The rest listened silently, aware that a vote for another was the priestly thing to do, yet tempted to make their own name one with the ages.

When the ballots were counted, Montini was four short.

Tisserant again struggled to his feet and said, "*Je suis de retour* [I have come back]." There was laughter. He looked around the chapel slowly and said, "Tonight I would speak with you."

He was visited all through the night by small groups of the Church's elite. He endorsed Montini, he told them. But Montini was not yet sixty. There would be time for him. For now, Tisserant said, let him continue in his new post as archbishop of a great city. Let him learn about the Church outside as he had about the Curia. Then he would be ready to become a great Pope. For now, he concluded, choose an old man who will sit quietly and keep the Chair of Peter occupied while Montini learns.

Tisserant knew that arguments in favor of old age and caution would always be persuasive to the College of Cardinals. He also knew who it was that would have to be chosen, and he had some idea of how that man would act. Tisserant had spent the night before the election with this man, Angelo Cardinal Roncalli, sharing coffee and cognac and exchanging reminiscences. As the hours passed, the courtly Frenchman realized that all of the joyous human contact he had been denied by his career was a part of this little man. Somehow he had served God and enjoyed humanity. It was this man, Tisserant knew, who should be Pope. But Tisserant was too experienced a curial diplomat to suggest someone who had rarely served in the Vatican. Instead, he only offered suggestions and went to sleep confident of what the next ballot would bring.

While he slept, Tisserant heard, as he did each night, the screams of Jews being taken by the Nazis from Nancy to the death camps. There was no voice in the dream to articulate their screams into compassion. Most throats had been frozen in fear. Tisserant's own silver tongue had been stilled, stupidly, unforgivably silent, because of his obedience to Pius. Perhaps now, he thought, on the evening before the third ballot, part of the debt would be paid.

More ballots were taken. Eventually, the master of ceremonies counted the ballots and announced that a new Pope had been elected. As the master of ceremonies approached the winner, the cardinals heard the canopies above their thrones begin to drop. Tisserant smiled as he saw Roncalli poise on the edge of his throne so that he could be the first to go to the new Pope and swear obedience. As the master of ceremonies approached him, Roncalli realized that his canopy had not fallen. He stood and screamed, "No! No! I beg you." As he cried out, the others came forward to do homage to Pope John XXIII.

John was old and he had not made his career in the Curia, but he was not a quiet, malleable Pope. Like any activist, much of what he did was the product of fervent ideas and poor thinking. He wanted to nationalize all the world's property without concern for who would run it. He believed that communists were friends who had merely made some doctrinal errors. His style was that of a ham-fisted peasant priest suddenly among clergy who do not have tomato stains on their soutanes. But these were not his worst offenses. These the Curia could have forgiven. What could not be forgiven was his concept of opening the Church up to the world. *A universally loving God. The freedom to choose one's own religion. The idea that the Jews had not killed Christ.* These execrable notions ran counter to a millennium of curial development: the Church obtained its ends by demanding; it did not negotiate. If the Church's opponents did not come around, they were condemned. John's entire papacy was an attempt to eradicate the formalized structure of nuances which had served the Church so well for so long. All future popes, it was decided, would be men trained by and loyal to the Curia.

When John died, Montini was swiftly elected and crowned Paul VI. He managed to roll back too many reforms to suit the young and not enough to comfort the conservatives. Catholics stayed away from their Church in droves. Paul hung on too long and died unregretted.

Before word of Paul's death was flashed to the outside world, cardinals were on the phone. Some of them were troubled by the Church's drift. They were not persuaded that it was enough to condemn one's enemies and ignore them. To these men, it was necessary to respect the wishes of the laity and choose a Pope who was a pastor, not a bureaucrat. Using the logistical advantages of being in Rome, these cardinals combined to guarantee the immediate election of Albino Cardinal Luciani, who took the name John Paul I.

It seemed at first that his choice of name was a public relations master stroke. (No matter that he should not have been called the first until there had been a second.) It was a name which indicated that he would serve the Church's people with John's love and Paul's concern for certain immutable truths. It became quickly apparent, however, that the name was not puffery. It was truth. John Paul I planned to bridge the gap between the Church and the people.

To do this, he went his own way. He made speeches extemporaneously rather than clearing them through the Curia. He took advice from no one, joked with altar boys, and ignored paperwork. The curialists did nothing. John Paul I wrote letters to Mark Twain, compared the soul to a car, and called God our Mother. The curialists did nothing. He even admitted that he spoke with Pinocchio about moral problems. Again they did not act. Then, barely a month into his papacy, John Paul I told an interviewer that he had been taught by Cardinal Ottaviani, premier policeman of the Church, that heaven was closed to all but Catholics. Over the years, he told the interviewer, he had seen all manner of men and had come to learn that Ottaviani was wrong, that heaven was open to all who followed their conscience to God.

In the morning the Pope was dead. Following his sudden death (and the Vatican's refusal to allow an autopsy), the cardinals returned to Rome. Those men who had engineered the election of John Paul I fell to squabbling among themselves. The cardinals who had not been Pope makers caucused and found unanimous anger at the preceding prearranged conclave (although there was also almost universal love for the man it had elected). These cardinals felt that it was time for the Church to face the reality and dangers of communism and to continue to attempt to bring the joy of their faith to the world.

Chemicals were used instead of wet straw. Argument was employed instead of Roman fawning. A Pole was elected instead of an Italian.

John Paul II alienated his principal American supporters by reactivating the recently renamed office of the Holy Inquisition. He won over much of the Church, however, by opening communications to the communist bloc countries. He was unfeelingly conservative, although he recognized, as the media do not, that certain truths are immutable. The Pope can allow the ordination of married men, and of women; he can allow the Mass to be said in the vernacular and permit any other change which does not contravene Christ's teachings. Those things which the Church finds to be rooted in doctrine rather than tradition—the sanctity of marriage, the right to life of the fetus—cannot be tampered with by any man. While attending to one of the things which man may touch, a political question where his assistance had been requested, his plane crashed and his papacy was cut short.

When the Sacred College next met, there was, for once, agreement on an issue: the new Pope should be an Italian. The Church remembered the awful dissension of the Middle Ages, when every country wanted one of its own on the Chair of Peter (and when as many as three men claimed simultaneously to be Pope). The election of John Paul II ignited cries of nationalism which the cardinals ignored at the next conclave. They would not risk ethnic factions again.

With that issue agreed upon before the election, the curialists acted quickly to choose the next Pope. As every cycle of activity in history precedes an era of calm, they argued, so too should the Church be given a period of reflection. The more progressive agreed and were duped into electing Benedict XVI, the former Cardinal-Grand Penitentiary, who ruled on problems of conscience. He believed that the best way to end the divisions within the Church was to condemn them, ignore them, and trust in God. At his death, the Catholic traditionalists had established separate churches in five European countries and America, no Protestant churchman of note would talk to a member of the Catholic hierarchy, and what slight religious activity had been allowed in communist countries had been crushed.

Benedict managed to rigidify the Church for eight years. His death brought Leo XIV to the Throne of Peter. Leo had been Cardinal-in-Chief of the Holy Roman Rota, the Curia Office which administers and interprets the Church's law of marriage. This office is concerned with resolving whether or not a sexually potent man who has had a vasectomy is theologically impotent. The Rota has also decreed that a Catholic who recognizes divorce for the unhappy, but enters into a happy marriage of his own, is probably not validly married. Most interestingly, the Rota enforces the Church's teaching that the absence of love is irrelevant to Catholic marriage law.

With this background, Leo was totally unprepared for the shambles which confronted him on his election. Two years later he was dead of a heart attack.

The members of the Curia had agreed that their cardinals would vote as a bloc for Pietro Cardinal Robustelli, Chairman of the Sacred Commission on Ritual. The outsiders were split. The traditionalists relied on this split, expecting that it would continue through ballot after ballot, assuring Robustelli's election.

On the morning of the first day of the consistory, the youngest member of the college, Antonio Cardinal Sebastianelli, broke all precedent, ignored form and ritual, and stood to ask that the first ballot not be used to honor faithful service. For thirty minutes he decried the foundering vessel of faith in which they had imprisoned themselves. It was time to end the Church's isolation, he argued. The world was not an evil place. It was God's creation, and only men and inaction made it evil. It was time for a man of action, one who had mastered the Curia without being sucked dry by it, one who understood the problems of priests and nuns and laity alike, who had visited the world's capitals and had found them inhabited by men willing to talk if not agree. He ended by saying that it was time to use the first ballot to show unity and elect Giancarlo Cardinal Ferrari.

John Cardinal Flynn, Archbishop of New York, sprang to his feet, pointed out Ferrari and shouted, "*Ita* [Thus be it]!" The four other American cardinals quickly followed. Graeme Cardinal Deerfield, Primate of England, joined them. And then France, Western Europe, South America, Asia, Africa. Only the Italians, the masters of the Curia, remained seated. Their objections were not enough. The canopies began to fall.

Giancarlo Ferrari was the only son of an undistinguished member of the Italian nobility. The father, Massimo, had been educated as a

112

geologist and upon graduation joined a minerals exploration company with offices in Milan and operations in Ethiopia. Massimo spent three years in Africa and returned to Italy in time to marry another impoverished member of the nobility, Lise Canale, and to father a son. In time, because four days after Giancarlo's birth Italy entered World War I.

One of the many things that made the army unique was its use of priests as combat soldiers. One of those draftees, a man who rose to sergeant in Tenente Ferrari's platoon, was Angelo Roncalli, the priest who became John XXIII. Ferrari, unlike most devout Italians, did not combine his unlettered love for his Church with a healthy streak of anti-clericalism. He did what he could for Roncalli, although the priest never asked for favors. Ferrari's kindnesses were small but appreciated by the fat peasant. These little acts, and the two soldiers' academic backgrounds, rare in the infantry, made them close.

When the war ended, the two men made the vow of thousands of comrades in arms: we shall never lose touch. It is a vow which endures until the first time a wallet or notebook is cleansed of its excess paper. Addresses are forgotten, names blur, all incidents somehow become amusing in recollection, random meetings in later years are uncomfortable at best. But for whatever reasons, Ferrari and the priest kept their promise.

Roncalli spent the two decades between the wars slowly winning a reputation as a capable administrator, a priest with the common touch who worked well with the Vatican. Ferrari returned to Ethiopia with his wife and child. The parents divided their efforts with the boy: Massimo attempted to develop him into a scientist, Lise fought to make him a model of the effeminate, superstitious Catholic so common among the Mediterranean clergy. Like many children raised in such circumstances, young Giancarlo stood back from the fray and took a bemused view of it all. To please his father, he agreed to be trained as a geologist. On his graduation, to please God, he became a priest.

By 1938 Massimo had seen enough of the new Italy in Africa to be persuaded that he would have to go underground. He made arrangements for his wife to emigrate to America, where he had already secretly banked enough money to allow for her needs. He arranged for Giancarlo to join the staff of Archbishop Angelo Roncalli. Then Massimo disappeared. He joined the partisan band of Enrico Mattei, an Italian businessman with a particular interest in petroleum. Mattei made certain that Massimo worked as hard at geology as he did at warfare. On every operation, rock samples were taken and soil specimens collected. Late in the war their efforts were rewarded: in the Po Valley the two men discovered a small pocket of oil. They kept their discovery secret until the war's end, when Mattei arranged to have himself appointed head of the Italian national oil company, AGIP. Massimo became his chief of exploration.

The deposits were small, but in resource-starved Italy the power of men who could make such a discovery became almost mythic. By remaining aloof from Italian politics (they were, after all, intelligent men), they amassed great political power. They were patriots who wanted to gain entree for Italy into the councils of the world's wealthiest nations. They obtained their entree by exchanging certain Italian trading rights for concessions in Russian and Iranian oil. The revolving governments needed them, and the two men prospered.

While Mattei and Massimo used Italy's postwar industrial strength to make themselves wealthy and powerful men, Giancarlo used his father to advance his own career in the Church. His assignment during World War II had been to serve as Archbishop Roncalli's secretary. It was a fortuitous duty, keeping him away from the inner workings of the Vatican. Sensitive to man's needs and obligations, Giancarlo would have been unable to keep silent in the face of Pius's conduct. Roncalli, knowing both the Pope's attitudes and those of his young secretary, wisely kept them distant.

By 1953 Giancarlo was a monsignor and Roncalli a cardinal. Rather than hold the younger man to him, Roncalli arranged that he be assigned to the Vatican's Foreign Office. With his own skills and his father's connections, Giancarlo proved invaluable in obtaining concessions from Middle Eastern nations, concessions which allowed the Church to enjoy the status of a tolerated visitor in Islamic lands.

In 1956 Pius XII elevated Giancarlo to the rank of bishop *in pectoris,* a bishop of the heart, with all of a bishop's powers and authority, but with his rank held secret in the heart of the Pope. With this secret power, Giancarlo was able to travel to Eastern European countries as a minor functionary of the Vatican Foreign Office. After each traditional round of futile visits to communist state officers, he would by prearrangement meet local priests whose loyalty to the Vatican was absolute. These men he secretly elevated to the bishopric, thereby empowering them to ordain priests and consecrate new bishops. In this way did the Church continue. After each trip, the Vatican press was careful to note that Monsignor Ferrari's trip had been cordial but unproductive. The communist host country diplomat accredited to Rome would clip and forward the press release. The priests who were known to be loyal to the Vatican could once again be safely ignored.

After Roncalli's coronation as Pope, his first act was to go through the ceremony of consecrating Ferrari a public bishop. Shortly thereafter he elevated him to the rank of cardinal and assigned him to be Secretary of Congregations.

From his father, Ferrari had learned how to respect all cultures, how to be at home with men whose lives and values were different, but whose assistance was needed. From his own deep humanity, he learned how to use the power of the Church to help others, not oppress them. These qualities, and his father's fortuitous friendship with Roncalli, guaranteed that he would rise within the Church. And that he would be in, but not of, the Curia. His appointment as Secretary of Congregations was his first task within the Curia. As such, he was the final arbiter of all questions involving the conduct and administration of the Church's myriad orders of priests, brothers, and nuns (although it was rumored that the one thing God did not know was how many orders of nuns there were). Every individual who served God by serving in an order lived under the Rule of Life drawn up by the order's founder. Giancarlo Cardinal Ferrari, who belonged to no order, determined what the rules meant.

One of his secretaries was Charles Halloran, chosen by his Jesuit superiors for his brilliance and sanctity. He so impressed Ferrari that when his two-year rotation was concluded, the cardinal arranged for him to be permanently assigned to his staff. Two years after that, Ferrari was named the Vatican's Secretary of State and asked Father Halloran to be his first deputy, with the rank of bishop.

It had been a dazzling prospect. At the age of thirty-seven, the boy from Washington's slums would be elevated to a bishopric, removed from the anonymity of his Society (which permitted the elevation only in extraordinary circumstances), and made a major force in the diplomatic efforts of the Church. His superiors urged him to accept. Not only would it be good for the order, it would bring an American into the Vatican Foreign Office for the first time since the election of John Kennedy had required their removal. His superiors, however, could only urge. Ferrari had made it clear that the choice must be Halloran's.

To the surprise of everyone but Ferrari, Halloran chose to return to America and reassignment by his Society. In keeping with the custom of the Jesuits, Halloran knew that four years in soft and prestigious posts would lead to eight in a mission land. As brilliant as his mind was, that simple was his faith. Christ had not taken the easy route. Neither would Charles Halloran.

When informed of his protégé's choice, Ferrari invited him to his office in the Vatican, hoping to dissuade him from returning to America. Ferrari rose from a Queen Anne chair as Halloran entered, caught him as he knelt to kiss the cardinal's ruby ring, and led him to a tea cart.

"I'll pour," Ferrari said. He measured out two cups of tea with lemon, handed one to Halloran, and said, "I have always wondered why my fondness for English tea does not offend your hot Irish temper."

"The English have given us much that is good, *Eminenza.*" As a protégé, he was allowed to use the familiar term of address.

"Such as?"

"Good Queen Bess, without whom the Church would have been denied so many Jesuit martyrs."

Ferrari smiled and crooked his finger. "Charles, you are more brilliant than any priest I know. You have the gift of languages, a love of literature, and a burning desire to serve God by serving man. You also have the touch of a rapist."

"Any observation by Your Eminence is welcome as valued and fair."

"You make me a liar." Ferrari laughed.

"I do not understand. But of course I do not have Your Eminence's fine Roman nose for the politic."

Ferrari rested a finger on his hooked nose and smiled again. "The touch of a rapist."

"Then I have restored Your Eminence to grace."

"You are playing with me." He was laughing.

"I am a Jesuit."

"Of that there is no doubt."

The two men sipped their tea. Finally Ferrari said, "Charles, come with me to the Foreign Office. I need you. It is no sin to be ambitious to serve God."

"Ambition is a weakness in any man. In a priest it is fatal."

"Now you do wound me."

"I do not mean to do so. You have certain skills; it would be wrong not to use them. My time is not now."

Ferrari opened an envelope, the black wax across the flap popping as his finger separated the folds. "This is your new assignment. I know what it is. Come with me, my friend."

"My time is not now. I need to serve God by serving his people in the fields, not the corridors of the Vatican."

The cardinal flipped the sides of the envelope and spoke in Latin the words that would send Charles Halloran to a leper colony near Jakarta. "Did you know?"

"Humility follows exaltation. As a Jesuit, I expected it." He rose and crossed to Ferrari, then knelt for his blessing, which was freely given.

The cardinal escorted the younger man to the door. "Your time will come, Charles. And you will not be able to say no."

"I have taken the fourth vow, *Eminenza*. I think you know that my total obedience will one day be yours."

"In that, Charles, I hope that you are as wrong as any man can be."

But he had not been wrong. It had happened, as they both had always known it would. And now Charles Halloran, a man of obedience, had come to advise his friend, the Pope.

Father Agnelli entered and inclined his head. "Holiness, Father Charles Halloran."

The Pope nodded and Agnelli went to a desk, opened a drawer, and removed a hand sweeper. The conversation which Xavier and Halloran were about to have could destroy the Church if discovered. And each man in the room knew that Robustelli was capable of discovering it. The hand sweeper was designed to emit a loud beeping sound when passed over a listening device. The young priest carefully swept the entire room while Xavier crossed the floor to greet his guest. "Good friend. We are honored."

"The honor is mine, Holiness." Halloran's simple black cassock twisted in the evening air as he genuflected and kissed his Pope's ring. His Pope, he thought. Pontiff. *Pontifex.* The bridge builder. The link to God. Inheritor of the Chair of Peter. "Thou art Peter," Christ had said, "and upon this rock I will build my Church." Peter. *Petrus.* The rock. Not a pun. A promise. And it had stood the test of time.

As had their friendship. Through all the years, Ferrari had been careful to make no attempt to influence the Society of Jesus on behalf of Halloran. The cardinal knew too well how jealous of its prerogatives was the largest order of priests in the Church. And how powerful was its Superior General, the Black Pope. But the Jesuits had known, of course, that Ferrari was the younger priest's friend, and they had been careful to recognize his talents. His term in a leper colony had been cut short when the presidency of the local Jesuit university had become available. After a total of nine years in Jakarta, Halloran had returned to lecture on church-state politics at the School of Foreign Service at Georgetown. A two-year term as the school's dean had been followed by his successive elections as the local provincial, superior of the American chapter of the order, and finally the Jesuits' first American Superior General.

Agnelli cleared his throat. When Xavier looked to him, he nodded. "We may proceed, Charles."

"There are vaulted rooms, Your Holiness."

"We will not hide in the Vatican. Bad enough we go through these searches." Xavier nodded his thanks to Agnelli, who withdrew, closing the door.

Halloran looked at the table beside the Pope and studied the untouched food. This once he decided to use the term of endearment which Xavier encouraged, but which Halloran found uncomfortable, almost disrespectful. "*Papa,* you should eat."

"We are rarely hungry. There is so much to trouble me."

"When Your Holiness is troubled, he does not eat. When you do not eat, your flock worries. When you see your children worried, you are troubled. The only solution is to eat."

Xavier laughed. "Charles, if ever a man was born to be a Jesuit." Halloran smiled. "We are glad that you can smile, Charles. Your knowledge of world events must be troubling indeed."

Halloran nodded his acceptance of the Pope's invitation to speak on the subject which had brought them together that evening. Now Xavier would not be *il Papa,* his longtime friend. Now they were Pope and adviser.

As they took their seats, Halloran said, "The British have McHenry. The Chinese will also act. My sources are certain."

"And?"

"And we must move."

Xavier smiled. "Charles, you would never have made a curial diplomat. Such a man would have said, 'We should lend ourselves to prayerful contemplation of a possible temporal course of action.' "

"And what would a curial diplomat say of the chemical formula? Would he admit that it is ours, that it was discovered by a Jesuit priest working in a laboratory financed by the Church. More importantly, what would he say of our acting now?"

"All of the Curia would oppose action.

"The world is collapsing into a moral cesspool and they send us learned tracts detailing philosophical objections to the evils which torment our flock. We point out the divisions, the persecutions, the spiritual collapse, and the Curia tells us to do as our predecessors did for two thousand years: condemn and ignore; then the problem will go away."

"Then I can act?"

Xavier held up his hand. "It is not the simple choice it appears to be. It is not between you and the forces of evil. The men in the Curia, for the most part, are not bad. They are only too isolated from reality to be of assistance to us."

"For the most part?"

"If I die tonight, do you know who will succeed me?"

"Robustelli."

"Yes. Robustelli. And if he learns of this plan, or it fails, he would force a convocation of the Sacred College and I would be turned out of office."

"He would not do such a thing. True, he represents a reactionary force within the —"

Xavier raised his hand. "It is not that. And it is not merely that he fought my election. He is a vicious, evil man."

"He is a cardinal."

"So were many of the Borgias."

Halloran nodded. "Go on."

"Charles, in the archives are the files on every priest in the Church. You know that."

"Yes."

"One of them is Robustelli's. The first entry after his assignment to the Curia is a letter from a foreign ambassador to Pius praising Robustelli for a moving sermon he gave to reluctant troops before their first assignment." Xavier covered his eyes and began to cry. He heard Halloran move and shook his head. "No, no, Charles. We are composed." He breathed deeply, took a silk square from the sleeve of his soutane, and wiped his face. "The soldiers were the men of the Death's Head S.S. They were about to start the ovens at Ravensbruck."

"Oh, God." Halloran bowed his head, devastated.

" 'Go forth,' he told them, 'and do the work of Christ in whatever ways are necessary.' "

"Perhaps, in his maturity—"

"He is worse now. If he ever learns of the mission, he will use it to drive me from the papacy and start the Church moving backward, inexorably marching to its own destruction."

119

"My sources are secure."

"Charles, the Jesuit network in China is staggering. But there are other ways for the plan to become known."

"It is worth the risk."

"We are not persuaded."

"*I* am. There is only one issue. Not your papacy, not my network of covert Jesuits, not Robustelli's nostalgia for the Nazis and Pius. You have years left to restructure the Church, achieve a modus vivendi between the many warring factions. You have already made strides in that direction. The restructuring of the splintered Church can be accomplished only over time. The question of five million American abortions each year must be addressed now. The United States can no longer afford to import endless rivers of Middle Eastern crude; and what there is of that will soon be as dry as the rest of the earth. We can give the Americans the formula. It can all be done through George Ingersoll. All we ask is a Presidential order on funding. That will give Ingersoll time to work the other levers, to seek a permanent resolution."

"It may fail."

"It may succeed."

"It has become a political issue."

"That is what Pius said about the Jews."

"You are a cruel man, Charles."

"Yes or no?"

"Do you have the men?"

"I have the man."

"Do what you must."

When the Pope had gone to bed, Father Agnelli returned to Xavier's apartment. As he did each evening, he adjusted the window levers to allow just the correct flow of air into the room, lifted the Pope's breviary from the night stand and opened it to the next day's first reading, and left the nightly cable summaries from each apostolic delegate around the world.

The young priest quietly entered the small confessional. On the penitent's side was the Greek Orthodox crucifix. Agnelli moved the resting pad beneath the nailed feet slightly, turning off the tiny motor. He then placed his fingers on the metal sign which read "INBI." The letters were an abbreviation hung over the head of Jesus by the Romans—who alone had the power of crucifixion—and which were meant to specify

120

the mocking title, Jesus of Nazareth, King of the Jews. Agnelli slid the sign out of its clips, removed the tape disk, replaced the letters, and left to call Cardinal Robustelli.

Chapter Eleven

Marshal Kiying put down his ragged copy of the *Ping Fa* and lit a cigarette. He detested the Chinese brands. Tobacco was his one great weakness and he disliked squandering his only vice on something so inferior. He realized, however, that more than one communist intelligence chief had gone to his death after developing a taste for things Western; he would smoke the nation's best and be silent. Kiying used his thumb and middle finger to pick a stray piece of tobacco from his tongue, lifted a tissue from the box on his desk, and cleaned his finger on it. He wadded the tissue and threw it away. After drawing on the cigarette, he looked at the *Ping Fa,* then pushed it aside. His teeth hurt.

Goddamned cigarette, he thought. Rolled dog shit wrapped in the hair of revisionist dissidents. No, dog shit would taste better.

He placed a huge index finger along each side of his mouth, bit down and enjoyed the painful release. The marshal wished that he had bought a piece of candy. He needed something to distract him from his teeth, his cigarettes, and his thoughts.

Aside from his gums and teeth, Kiying's health was excellent. Nearly seventy, he remained the large strong youth of the Long March. He had been bald almost since childhood, a result of one of the innumerable infections available to the Chinese peasantry. As a result, people remembered him as having always looked as he did now, at the final moments of his career. It was said among the unlearned of the government that he possessed a magic root which, when chewed, released marvelous juices into his system. These juices, it was believed, kept him young. The legend flashed through his mind and Kiying smiled, wondering if devil root could ease the pain in his teeth.

The pain of his thoughts could not be so easily brushed aside. He would have to find a way to dispose of Major Lung Ch'ien. The young staff man was a source of constant regret to Kiying. He had come to the marshal's attention through Lung Ch'ien's excellent work in preparing the daily summary of the Party Channel branch. That office, along with the Central External Liaison Department and the State Council, constituted the Central Committee of Intelligence, of which Kiying was chief.

Lung was career army and had been on rotation through C.C.I. when he was first brought to Kiying's attention. The marshal did not recruit from the career army. Like their brother soldiers around the world, the Chinese army's best men were intellectually indolent fascists. They all seemed to come from the communes, where they had slaved to attain high productivity while memorizing all the right tracts. Once commissioned, they divided their time between projecting the image of a humble, unassertive servant of the party and scheming to create new adventures to bring them advancement. Lung seemed at least superficially different. His record indicated that he had been born in a commune which had later been lost to a localized epidemic of typhus. Lung was found at the village and nursed to health at the provincial hospital. There were no records for him at either party headquarters or the medical center, but this was not unusual in the more remote provinces. One thing was obvious: the youth was bright. The local party cadre knew enough to advance him. After schooling, he performed his compulsory military service, volunteered for career status, and was commissioned.

Kiying was drawn to the younger man's lucid prose and insightful comments. He arranged Lung's transfer to his staff, only to find that he had acquired a fraud. Lung's restrained analysis was only a sham, an exercise undertaken to assist him in moving out of a menial job. Once promoted to Kiying's staff, Lung used his post to lobby constantly for action.

The marshal was not only tiring of Lung's craving for action; he was beginning to find it dangerous. To Kiying, the soldier's virtuous love of combat was a deadly virus in a spy. Kiying loved the game. Lung loved the kill. Worse, he wanted to kill, then return to Kiying's staff, a military hero sitting at the right hand of China's intelligence chief. Kiying had seen it before, in one form or another: the battle chieftain, the popinjay, the party philosopher, each attempting to use the C.C.I. for his own advancement. Such men and their plans, the marshal knew, had inevitably meant disaster for the Central Committee, or one of its operations. And more than once had almost brought death to Kiying himself; and the marshal had no desire to court disaster. He was an old man, true, but not yet ready to die. Not that anyone ever was. But he still enjoyed the game and wanted to go on playing it.

No, Kiying thought, Lung would have to go.

Kiying encouraged younger men and often advanced their careers. In many cases they brought a freshness of view and willingness to experiment which older officers lacked. In all cases they were available as scapegoats if a project failed. The marshal, however, preferred not to reach that point. He was always happier when the men served a more constructive purpose. Such a man was Colonel Feng Yao. Major Lung shared Feng's nondescript personal background, but there the similarity ended.

Feng had been chosen by Kiying personally. The younger officer had established an excellent record as an aerial intelligence analyst, a skill that Kiying happened to need at the time. Feng was also a pilot, a skill which the survivor Kiying knew might be needed at some time of future upheaval.

It was Feng who had encouraged Kiying to learn to fly. The marshal had accompanied his aide on a routine helicopter qualifying flight. At three thousand feet Feng asked, "Would you like the controls, sir?"

"Not unless you want us both killed."

"China would mourn your loss, sir, and applaud the instantaneous justice meted out to the one who caused it."

Kiying turned, upset at the blatant flattery. But as he shifted in his chair he saw the smile in Feng's eyes and began to laugh himself. "You keep my rank in perspective," Kiying said.

"I am an intelligence officer. I keep everything in logical perspective."

"How logical is it to expect a sixty-five-year-old man to learn to fly?"

"As logical as it was for the American Admiral Halsey to learn at about that age." Feng looked out the window. "Of course, he was quite active."

"Damn you," Kiying said, then burst into laughter. "What do I do?"

And so it had always been in his relationship with Feng. The younger man had an obvious respect for his superior but lacked any sense of awe or desire to fawn. He had precisely the right approach to Kiying, a man

123

whose survival had been achieved in part by fending off the false and flattering.

The two men shared a passion for Chinese literature and a deep knowledge of the troubled country's history. In a profession where friendship is fatal, they had formed an intellectual bond, a relationship of respect for professional achievement and disregard for the exaltation of theory and personality. Kiying had once thought that Lung could share in that bonding, but it was not to be.

Feng himself had a distaste for Lung. Major Lung Ch'ien seemed too quick to please, too anxious to prove himself, whatever the cost to the greater good. Feng, however, kept these feelings to himself. He did not advance himself at the cost of other men's careers, although he made permanent mental notes on them. There were always stories about the officers, such as the legend of Kiying's hair. And the story that Kiying reputedly had only one name. In fact, Mao had once mentioned Kiying by the one name in a dispatch written under fire. Whatever other name he might have had was lost to legend. Feng knew that he could joke with Kiying, respectfully, about his hair and name. But not about his teeth.

Kiying smelled roast pig being prepared in the commissary. He could never eat it, not with his gums. His teeth would have to go before Lung did. He hated dentists. Thirty years before, it had taken both novocaine and gas to calm the marshal long enough for the implantation of a cyanide-filled false tooth. Surgery had been required for its removal. Kiying had been starved, imprisoned, whipped, shot, and twice knifed. But dentists. Perhaps, he thought, he could send Lung to a dentist.

Kiying's secretary announced the presence of Major Lung. The marshal lit another cigarette, lifted the *Ping Fa* from his desk, and buzzed for Lung to enter. The aide knocked twice, which was not necessary, and entered smartly, standing like a British sergeant-major on parade. Kiying smiled. He had held many posts in the army, none of them anything but a cover for his real work. He loved precision and detested militarism. On occasions such as this, he envied the memory of men like Allen Dulles. It must have been so nice, he thought, when intelligence was a club.

"Please sit down, Major. When you stand, I am reminded of my elevated rank and thereby my elevated age." He smiled at Lung, who took his seat as precisely as he had quick-stepped into the room. Kiying studied the stiff young man and said, "I am so glad you feel at ease with me. What news of our opponents?"

124

"The British plan has worked, sir. They have McHenry and he will cooperate."

Kiying frowned. "Unfortunate. He will make our task much more difficult."

"He is not a professional, sir."

"No, but he possesses the talents necessary for this assignment. That is regrettable."

"I would prefer, sir, to face a brave enemy rather than a foolish amateur."

"Then it is your enemy, Major, who faces the fool." Kiying watched the tall, handsome young soldier bristle, then decided to soften the blow a bit. An idea was taking shape. "Major Lung, permit me to explain my comment with an observation by the great critic Chin Shengt'an: 'I wake up in the morning and seem to hear someone in the house sighing and saying that last night someone died. I immediately ask to find out who it is, and learn that it is the sharpest, most calculating fellow in town. Ah, is this not happiness?' "

Kiying's strong body shook with appreciation, but his eyes never left Lung's face. The younger officer had no idea of what had just been said. Kiying ran his hand over his bald head and scratched vigorously. "Major, I have just told you to take any victory which presents itself."

"Yes, sir."

"As a soldier, you may feel that you obtain no honor from vanquishing a weak opponent. As an intelligence officer, however, you must be content with the victory. How and over whom are not important."

"Yes, sir." Lung was impassive.

Kiying realized that it was no use. He also knew that admitting an error in choosing personnel was dangerous. Perhaps Lung would spare him further efforts in instruction. "Major, I know that you would take no pleasure in facing a homosexual from M.I. Six or an assassin from Langley. But I also know that until your entirely commendable desire for combat is satisfied, you will be limited in your effectiveness here. Perhaps, and this is only a suggestion, you would care to represent me on the Antarctic ice. I am most reluctant to spare you to assist in the battle with McHenry. He is not worthy of you, but—"

"I am honored, sir."

Kiying could see that he was. "Good. Good. You will be informed."

Once Lung had left, Kiying reflected that the assignment was indeed a good one. Lung Ch'ien was exactly the sort of zealous simpleton who would precipitate action at the South Pole. Exactly the right sort to die in place of better men. And if the mission went badly, Kiying could always point out that Lung was regular army, not C.C.I.

It made it easier for Kiying to send Lung to his death because he felt nothing toward him—not anger or fear or resentment or, much more debilitating, love. It was the total absence of emotion which had made Kiying so successful. Celibacy, he knew, had been invaluable in his rise. A family provided a hostage to one's enemies and took time from work. It was a strength recognized throughout history. Saint Paul had said to make oneself a eunuch for Christ's sake. The Russians still had the Skoptsy, men like Malenkov, Beria, and Khrushchev, who had had themselves castrated in middle age to prove party loyalty. Kiying, somewhat less painfully, had simply chosen celibacy. A virtue, the computers reported, that was lost on McHenry.

There was, to be sure, loneliness. But if he had had a child, Kiying knew, the boy or girl would have had to live through disease and famine, endure the Long March, and overcome the Japanese, the Kuomintang, the Koreans, the Cultural Revolution, and the tortured years of upheavals since Mao's death. Perhaps, he often thought, there was a God, to have spared at least one child's life.

"But enough of such melancholy," he said aloud. It was ten o'clock and time for that day's reading of the *Ping Fa*.

Lung Ch'ien betrayed no emotion as he walked the halls of C.C.I. to his office. Only after he had safely closed the door and raised that day's issue of *Jenmin Jih Pao* to his face did he smile. It had been so easy.

Revolutions, he believed, were made by young men and lost by old ones. Kiying was an old man and he had blundered. Not that Lung Ch'ien thought him a fool. The marshal had survived too many purges over too many decades to be underestimated. But he was growing old and had made a mistake: he had allowed Lung Ch'ien to make himself unbearable. And because Kiying was old and wanted no problems, he had allowed himself to be goaded into assigning Major Lung to the McHenry mission. And it had gone so well.

For his part, Lung Ch'ien was still amazed at how easy it had all been: the creation of a false identity; being dropped into a village too remote, too decimated by disease to be checked; advancing along a predesignated route to Kiying's staff; the carefully orchestrated fall from grace which would allow him to do what needed to be done. If he had been a worrier, Lung Ch'ien might have thought that it had all been easy because Kiying had allowed it to be so. Indeed, there were entire mathematical tables constructed out of the spy's quandary: if I send the message, they will know I am a spy. If I do not send it, they will have deceived me. So if I send it, it is because they have allowed it. So I will not send it. Which is what they want, because the message is correct. But if it is accurate and not sent . . . Ad infinitum. There were certain decisions which a spy could make by computing the number of variables. The seesawing of variables was so technical as to be almost amusing.

What was not funny was overconfidence. He knew that the first manual on torture had been prepared by the eunuchs of the Empress Wu Chao. It was said that a copy had found its way into Kiying's hands. Lung had no desire to learn the truth or falsity of the rumor. He had only a desire to fulfill his mission. In any event, antiquities of Chinese writing were of no interest to him. They appealed exclusively to the marshal, who buried himself each day for at least an hour in the totally irrelevant contents of the *Ping Fa*.

In the year 510 BC, Sun Tzu, a philosopher of the Kingdom of Wu, then ruled by Ho Lu, wrote a work of eighteen *p'ien,* of which only thirteen chapters survive. This work, the *Ping Fa*, or *Principles of War*, was dedicated to the King by the philosopher, who begged permission to bring his book to court and demonstrate to Ho Lu how his philosophical theories would work.

Ho Lu was then the master of the three finest generals in China, Wu Yuan, Po Pei, and Fu Kai. While he respected them and their successes, Ho Lu realized that he could not win war after war simply by throwing bodies before his enemies. Even a tyrant's decree could not hasten the period of gestation. Ho Lu also knew, however, that even a philosopher could appear talented if given command of the armies of the Kingdom of Wu. For that reason his invitation to Sun Tzu carried an unusual restriction: the philosopher would be given freedom to demonstrate his theories, but not on trained soldiers; his command would consist of slave girls. Sun Tzu agreed.

The king's generals awaited the philosopher with some amusement. They knew little of the contents of the *Ping Fa,* only that the author had devised a new system of waging war. They did nothing to detract from Sun Tzu's scheduled performance; they knew that nothing could replace masses of men in combat. The philosopher could only fail.

When Sun Tzu arrived at court, he was presented to Ho Lu and permitted to pay homage. Because it was evening, the King instructed Sun Tzu to rest, then ordered his eunuchs to prepare 180 slave girls. They were to be brought from the concubinate at dawn and divided into two groups, each under the command of a favorite. To test the philosopher's powers of concentration, the eunuchs were ordered to present each of the favorites naked, her body anointed with oil to catch the sheen of the great fireplace which both heated and illuminated the hall. No one but the King, the philosopher, the women, and the eunuchs was to be present.

In the morning the women were brought before the King, paid homage by kneeling, and remained in position, heads to the floor, while the favorites were brought forward. Sun Tzu, who was standing at the foot of the throne, ignored the women's beauty and instead asked the King's permission to assume command of the slaves. Ho Lu nodded, and the philosopher ordered the women to stand, a favorite at the head of each group. He then satisfied himself that each woman knew right from left, and explained the rudiments of drill. Sun Tzu ordered the women to perform a right face. The concubines fell to chattering and laughing at the ragged teacher.

The King said, "They will not obey a philosopher."

"Your Majesty, if words of command are not clear and distinct, if orders are not thoroughly understood, then the general is to blame."

Ho Lu nodded to try again. Sun Tzu again explained the drill. Again the women laughed at his commands.

"They understand strength like mine," the King said. "And whips such as those I give the eunuchs. They do not understand reason."

"If a general's orders are clear and soldiers disobey, it is the fault of the troops," Sun Tzu said. He instructed the eunuchs to bring before him the two favorites, who were marched forward and made to kneel. From beneath his ragged cloak Sun Tzu drew a saber and, in two strokes, beheaded the women.

Ho Lu leaped to his feet, shouting orders to the eunuchs to seize Sun Tzu.

The teacher stepped forward. "A moment, Majesty."

The King, realizing that punishment delayed is more enjoyably observed, nodded to the eunuchs. He looked to Sun Tzu, who chose a girl from the ranks of slaves. Pointing to the giant fireplace, he said, "Walk into the fire." The girl walked forward, stepped onto the brick apron of the roaring blaze and walked toward the flames. As she was about to take her last step, Ho Lu waved a eunuch forward and the girl was saved.

Sun Tzu bowed and said, "May I suggest to Your Majesty ways in which the philosopher can assist in war."

"She obeyed only because she was afraid. Any eunuch can do the same thing if he is cruel enough."

"No, Majesty. She obeyed because my power was unexpected and terrifying in its surprise. Your own troops are most afraid when your generals, the most magnificent in China, send them into battle without knowledge."

"Knowledge is obtained by overrunning the enemy and torturing prisoners."

"Majesty, would it not be simpler, and less costly, to know all about the enemy before you lead your troops into battle?"

"Is that what your book will tell me?"

"Yes, Majesty."

"Then speak."

The essence of Sun Tzu's philosophy was that men should fear the subtle and have their fears allayed by the obvious. Endless waves of human fodder did nothing but thin the population. Spies, he taught, could win wars. He presented to the King the types of intelligence most needed, and his suggestion as to the kind of man necessary to obtain such knowledge. Most importantly, he listed the type of reward necessary for each kind of spy: patriotic honors, vengeance, wealth, love of the game. With the King's aid, Sun Tzu found the necessary men and established a program of rewards for them. Ho Lu then deployed them against his enemies, holding his generals in check until the undercover beggars, priests, jugglers, and adventurers returned to court. Sun Tzu collected and evaluated their findings and gave what he had learned to the generals.

When Ho Lu struck, the chronicles record that it was as if he had suddenly appeared through a crack in an impenetrable wall. As a result, the King ordered his calligraphers to create a Mandarin character for the word spy. It symbolized a crevice. Sun Tzu approved; he wanted his enemies to live in fear of a dark eye studying them through an unseen crack in the walls of their lives.

When all of this was done, Sun Tzu reminded his master of the incident of the slave girls. They had never expected a bedraggled philosopher to possess the power of death. The concubines, after all, were pampered and protected and, in their own way, powerful. Each of

China's many kingdoms, Sun Tzu argued, was like a concubine. It was one with its ruler, a pampered prince who was protected by others and was, in a way (but not Ho Lu's way), powerful. China was too vast, the number of effeminate kings too great, for force to be a believable threat. It would always be necessary for power to be skillfully concealed and swiftly applied. No matter how unified China became, its needs and people would always be too numerous for direct action by military force. Success would always come by indirection. For as long as Sun Tzu lived, the lesson was believed. But then he died.

For two thousand years the teachings of Sun Tzu were ignored until in the early 1640s a Jesuit missionary rediscovered the *Ping Fa* in Canton. Trained from the first days of his novitiate to understand the concept of victory through intellectual stealth, he seized upon the ancient work as the key to opening China to the Church. With the consent of his superiors, this priest, Adam Schall, made his way across China to the camps of the Manchu warriors who were about to invade the country. He eventually obtained an audience with the Emperor Shun Chih.

Schall emphasized to the Manchu leader what he already knew: the Chinese could not withstand their arms, but they could impede the Manchus for a thousand years by bifurcating Chinese society. The Chinese looked down upon the Manchus as barbarians. Conveniently forgetting their own society's inhumanity, the Chinese had decided to cooperate with the imminent Manchu empire only enough to be spared the lash. All except those directly concerned with the foreign occupation would ignore the Manchus. In a land where time is the only commodity in greater supply than human life, the Chinese could afford to wait. In time they would be strong enough to rise up and destroy the Manchus, or, more likely, they would simply absorb them. It had happened before; it would happen again.

If Shun Chih did not wish to wait, Schall argued, the Chinese could be won over if they became convinced that the Manchus were as intellectually advanced as they were. It was necessary, he said, to persuade the Chinese that the Manchus were a people of greatness with whom their country could be shared. Only in this way could cooperation be assured. To that generation of Chinese, as to all since, mathematics and astronomy were the greatest of the disciplines. Schall was learned in both. He swore to ask his God to bless the Manchus before battle and bedazzle the Chinese afterward. All that he asked in return was to be allowed to preach at court. The bargain was struck and the dynasty established.

Schall represented the Emperor at all meetings with Chinese intellectuals. He challenged their greatest mathematicians and astronomers to public tests of their skills, and always won. The Jesuit tutored each of Shun Chih's many sons in the arts as well as the sciences. Schall prepared a calendar, a table of tides, and explained how to calculate the approach of an eclipse—a momentous event even today. Many courtiers thought that Schall himself had made the sun disappear.

The Chinese were not happy with Schall's success, but he gave them an excuse to counsel their own people against the armed rebellion that could only be disastrous. The Chinese would wait and assimilate the Manchus. The Jesuit did not wait.

Within a year, Schall, who had access to the entire palace, had converted fifty of the Emperor's concubines, forty eunuchs, and one hundred courtiers. Shun Chih secretly began to take instruction in Catholicism.

In time, the Chinese astronomers and mathematicians found a way to avenge Schall's assistance to the Emperor's victory. Through a series of false rumors and a campaign of subtle, widespread vilification, the Chinese were able to destroy Schall's reputation. It was a process which consumed more than a decade, a period of time hardly worthy of mention in a land where patience is the greatest strength. Schall was condemned to death by dismemberment, but because of his age, the sentence was commuted to banishment. The Emperor, remembering his debt, relented slightly, and Schall was permitted to pass his life under house arrest in Peking. Catholicism was banned, although a few Jesuits lingered in China.

Two years later, the Emperor was succeeded by his fourteen-year-old son, K'ang-hsi, who asked for a priest to be brought to court. The only Jesuit remaining in Peking was Schall's assistant, Father Ferdinand Verbiest. The young Emperor demanded that Verbiest make the sun disappear, as Schall had done. When the priest explained that such a feat was not within his power, the court astrologers sensed their chance. They demanded Verbiest's death for failing to please the Emperor.

Verbiest, knowing that the Manchus were still sensitive to charges of barbarism, appealed to the Emperor's sense of fair play. K'ang-hsi asked what Verbiest would consider a fair test. The Jesuit, of course, challenged the court astronomers to produce an eclipse. When they could not, he engaged them in a series of mathematical games, all of which he won. As a result, the court astronomers were arrested and Verbiest was made chief of the Astronomical Bureau.

Over a period of years, Verbiest became the young Emperor's personal intelligence officer and received a commission to write a Manchu grammar. He used his dual charge to travel over the entire empire and establish the first truly national intelligence network in China. In 1682 he became assistant director of the Board of Works, a post he used to develop a modern system of armaments and border security for China. This work brought him into close communication with Russian officials, laying the groundwork for an intelligence system which the Chinese still exploit.

Verbiest was killed in an accident in 1688. Two years later, Jesuits, using his contacts, drew up the Treaty of Nerchinsk between China and Russia, a treaty which ceded valuable trade concessions to Peking. As a reward, an edict of toleration was issued and the Jesuits were given authority to operate purely religious missions throughout China.

By the time the Jesuits were suppressed a century later, their missionaries had established orphanages, schools, churches, and seminaries all over China. Peking had come to rely so heavily on their influence over the people that the Emperor sent a French Jesuit, Jean Joseph Amiot, to the Vatican to present China's plea that the order be restored. The Emperor's gift to the Pope was an original sixth century BC manuscript of the *Ping Fa*. The Pope granted the Jesuits permission to operate as individuals in China and sent to the Emperor, through Amiot, a signed copy of Saint Ignatius Loyola's *Spiritual Exercises*.

When the order was restored, it quickly set about protecting itself, and the Church, against future dissolutions. A network was formed to enable talented young Chinese to be ordained deacons after minimal study. This office permitted the Chinese youths to distribute communion, perform weddings and baptisms, and hear confessions. It was also arranged that a group of secret bishops would be placed among the peasantry. Because of the bishops' unique power to ordain priests and consecrate new bishops, the Church guaranteed itself a continuity of men within the country.

When the century turned and the Boxers liquidated almost all native clergy, the Jesuits realized that an infiltration system would be necessary. For the remainder of the twentieth century—through partition, two world wars, a revolution, and the establishment of communism—overseas Chinese were returned, infiltrated, and forgotten. They took advantage of riots in cities and plague in the provinces to establish themselves in places where they might otherwise have been suspect. Because the Pope may permit priests to marry and married

132

men to be ordained, the clergy who burrowed their way into Chinese society were free to establish families and avoid suspicion. And because the end of serving God is superior to all others, secret priests worked at all types of occupations, going where the party sent them and on occasion joining and rising through the party itself. None of these priests and bishops was expected to come out alive. All were Jesuits.

The government had recognized the historic value of the Jesuits as late as 1979. Early that year, the opening to the West included an invitation to the Society to return to the mainland and open a medical school. The Jesuits had accepted immediately, and within a year had begun their new assignment.

Like Jesuits before them, however, the new professors could not accept the limited nature of their charge. They were allowed the freedom of the city, more substantial unescorted travel privileges than those offered other visitors; and, of course, there was never any interference with their practice of Catholicism. *Their* practice of *their* religion. It was made clear to the Society at the time of the invitation that they were to teach medicine, not religion. They could not accept that. The reports which filtered back to Kiying made it clear that the priests almost immediately began activating a network of Catholics to spread the word. None of the already placed secret priests or bishops was contacted. They might be needed again. The new workers were laymen whose interest derived from a family tradition or contact with a Jesuit teacher.

The state permitted this type of contact to see how far the Jesuits would go. Nothing was done when the curious came to see the legendary priests, or when the intrigued visited a Mass or stopped a Jesuit for conversation. Nor was anything done when the Jesuits involved themselves in the non-academic aspects of their students' lives. Such conduct could be expected from any dedicated teacher.

Action became necessary only when the priests began collecting information and sending it out of the country. They could not escape their traditions. Economic data, military secrets, the private failings of leaders: all were grist for the Jesuits' mill. They would collect facts, send them to the Vatican, and the Pope would negotiate for ever greater and greater concessions. It could not be tolerated, and it was not.

In 1983, less than four years after the invitation to return, China, as it had so often over the centuries, once again expelled the Jesuits. Every country in Europe, Russia, and several South American states had either expelled or suppressed the Society. In each nation the Jesuits had left behind a secret network. They had done so often in China. They did so again, leaving intact not only the formerly placed priests but also many new converts.

No one knew better than Marshal Kiying just how widespread the Jesuits were. From time to time one of them made a mistake or was betrayed to the C.C.I. It was never more than one, however, because each knew only his bishop, the bishops knew only ten priests each, and a bishop had never been captured. Or so it was believed. It was a part of Kiying's duties to supervise the torture of these men. They revealed nothing. To his superiors, that meant that no bishop had been captured, because they believed that any man with information would speak to end the pain. Kiying was not as certain. He had read the *Ping Fa*. But he had also read the *Spiritual Exercises*. He believed that the Jesuits had a mission to accomplish, and torture would not deter them.

In a way that pleased Kiying. He was not a sadist. The sessions repelled him. He preferred other methods, the methods of the *Ping Fa*. He had learned many years before that Sun Tzu had been right about so much. There were agents for whom patriotic honors were the highest reward. These buffoons were given the most unimportant, most deadly missions, in exchange for which they received a hunk of tin and a citation. There were the glory seekers, like Lung Ch'ien, who would gladly risk his life at the South Pole when indirection was all that was needed.

Those who preferred material comfort became seeded agents. These men and women were planted in colonies of overseas Chinese throughout the world. In exchange for the better life of Europe or America, they gave up family, friends, and cultural ties; but they were invaluable, providing, as they did, an endless flow of information.

Finally, just as taught in the *Ping Fa,* there were the ultimate agents, men and women willing to spend their lives in preparation for one mission. These agents were placed so that they might be used in an assignment of such complexity and importance that it could change the world. These ultimate agents were distinguished by their ability to practice China's greatest character strength, patience. China was a land which had recorded its first Golden Age twenty-three centuries before the birth of Christ. Its people had from antiquity endured warlords who began conflicts merely to reduce the burden on arable land. They had borne endless cycles of floods which followed droughts and preceded smallpox, the black plague, and infestations of rats the size of dogs. They had accepted nearly a dozen nations as conquerors and in the end conquered them all by absorbing them through patience. The Chinese were ideally suited to provide agents willing to wait a lifetime for a call that might never come. Kiying shared this great character strength, this endless reservoir of patience. That was why he never regretted the forty years it had taken to develop Vultan.

Chapter Twelve

McHenry took a house in Belgravia. He was determined that if he had to run the operation it would not be from an M.I.6 safe house. He knew enough of British budgetary problems to be certain that Dole's houses would be filled with motley staffers in various states of disrepair, lounging about space-heated bed-sitting rooms with faded wallpaper. In any case, he knew, Langley would be paying the bills. A quick call to George Ingersoll had confirmed that. The old man knew nothing about the project, except that he was to consider McHenry on detached duty, and likely to come in contact with some very large new clients.

It bothered McHenry that the British had control of the operation. His C.I.A. runner in S.O.G.-South had made it clear that, from the 1930s on, the British Secret Service had been one very large, very gay sieve. But, he thought, they did own the formula. Or did they? Certainly the Chinese, who had financed the priest, had some claim to it. And certainly the Jesuits, who had sent the missionary to Peking, had a claim. If they knew about it. McHenry smiled and lit a cigarette. They knew.

Dole had said that it would be three days until the Belgravia house could be considered safe. Then he would deliver the diary. Until he had the book, however, there was enough to occupy him.

McHenry went first to Fribourg and Treyer and purchased ten cartons of Camels and five bottles of The Glenlivet. He returned to the house, emptied two of the bottles into ice trays and set the Scotch to freeze. Stepping back into the London afternoon, he hailed a cab and told the bullet-headed Pakistani driver to take him to One Savile Row, the home of Gieves and Hawkes, the only bespoke tailor in London with a complete line of ready to wear. Gieves, Britain's senior naval tailor, had been invited by Hawkes, the premier military tailor, to join it after a random I.R.A. bomb had blown out the former establishment. Hawkes was legendary for its design of the Indian army helmet which kept the heat from a soldier's head and, when tipped over, held grain and water for his horse. McHenry knew that the firm could outfit him not only for London but for his special needs on the ice.

At Church's he ordered shoes, walked down the Burlington Arcade to Simpson's for pipes and tobacco, then strolled at a leisurely pace to Garrard's, the crown jewelers, for a specially fitted cigarette case and gold collar stays. Then he turned toward Belgravia.

On the way, he began the calculations necessary for his own protection. It was reasonable to assume that every operation, particularly if run by M.I.6, had a leak. One. The Chinese wanted the formula and so might well, probably did, know about him. Two. And Colonel Sharp would not forget his humiliation before Dole. Three. It was, McHenry knew, best to minimize the risks before going into the operational phase of the mission. He had begun to do that. The day's shopping had been pleasant, but it had also left behind enough sales slips with his address, enough delivery tickets with instructions, enough information on his habits to make it almost irresistible for someone to act now and find him.

And McHenry wanted to be found. He had known from the moment that Dole had allowed him to humiliate Sharp that the danger would begin immediately, long before they were on the ice. From that instant, he had begun to feel that sensual response which only danger brings.

He had felt it first going out of the jump planes at Fort Benning: the knowledge that all of the technology and planning could be destroyed by a sudden breeze that might whip him into a high tension wire. It had returned again and again after that: rappeling down mountainsides at Ranger School, brief engagements in the jungle with Chechoweo, the machete fight with the Lobo. It had not occurred since he had left the army, and now there was no mistaking its presence: the straining of every muscle, the constant wariness toward all around him, the heartbeats that hammered at every unexpected sound. It was composed of all the elements of fear, but was its exact opposite. He had missed it and now wondered if, as on the morning of his first jump, it would make him come.

Inside the house he showered and shaved for the second time that day. There would be no shaving at the South Pole; he knew that. Basic military hygiene taught that a clean-shaven man stood a better chance of surviving the infected face wound, but the cold would not allow it.

He smiled. If Sharp or anyone else made his move on the ice and was successful, McHenry would be dead and frozen before infection could even begin.

At that moment the bell rang. A messenger delivered the first of his packages. McHenry tipped him and carried the shoes upstairs, where he treed them and set them in a row. He went back down to the kitchen and broke open an ice tray, filled a glass with cubes, and poured in three fingers of The Glenlivet. For the next ninety minutes he sipped Scotch, smoked cigarettes, and took delivery of all his purchases.

It was late enough then to call Elspeth. He was certain that he recalled her schedule sufficiently to know that she was incoming that day. If he was right, she would have made the perfunctory crew member's walk through customs and reached her flat. He dialed the number.

"Hello."

"Elspeth?" He knew that it was not.

"No. Elspeth had to fill in on today's back shuttle." He smiled at the British view of the trip to America. "Who is this, please?"

"Simon McHenry. Who's this?"

"Caroline Somerset. Elspeth's roommate."

"She mentioned you."

"And you. Back from Europe already?"

"Yes." There was no alternative but to let the story stand.

"Oh! And faced with a night alone."

"Would you do that to me?"

She wouldn't, of course, and didn't. He promised to call for her in forty minutes.

He dressed in blazer and flannels, candy-striped shirt and maroon tie, then called the Zoo for a dinner reservation. McHenry walked down the servants' stairway to the garage and studied the Mercedes he had had Dole deliver. He ran his finger along the door of the garage and found the long blond hair he had stuck with spit to the roller. That meant only that no one had come in from the side street. He lifted the hood, followed the starting wires to their terminal, then fell to the floor, landing on his palms and toes. No wires ran to the back of the car and no plastique had been affixed to the tires. He rose, closed the hood, walked to the boot, opened it, and searched inside. He slammed it and entered the car. There were no wires in the cigarette lighter or glove compartment. He started the car, got out, opened the garage door, drove into the street, closed the door, drove to Elspeth's apartment, and picked up Caroline.

He took the long way to the Zoo, a new restaurant owned by an Oxford friend who had grown tired of progressing respectably toward senility at National Assurance. With twenty thousand borrowed pounds he had opened the restaurant and bar across the street from its namesake, furnished each room with splendid photographs of the country whose name the room bore, and left one table open each night in the event a backer, like Simon McHenry, might call.

The girl assumed that the American was going the long way around merely to give them time to become acquainted. She liked that. She knew that her full body, black hair, and violet eyes attracted McHenry, and she wanted it that way.

Simon took a long route from her apartment, driving roundabout to Fleet Street, up the Strand, north into the Aldwych and up Drury Lane to Saint Giles Circus. He turned along side streets to Tottenham Court Road, took a quick left-right-left combination, and came out on the approach to Regent's Park, around the semicircle, then pulled into the restaurant's lot. He had never broken the soft, inquiring, amusing conversation that they had set up; had never paid too much attention to his rear-view mirrors; had not spotted a tail.

Dinner was graced with the same flow of conversation they had set up in the car: gentle, inquiring but not personal, concerned but not involving. They enjoyed one another and would continue to do so. Elspeth, they both knew, was three thousand miles away and would not care.

When they had undressed, they stood on her living-room floor and McHenry took Caroline's small, tightly furrowed brown nipples in his fingers and moved her forward.

"Not yet," she said. "Bathe me." Then she led him by his firm penis into the bathroom. She turned on the shower, stepped in, and waited for him to join her beneath the fine misty spray.

McHenry twisted her perfumed soap in his muscled hands, then laid them, like knotted sponges, on her shoulders. He turned her around, working his way gently down her spine, kneading the flesh and bone into one. She moaned and reached for the towel bar, firmly grasping it as he cupped her breasts and began to work them with his palms, stroking and stretching every aspect but her nipples. When her grip on the bar tightened, he pinched the nipples and she moved forward, involuntarily weakening her legs. He entered her from behind, one hand lying across her matted hair, forcing her backward, while the other held her firmly in place. She had superb control of her internal muscles and worked them as McHenry moved inside her. In another moment they came together.

Caroline reached down and felt his penis grow smaller and slide out of her reach. She turned and buried her face in his chest as he silently reached behind and threw the knob. Water poured into the tub. He helped her down, stepped out and knelt beside her. Again he massaged her and she slipped quietly into total relaxation. He took a cloth, soaped it, and cleaned between her lips.

As the warm water quickly loosened every muscle and drew her down in quiet appreciation of his skills, she allowed herself to half-doze, knowing, as women who take such baths at such moments do, that she would bob safely. Caroline barely heard McHenry open and close the medicine chest, say that he was leaving for a moment, that he would be right back, or his first words when he was again kneeling beside her.

"What?" she asked.

"I'm very sorry."

She turned her head, slowly opening her eyes and focusing on two strips of gold. "What are those?"

"Collar stays." He placed them on the sink. "As you know, I wasn't armed."

"I don't understand." She started to struggle up but his hand knotted her hair and jerked her back into a seated position of attention. His other arm locked her elbows behind her back.

"I apologize for the pain, but I can't leave any bruises. This way is cleanest."

"Oh my God!" she cried.

"Don't be surprised. You knew the risks when you accepted the assignment."

Caroline twisted once, but McHenry's fierce grip on her hair prevented any serious forward movement. "Let me go," she begged. "I'll drown."

"No you won't. We have to talk first."

"Please don't kill me. Please don't. I don't know about any assignment."

"Sharp didn't have me followed tonight, that means that you were covering me for him. Or was it someone other than Sharp?"

She wrenched her upper body, and her soap-covered arms slid just enough for one hand to pull free. She drove her nails into his now flaccid penis, looping her fingers around his testicles as tightly as possible. McHenry locked himself against the tub, enduring the pain for longer than he would have deemed possible. At last he said, "Let go or I'll drown you." He twisted her head down toward the water.

Through her terror, Caroline forced herself to think. If she held on, he would break and have to strike her, thereby ruining whatever plan he had. But she would surely die. If she let go, he might let her live. She released him.

"Aaghhh!" McHenry twisted his head violently as the pain flowed out of his groin. He locked her again in his grip and said, "Now tell me."

She shook her head desperately. "Sharp! It was Sharp. But I was only to compromise you."

"Like Gourley?"

"No, no. He only—" She stopped, realizing that she had said too much, that McHenry knew that she knew, that she was only a way station on the road to Sharp's ultimate tortures. "I'll do anything," she whispered.

"You already have. A man is dead because of you. You arranged his death so that people could get to me. We both owe him this."

"He would have died anyway. Dole gives Sharp someone each month, to keep him loyal."

McHenry was once again, he knew, the strongest boy in the orphanage, protecting those who could not protect themselves. That much was the child's code. But he was also protecting himself from a woman who would gladly set him up for a fee. That much was adult realization. "Does Dole know about this?"

"No. Sharp is still angry about how you made him look at the hotel. He's there, waiting to kill you."

McHenry let go of her hair, reached across, and lifted one of the golden stays from the sink. "Elspeth?" he asked.

Caroline shook her head.

"I'm glad."

"Oh, please!" she screamed. "In the name of the almighty God." Her body convulsed as she realized that she would soon be dead.

He forced one hand to the side, holding the heel of the palm and wrist apart with his fingers. As she moved to bring her other hand around, he pressed the stay against her flesh and watched the blood pop out in a small clustered spray. Then it ran into the tub. He pushed her other arm back while the blood pumped in large obscene spurts into the water. After a moment, he cut open the other wrist. Caroline, in total shock, merely watched her life drain away.

"I'm only thirty-one," she said. She stared at him, unbelieving, then died quietly.

"I'm so sorry," he said.

McHenry gently laid her back in the tub and spread her hair so that there would be no sign of his attack. He knew that there were no razor blades in the cabinet, so he left the bathroom for a second time, dressed, and walked to a nearby chemist's. Moving past the nodding lines of registered addicts, he purchased a package of blades and a nail clipper with the exact change and left. No one would remember him.

Once back inside the apartment, he stripped and carried the blades and clipper into the bathroom. He opened the clipper and cleaned the residue of his skin from beneath her nails. He put it on the sink, slipped a blade from the pack, wiped it clean, then pressed it into each wound, put it between the fingers of each hand to show that she had cut both wrists, and let it fall beside her buttocks. He wiped the apartment clean of his prints, dressed, and left.

From a pay station near the house he called Dole.

"I can handle it with the police," Sir Fraser said. "At least you've left it right for an autopsy and the press."

"That was the plan. Pull Sharp out of the hotel or you'll have to dispose of two bodies."

"Done. But I can't terminate Sharp. I need him."

"I can wait."

"Yes. And I imagine you will."

"I will. I want to see the diary. There's no point to my staying in London waiting for you to set up your end."

"I'll send it over tomorrow."

"Good. And Dole."

"Yes?"

"When you see Sharp, tell him that now he owes me two lives."

Cardinal Robustelli took the violin from beneath his chin and lowered his bow. "Good," he said with a slight smile. The music of Haydn always soothed him. He turned from his secretary, Father Esteban, who was seated at the piano, and inclined his head over his shoulder. "You have been so still, Luca. I could not tell whether you were entranced with the deathless tone, stupefied by my lack of talent, or simply reluctant to speak."

"The first, Your Eminence," Monsignor Luca Bello, Robustelli's chief of staff, said. "And the last."

"What is it?"

"The English slut is dead."

"Ahh." Robustelli shook his head. "I see." He rose, laying the violin and bow on the piano. Father Esteban put them in the case, walked to a bucket of ice, removed the bottle of champagne, opened it, and poured a glass for the cardinal. Robustelli had walked to his favorite chair and sat down heavily. He sipped the champagne, then asked, "Did she implicate us?"

"It is unlikely, Your Eminence. There was no way for her to know that I was a priest. And, if there had been a slip, we would have been visited by the Swiss Guards."

"I agree. Was it that psychopath Sharp?"

"No, Your Eminence. He still knows the girl only as a stewardess and a prostitute. It was McHenry."

Robustelli stirred in his chair. "Why?"

"She was apparently to delay McHenry while Sharp set up an ambush. Both men are alive and going forward with their plans, so Dole must have intervened."

"McHenry's death would have been convenient, but I have every confidence in our plan."

"Yes, Your Eminence."

"The taping equipment has been removed from the girl's apartment?"

"Yes, Your Eminence."

"Good. I see nothing that is changed by her death."

"The plan is leading to violence, Your Eminence."

"I had thought that canon law forbade the ordination of eunuchs."

"Forgive me, Your —"

"Be silent! The plan is brilliant. If we fight Xavier publicly, he will win. This way, our man in China works backward and exposes Halloran's network, and gives us the formula. We can then expose Xavier's maneuverings and end his misguided love affair with world Jewry." He smiled. "The Arabs would love the formula."

"But the woman is dead."

"The *whore* is dead. No matter! We have men in China, in the Vatican, everywhere, dear Monsignor. Everywhere. Do not be concerned."

Simon McHenry drove over the Kirkstone Pass, into Patterdale, and along the bank of the Ullswater. The modest peaks of the Lake District, the oldest mountains in the world, rose all around him as he proceeded to his rendezvous.

He turned up a private path, along a modern road to a plain near the top of a rise. He parked and stepped from the car. The blue evening air was heavy with mist, a gift of the Irish Sea. At the point of the peak was the man who could provide McHenry with the guarantee he wanted: His Grace, the Earl of Somerville, Francis Henry Stuart, V.C., D.S.O., M.C., last collateral male descendant of Henry Stuart, Cardinal York, late Pretender to the Throne.

Past sixty, taller than McHenry, gaunt, he turned and offered Simon his firm hand—not merely a greeting but an aid. Stuart led Simon to the edge and said, "Defoe called this the wildest, most barren, and frightful county in England. We financed that tour, and benefited from the book. When it was time to hide, we hid here, and when it was time to build, we came to stay."

"Did you finance Wordsworth and Coleridge too?"

"Most likely. But that would have been for reasons of art, not politics."

"And the two should be kept apart?"

"It depends on what you mean by politics. It depends on what you mean by art."

"Sir Fraser Dole is a craftsman. An artist would not leave spaces."

Stuart knew that McHenry did not want to undertake the mission and that the American was offering him an opportunity to persuade him to do so. "Do you know how many books have been written about my ancestor Mary, Queen of Scots? I do not. But in all that I have read—novels, poetry, biography, even the score of an opera—the great space is that caused by the fact that she never met Elizabeth. We do not know what might have happened if they had spoken."

"It is unlikely that two strong-willed people convinced of the rightness of their position would have yielded. But to repeat the past is tragic."

"Good. May I offer you dinner?"

"No, thank you."

"Then let us walk."

Stuart led him along the cliff to a pasture, through the field to a small enclosed cemetery. The view of the vale and the water beyond was soft, distorted by the shadows of the evening sun reflected from the knolls. The graveyard itself was unforbidding, pastoral, a thought which displeased McHenry.

"We have buried here for generations. Except those burned by the Crown for imagined wrongs, or enshrined by it for equally imagined achievements."

"It would seem that the Crown, like my firm, always pays its debts, whether real or imagined."

"Is that why you insisted that the Vatican be given its share—because Ingersoll and Constance pays its debts?"

"Yes."

"Yet I am told that you have love for neither the Jesuits nor the Church."

"That is correct."

Stuart smiled. "And yet you insisted. Could there be some vestigial trace of Catholicism, Mr. McHenry? Or could there be some realization that, even in America, even for a partner of Ingersoll and Constance, some doors are slow to open, some privileges are never conferred?"

He turned from Simon and led the way along a row of stones. McHenry read briefly of the soldiers and priests, farmers and wives and barristers who rested beneath his feet. Every marker was perfectly cut, stating each person's dates and achievements and bearing a quotation from scripture or literature.

"The question of religion and privilege interests me, Mr. McHenry. In less tolerant times, members of my family were drawn and quartered, hacked and burned, for every treasonous gambit from revolution to attending Mass.

"But this is a more peaceful era. We are older than the Crown, Mr. McHenry, but outside of society. The charities that we sponsor, the schools we attend, the Church we honor, all are kept at a remove. When I was a child, it was an easily accepted difficulty, if only because nothing else was expected. But in my children's time it became more difficult. Society was pluralistic. They were given some deference, but always as anomalies. It was too difficult. And so they drifted.

"Interestingly, Mr. McHenry, my first loyalty is still to England. It is perhaps for that reason that I am His Majesty's Secretary of State for National Defense."

Simon started.

"Yes, Mr. McHenry, I am a Member of Parliament and a Member of the Cabinet. And no, Mr. McHenry, Dole and Sharp do not work for me, nor do I control them."

"Then why were you told of the mission? It would not be discussed at even the highest levels of government except on a need-to-know basis. What is your need to know?"

"I need to know so that I can convince you to go. For the reasons which Dole has given you, the mission cannot succeed without you. And there is not time to replace you.

"My country desperately needs to have the mission succeed. As does the Vatican. I am the premier Catholic peer of the Realm. As such I enjoy certain confidences. The Papal *nuncio* tells me things, as does the King. Each expects total secrecy, except insofar as I may find it necessary to be conversational. The Vatican knows of the diary. If it is not included in the operation, it will take steps to neutralize Dole, and the mission he fields. Dole has promised to share the formula with Rome, but only if you go. And so, you see, each side can make it difficult for the other."

"And which side do you represent?"

"Both. I want the mission to succeed for reasons of state. And reasons of the soul."

Stuart walked toward the front of the graveyard, stopping by one of the newer stones. "I said that England needs the formula. So does the United States. Dole would as soon use you and dispose of you, with apologies to Langley, of course. Whether or not you return, the Jesuits will make the formula available to America on a political basis. The formula will be used to influence legislation in order to bring about an end to abortion."

For the first time, McHenry was affected. "Even an orphan has the right to struggle toward life," he said.

"Precisely." Stuart knew that at last he had reached him.

"What guarantee do you offer against Dole, and that *vermin* he commands?"

"You will take one of my children. An adult, of course, and fully qualified for the mission. Certain wireless transmissions will be arranged. If they are not sent, the Vatican will use all of its political and commercial resources to destroy both Dole and any chance of Britain's using the formula.

"If the messages are sent, and at least one of you returns, I will guarantee to share the formula. And it will be my decision to make: you will obtain the formula and share it only with the person I appoint."

"Your faith is that important to you—that you would risk your child?"

"My faith is everything. And this sin is the worst in its cognizance." Stuart looked out over the water, then said quietly, "We should go back."

"No," McHenry said, "I think that you want to stay here."

Stuart turned and saw McHenry look up from the new gravestone. It bore no name, no date, only an inscription, which McHenry read aloud: " 'O pardon me, thou bleeding piece of earth, That I am meek and gentle with these butchers!' "

"My God!" Stuart said. His voice was filled with fear as he

whispered, "No wonder they want you."

"Do you want to tell me?"

"My older daughter, Angela, is married to an art dealer. They travel. They are surrounded by beauty. They have health. You see, what begins as an alleged help for the poor becomes instead an excuse for all. The child would simply have been an inconvenience. They told the doctor to throw it away. I brought it here for burial."

He began to weep as McHenry softly completed the passage:

> "O pardon me, thou bleeding piece of earth,
> That I am meek and gentle with these butchers!
> Thou art the ruins of the noblest man
> That ever lived in the tide of time.
> Woe to the hand that shed this costly blood!
> Over thy wounds now do I prophesy,
> Which like dumb mouths do ope their ruby lips
> To beg the voice and utterance of my tongue,
> A curse shall light upon the limbs of men."

"You *will* go, Mr. McHenry?"

"I would like to meet your son."

"No, Mr. McHenry. My daughter, Elspeth."

McHenry opened the door to Elspeth. He led her into the library, closed the door, turned, and struck her face, sending her down hard against the floor. "Don't get up yet," he said. "I haven't decided if I'm through with you."

She touched her fingers to her jaw and instantly pulled them back. Her mouth burned and her throat was becoming clogged with blood. She choked, inhaling phlegm and blood and her fear of his anger. He had used only his open fingers, yet the blow had been horrible. His physical powers, like his hatred, were perfectly controlled.

"I didn't believe you'd killed Caroline that way," Elspeth said. "I thought it was Sharp on one of his tears." She looked down. "Now I know better."

"She was loyal. She didn't implicate you."

"She didn't know."

"I *am* impressed. You fooled your own roommate."

"I'm a professional. Like you."

"Oh, no. I'm an investment banker who once trained in the Arctic. But you, you are an accomplished whore."

"I do what I do for my country. And my Church."

"Ahh. A sense of humor. Then please rise; I'm impressed with your nonchalance."

Elspeth rose slowly, terrified that the attack might resume. She was well trained but knew that McHenry not only possessed greater strength; he was motivated by a flow of crystalline hatred. She knew enough to fear him.

He read her mood and said, "Don't worry. I won't hit you again. But tell me the real reason you're so good at what you do: nymphomania, a faithless lover, vengeance on all men for an unwanted pregnancy? Or are you willing to admit that you're a dyke?"

As he had hoped, she began to cry. He had hurt her enough for now. What she could not know was why. But then she asked why.

McHenry turned away. He too had been hurt enough. It would have weakened him beyond recovery to admit that she had done what no one else had ever come close to achieving—she had pierced his armor exceptionally well. Dole had told her of his early life, and the shell he had erected for himself. And so, not content with helping to set him up—which, oddly, bothered him not at all—she attempted to involve him emotionally. And she had succeeded. What she had done—no, how she had made him feel, at the hotel—that was unnecessary. And she had done it with such obvious pleasure. She enjoyed her job too much. She went too far. And now he would have to withdraw again into his shell. He could not risk another commitment. That was why he hated her.

"I think I know," she said. "Did it occur to you that what grew between us in the hotel was not planned, that I felt as you did?"

Yes, he thought. "No," he said. "That did not occur to me. And it does not."

"I see. Then you will kill me." It was a statement, not a question.

"No. If you hurt me, I permitted it. I share your guilt. I won't kill you." He turned and lit a cigarette. "And what of Dole? Are you safe from him?"

"He has agreed to my father's conditions."

"Then you will return safely. The question becomes: what of Sharp and me?"

"Is he coming?"

"Not with me. But he'll be somewhere about at the end."

"But surely Dole—"

"I am not under discipline. There can be no leaks. George Ingersoll is a conduit who will eventually profit from his ignorance of the operation. I am an agent who can be taken by the oppo and turned. But for now"—he snapped the cigarette in two—"give me the diary."

Elspeth handed him a briefcase, removed a clasp bracelet from her wrist, and structured the links into an X-shaped key. She inserted both prongs of the key into the briefcase, removed it, and said, "Open it normally. It's defused now." He removed a manuscript. It was typed on fresh bond and bound with plastic spindles which looped the purple cover. The lettering on the white label read, "Simon McHenry, For Your Eyes Only."

She said, "It begins with an introduction by Churchill, then the Painter's diary, and a concluding entry by Churchill."

McHenry sat down and said, "You know what I drink. Fetch it."

THE DIARY

Chapter Thirteen

EXTRACT FROM THE PRIVATE PAPERS OF WINSTON CHURCHILL

Immediately after the announcement that I was to become Home Secretary, I was visited by, of all things, a priest. And not just a priest, but a Jesuit. There was, of course, no longer a danger of being called a traitor for merely harboring a member of that remarkable Society. Nonetheless, I found the very fact of his visit to be politically troublesome, my own views on the only possible fate for the dogs of Ireland being well known.

The priest's card indicated that his name was Edmund Campion. This amused me greatly. Like any well-educated Englishman, I was familiar with the true Campion, a man I am forced to admit was admirable as poet, priest, and patriot. There have always been rumors that Campion's youthful poetry brought him to the attention of Elizabeth, and she made him briefly her favorite. Whether or not this is true, I do not know. It is true, however, that Campion left England for the Jesuit seminary at Douai, where he was ordained. Elizabeth's spies in France sent word that Campion and his superior, Robert Parsons, were to arrive in Dover. The harbor master later received word that an incoming ship's captain had further information on the Jesuits' arrival. The captain, back from Calais, provided the harbor master with sketches of the priests and details of their wardrobe. In exchange, he asked only that his business partner, an Irish merchant named Patrick, be sent by the port office to the captain's London home when he arrived. The harbor master was so grateful that he met Patrick and his servant at the boat, passed their papers, and stood them to dinner. Then the Jesuits rode on to London.

Campion was particularly successful in eluding the Queen's police. His mastery of dialects, disguise, and simple horsemanship, kept him alive for longer than any priest before him. His brilliance as a preacher made him a particularly desired fugitive. At last, a servant's mistake gave away his hiding place.

Elizabeth herself questioned him, being particularly concerned with whether or not he recognized her as Queen.

"I do, Your Majesty," he replied.

"The Pope says that I am not Queen."

"The Pope is concerned with Your Majesty's father's marriages. Such intricacies are of concern to Italian theologians, not loyal Englishmen. You are my Queen."

"Then you will accept me as head of the Church?"

"No, Your Majesty."

"Then you reject me as your Queen!"

"Your Majesty, you are my Queen, and as such, mistress of my temporal fate. Nothing less, but certainly nothing more."

Elizabeth, outraged, ordered Campion put on the rack. Further torture included having spikes driven between his fingernails and shins and being trussed up so that he could see his toenails being turned back. He was then condemned to be hanged and let down alive, his penis and testicles cut off, his bowels pulled out and burned in his sight, then beheaded. As he stood on the gibbet, his final words were for the grace of God to give Elizabeth a long and prosperous reign. Then he smilingly invited the executioner to send him to heaven.

And now the Church had sent another Jesuit to England on a mission of importance to the government. Or so I assumed, else why would the priest have sought me out. I looked forward to meeting the man, both for his wit in the choice of a cover, and also because he was probably English. I could, therefore, hope that he would not be one of the dreary continental clerics one sees in these times, brown head bobbing beneath a broad-brimmed Spanish hat, uncovered spindly legs visible beneath a sweat-soiled soutane. His appearance proved me correct. Campion was tall, slender, handsome, and garbed in a suit which, while it may have been plainly clerical, was, nonetheless, unmistakably from Huntsman's. It was manifest that he was one of those Oxford boys who had been much taken with John Newman (although I do not know why, having always considered his *Apologia* bright enough, but a bit mawkish in tone).

Many good men, of course, were influenced by Newman and, later, the Jesuits. The Pretender himself, Henry Stuart, Cardinal York, last direct descendant of Mary, Queen of Scots, had been brought along by the Jesuits. It was widely known that the only reason he did not join the Society was that Jesuits may not normally accept high Church office, and the Vatican had great plans for him. Before his death, he had so restored dealings with the Throne that he left his Crown Jewels to England. His royal manner did much to normalize relations with the Vatican.

Once he had been shown in and seated, Campion had the good grace to congratulate me on my appointment. I thanked him and asked if he proposed to pray for my success in office.

"That depends on what you plan to do in office."

"I plan to do nothing about Ireland but hold it exactly as it is."

"I couldn't care less," he said.

At *that,* I stirred in my chair. "Father, you have the gift of surprise."

"I am English, Home Secretary. It is a matter of indifference to me if you systematically starve the people and destroy the economy of a sister island."

I was beginning to positively *enjoy* this fellow. Of course, I offered him a cigar, which he refused. "Sherry, then?"

"Cognac."

"Father, you are not typical."

"That is why I am here."

I poured the cognac into the snifters and handed one to the priest. "Did you know that I, like you, studied both Latin and Greek for several years?"

"Yes. And unlike me did poorly at both. Do not retreat from your realization that I am not typical."

"It made me feel secure to do so. I shan't make such a mistake again. Tell me, is liquor actually permitted to you?"

"Of course. But, in any event, like Wilde, I can resist anything but temptation."

"A priest who reads Wilde."

"Why not?"

"The Index, of course."

"The Index protects the unlearned from books which they cannot understand. The rest of us read what we like."

"Including my despatches from the Boer War?"

"A very vain effort. Your ego weakened it greatly."

"But then you did not come here to discuss books."

"Indeed I did."

"Go on."

153

"As Home Secretary you are nominally the supervisor of Scotland Yard."

"Yes. One of the more inviting aspects of my new post."

"Then you may, if you have not already done so, become familiar with Peter the Painter."

"Legendary anarchist assassin who escaped from Russia in the late 1890s. I've often wondered how he did that."

"No doubt."

"*You* know, don't you?"

"Of course. And much more."

"Go on. Please."

"Peter came under our tutelage at an early age. He went bad and became the notorious character of whom you know. After his escape, he again came under our care. We asked him to do a good thing, and this time he did not betray us." Campion smiled. "We want something."

"What?"

"We don't know."

"You will tell me the end of this bizarre adventure if I promise to give you something, the identity and nature of which are unknown to you?"

"Yes."

"I could be out of office in a month."

"Oh, we think that you will *often* be out of office. You are a bellicose, imperialistic, narrow man. But you will also hold office in times of crisis, because you are a great man. At one of those times, we shall call on you."

"I will do nothing to hurt England."

"Do not insult *me, politician!*"

The priest's face was venomous. I knew that I had, again, misjudged him. "Forgive me, please." He realized that I was sincere. I can think of no worse thing than to insult a man's patriotism.

Campion sat back and said, "That's better. Now, do we have a bargain?"

"You have a bargain. You have my word."

"Very well. We believe that Peter is soon to make his way to England with two medical students who have fallen under his still very considerable charms. I doubt that we will know where or when. We will, however, have information on his present appearance, which will be helpful to your people."

"You give me nothing."

"Be silent and we will give you everything." Campion sniffed the brandy and said, "He represented us on Basil Hawkeland's last mission."

I crashed my hands onto the desk. This was *wonderful*. Positively *wonderful*. "Go on. Please go on."

"He survived the Antarctic expedition."

"Everyone died."

"Forgive me. I've taken up enough of your time."

"Oh, no, no, no. I'm wrong. He survived." The oil, I thought. The Jesuit can put me onto the oil!

"And made contact with one of our priests years later in Cairo. From time to time he has again been in touch with this priest, Father Teilhard de Chardin."

"And now?"

"And now we believe that he is on his way to England. He has spent a lifetime being consumed by hatred. His entire career has been fueled by this madness. In recent years, drink and disease have taken their toll of him. He still retains, however, a kind of romantic grip on some members of the International." Then the priest stopped. I shook my arms at him to continue. He wrinkled his nose and looked away. Impatience was obviously the wrong approach. "I was agitated," I said. "Excited. I was most certainly not waving you on." *Vain bastard!*

"I understand." He looked at his snifter. "Tell me, Home Secretary, does this truly remarkable Hennessey come in splits?"

"Mmm? Oh, no, no. Not at all. Please forgive me." I poured another four fingers for each of us, then said, "What is there next in this extraordinary story?"

"Be silent, I said, and you will learn it all. He carries a diary which records his entire life, and the true story of his voyage with Hawkeland. Including, we think, the formula. If you merely send the police after him, you will wind up with three bodies. Knowing about the diary, you may end up with it."

"Then all the stories, the legends of the Hawkeland mission, the veiled references in government papers . . ."

"All true. And if the formula is in the diary, half the profits go to us."

"I have given you my word."

The priest cast a sere laugh. "No, my dear fellow. You promised us what we have not yet decided to request. The profits are already ours by prior arrangement with the Crown."

"And if I refuse?"

"In his capacity as Primate of England, His Eminence, the Cardinal Archbishop, will take to the pulpit to blame you for every death, from whatever cause, in Ireland. Thousands of Catholics will move to your borough and vote you out of office. If you move, so will they. Our coffers are quite deep.

"In his capacity as Premier Catholic Peer of the Realm, he will advise all who meet him socially, including his friend the King, that you have fallen heir to a most unfortunate disease."

"You *bastard!*"

"I know."

I settled back. "You play the game well, Father."

"I enjoy the game, Home Secretary."

"The diary may be useless."

"You have given me your word. However, we seek only to be reimbursed on a theory of *quantum meruit*. We will not take advantage."

I snorted at that. "You have my word."

"Excellent." He stood to leave and I walked him to the door. "Tell me, Father," I asked, "do you ever fear that your tactics may condemn you to hell?"

"About as often as you do, Home Secretary. Good day."

This new Campion was every bit as spirited as his namesake. The original, as I recall, was beatified, one step below sainthood. The process of canonization takes centuries, and Campion's cause was not dropped until the late 1800s. Now I knew why. Both the Church and England had matured enough to know that one does not argue over a martyr's blood before undertaking to negotiate.

A few days after my meeting with the extraordinary Jesuit, the diary fell into my hands. It was a delightful way in which to begin 1911.

Chapter Fourteen

THE DIARY OF PETER THE PAINTER

I became an anarchist on my sixth birthday. My philosophy was a gift from the Tsar, who provided it to me as he provided amusement to eighty thousand others that day. The occasion was one of the greatest street carnivals in the saga of the Romanovs; the festival was the last public hanging in Russia.

It seemed that for every onlooker there was a peddler. Vendors moved through the delighted crowd offering cheap icons, unattractive two-dimensional renderings of the Jewish boy-God and his mother. Old ladies moved slowly, bent over by huge wooden tanks of hot colored water, samovars filled with tea, or flasks of vodka. A few coins, or perhaps even a bit of bartered food, would bring enough scalding liquid to make the day more festive. All along the way, kiosks had been set up; behind them farmers offered roast pork skins and bits of sausage. The masses of people, steaming in greatcoats and astrakhans, blankets and caps, their breath fouled with coarse food and plum wine, moved about jubilantly, crushing, jostling, talking in a fellowship of warmly anticipated enjoyment.

At the far end of the circus, in place of the ring where fire eaters or pony riders might have performed, a giant platform had been erected. On its planks stood six stools. Even from a distance, my view distorted from the angle one perceives when sitting on another's shoulders, I could tell that the flimsy stools were newly carved: there was not a mark or stain on them. They seemed more suited to a shopwindow than a gallows.

This entertainment, so necessary for the diversion of an unemployed and starving citizenry, had been occasioned by the assassination of Tsar Alexander II. It is ironic to realize that all previous plots had been conceived, mounted, and staged with some degree of skill. The unsuccessful plotters had moved only after reflection, reconnaissance, and practice. The poor students who were to be dispatched at the carnival, however, had botched everything about their plot, and, by accident, they were successful. And also by accident they killed Alexander only hours after he had signed the Loris-Melikov reforms, a bill which would have moved Russian society further into sanity than it had traveled in a millennium.

The student assassins knew nothing of this, of course, but I doubt that it would have made any difference. They were idealistic, you see, and idealists never think. Except, perhaps, when they are about to die. At that moment, each was shown a copy of the now-revoked reforms. They were permitted to carry into eternity the realization that they had destroyed forever the enlightenment for which they had killed.

This group of bungling assassins had grown out of the Tchaikovsky Circle. They had earlier attempted to shoot the Tsar, blow up the Imperial train, and dynamite the Winter Palace. Each attempt was more ludicrous than its predecessor. Until, late in 1880, Sophia Perovskaya joined the circle. Like most true revolutionaries, she was from the upper middle class. (Beyond all the rhetoric, reformers do not enjoy the company of people who sweat.) Her father had once been Governor-General of Saint Petersburg. He had later been dismissed from the post, but remained ever loyal to the Tsar. He felt no affection, however, for his daughter, and this infected his every dealing with her. When the pus of his love had spread far enough, she knew that there was no alternative but to cut it out. To do so, she joined the Circle.

Sophia was shocked to find that, despite its reputation for foolhardy violence, the Tchaikovsky Circle was a collection of endlessly chattering students. Like most students who plan to stir the world, they had difficulty stirring their bodies from chairs. They talked, they smoked, they drank tea, and they bungled.

She soon became the scourge of the group. If they wished to drown in tea and suffocate in theory, she said, so be it. She would save society, with pride in her courage and regret that her comrades were not really men. In time, to save their wounded honor, the men agreed to take action.

The group tracked the few public movements of the Tsar and soon learned that Alexander always traveled along the Maly Sadovayo when entering and leaving the Winter Palace. Despite the repeated attempts which had been made on the Tsar's life, security was weak, and the Circle was able to rent a basement room on the route. Above the room was a cheese shop which the anarchists could not afford to stock with even a small selection. Three members of the group were arrested while loitering on the Maly Sadovayo, imprisoned, tortured, and questioned. Incredibly, they said nothing. Even more startling, the police failed to investigate either the empty cheese shop or the warren of rooms which was known to exist beneath the street.

The Maly Sadovayo was tunneled under and mined. The remaining members of the anarchist group learned how to throw bombs. And everyone waited for his courage to equal his resolve. Sophia stood ready.

They moved on a Sunday morning in early spring. As he did each week, the Tsar had set out for the Michael Riding School, where he went to applaud the horsemanship of his guards. The mine was ready. The bomb throwers were stationed along the various turning points open to the Tsar's carriage. Sophia stood at a central position, in view of all the terrorists.

As the Imperial carriage moved rapidly toward the Winter Palace, the driver, for no apparent reason, turned off the Maly Sadovayo and proceeded along an entirely new route. Sophia gave her signal. One bomber did not see it, as he had already fled. A second, the eighteen-year-old Rysakov, threw his missile from fifty feet away, killing a baker's boy in the crowd and mortally wounding a Cossack outrider. Several other of the Imperial horsemen captured Rysakov.

Alexander, against the advice of his guards, walked back to see the man who had tried to kill him, then went to comfort the casualties. "Thank God Your Majesty is safe," a policeman said. As he walked through the slush and muck of the streets, a third anarchist stepped before him and said, "Rather too early to thank God," then threw a bomb between Alexander's legs.

The Tsar's horribly mangled body was carried to a sofa in the Winter Palace. He died two hours later. The bomber's wounds were almost as severe, but he lingered for eight hours before dying. At least twenty bystanders, innocent men, women, and children who had come out to cheer the Tsar, preceded the Emperor and the anarchist in death.

Weeks later, the carnival was held. The authorities had done all they could to break the group's members, and they had failed. Except with Rysakov. The eighteen-year-old boy had broken down in prison, confessed, and begged for mercy. As a punishment for his weakness, the others turned from him on the gallows and left him to die alone in public.

The bungling continued even unto death, but now it was the government's turn. The carpenters had forgotten to build a drop into the scaffold, so the stools had to be kicked away. The executioner, who was drunk, had not weighed the victims properly. As a result, one youth's noose slipped twice and he had to be rehanged each time. The crowd was provided with great entertainment, as it took each conspirator twenty minutes to strangle to death.

The mob moved forward to grasp a piece of each victim's rope, in the belief that such a souvenir would bring good luck. The Cossacks, however, held them back, and cut down Rysakov, my brother.

I cannot describe how close I was to my brother. Despite the ten-year difference in our ages, we were inseparable. My father, a landowner and bureaucrat, went into a long and irreversible period of mental decline shortly after my birth. My mother was ill. As a result, Nicky raised me, serving as both father and brother. All of the pleasures of my youth flowed from the time that he spent with me and the things he taught me. When he went away to school, his letters were constant and my admiration unbounded. I knew nothing of the anarchist group, of course, until it was too late.

I had been taken to the hanging by Father Arkady, our priest. He lifted me onto his shoulders so I could see my brother's final moments, and brought me down only at the end. He said only one thing that day, an admonition whispered as my brother twisted in the wind. "Remember this, Peter. The day will come for your vengeance on the Tsar."

These words greatly shocked me. It was understood, even by children such as myself, that priests were part of the government. Religion survived in Russia only because of its dual accomplishment: it was a comfort to the serf and a justification to the master. Yet Father Arkady with a few words had placed himself outside this twin function. It was even more shocking than might have been the case, because of his unique position.

Father Vladimir Arkady was, first of all, a mitered priest. This is a rank unique to Orthodoxy, placing the designee between a common priest and a consecrated bishop. It is a rank open only to those of legitimate birth (the priesthood is not similarly restricted); and the designee must be literate (which many priests are not). Father Arkady was unusual also in that, contrary to custom, he kept no concubine; nor was he ever married, which is a privilege extended to Orthodox priests. As I grew older, I found that our village priest was different from the Orthodox clergy in one other important respect as well: he was a Jesuit.

Because of the strange role which the Society of Jesus has played in my life, I feel it essential to set forth something of that group's history in Russia.

In the year 1580, Pope Gregory XIII sent the greatest Jesuit diplomatist of all, Antonio Possevino, on a mission of supreme importance. The mission was undertaken in response to a request from Ivan the Terrible. The Tsar requested the intervention of the papacy in Russia's losing war with the Catholic, pro-Jesuit Polish king, Stephen Bathory. In exchange for the Pope's aid, Ivan promised to join in a papal campaign against the Sultan.

For centuries, the Papal See had desired to promote a new crusade against Islam. The plan had always been frustrated by the desire of the Christian princes to speed each other's Catholic subjects to heaven. The Pope realized that blunting this otherwise commendable desire would free a massive bloc of Christian soldiers to move against the infidels.

Equally important, the Pope thought that a peace which saved Russia might lead to the granting of religious concessions. For that reason, he turned to Possevino, who had just negotiated the supremacy of the Catholic Church in Lutheran Sweden. It was a brilliant choice.

Possevino stopped first in Venice, where he appeared before the Council of Ten, which had refused for decades to support papal militarism. He spoke for hours of the commercial benefits which the *signoria* would achieve in their new Russian markets. The gains which he promised so far exceeded the needs of his mission that, for the first time in a quarter-century, the Doge and Council agreed to finance a papal mission.

The Jesuit traveled through Graz, Vienna, and Prague, arranging alliances, offering commercial concessions, and striking deals on behalf of the Pope. By the time he arrived in Vilna, King Stephen was in the midst of a series of great victories. He possessed no desire for peace, and a sour disposition for a victorious warrior. Possevino waited. And observed.

A few weeks of silence brought gossip which enabled the Jesuit to ascribe King Stephen's dour demeanor to his political marriage to the fifty-four-year-old Princess Anne Jagiellonika. Possevino observed

161

that this unhappy temperament carried over into the King's personal life; he ate boiled beef and cabbage, wore plain clothes, and tolerated only direct talk. The priest added this to what he already knew, that the King, through another title, owed partial allegiance to the Sultan.

It was five weeks before the King's victorious march ground to a halt, having completely outrun its supply lines. Only then did Stephen agree to see the Jesuit. Possevino came to the King's tent clad in a tattered soutane. He insisted on a meal of beef and cabbage, stating that anything else would have been a violation of his vow of poverty. The King was deceived and asked the priest to tell him what the Pope wanted.

"His Holiness desires only an end to the bloodshed between his children."

"Ivan's father is the devil."

"Satan would claim us all if he could."

"And who would claim our land?"

"Not the Pope."

"Not Ivan."

"That will be guaranteed."

"We cannot enter into a guarantee with Ivan. It is a question of honor."

"It is well known that you are an honorable man."

"Then know this: If we agree to the Pope's peace, Ivan will repay the Vatican by marching on the Sultan. I am Voivode of Transylvania, which means that I am a vassal of the Sultan."

"His Holiness knows of this alliance. And approves."

"The Pope approves of a Catholic King being in bed with the all-high of the infidels?"

"The Holy Father's approval or disapproval means nothing. Peace is everything."

Stephen studied the priest. "Peace? You are a witty one. Ivan is a syphilitic slayer of his own children, who would not know peace if it appeared as a dog and bit his ass. You can take these terms to our brother monarch: we will cease our war if he will. There is nothing else to discuss."

The priest agreed. In the morning he left for Ivan's residence in Tsaritsyn on the Volga. His welcome was the most ornate of his career, so filled with Tsarist excess that he refused even to report specifics to the Holy See. What he did report was his conversation with the Tsar.

"What does the Sultan's Polish eunuch want?" Ivan asked.

"Peace."

162

"*Hah!* He wants to keep my armies tied down endlessly so that they cannot go forth to do battle against the infidel enslaver of Christians. I tell you, priest, if you can free me from this vexatious war, which is my only reason for seeking your aid, I shall turn my fury on the Sultan."

"Such a peace would dishonor you, Magnificence. Many would say that you attacked the Sultan only after using the Pope's treaty to neutralize the infidel's European ally."

Ivan cocked his eye and smiled. "Do you want a woman?"

"No, thank you."

"Uhh." He turned away. From over his shoulder he called, "Then the Pope will not help."

"He will do whatever will aid Your Imperial Majesty."

Ivan's face clouded. "I understand, of course. But the specifics . . ."

"King Stephen asks only that your two armies stand in place and put up their swords. No reparations or continued hostilities. His Holiness prays that both magnificent princes will simply end their war."

"And the crusade against the Sultan?"

"It need not be undertaken."

"Will Stephen meet me?"

"In the village of Jam Zapolski."

"No. No. That is a despicable hamlet. There is no safe place to meet there."

"I could build a church."

Ivan snorted. His ridicule slowly turned to appreciation, and then pure humor. He had been gulled and he knew it. "And then what?"

"Freedom for the Jesuits to operate in Russia."

"Done."

"Schools, seminaries, our own bishops. Everything."

"Everything."

"And recognition of the Pope."

"As a sovereign."

"As head of the Church on earth. Supreme over Orthodoxy."

"Never. If God didn't strike me dead the priests would."

"Then as a sovereign only. But we can go where we like and convert anyone who believes. Even at the highest levels of court."

"Done, done. Send word when the church is built."

It was soon constructed, and the two monarchs met and concluded their treaty. Each man then went back to the business of consolidating his rule.

In Poland, Stephen was eventually succeeded by John II Casimir.

163

The new king had been raised in Rome, entered the Jesuits, received permission to become a cardinal, then resigned from the Society and the Church to marry the Dowager Queen, thereby becoming King of Poland. He remained close to the Jesuits, favoring them in his policies, and giving the Society a safe base from which to launch operations against Protestant princes. They used the base many times.

In Russia, following the deaths of Ivan and his feeble-minded son Fedor, Boris Godunov schemed his way to the throne. He had convinced the Zemsky Sobor that convened to elect a Tsar that none of Ivan's issue had survived, the only other male, Dmitri, having died at the age of two. He did not mention that his men had killed the child. Godunov's reign is described by most historians as the Time of Troubles, a coming together of political unrest, foreign travail, and a devastating famine which lasted from 1601 through 1603. The people were, of course, discontented. Relief appeared in the form of the teenaged Dmitri, second son of Ivan.

Word spread throughout Russia that Boris's men had killed the wrong child. Immediately behind the rumors came Dmitri himself, leading four thousand men into the Ukraine. This area, already under the twin pressures of ethnic consolidation and conscription, was most eager to join Dmitri. Thousands of Cossacks flocked to his banner, garrisons declared for him, and an independent force struck northward, in his name, against Moscow. Boris died of a heart attack and the stage was set for the accession of Dmitri.

Maria Nagaia, widow of Ivan, embraced the youth; the boyars swore their allegiance; and the people proclaimed Dmitri Tsar. He repaid them by driving out Godunov's hated court, killing Boris's wife and child, and dispensing money lavishly to the poor. Dmitri then proclaimed a national holiday as he married a Polish bride, Marina Mniszek, before two Polish Jesuits, Father Czyrowski and Father Sawicki.

It was this Jesuit connection, as well as a fear of a return to Ivan's terror, that most alarmed the boyars. They were concerned over the priests' constant presence and their insistence on chatting in a strange tongue to the new Tsar. Orthodox priests studied the odd language, recognized it as a code, and learned that it was a method the Jesuits had of communicating with the new ruler. They also learned that Dmitri was an apostate Russian monk named Grishka Otrepiev, who had been persuaded by the Jesuits to accept Catholicism and claim the throne for the Church.

164

Less than one year after his accession, Tsar Dmitri was murdered by the mob, and his body dragged through the streets. The Jesuits, incredibly, survived.

For more than a century, the Society flourished in Russia. Not only did Jesuits build great centers of learning in Saint Petersburg and Moscow, they carefully worked to overthrow the Orthodox Church. It was a task in which they enjoyed the unwitting help of the Tsar.

Bringing to the throne a great love of the West, Peter the Great consistently attempted to advance priests with Roman leanings. Foremost among these, of course, were the Jesuits, who had earlier received Imperial protection from Sophia. Although the Patriarch Ioakim, who supported the young Peter, and Ioakim's successor, Adrian, wished to begin an assault on the Jesuits, Peter waited.

When Adrian died, Peter chose as his successor Stephen Yavorsky, metropolitan of Ryazan. In his youth, Yavorsky, a little Russian, had pretended conversion to Roman Catholicism in order to secure admission to a Jesuit college in the West. Ironically, he came to believe what the Jesuits taught about the Roman Church. Yavorsky could not, however, reject completely his love of Orthodoxy. The Jesuits understood this (as they had understood his false conversion), and encouraged him to return to Russia and spend his life as an Orthodox priest. It was a wise decision. Yavorsky's love of things Western meshed well with Peter's desire to open Russia to the world. Yavorsky became Vicar-General, although even Peter's support could not persuade the Muscovite hierarchy to forgive Stephen's false conversion and make him a patriarch.

Yavorsky eventually became head of the Holy Governing Synod. In that post, he encouraged the teaching of seminarians in accordance with the Jesuit *Ratio Studiorum,* and made mandatory the study of Loyola's *Spiritual Exercises.*

On July 21, 1773, this progress was threatened. Acting under great political pressure, Pope Clement XIV published *Dominus ac Redemptor,* which proclaimed the complete suppression of the Jesuits. The members of the Society who were operating in Russia persuaded Catherine to permit them to stay. On the surface, they were welcome to operate their colleges and aid the advancement of learning in Russia. On a more serious level, Catherine saw protecting them as a chance to ridicule the Pope's authority.

At the Society's request, Catherine named one priest, Father Siestrencewiecz, Bishop of Mohilow, and another Jesuit, Father

Benislawski, his coadjutor. She then dispatched Benislawski to Rome to ask for the Society's recognition in Rome. Clement refused, and threatened to excommunicate them all.

Benislawski, aware of Catherine's desires, asked, "Am I to understand, Holiness, that you condemn a band of priests sworn to serve you, but that those priests will be defended by a queen who is your enemy? What a spectacle to present to the heathen!" He turned to leave.

The Pope told him to halt, then walked to a desk, took out paper, and dipped his quill. He wrote, "*Approbo Societatem Jesu in Alba Russia degentem; approbo; approbo.* [I approve the Society of Jesus residing in White Russia; I approve, I approve.]" Then he sealed the document, spat upon the floor, and left.

The Jesuit Superior in Russia at that time was named Grouber. He restrained his men from proselytizing, and instructed them to busy themselves in their schools. He later undertook a series of secret diplomatic missions for Tsar Alexander I. Grouber perished in a fire in 1805, and his men went back to working among the people. So angry did Tsar Alexander become as they converted thousands of the Orthodox, he placed the Society under tight constraints. By the time of the Jesuit Restoration in 1814, the members saw their power declining in Russia.

The following year, the Tsar turned to Pietism, a sect which drew on Catholicism, Masonry, and Protestantism. Pietism's greatest teacher, who had been Orthodoxy's greatest theologian, was Simeon Todorsky, the converted son of a Jew who had been educated by Jesuits. Alexander turned the Society out of Moscow and Saint Petersburg in 1815. Five years later, they were expelled from Russia.

Not surprisingly, some stayed on secretly. They established a chain of command and communication which was controlled by Jesuits working out of the Polish sanctuary. There, priests and bishops developed youths of good family and Catholic leanings, ordained them, and sent them back to become Orthodox clergy. These men in turn kept alive the Roman Church and searched constantly for new candidates for the priesthood. One of these Jesuits was Father Arkady.

I learned later that it had been Father Arkady's hope that taking me to the hanging would instill in me a deep hatred of the Tsar and his Church. His wish was granted.

Arkady's own hatred, of course, was not really for the Tsar. Like most Jesuits, he was concerned with controlling the thought processes of the man on the throne, not whose buttocks warmed it. The Romanovs, after all, were not Protestants or infidel defilers of the Church. They were, rather, misguided Catholics, rulers who could be placed on the road to God only if their Church was toppled. That could be done only by missionaries, and missionaries came from youths like me.

With the consent of my slowly failing mother, the priest undertook my education. I spent part of each day attending the village school, but that was only to learn the rudiments of scholarship. Arkady, in his house, spent each afternoon teaching me Latin, Greek, and religion. It was one of the decisions of nature that I should master languages easily. It was my decision to resist accepting the subtleties of God's ways. I could not believe that a subtle God would permit my brother to be strangled. We sparred over this point for months. Arkady then spoke of my debt to the Jesuits for the first time. He told me that he recognized my love for my brother, and applauded it despite Nicky's conduct. For what the Jesuits had given me, however, he asked that I recognize a debt, and pay it in part by promising never to engage in any prohibited conduct without Arkady's consent. To a youth my age it seemed an easy enough request. I made the vow, and I was to keep it. And Arkady was right, the debt was great.

The lands and liberties of the family of a regicide are forfeit to the Crown. New Tsars frequently remitted the bills of attainder in order to appear more merciful than their lineage would indicate. My brother's friends, however, through their gross incompetence, had butchered not only the Tsar but a score of innocent citizens as well. As a result, bills of attainder were applied to the families of all the conspirators. Yet we were spared. Father Arkady told us only that it had been arranged.

Along with the subjects which I have described, and others which made up the Jesuit plan of studies, the *Ratio Studiorum,* Father Arkady encouraged my interest in painting. This was entirely in keeping with the Jesuits' history. Loyola himself was a friend of Michelangelo, who, at the age of eighty, offered to design a Jesuit church in Rome, although he died a short time later. Rubens painted "Ignatius Cures One Possessed," and presented it to the Society. Van Dyck engraved devotional books for Jesuit friends. Bernini, Baldinucci, the Chevalier

167

de Chantelou, Giacomo della Porta—the list goes on, through the years and through many forms of expression. To the Jesuits, all forms of skill were to be used as demanded by their motto, *Ad majorem Dei gloriam:* for the greater glory of God. My fear was that my glory would never be exposed.

As the years passed, I argued constantly with Arkady that my talent was wasted in the village. I wanted to go to Moscow to study. He told me to bide my time, that while the bill of attainder was no threat, it was still too soon to move to Moscow. He kept me in the village, but arranged frequent trips to Saint Petersburg, where friends of his guided me through the great museums. At home he helped me to prepare for my university examinations. With his help, my grades were the highest recorded that year. Through it all, however, I knew that he wanted me to be a priest. I said nothing, knowing that my entire being belonged only to art.

As important as my studies was the physical preparation which Arkady forced upon me. He insisted that I undertake a regimen of exercise which soon enabled me to perform at a high level of endurance. I could not but imagine that he did this because of his desire that I be able one day to successfully evade the anti-clerical police of the world. His training enabled me to do that, but for reasons he could not have foretold, and in a way that he could not have imagined.

The month before I left for the university, Father Arkady called me to his bedchamber. "Peter," he began, "you know that I had hoped to develop you for the Society. I have given up on that hope. There is room in the priesthood for many kinds of talent, but when a talent consumes all of a man's being, it would be wrong to detract even a whit and direct it to another calling." He saw my eyes widen in surprise at how well he had read me. Before I could object, he raised his hand for silence and continued.

"I have, therefore, arranged for you to go, not to university, but to Moscow. We have arranged it at this time because we think it is safe for you. There is a man there, perhaps you have heard of him: Serov." Arkady smiled when I gasped. Serov was one of the best-known artists in Russia. His "Girl with Peaches" was considered by many critics to be second only to the "Mona Lisa." What Surikov was to heroic scenes and Vasnetsov was to rendering the life of the peasant, Serov was to pure painting.

"I thought you would be pleased," the priest said. "Now I am going to do something which will shock you, but as a matter of discipline you

168

will obey without question." I nodded. "Stand up and strip," Arkady said.

Like all young men, I had heard many stories of the danger posed by womanless priests, but I had faith that Arkady was not so inclined. I did as he commanded. My trust was rewarded. He appraised me with no more passion than an ostler observing a horse. From the folds of his robe he took a small metal tube not much longer than a rifle shell. Then he commanded me to turn.

"Bow forward," he said, "and grasp the bureau." I did as I was told. "This will hurt," he warned. An instant later the tube was inserted in my rectum. I jumped forward, hitting the bureau. Father Arkady jerked me back into position, then slapped a sticking plaster over my ass. "Get dressed," he said.

I must confess that when I turned to face him I was ashamed. He sensed this and quickly said, "This has its reason. Keep the tube in place until tomorrow, no matter what. There is a reason." I did as I was told.

Each day for the next two weeks he removed one tube and inserted a wider one. By the end of the fortnight, Arkady was able to insert a cylinder the size of a small fist. He told me to keep it in place for five days. The physical and emotional distress were great. I knew only that Arkady had a reason and that the power of reason dominated the life of a Jesuit.

On the night before I was to leave for Moscow, I visited Father Arkady one last time. He handed me the large cylinder. It was heavier than I remembered. We went through the process of insertion. When I was dressed, Arkady spoke. "You are leaving to study art. That does not displease us. We admonish you, however, to remember whence your education has come. You are in our debt. You will repay us by undertaking a mission. The tube will finance you, or your escape, if necessary. Although painted black, it is made of gold. Inside are ten one-thousand-ruble notes. Do you accept the existence of your debt, and your obligation to repay us?"

I nodded. Arkady knew that I would not betray him. "Very well," he said. "You are to represent us before Pobedonostsev." Arkady listened to my gasp, then laughed. Constantine Pobedonostsev was Procurator of the Holy Synod, in effect the Grand Inquisitor of Russia. Although a layman, he ruled over Orthodoxy for the Tsar. The slightest deviation from the concept of religious subservience to the House of Romanov was reported to the Procurator. Mitered priests, archimandrites, metropolitans, all lived in fear of him. Pobedonostsev could reassign or jail any cleric in the Empire. What he did was done in the name of the Tsar. And done ruthlessly.

Russia was then not the monolithic religious entity many believed. There were always sects flourishing and heresies waiting to hatch. The Duchoborzen, or spirit seekers, believed that God and man were inseparable, with the deity always within the human. They were banished to Siberia, or drafted en masse into the army for periods of twenty-five years.

An offshoot of their sect was the Molokanes, the milk eaters, so named because they drink milk during periods of fasting. Theirs is a religion without ceremony. Pobedonostsev made them a people without freedom.

For two centuries the Stundists, rejecting both the Old Testament and priests, have been persecuted. Pobedonostsev raised their torment to an art, banishing thousands, and authorizing local officials to treat them with open cruelty.

No group suffered more horribly under the Procurator than the Jews. Pobedonostsev acquired control of the Jews in 1889. He and his enforcer, Vyacheslav Plehve, of whom more later, assigned editors to whip up resentment against the Jews. Once the mob sniffed blood, he gave it to them. Troops butchered the Jews of Kishnikoff, Homel, and Odessa. Pobedonostsev and Plehve forced the passage of Article 13 of the Passport law, which forbade Jews to live in the provinces of Don, Kuban, and Tereh. They were also forbidden to use health springs, medicinal water, or gentile doctors, or to participate in the rural assemblies.

Under Pobedonostsev, the Jews were driven out of metropolitan areas, their homes and possessions forfeit. In Kiev, they were allowed to pay their licensing fees, then barred from employment. Whole factories were expropriated, and the Jewish educational fund for Diniaburg was confiscated for use by the Church. The most tragic abuse occurred along the frontier, where Jews were forbidden to live more than fifty versts from the border. The official reason was Jewish involvement in smuggling. The true aim was to crowd the Jews into camps, where starvation and disease killed off almost all the children.

Unlike most Russians, and most Catholics, I have no animosity toward the Jews. The reason for this, I suppose, is the deep impression made on me by Father Arkady. He constantly emphasized the respect which he had for Jews. His approval was grounded in the common approach to God and theology of the Jews and Jesuits. From the earliest days of the Society, the Jesuits had drawn heavily on the Jewish Mishnah for theological examples. Both Jesuit casuistry and Talmudic subtlety are similar in their application of general moral precepts to the individual case.

Catholicism rejects any question of caring about an individual's spiritual torment. It is concerned only with abstract morality, which is applied only in the negative. Catholics are taught to live in fear of a vengeful God who sits in waiting for each infraction of His rules. The Jews, however, view God more as a neighbor with recently acquired wealth and power. As a neighbor, He may not do enough to alleviate the suffering or advance the causes of His less fortunate friends. But a friend He remains, one to whom thanks can be offered and complaints made without rupturing the delicate relationships between the parties.

The Jesuits, alone among priests, take something of this view. They never forget that God is above them, but believe that because He made them and is all powerful, they have the right to talk to Him, to give thanks and offer complaints.

To Pobedonostsev, the Jews were a vehicle, an engine which he could ride to even greater control of society. He had tutored Alexander III and became his prize henchman. His barbarism toward his enemies was such that I could only assume that Father Arkady had signed my death warrant.

"Afraid?" he asked.

"Yes, Father."

"With good reason. And yet the man is not beyond redemption."

"You expect me to convert that animal?"

"In a sense, yes. Unlike most zealots, Pobedonostsev is not without reason. And, again unlike most zealots, he is complex. He stands for the harsh, ruthless Church of the state; and he has translated the *Imitation of Christ,* warmest of books on God. He moves his priests from church to church, concerned not with men's salvation but only with guaranteeing an undiluted stream of reliable information. Yet he does everything with the belief that it will save men's souls. He presides over a bureaucracy, the alpha and omega of which is corruption. But he lives simply, without goods or women. Pobedonostsev appreciates art and music, and has set out to destroy every ethnic contribution to culture produced in the Empire.

"And that is why he must be approached.

"Russia is destroying itself with its refusal to advance one step beyond the prerogatives of the Throne. Pobedonostsev is attempting to Russify God and culture. Take a man's home, Peter, and he will build another. Steal his food and he will grow more. Enslave him and he will dream of freedom. But take away his God and man is hopeless.

"Neither socialism nor anarchism nor syndicalism can replace God. They merely omit Him. Communism, however, is wise enough to offer a new god, the state, in place of the old. Men without hope are easily ground beneath communism's wheel. Communism is the greatest danger the Church will ever face. That is why Pobedonostsev must be persuaded against his present course of conduct."

"Persuaded?"

"Peter, you of all people realize the futility of assassination. And to that end I remind you of your vow to abjure politics except as I direct you. The Society once came close to obtaining great concessions from the Crown. An assassination stole our gains. That was long ago. We no longer have great empty episodes of time. We cannot kill Pobedonostsev and hope for a better replacement. I cannot safely approach him. A diplomat would be rebuffed; a suborner rebuked.

"But you, Peter, you have a chance. You have a shining talent. Serov is loyal to us. Pobedonostsev is his greatest patron. An introduction will eventually be arranged. You can win his eye with your talent. Win his ear with the logic that I have taught you. Win his heart with your purity. Or you will lose Russia for the Church."

One cannot appreciate Moscow if one is not from a farm. My first vision of the city came during the carriage ride which followed my train trip. I had dozed off, and as we bounced over a rutted street I was jolted awake. I stirred myself enough to glance out the window, and I saw a church of incredible beauty. I asked the moujik about it and learned not only its name but also its history. The driver told me that Ivan the Terrible had retained an Italian architect to design it. So overcome was the mad Tsar by the church's beauty, so intensely proud was he of its originality, that he ordered the Italian blinded. Months later I learned that the cathedral had been designed by Russians who had suffered not at all for their success. Thus I learned my first lesson about Moscow: everything was a lie.

As an artist, I could not help but be overwhelmed by the city's architecture. Three and a half centuries before, Moscow had been a town of wood, "the burning city." On my arrival it was a city of two entirely dissimilar parts. The first was the enclave of privilege which radiated out from the court. As a student of Serov, the Imperial favorite, I would become a member of this charmed circle. Here homes were well heated, clean, of polished wood and stone. Churches were for worship, not despair. And they were works of art, like the Sobor Vasiliia Blazennago, an assembly of nine churches in honeycomb fashion. The structures were capped with brick steeples reminiscent of portraits of Protestant churches in New England, yet bearing the onion cupolas so common in Russia. Indeed, if one lived in what was to become my circle, one could easily compare Moscow to New England: the weather was harsh, the scenery beautiful in a desolate way, the food plain but plentiful, the life good.

The second Moscow was entirely different. It was a city which shared the mass of Russia's industrialization with Saint Petersburg. The difference was that the latter city was set at a distance and drew workers from wherever it could. Moscow was the most overpopulated area, the area where the need for jobs was greatest. As a result, Saint Petersburg paid more, was forced to develop technologically, and child labor and night work were almost abolished. The factories in Moscow drew on an endless supply of bodies, and so were backward, and extracted the last drop of strength from each worker, eighteen hours a day.

The unluckier laborers were required to sleep in the workrooms, and after a 126-hour work week were paid in scrip, redeemable only by the company. They were subject to large fines for small infractions of company rules. The more fortunate laborers, however, lived off the factory grounds, which they counted a great favor. They were jammed into tiny, filthy cubbyholes. There, consumptives died, their choking rousing infants who slept on the floor between parents, who themselves ate, defecated, and fornicated all in one cubicle. These cursed people fought on and reproduced, living on the edge of death until they were fortunate enough to fall into its gift of eternal rest.

My body lived in the first Moscow, my heart in the second. I was, however, wise enough to know that nothing would be gained if I left Serov and went to work in a factory or, even more foolhardy, distributed pamphlets at the workers' entrance.

A number of students had gone to join the workers after the passage of the University Act of 1884, which dispersed faculties and ended academic freedom in Russia. On arriving in the fields, the students discovered that the peasants were not noble workers but exactly the smelly, surly, suspicious louts that should have been expected after centuries of enslavement. I had no desire to repeat the noble experiment.

173

Serov kept me fully occupied the first few months. I learned little of him as a man, except that he was both intensely religious and amorally sexual. It never seemed to occur to him that there was any conflict between the two passions. Models, patronesses, visitors, anything suited him. Indeed, his one dissatisfaction with my performance was ⁺hat I had no interest in joining him. This is not to say that I was not desperate for a woman. I was. I merely wished it to happen naturally, not as a result of Serov's passing along a hungry young model.

Between his private oratory, his bedroom, and his studio, it seemed that Serov never went outdoors, although he kept a coach and team. It was with some surprise, therefore, that I received an invitation to join him for a turn around the city one Sunday evening.

We drove about for some time. Even in the carriage the incredible cold cut a path down my throat and seized my groin. I could only hope that with the passage of time my system would become more accustomed to the godless cold. It did not. I was, as a result, somewhat reluctant to join the maestro when he suggested a walk by the riverbank. But join him I did, running to maintain his pace as the carriage fell behind. An instant later I heard a splash.

Someone had fallen into the water a few yards back. I turned quickly and ran to where a black bundle was rapidly moving away from shore. Without a moment's hesitation I stripped off my coat, threw it down, and plunged into the water. A few yards from shore I was able to grab the man's scalp. He twisted once and I lost him. His panic-stricken movement had thrown my hand free. As I lifted it above my head to try again, I was sickened to see creatures crawling along my fingers, and maggots which had themselves become encrusted with filth. Repressing the need to vomit I again reached for the man and caught his collar. With the terror of the drowning, he fought savagely to be free, twisting again and again, pulling my face below the black water. As he struggled, we became entwined and began to crash through the ice crust which was several yards offshore. A sudden blow by the demented man forced my head below water. As I fought to rise up and gain the air, a shard of ice caught my ear, which immediately began to burn and bleed. Furious at his stupidity, I looped my arm over his throat and, with my free hand, thrashed our way to shore.

I pulled the sorry beggar onto land and saw that a crowd had gathered. While I neither expected nor deserved cheers, I thought that some assistance might be proffered. I was, instead, subjected to the withering glare of the small mob, which is what I now perceived these people to be. An intense silence enveloped me, a silence which was not still, but seemed to palpitate on the hatred of the onlookers' eyes. Even Serov stood back. I heard a second splash and turned to see that the madman had again plunged into the water.

Serov was lost in the pack. Turning to the crowd, I shouted, "Brothers! Help me! I am tired." This last was the truth. The effort of struggling with the wretch in the icy water had weakened me to exhaustion.

No one moved. I had no choice but to plunge again into the river, leaving the mad throng on the shore. This time I caught the man only feet from land and had no difficulty dragging him back. By then the police had arrived and were shouldering their way through the onlookers. Those stone-hearted citizens soon disappeared, and I was left alone with the madman and the police, who insisted that I turn him over to them. I refused, pointing out that attempted suicide was a Church offense. I did not point out that he would receive at least some mercy from the priests, and none from the police.

Ignoring me, they took him and threw him into a transport. I could not let a madman go to prison, so I shouted to the police, "Let me give you my name. The priests will want evidence that he is mad." A policeman stepped into the transport, and as he slammed the door he laughed and shouted, "Don't freeze, little brother." Only then did I realize that my greatcoat had been stolen.

I looked desperately about, wondering how I would avoid freezing to death. From the roadway I heard the clapping of a single pair of hands, three times mocking my solidarity with the poor. I turned and saw Serov standing by his carriage. He took a cigar from his mouth and laughed. "Bravo, little brother! Bravo!" He carefully lit the cigar, then said, "Please join me."

He opened the door to the carriage as I ran up the embankment and jumped past him into its comparative warmth. He removed his coat as if it were a musketeer's cape and twirled it over me. "Home," he shouted to the moujik, then stepped inside and shut the door. The carriage began to move.

He took a flask from his coat pocket, opened it, and poured a large measure into the gold cup which served as the cap. I quickly downed it, and felt it rise almost as quickly. I forced it back and gasped as its warmth started down through me.

"Cognac is to be sipped," he said. "But I thought that a member of the burmistry would know that."

175

"The burmistry? What are they?"

He smiled again, and I saw that his amusement at both my aquatic performance and my ignorance was not of the spiteful kind. It revealed more a bemused detachment.

"Forgive me, little brother. I know that you are not of the burmistry. Indeed, they no longer exist as such." He passed the flask to me, and I poured a second drink, taking care to toast him and sip the cognac. Then I waited. I knew that he was enjoying this. "The burmistry were originally created to collect taxes for the merchant class. The government even then recognized that it could not trust its own revenue service. The burmistry kept accounts straight between the two sectors." He paused. "And dragged unwilling peasants back to work."

I glared at him. "Then he was *not* mad?"

"Oh, no. He knew what he wanted and had the courage to seek it out. At the edge of youth, he preferred to strangle in silt."

"That is why the others hated me."

"Mmm. It was quite clear to them that you did not care to see him at peace. They envied him, and hated you. Now they must hate him also, because he has failed, and denied them a hero."

"What will happen to him?"

He shrugged. "Some illiterate monk will obtain his release from the police, then slowly torture him to death in the name of the merciful Jesus." He flashed a bitter smile. "You should have less respect for the oppressed."

"*You* did nothing!" Maestro or not, he would have let us both drown.

"I was capturing it all in my mind, Peter. I may render the scene one day. My work is more important than that poor boy's life, or your own."

"If nothing moves you but painting, art demands too much."

"Easy, boy. What you did tonight is exactly what Father Arkady warned me to watch for in you. I know about your brother. And it is sad. Sadder even than I could capture on canvas. But he is gone. You mourn him still, and I cannot fault you for that. But you are still young enough, still child enough, to be easily swayed by the sad or romantic moment.

"It is just such moments as this that Arkady feared. You gave him your word to do nothing political."

"*I saved a man's life.*"

"Not intending it to be a political act, although it was one. But

176

tonight could ignite you. You could go out looking for one of those nameless bands that periodically bring terror to us all. I beg you to be calm, Peter. Wait for Arkady to put you to use. Wait for me to arrange for you to see Pobedonostsev. Do not let tonight drive you to anarchism.''

Pierre Proudhon gave name to it, in the manner of a Jesuit, by affixing the alpha-privative to a present thought. He called it an-archy. No government at all. Its greatest preacher, Bakunin, believed that society would accept the absence of government through the dictates of reason. This was itself illogical, yet was the linchpin of Bakunin's thought. Perhaps this was as it should have been for a man who escaped from hopeless imprisonment, inflamed the world with his passion, rejected Marx as too structured, and influenced Wagner in his characterization of Siegfried.

Illogic was the strength and weakness of anarchism. It was so disorganized, so inherently resistant to structure, that its cells were virtually immune to infiltration, yet totally unable to agree on means. Only Sebastian Faure, the Jesuit-trained anarchist philosopher, was rational. Revolution, he wrote, leads only to the establishment of a new ruling class. To follow it was almost self-defeating. Yet follow it thousands did.

My exposure to anarchism was exclusively passive: hours spent reading *Germinal, Talk Between Two Workers,* and an occasional smuggled issue of *La Revolte.* I rejected anarchism for its anti-intellectualism. Goethe had written, *"Im Anfang War die Tat* [In the beginning there was the deed].'' For me, trained in logic, action should only follow thought. Yet Serov had been right. The sight of the youth attempting to drown himself reminded me of Bakunin's thought that "the urge to destroy is also a creative urge.'' There were many students about who were anarchists, including the many apprentices I met at galleries where we went to learn by copying masters. With only a word I could have joined any of them, but I did not.

The idea of violence as a method of reform was as old as Russia itself. Our own nineteenth century began under the lunatic reign of Tsar Paul. His handsome, liberal, reform-minded son, Alexander I, wished to replace him on the throne—which he did, after arranging for his father's strangulation.

Alexander accomplished nothing. He allowed himself to be guided by ministers who flattered him into thinking that he was the hope of the future, while they were the anchor to the present. The anchor was never weighed, and Alexander died unexpectedly at forty-seven, having achieved no reforms. His passing set the stage for the first significant modern move against the Crown.

The childless Alexander's brother, the Grand Duke Constantine, was next in line to the throne. His most imperial quality was that he had inherited his father's pug nose. (Paul had founded the Pavlovsky Guards, all of whom were required to have pug noses. Ironically, I share that feature with them.) Constantine, however, had already divorced the Princess of Saxe-Coburg and married the slatternly Countess Grudzinka. He had been required to renounce the throne because of this, but for reasons of state his renunciation had been kept secret.

Even after his brother's death, Constantine refused to make public the renunciation. The only possible explanation for this is that he was a simpleton who was amused by all the wrong things. His brother Nicholas knew, of course, but would not act while Constantine kept up his game of refusing the throne without saying why. Nicholas, less popular, was then offered the throne, but also refused, knowing that to claim it could mean violence, but that to be coaxed onto it could mean absolutism.

Finally, on December 13, 1825, Nicholas let it be known that he would take the oath the following day. A thousand miles to the south, in Kiev, a revolution was supposed to march into action. But its leaders, like anarchists, could agree on neither goals nor tactics. At the scene of the coronation, the Moscow Regiment of Foot, with elements of the Grenadier and Marine Guard, formed up across the square from troops loyal to Nicholas.

Many of these common soldiers—drafted at random for twenty-five years, degraded, ill-paid, without family or future—lived only for their loyalty to the Tsar. They had been told that Constantine had never renounced his throne, that Nicholas was a usurper, and that they were fighting for the legitimate succession. When their officer raised a cry of "*Konstitutia* [Constitution]!" these foot soldiers thought that they were cheering the wife of Constantine. Then they walked to their deaths.

Nicholas emerged from the abortive revolt as the master of Russia. Some have argued that he should have quickly accepted the crown and averted the Decembrists' revolt. I disagree. I believe that Nicholas wanted the plot to go forward so that he would have further justification for a reign of repression. Ironically, he showed mercy to the

178

families of some of the Decembrists, but acted cruelly toward his own country.

In the decades which followed, Nicholas did in fact use the Decembrist conspiracy as justification for a regime which inexorably added increments of repression. His successors did little better. Serfs were freed in name and remained slaves in fact. Women were denied education, and so went abroad to study. Men who resisted the authorities joined the women, and soon thousands had gathered in Zurich. The city became a center of the International, and a source of concern to the agents of the dreaded Third Section. The police, in their inestimable wisdom, arranged for the publication of an Imperial ukase in 1873. This order required the students to return home or lose their passports. Suddenly, hundreds of anarchists, socialists, and nihilists who had thought Russia forever closed to them entered openly. And disappeared.

As I have indicated, the students could be called by a number of titles. What they had in common, however, was an ability for random violence. There was a consistent belief among them that eventually one act would be committed which was so outrageous, so horrifying, that the people would rise up. Of course, anarchy lacked all ability to plan such an act so that it would reach beyond its immediate impact. The cells did not, would not, work together. Instead they embarked on a reign of random terror.

The police did not know how to combat the suddenly arrived students, so they arrested them. In the mad summer of 1874, fifteen hundred students were dragged to various police stations. The treatment meted out to them was so horrifying that many assaulted their guards in order to be transferred to the ranks of common criminals and entrusted to regular warders. Others died, killed themselves, or went insane.

In 1877, forty were tried for no offense but their beliefs, the least codified, most ancient of crimes. A year later, one thousand were arrested and tortured. Nearly 10 percent took their own lives. Fewer than two hundred were eventually charged with making anarchistic speeches, and most of these were imprisoned.

At the time, the police prefect in Saint Petersburg was one Trepov, a torture master who directed his most creative efforts at students. His crimes were so heinous that an apolitical woman, Vera Zasulich, made her way to Trepov's office and wounded him four times. When she was brought to trial, the jury acquitted her. The police, expecting this, had arranged to rearrest her outside the courthouse. As she stepped through

179

the door, Vera Zasulich was pulled into the crowd and disappeared.

Alexander II, despite his earlier attempts to ameliorate the lot of the people, responded to the Zasulich acquittal in repressive fashion; he ordered that everyone connected with the terrorists be hanged. In reply, the students passed a death sentence on the Tsar.

Now the anarchists had entered a new phase. They were in the realm of *realpolitik*. They had taken a lesson from the Crown: A corrupt regime can only be destroyed by regicide. Plans to kill Alexander by dynamiting—first a train, then a bridge—failed. The students decided that if they could not kill Alexander in the field they would kill him at home.

A conspirator named Khalturin had obtained employment as a waiter at the palace. Learning that the waiters' residence was beneath and at an angle to the Imperial dining room, he smuggled in small parcels of dynamite. In time there was enough to lift the floor and blow away the eating area. Incredibly, the police suspected nothing, even after capturing an anarchist who carried a map of the palace with an *X* over the dining room. A few of the staff were questioned but not searched. The dynamite smuggling continued. Finally, Khalturin said, "*Gotovo* [It is ready]."

The explosion destroyed the lower chamber, killing at least thirty servants and soldiers. The Tsar, of course, was unharmed.

Alexander, the man who had freed the serfs, abolished the whip, and imported the jury, was now hunted even within his own palace. There were two routes open. The first to crack down even harder, the second to liberalize in fact, not only in form. He chose the second path.

The man who was to lead the way was Mikhail Loris-Melikov. Appointed to head an executive committee to inquire into the causes of anarchism, Loris-Melikov found the truth all too ugly. He began a program of wheedling, cajoling, bullying, and promising, all directed at forcing through a set of reforms which would bring Russia into a period of enlightenment. On the day that Alexander signed this invaluable document, my brother killed him.

The periodic assassinations and mass arrests gave way to a war of brutality. The commandant of the Tsar's forces was Vyacheslav Plehve.

This most extraordinary policeman began his career in the home of a wealthy Pole who educated and advanced him. In appreciation, Plehve denounced his benefactor to the Polish authorities as a leader of an 1863 insurrection. The grandee was sentenced to death by strangulation, and Plehve joined the Governor General's staff. He rose quickly.

It was Plehve who prosecuted the arraignment of my brother's group. He then joined the Procurator of the Holy Synod, Pobedonostsev, who made him Secretary for Finland. In that post Plehve curbed all resistance to Russification.

Promoted to Minister of the Interior, he established secret courts-martial for civilian offenses, extended the death penalty to non-capital crimes, and devised a method of fighting the anarchists. There was, of course, no central committee which Plehve could infiltrate, no unified set of plans which would enable him to turn the conspirators' designs back on them. He therefore decided to deploy a series of agents who would join individual cells and betray them. Where the members proposed nothing more violent than conversation, the agents themselves were to suggest acts of terrorism. Once these acts were carried out, usually against Plehve's enemies, his agents would denounce the cell, and Plehve would claim credit for the capture.

Plehve had one other method for combatting the reign of terror: He blamed everything on the Jews. This not only provided the Crown with a convenient scapegoat, it also endeared Plehve to the Procurator of the Holy Synod, Pobedonostsev. Ironically, the Jews, who had been good citizens, now took an interest in the underground, realizing that there was no hope for true freedom under the Tsar.

It was within this atmosphere of political repression that I lived and worked. As a student, I wished to be active; but as a rational man, I knew that anarchy offered nothing. As Nicky's brother, I wanted to reach out and accomplish some concrete result; and yet, as an artist, I knew that Serov was right, that what he and Arkady offered me would eventually satisfy many of my desires.

One aspect of my creative forces, however, continued without hope of requite. All around me there was beauty. Repin and Vereshchagin were at the height of their powers. Surikov was catching history on canvas while Vasnetsov was progressing from the maudlin to an artistic rendering of the national folk spirit. And the premier portraitist remained Serov. He dominated my days. One of his clients would soon dominate my nights.

Princess Irene Dolgoruky, first cousin to Alexander's own mistress, had come to the salon to commission a portrait of her husband, Prince Felix, then on assignment as commander of the military region of the Dnieper. Her reason for wanting the portrait was explained to Serov as I stood behind a partition, cleaning the maestro's brushes.

"It is to be a gift," Princess Irene said. "There are enough portraits and photographs from collodion plates for you to study. I will require that it be completed before my husband returns in eleven months."

"I am flattered, Your Royal Highness. But I do not paint from other people's work."

"I would not have bothered you, maestro, if Repin had been free."

"I am indeed grateful to be thought of after the great Repin, who so brilliantly depicts bargemen and religious fanatics."

"If you do not need a commission of two thousand rubles . . ."

To defuse the argument that was about to begin, I stepped from behind the partition and saw Princess Irene Dolgoruky. She was taller than most Russian women and even in her mink coat displayed none of the bulk they achieve to protect themselves from the winter. She wore her black hair tucked under a broad-brimmed sealskin hat, which had been dyed to match perfectly the maroon luster of her furs. When she saw me, she stepped and half-turned to Serov, who pronounced my name tenderly, as if afraid that a strong voice could summon up memories best forgotten. I inclined my head slightly, placing my gesture in the category of deference one would give to a princess or a grandmother. "My lady," I said.

"Your Royal Highness, you mean." She glared, then slowly raised her chin and awaited my surrender.

Forgetting my original role of peacemaker, I allowed the bitch to provoke me and said, "I was not aware, my *lady,* that a particular title was an essential aspect of nobility."

"Apologize!"

When I said nothing, she turned to the master and said, "Serov, make him apologize."

"He is a lout, Your Royal Highness. And certainly a disrespectful buffoon. But no serf. I can talk to him. But make him . . ."

She said, "I will expect you at my home tomorrow at ten. You will apologize or I will take steps to end your misbegotten career."

And so it was arranged, as simply as that.

Most homes in Moscow then were only two stories in height. The Princess Dolgoruky lived in a five-story mansion reached by passing through a gate and walking down a path, across a courtyard, and into the house. There I encountered my first elevator. Stepping into the rosewood lift, I pressed an ivory key for the first numbered floor. A great weight dropped and I ascended. When the car stopped, I was behind what appeared to be a massive door. I touched its handle and it opened instantly. I stepped past the perfectly balanced panel onto the landing and admired the carving on the front of the door. Each of its panels depicted an important moment in man's limited attempts at flight. Icarus, Galileo, Michelangelo, even Benjamin Franklin. The carvings were both delicate and utterly realistic. The prince was a man of both taste and wit.

This impression was strengthened by the simple elegance of the foyer. Its marble floor was bare except for a harp which stood by the wall. The gold instrument was reflected on the black floor, giving the entrance an odd cast. I approached and, like all before me, I suppose, plucked a string, then turned from the foyer to my left. A series of drawing rooms opened beyond me, ending at a floor-to-ceiling glass wall which overlooked the street.

The first area was furnished as a music room, with a grand piano just off the foyer. Two rows of slender chairs could accommodate either sleeping aristocrats or twenty-four musicians. A stand against the wall attested to the harp's use in musicales. As I moved forward into the next room, the seating area was barren except for a circular sofa of Wedgwood blue with an ivory column surmounting it. The final area was a parlor done in the Directoire style. The only constant was the far wall, an unbroken series of bookcases. The effect, as I have stated, was unique. The artistry was clear. Princess Irene had been given a cavern by her husband and had made it fit for any type of society. There was a rustle behind me. I turned to see a grandmotherly woman walking toward me.

At fifteen paces she stopped and bowed. "My mistress will see you now, sir."

"Thank you." I turned and followed the servant back into the foyer, across a bridge over a rear courtyard, through the family dining room, and up a flight of stairs which was hidden between the dining area and a small pantry. At the head of a double flight of steps the servant stood back. I passed through a door, which then closed and locked behind me.

The room was the color of opals. I do not know to this day how the papermaker achieved that particular tint, but his creation was breathtaking. Almost as much so as the appearance of Princess Irene Dolgoruky. With her hair swept up into place by a single pin, and her transparent peach-colored gown, it was obvious that she had just stepped from her tub. I executed a sweeping mock bow and said, "Your Royal Highness."

She placed her index finger beneath my chin, lifted my head, and drew my mouth closer. I gently slipped my tongue against hers. In one moment I was lost in her. In the next instant I was red with pain. The slut had clamped her teeth down on my tongue. I forced my fingers between her teeth and slowly, with great agony, pried open her mouth. When I was at last able to suck my tongue free, I inhaled a glob of blood. Irene was laughing madly as I hopped from one foot to the other, shaking my head with the pain. After I had regained some semblance of self-control, I gasped, "Bitch!"

She laughed again. "You have a disrespectful tongue."

I brought my hand up to her face and struck her hard enough to drive her to the floor. Her robe fell open as she rolled from her side to face me again. I gently placed my booted toe on her nipple and softly said, "Bitch."

She nodded and I moved my foot. Irene rose and came to me. She drew herself erect and said, "Whatever we do in bed we do. Pleasure and pain are one to me. But I *am* a princess royal, bumpkin. So created by God. Strike me again in anything but passion, and you will be my eunuch."

I picked her up. Irene nodded and I carried her to a door beyond a tall screen. Her bedroom was a pale yellow, as was the silk canopy over her bed and the coverlets on it. I placed her on the bed and drew off her wrapper. The sable coat had been a prankster. Her body was not slender, as I had imagined, but possessed such a fullness that I became rigid immediately. It was just as well, for she drew me into her the moment I was on the bed. I pulled her buttocks up and was enveloped by her muscled thighs. As I stroked, she began to come, as I did an instant later. I knew that there was no need to apologize for the quickness of our act together. There would be many more. But first we would talk.

Prince Felix Dolgoruky had been born in 1839, the same year, and in the same province, as Mussorgsky. At seventeen they both became officers of the Preobrazhensky Guard regiment. Although Mussorgsky resigned two years later, Prince Felix remained with the Guards. He won a posting to Alexander II's staff, worked on the Prussian military reforms of 1874, married and became a widower, and fought with distinction in the Turkish War. He had been assigned to the personal guard of Alexander III, but his fierce temper and love of action had made him intolerable to many civilian leaders. He had eventually been shunted to the Department of the Dnieper, leaving his beautiful second wife, thirty years his junior, in Moscow. I had no illusion that I was anything but the latest in a series of serviceable bucks.

All of this I learned before we made love the second time and fell asleep. When we awakened in the evening, I asked her about the advisability of my staying even for an hour.

"Are you worried about scandal, darling?" She laughed. "Don't be silly. There is no scandal at this court. Except perhaps poor Nicky's utter fidelity to Sunny."

"Sunny?"

"Mmm. Nicky's name for the Tsarina. I was wrong about that one."

"What about her?"

"Mmm? Oh. Not Sunny. The marriage. Nicky had been so in love with Mathilde Kschessinska, the prima of the Imperial Ballet. Do you know her?"

"No."

"Such a bumpkin. But once he married Alex, there was no one else for him."

"What happened to the dancer?"

"The prima, you clod, is well kept. As you will be."

I ignored this last and said, "Well kept? I thought you said that the Tsar was faithful to his wife."

"Yes, Nicky is faithful, in his own way. He keeps Mathilde, but his love for Sunny is so great that the other relationship may really be platonic. Which ours will not be."

"If I choose to continue it."

She laughed hysterically, stopping as suddenly as she had begun. "Don't let your artistic spirit make you a boor. I can take you everywhere, introduce you to everyone, even get the great patrons to ignore the cow flop on your feet. *If* you are a dear boy and a good artist."

"You don't know that I can be either."

"You're right. I'll get an album of daguerreotypes of my husband. See if you can do a sketch."

I nodded. Irene got out of bed and crossed to a bureau. I was amazed at the strength of her body. Her breasts, for example, were disproportionately large for her body. Yet when she walked, she barely jiggled. The remainder of her form was incredibly firm. And, of course, she knew well the superb quality of her beauty. She moved about with no concern at all for my appraising glances. She knew that she was always in command.

Irene handed me the album. The prince had changed little from the youthful Guards days to the moment of his present splendor. He was a tall, thickly built, bull-necked man with a square face; his eyes were his best feature, showing, as they did, surprising intelligence for a soldier. His hairline had hardly changed in arrangement, only becoming more speckled with gray as he grew older.

I was discreet enough not to ask where Irene had obtained the pad and charcoal which she then handed me. We exchanged slight smiles and I began sketching. When I finished, I ripped the sheet loose and handed it to her.

"That's extraordinary. So quickly done."

"A rough sketch only."

"Don't be modest, dear one. The only earth the meek inherit is Siberian wasteland. This is *quite* good."

"Thank you."

"Except for the eyes."

She was right, of course. I waited to see if she knew why.

"They are so flat. Almost like those in an icon." Suddenly she laughed out loud. "Are you religious?"

"Somewhat. But my first art teacher was a priest."

"You poor child. Did he rape you?"

"No. Not all of them are like that."

"One can only hope." She studied the sketch again. "The eyes are simply too, too flat. Are all of your paintings like this?"

"Yes."

"Do you plan to improve?"

"Serov is an excellent teacher."

"I hope so. This garbage may be acceptable to a religious *exaltée* like Sunny. Otherwise it won't sell."

"Thank you."

She put it down and slid into bed beside me. "I *am* sorry, darling. It's for your own good."

"Is that why I'm here? My good?"

"You do have an insolent tongue."

"If you hadn't bitten me, I'd show you just how accomplished my tongue is."

"You're not the only one with an accomplished tongue, my love." Then she slid down between my legs.

I would like to offer some excuse, some explanation, for the months which followed; but I cannot. I allowed myself to be taken over completely by Irene, and I regretted not a moment of it. Indeed, even now, looking back, I cannot condemn that time. I had spent years in loneliness and study, paying the terrible price of permitting work to become almost my only pleasure. With Irene it was different; our pleasures were anything which amused the flesh. I was long overdue for it.

During this time 1 kept up my studies with Serov, talked anarchism with other students (but did nothing about my feelings), and met regularly with Father Arkady. He always stayed in a room over a stable owned by an adherent of the Roman Church. This arrangement gave him not only a safe home but also quick access to the means of escape if he needed to flee. In addition, it provided him with an opportunity to ride. His father had raised horses, and Arkady loved not only the animals, but everything about them. We would sit and talk by the hour while he stropped leather, polished trappings or cleaned his equipment. He never mentioned Irene.

My reputation as Serov's prize student grew. This pleased Arkady. He was also pleased with how quickly I learned the intellectual arguments he wanted me one day to present to Pobedonostsev. The day would soon come.

I had been with Serov five months, and with Irene two, when it was arranged for me to meet Pobedonostsev. To say that I was anything less than terrified would be a lie. Although I was to see him to discuss a commission, I would attempt to strike open some wedge of conversation that would enable me to begin my work of gentle prodding. I was, for good or ill, an agent.

Father Arkady had been right. Pobedonostsev did not live in luxury. His dusty apartment, typically, above his office, was shared only with a manservant. I was let in by the old retainer, who then moved as quickly as he could to his master, stepped sideways across his legs, and resumed tugging at his boots.

"Come in, boy," Pobedonostsev called as I stepped forward. He waved his arm. I had obviously arrived just a bit too early, or they had been delayed. This seemed hardly the condition in which the Procurator of the Holy Synod would wish to be seen. Nonetheless he cheerily called me forward.

I thought that the manservant would suffer a heart attack, so mightily did he strain at the remaining boot. Pobedonostsev pushed with a stockinged foot against the old man's buttocks. At last, the boot and retainer flew off. Pobedonostsev and the old man both laughed.

"Oskar, I feel we are both becoming too old for the outdoor life."

"*I* am not too old, Master. And these boots"—he kneaded the leather—"*they* are supple."

The Procurator laughed. "Get out, you old dog."

"Yes, Master."

The servant exited the room, and Pobedonostsev turned to face me for the first time. It shocked me to see that he was an average-looking man. Indeed, with his wispy hair, owlish spectacles, and bow tie, he resembled nothing so much as a provincial schoolteacher.

"So, Arkady sponsored you."

"Yes, Your Excellency."

"He is known to us. A good man, but with intellectual pretension."

"Father Arkady is most intelligent."

"That is not the same as being an intellectual."

"I agree, Your Excellency."

"Do you agree? Or are you agreeing?"

"I happen to agree. I would not simply be agreeable, Your Excellency."

"Good. Your Father Arkady obviously knows something about art, or you would not have been accepted by Serov. Which is why you are here. The maestro tells me that you are good and that, when necessary, you can be quick."

He breathed deeply, then walked with some effort to a samovar and drew a cup of tea. He placed a sugar cube between his teeth and drank the tea through it, then sat down heavily. "You know Tolstoy?"

"Yes, Your Excellency, his books."

"Aargh! He should have stayed with his books. Russians think he has grown since leaving fiction in novels for fiction in religion. They are wrong. He told me I am to be a character in his next book, *Resurrection*. I told him I would excommunicate him."

At that instant I thought the Procurator was strangling, until I realized that it was the harsh laugh of vengeance.

"All writers are fools. Do you know Dostoyevsky's Grand Inquisitor?"

"Yes, Your Excellency."

"I like that character. He exercised religious control through fear and power. Yet Dostoyevsky had Ivan Karamazov say, 'The Jesuits speak and write like the Grand Inquisitor.' The idiot! The Jesuits had nothing to do with the Inquisition, although God knows they've given me enough other problems."

I stiffened, but Pobedonostsev saw nothing.

"Writers! Aargh! Now Tolstoy is inciting people to what he calls a new Christian state."

"Surely that is what Your Excellency desires."

He inclined his head toward me. "You see that, do you?"

"Yes, Your Excellency."

"The alleged repression, the alleged political transfer of priests. Those things do not bother you?"

"They are beyond my understanding, Excellency. I know only that man is imperfect, and that God provides leaders when necessary."

He smiled, genuinely pleased. I had applied what Father Arkady had taught me was called a broad mental reservation, the truth as to the listener, but not as to the speaker. Not a lie, because a lie must be heard to be consummated. Theologically, a neat point. Politically, a good opening.

"Sit here, boy. I like you."

"Thank you, Your Excellency."

"You know, when those moronic students assassinated Alexander"—again I went rigid, and again he saw nothing—"I had my first contact with Tolstoy. He wrote to the new Tsar asking clemency for the conspirators. The letter would have been very influential, if I had passed it on."

"You did not?" At that moment I could have killed Arkady for sending me to treat with this devil, but I sat silent.

"No. I was undecided until I heard a sermon preached the week before the executions. The priest said that the true Christ was a man of strength, unafraid to exact vengeance when necessary. I realized that he was right, and allowed the executions to go forward."

By some process which I cannot describe, I restrained myself and kept only my mission before my eyes.

"And Tolstoy?"

"Hah! Mad Leo? He has begun to exalt the concept of the people over the person as individual. I care little for either, but the rabble are confused that they are no longer the center of his attention. That is why I have called for you. You will undertake the commission?"

"Yes, Your Excellency."

"Without asking what it is?"

"It is not my place to question the Procurator."

"Very good, very good. The peasants are fools, but they do love their Tsar. And they would turn from Tolstoy if they were again convinced of the Tsar's unwavering love for them.

"As you know, all priests report to me. With the information supplied by them you will draw murals for use in villages where Tolstoy is most effective. The pictures will depict the Tsar's, and God's, personal

189

interest in each clearly recognizable place, and each clearly recognizable village elder. That, of course, is only a first step. Tolstoy's ultimate destruction will come later, in ways that need not concern you.''

"Yes, Your Excellency. I am ready to start at your command."

"Good. Very good. I will destroy the Messiah of Yasnaya Polyana, and his doctrine of weakness."

"May I ask Your Excellency a question?"

"Of course."

"Would it be at all advisable to allow the people to deviate slightly from the norm, and remain diffuse in their errors? What if Tolstoy were replaced by another prophet, one less spiritual, more violent, like a Marx? Would not the danger be greater if all dissatisfactions were fused?"

Pobedonostsev drew back his head. "Perhaps." He continued to look at the ceiling. "Perhaps. But where do you set limits?"

"Your Excellency presents a difficult question. If I am not too forward, perhaps I could reflect on an answer and present it when I begin my duties for you."

"Good. We will talk again."

I never again saw the Procurator. The meeting had gone well enough. Indeed, perfectly. The respectful questions, the appearance of a youth eager to learn, the refusal to flatter emptily, all had been part of what Arkady had seen as the proper approach to Pobedonostsev. But I was now to embark on a path of death and deception which would take me far from the court and salons of Russia. Ironically, I was to be set on the path by the new Tsar himself.

Nicholas is the most dangerous of rulers, the weak-willed autocrat. Considered a dolt by his father, hectored constantly by his wife, he brought to the throne a deep-rooted inferiority complex and the delusion of grandeur that he could embody and achieve the desires of his people. Tragically, he believed that he could do these things by being an autocrat.

Although he had come to the throne a year earlier, Nicholas had delayed his coronation festivities until the spring of 1896. When he was finally moved to stage the series of events which would mark his accession, he decided to include a quarter-million peasants. They were to be feted, then carry back to their villages the message that the true Little Brother, the Tsar, was interested in their happiness.

190

On the fourth night of the festivities, a brilliant May evening, the Imperial commissary set up wagons on Khodynka Field. Twice the expected number arrived; and as the evening wore on, a half-million loyal and drunken subjects gathered on the field. Jews, gentiles, and gypsies shared campfires; commissionaires roasted whole boars and saddles of lamb; strangers danced together; entire villages set up as encampments. By order of the Tsar, free beer was distributed in coronation mugs. The beer flowed, and the level of the festivities increased. The entire field had become a blur of every ethnic bloc which exists in Russia. The people came together, giving off vapors of sweat and garlic and alcohol, allowing themselves to be enveloped in a belief in better times to come.

The hours passed, and everyone grew more and more inebriated as they awaited the Tsar and Tsarina: the couple who had been chosen by God to rule over them, the couple who had given them food and mugs of beer and what seemed to the poor to be an endless plain of recreation.

No one from the Imperial commissary remembered that the field had earlier been latticed by ropes of ditches, each of a varying depth, and each dug for use in infantry games. As the mounted police and Cossacks kept order, the crowd grew more and more inebriated. Suddenly it seemed to move. Only later did the government learn that a rumor had begun that the beer and mugs were running out. To a people unaccustomed to sufficient food, the prospect of losing free beer is a dramatic one indeed.

The field took on a head as those thousands closest to the police rose and turned to charge the commissionaires' wagons. Like a regenerating snake, the throng extended out, growing a body and power beyond the expectations of the police. At that moment a half-million men, women, and children were caught up and flung forward. The mob assaulted the first line of mounted police, clutching at braid and buttons, pulling down the guards. Wild peasants stepped on the police, flung themselves upward to the horses' saddles, and wrenched the stupid beasts down. Thinking that they had overcome a barrier to the beer, the mob pressed on.

Blooded now, brandishing weapons taken from the police, the crowd cheered as it moved angrily toward the commissary wagons. The Cossacks on the perimeters formed a cavalry line, drew their sabers, and charged. From all four sides of the giant field came the wild horsemen. Within seconds they had closed on the mob and begun to run it through. Mothers felt their babes impaled against their breasts,

191

young lovers were separated and crushed, children sped away from the horses, only to fall into the ditches.

Carefully avoiding the infantry trenches, the Cossacks turned and whirled at each quadrant of the field. They moved ever more slowly, more deliberately. With each turn the hopeless screams and sobs grew louder as children and parents were forced into the ditches. Once the mob was crushed, the Cossacks began to whirl and charge across the tops of the trenches. Skulls were thudded into by wild Cossack horses, split open and seared with the mounts' spittle as the faces beneath were driven into the night. Screams were stifled by the inhalation of dirt and pebbles. As thousands were slowly, intentionally, horribly buried alive, troops came forward and bayoneted any who still moved. As dawn creased the field, the only sounds were of infants caught in air pockets, slowly strangling; peasants blowing out their sphincters at the moment of death; old people moving fingers thrust up between bodies, their gnarled and spindly hands begging desperately to be pulled up from the entombment. Thousands died.

I had seen it all from Irene's passing carriage.

When Nicholas learned of the tragedy, he remarked upon his sorrow, then attended a ball given in his honor by the French. Twenty thousand roses had been sent from the Riviera. Moscow smelled like life.

I knew then that I would have to take some action. Whether by forming a cell with students or going into the underground, I did not know. But something had to be done. I was still bound by my oath to Father Arkady, but I had no choice except to seek my release. If he would not give it, I would have done all that I could to be true to him and could then consider myself free to act. When I next saw him, a few nights after the massacre at Khodynka Field, he was sitting quietly in his room over the stable, polishing a harness.

I crossed the room to Father Arkady and genuflected for his blessing.

"Peter, I bless you as I would any man, but I fear for your soul."

I stood and asked why.

"Your whore. Why do you think?"

"You know of her."

"We know everything, Peter: how well you are progressing with Serov, how pleased Pobedonostsev is with your talent, and how you are disporting yourself with this slut. It is worse even than fornication, Peter. She is married. The sin is adultery."

"I spent years without any pleasure, with only work. I will not give her up. I will not say that I am sorry."

"Without contrition there can be no forgiveness."

"I did not ask for your forgiveness."

"Then why did you bother to come?"

"Why did you wait until now to mention her?"

He smiled. "I trained you well. I wanted to see how long it would go on. Obviously you will not end it. I would have had no choice but to mention it tonight. As it is, you are obviously agitated about something. I thought it best to dispose of the woman first."

"I will not discuss her."

"Then why are you here?"

"To discuss my debt to you."

"You have an interesting way of paying your debts. The Society does not recognize adultery in satisfaction of obligations owed."

"Do not play games with me, Father. I am here to discuss my oath to you."

"In that regard we are pleased. You have done all that we asked regarding the Procurator."

"Your course is too slow. You know of Khodynka Field?"

"Of course."

"Long-term intellectual conversations with Pobedonostsev will not prevent future massacres."

"They might."

"They will *not!* Only violence can end the domination of the Romanovs. They are to morality as vomit."

"So you would kill randomly to elevate the moral plane of the state?"

"I do not know what I will do. I know only that I am honor-bound to tell you first of my desire for action."

"At least your brother had a plan. You propose merely to kill someone, *anyone!*"

"Leave Nicky out of this."

"Oh, no, Peter! This all repeats for me. We did for Nicky what we did for you. School in the village, recognition of his great technical talents, admission to the Saint Petersburg Mining Institute. And we asked what in return? That he await our request for assistance someday in the future.

"But he could not be grateful. He could not wait. He joined with that slut Perovskaya, Srinevitsky, and the others. Just like you: anything for action. Stupidly, wantonly, he defied our orders."

The priest stopped, realizing what he had said just as I did.

I turned on him. "What orders? What *orders?*"

Arkady knew enough not to lie. "We told him that we were close to a great breakthrough. That soon there would be major concessions for the Church."

"The ones that were destroyed by an assassin?"

"The reforms that Alexander signed on the day Nicky killed him. The ones that Pobedonostsev then destroyed. And your brother *knew* that it was all coming. He simply would not wait."

"Perhaps his only concern was not the Church."

"Then it is just that he died."

Suddenly I realized. "The sermon that persuaded Pobedonostsev not to pass Tolstoy's letter to the Tsar."

"It was given by one of my priests, Peter, with exactly the effect that we intended. Nicky knew of the letter. And Nicky knew of the sermon. Punishment means nothing if the culprit is ignorant of its source."

I leaped across the room and grabbed Arkady by the throat. He was strong, as I expected, but I had youth and surprise and the momentum of my attack. He fell to the floor, collapsing on my stomach. We wrestled for a moment, then I blocked his windpipe until he was unconscious. I took the harness he had been waxing and walked to a bureau in the room. I nailed the leather in place, walked back to the priest, and dragged him to the gallows. Pulling over a chair, I climbed on and hoisted Arkady, then quickly knotted the harness, jumped down, and pulled away the chair.

The pain of the fall shocked him into consciousness. He twisted violently, his fingers clawing at the straps, gouging out great wounds in his neck. But he was already weak from my first assault and could not leverage himself up to the beam. He ripped at his face, and blood washed down over his hands and shoulders. His eyes began to inch forward as he strangled slowly. All the while his legs were shaking desperately. He gagged loudly, then voided in his pants.

"Iscariot!" I said. And I was gone.

I remained in my room for several days, complaining to Serov only of an indisposition. In fact, I suffered diarrhea, nausea, and, I must confess, exhilaration. After a week I knew that I had to seek some relief, and so went to Irene's.

Her grandmotherly maidservant, Sonia, who had attended us our first night together, admitted me and quickly bowed. She normally spoke some word of greeting, but on this occasion merely averted her eyes and stepped backward. Whenever the poor woman had been the

194

object of Irene's pointless abuse, she reflected the pain in her eyes. As she bowed, I saw that pain.

Irene was in her bedroom lifting gowns and wraps, pulling hats and shoes, even jewels, out of her garderobes. She was bent forward, haphazardly littering the room with her belongings. She turned as I entered and said, "Oh, Peter, how difficult you are to arrive now. I am invited to the last of the coronation parties—I can't take you, darling—and I haven't a thing that's unworn."

I could not believe this insensitive woman's prattling. "Irene," I said, "are you mad? We saw hundreds of people *crushed* to death at a coronation *party*. And you are going to *another* one?"

"Darling, don't be tiresome. Nicky is giving each family a thousand rubles. Now put it out of your head."

"Out of—"

"*Peter*, I simply will not discuss it. They died happily, didn't they? Running after beer? And a thousand rubles! Which of them was worth one percent of that? *Sonia!*" She turned toward the door, which was immediately opened by the maidservant. "You stupid whore! Where is my new red velvet gown?"

"You ordered me to return it to the dressmaker, Mistress. For new buttons."

"I did no such thing, you idiotic bitch. I have nothing to wear. This humiliation is your fault. Come here."

The old lady walked forward. Irene lifted a long crop from the closet and struck the maidservant across the face. I could stand no more of Princess Irene. I walked to her and ripped the crop from her hand. As she turned to face me, I grasped the shoulders of her dressing gown and ripped it loose. Her rage at this humiliation rendered her speechless. Before she could recover, I struck her across the face, knocking her to the floor. Then I flogged her naked buttocks unmercifully. Perhaps at that moment I truly believed that I was protecting the old woman, or that I was avenging the victims of Khodynka Field. Now I know better. I was exorcising all the hatred I felt for myself. Sharing pleasure with Irene had been no offense. Blinding myself to her stupidity and telling myself that her wrongheadedness did not exist, those had been my sins. It had taken the coronation massacre to move me to action, and even then I had come back to her. I punished Irene because I could not forgive myself. When I had finally turned my lover's beautiful body into a mass of welts, I dropped the crop, turned to the old woman, and said, "Be well, grandmother."

195

She reacted not at all.

I was more than shocked when two days later a messenger brought me an invitation from Irene. The note said that she understood, forgave me, and wanted me. I knew that she would never forgive the humiliation I had inflicted in the presence of her servant. The grandmother! Of course, the spoiled bitch planned a vengeance on the old lady and wanted me present. I raced to the house.

The door was opened by a maidservant I had never before seen. That was enough to cause me to race to the elevator, which ascended almost before I could press the button. When it stopped, I opened the door to see Irene and a well-dressed civilian standing before a squad of six soldiers. From the base of the elevator shaft I could hear the sound of another squad moving into place. There was no escape. The civilian smiled and said, "I am V.K. Plehve. Perhaps you have heard of me."

Plehve! The most hated man in Russia. Torture master of the Tsar, exterminator of Jews, Poles, Finns, and Armenians because, he had once said, "It was more amusing than loosing falcons on sparrows." And now he had *me!*

He turned to Irene and said, "Is this the man?"

"Yes. I originally retained this man to do a portrait of my husband, Prince Felix. I saw him only when he would visit to study photographs of my husband. The portrait was totally unacceptable because of the childish, iconlike eyes. When he last visited me, he was quite mad. Your officers were kind enough to tell me why."

Plehve nodded his thanks and smiled again. "Shall we go?" he asked almost gently. I nodded and stepped back, then turned to look at Irene, who smiled and folded her hands demurely over her buttocks.

There were three police vans pulled up before the house. Men in civilian clothes were by the front door, each surrounded by soldiers. We were walked out in three groups, each civilian being put into a different van. I was quite surprised that Plehve had me transported in a common police wagon. It was nothing but a vendor's cart with a locked door. I assumed that Plehve had responded personally to Irene's summons only because of her rank, but that he would soon realize that he had absolutely no evidence against me. Then I realized that the other prisoners and their vans were only decoys. The question became not Irene's anger or why Plehve would act without evidence. The question was where I was being taken.

My confusion was short-lived. Rather than deposit me in Plehve's offices in the Kremlin, the transport clattered over a bridge and drew up in what sounded like a stone courtyard. When the door of the transport was opened, I took only a moment to realize that I was behind a train station. Guards lifted me from the van and threw me into a boxcar containing more soldiers. From there I was transported to the Fortress of Saints Peter and Paul and a cell in the Alexander Ravelin.

"Welcome to Gehenna," an officer shouted. "Your only fear now is that you will not die quickly, my anarchistic friend."

Few before me had been so fortunate, particularly anarchists.

The most famous anarchist to perish here, of course, was Nechayev. After only four years in the field, three of them abroad, he had been imprisoned here at twenty-five. For ten years he heroically endured the scummy water, maggoty bread, rat bites, and chains of the fortress. By the time he died, covered with the pustules of prison, he had convinced twenty of his warders that the revolution was imminent and that he would rise up to lead them. In a sense, he did. He so impressed one of our writing brothers that he cast him as Verkhonensky. It did not seem to matter that he had lied, deceived, and murdered at the expense of his fellow anarchists. It seemed to matter only that he did indeed possess the key to revolution.

He had been so charismatic and so wily that he had been able to persuade Bakunin in Geneva that he had established a secret group of cells within Russia, and to obtain from the great anarchist a document proclaiming him the leader of the future. He had also obtained most of the reserve fund which Bakunin had set up to one day prosecute the revolution. The secret group of cells, of course, did not exist. Nor, after a bit, did the reserve fund.

What had given Nechayev such a hold over young radicals was his theory that they constituted an anarchist elite. It is a simple matter to win over students by persuading them that they have the intellectual skills and moral courage necessary to change society. They believe that nothing has preceded them but failure; and, being young, they are not disposed to mercifully judge their elders.

The legend of Nechayev was so great that, even after his swindling and lying became known, groups of students planned to assault the Fortress of Saints Peter and Paul in order to free him. One of these groups, not even knowing if Nechayev was dead or alive, resolved that no greater act of revolution could take place than to attempt to free him. The youngest member logically argued that even if the great radical was still alive, the assault could only be a doomed gesture, but an assault on the Tsar might succeed. Nechayev died in prison. The students who listened to my brother were hanged.

My cell was a hole in the Alexander Ravelin, the original dungeon block of the fortress, an opening carved from the single piece of stone which makes up the Ravelin. Night and silence were total and constant: guards patrolled in soft-soled shoes, keys were oiled, all sound was forbidden in the cells and corridors. The only breaks in the pitched stillness were the scurrying of rats along my flesh and the trickling moisture which permeated the far wall; beyond that wall was the waterway which consumed the bodies of the dead. Other than my feral friends, the only visitor was the hand of one guard. This solitary appendage opened my food slot, inserted my chunk of maggoty bread and pan of water, then shut me away again in darkness. When the food was delivered I would crawl forward as far as my chains allowed, then reach for the bread and water. My first task was to pull out from the loaf as many maggots as I could find in the darkness. I would gobble what was left and bolt the water. If I did not, the rats would have consumed it for me.

I do not know how many months I served as food for the rodents. I could only sit and wait to see their glowing eyes and attempt to swat them away. With limited mobility, my attempts usually failed. After a short time the beasts learned this; and when it suited their purposes to gnaw at me, they came in packs, one or two in front, the rest at my neck or back or buttocks. My principal concern, of course, was to protect my eyes and genitals, which I was generally able to do. They attacked only when they thought I was sleeping, so I spent my waking hours moving at least slightly. This kept me in a state of constant weariness, of course, but also encouraged the rodents to visit other cells more often than my own. Bread and rats occupied almost all my attention during those tortured months. Bread and rats and thinking. My thinking prepared me for what I had to say when Plehve finally appeared in my cell.

I did not hear him coming. That was just as he had planned it. I did not hear the key enter the lock or turn it. My first indication of his presence was the sharp grating of the cell door on the floor and the point of light which pierced my eyes. I struggled to rise as two guards entered and announced the presence of my keeper.

"You must forgive me, Your Excellency," I said. "Had I but known of your visit, I would have dressed for the occasion in my best pustules."

"You should have kept your sense of humor about you when dealing with the lady."

"Apparently. I did not know that she would connect me with the priest's death."

"She did not. The Procurator caused my agents to investigate. They quickly found links between you, the priest, and the princess. A suggestion from us, and she told us how bizarre, how *criminal,* your conduct had become. All noticed after a lover's quarrel, I dare say. Using her to arrange your arrest was merely a matter of administrative convenience."

"Then why the complexity of execution? Why not simply have done with it?"

"Would that we could. You should have killed a minister. Or assassinated the Tsar, like your brother. Oh, yes, we know. For those crimes we could have tried you in private and hanged you in public. But you killed a priest. An insignificant priest, to be sure, but a cleric nonetheless. The Procurator was personally offended, both because it was a priest and because he had begun to like you."

"I am sorry to have disappointed the merciful Pobedonostsev."

"Oh, he is not killing you out of a sense of outrage. Only impatience. You see, priests are essential to us. They keep the masses in their place. They spy for us, preach for us, keep the caldron from boiling over with anger. When you kill one, you hurt our plans, and the punishment must be an example. That is why the Tsar is taking part. Why he is at Tsarskoye Selo this time of year I don't know, but it is convenient. A good reason to transport you in the Death Box."

Plehve watched my face shrivel and said, "Don't be deceived by the peasants' stories of how quiet it is to die by freezing. Only living men tell that tale. We will keep you alive long enough to freeze slowly. And if you survive the ride, the Tsar can supervise your execution and show his deep commitment to the sanctity of the priesthood. You will be hanged before the Tsar. Your corpse will receive six thousand lashes, after which it will be transported through all the Russias. We will display your carcass to the peasantry so that they may see that the *liberator* who killed so many—"

"I killed only the priest."

"Oh, no, boy. You killed several police agents and attempted to kill a minister. Your capture has solved many crimes and will break many spirits eager for revolt."

"I will never sign such a confession."

"I will attend to that ministerial detail for you. But if I wanted you to sign, Peter, and had the time, you would do so. I will promulgate the writing, boy, and make you the *second* most feared man in Russia."

Then he drove his booted foot into my naked groin, spat on me, and was gone. His only words to the guard were "No visitors."

Plehve was wrong about one thing. I was to have one visitor. I do not

199

know how much time passed between his visit and my mother's, only that the waiting was at last endurable: I knew that I would soon die. I thought that I could stand that; I could not have borne up under an indefinite sentence to the Alexander Ravelin. The guard who came for me was almost gentle. When I told him that I could not face my mother, he said, "Go and see her, boy. For her sake, if not your own. Give her these last moments. And take something from the meeting for yourself. You know what they're going to do with you. After this, you'll be all alone."

I nodded my thanks and stood. The guard attached a chain to the ring on the front of my collar and led me like a performing bear, almost blind from the darkness, to the office of the fortress master. As we moved along the corridors, I asked the guard if I could not be given some cover for my nakedness. I heard him say that he was sorry just as he began to form in my cloudy field of vision. The back of his head assumed a recognizable shape as we marched toward sharper light. By the time we reached the master's office, my eyes had recovered from the months of constant night. The first thing that I saw perfectly was my mother's face.

I stood before this sick and broken woman, naked in my chains, and turned my head away. Twice she had endured nine months of pain and twenty years of hope, only to have the travail end in death, skewered on the ego of ungrateful children. Because she was my mother, I could not ask forgiveness, but only hope that she accepted me as I was. And because she was my mother, I thought that perhaps she had come to help me. Held back three feet, she only cried and said over and over, "My son, my son. There is nothing I can do."

I nodded and said, "I must go now, Mother, to my death."

She leaped forward, screaming my name. She managed to clasp her hands about my neck, but was instantly pried loose by the gentle guard, who stayed behind with her. I was led out. Nothing had passed between us.

In the hall the guards amused themselves by humiliating me with a thorough body search. My mouth, genitals, every crack and crevice where something might be hidden, all were examined in loathsome detail. Finally the most junior guard stepped behind me while the others held me in place. He spread my buttocks and inserted his fingers. His hands were strong and he had no difficulty separating the cheeks. I thought his fingers would never stop inching forward when I realized that he was inserting a tube up my buttocks. I expressed nothing but the

200

shame that was to be expected. When he had finished, another guard said, "A dirty job, Anatoly."

"Yes," the junior warder replied. "But it is easier if you do everything for Russia, and the greater glory of God."

They all laughed at what they thought was his cynicism. I too smiled at the sound of the Jesuit motto.

Once I was alone in my cell I began to practice moving the tube in and out. It had been months since I had carried Father Arkady's gift in place, but I had become so accustomed to it that with only a little work I was able to insert and expel the tube easily. Its contents offered only a slight hope. A file, a pliers, and a key. For some unknown lock, I assumed, because it did not fit the cell door or any of my chains.

Three days later I was led, chained hand and foot, down the halls of my prison. The weather was cold for spring, and the blanket in which I had been wrapped offered little protection. I could tell only by the descending staircases, opening doors, and bitter wind that I had been brought to the courtyard. My hood was removed and the prison master spat in my face. Obviously he believed what Plehve had put out about me. I returned the salute and was struck twice across the face. Then I was hooded again and placed in the Death Box.

I waited until we were under way for thirty minutes before moving. Ironically, the Death Box was so finely constructed that the tight quarters caused me to sweat. This made it easier for me to stay relaxed internally and expel the tube from my buttocks. Once I heard it hit the floor I waited. The metal sounded outrageously loud against the floor, and I feared that the next noise would be the guards sliding back their peephole. But I heard nothing. I maneuvered the tube with one kneecap, until I could feel the cylinder between my legs. Although I could not see, I felt the damned thing touching my penis. I wished desperately for an erection, but, whether from the cold or fear or both, my shriveled fellow was as curled up as a sprout. I slid back farther and the tube remained still. Another backward movement and it was between my knees. I brought them together and held the tube in place.

I sat back on my buttocks and lifted my legs to the slight degree allowed by my chains. I pressed my head forward, opening my mouth to the greatest extent allowed by the hood, until I could bare my teeth. My shoulders and hands throbbed from the rocklike embrace of the pinion. I pushed down, feeling the terrible strain on my breast and midsection. Finally I was able to grasp the top of the tube with my teeth, twist and twist again, then lift my head, the cap securely in my mouth.

I lowered my legs gently and placed the tube on the floor, placed my face flush with the ground, and stuck my tongue into the tube. It fell upon the key, which I worked out. I turned and bowed down, my hands still trussed up behind me. As my shoulders came down, they scraped the floor, then moved over the key. It stuck to my flesh, buried in the skin and sweat. I rubbed my shoulder hard along the floor, cutting the flesh but loosening the key. I carefully brought my hands down to hover over the area, and began to feel about. After several seconds I found the key, twisted it around, grasped it, and slowly moved it up and into the lock. But I could not turn it. I placed my two thumbs against the key and crawled to the wall. I felt for a crevice in the frozen hay, turned and placed the key in it, and slowly twisted my body. I laid my hands between the key and worked it up into the lock. I went up, turning the key with my flesh, rocking my body into a contortionist's stance. When I could no longer endure the pain, I twisted in reverse and felt the lock snap.

Once my hands were free, I pulled off my hood and crawled back to the center of the wagon. I massaged my hands, arms, and feet and thought through my next moves. If I completely unchained myself, I would almost certainly be caught if there was an inspection. By leaving everything but the pinion in place, I could assume at least some chance of escaping detection. A quick look backward through the driver's slot would destroy me. But if we stopped, I had time to close and insert the tube, pull on the hood and hold my hands behind my back. I set to work.

There was a small door in the bottom through which a plate of water would be passed occasionally. It was not large enough to escape through, but neither was it terribly secure. It had been cut from the floor and a small spring door inserted. The area around it was not reinforced; one could tell that from the loose installation. I decided to cut around the door. When I was finished, I would use the pliers to cut the metal bands which held the hay bales in place.

I have no idea how long I cut. I did, however, work ceaselessly and, by what I assumed was the end of a day, had cut a surface line into the straw. Then I put away my tools, put on my hood, and slept in a corner with my hands behind my back.

Sometime later we stopped. The sudden calm waked me up, and I assumed a fully bound position. It was necessary. The door in the floor was opened and water put inside. A voice called me over, and I crawled to the opening. I was commanded to bow my head and drink. I slurped a bit of water and stopped when told. The pan was removed and the door locked. Moments later we moved again. I immediately set to work.

Time after time I worked the knife slowly into the straw and jiggled, stroked, and pled and cursed it back and forth. It seemed that each new insertion was only tempting the certainty that the knife would snap. It did not. After what I believe was an entire day, I had forced a cut around the trap door. The new outline would permit me to wedge myself through. I had only to await the moment.

I used the blade to pry the locks on my manacles, then took the pliers and snapped the wire bands which held the bales together. Each quiet sound was, to my ears, the roar of a peasant battalion. But still we bounced along, the sound obscured as the wagon managed to hit every rut and stone in the ground. Once the wires were loosened, I stepped over them, knelt on the square and slowly, painfully forced my fingers down between the bales. The pressure on my fingers was terrifyingly heavy, but I continued to shove down. I had buried my arms up to their elbows when, at last, I felt my fingers claw through to the bottom.

As the wagon bounced along, I could feel the chunks of ice and snow being thrown back by the horses' hooves. My fingers were now not only caught in a vise, they were burned by the wind and wet particles of waste.

I locked my knees behind me and began to force the hay down with every heaving, stinking particle of my body. One corner began to sink. It separated from the body of the bale at mid-point. Half the area I had cut away and the door were coming loose. They began to drive downward, carrying my arms and head behind. I pushed the floor away and heard it hit the ice. I twisted sideways and hooked my hands on the underside of the carriage. Gasping desperately, I pulled myself forward, ripping my chest and sides. Suddenly, as my legs flailed and sank through the hole, a rush of wind froze my face and blocked all sensation as I fell. My neck and shoulders wrenched around as I hit the ground. My trunk was pulled along in the ice, opening the prison pustules. I watched my own blood spreading on the snow as I slid forward. When I turned my head, I saw too late the massive stone that rose before it.

203

As my eyes slowly opened, the black of unconscious stupor yielded to the gray of hazy awareness. I turned my head slowly, hoping to clear the mists from my brain while I brought my eyes into focus. Forms soon came into view. I raised my arms and attempted to swim up to the figures sitting over me.

"Not yet, Peter," a voice said. A pair of hands embraced my shoulders and slowly lowered me back onto the bed. "There will be time."

"Where am I?"

"Jam Zapolski."

I whispered, "The Jesuit village?"

My benefactor laughed heartily, then leaned forward and came into focus. He was a large man, middle-aged, with the chiseled, swarthy features of an Italian. "Yes," he said. "The Jesuit village, although nothing historic has transpired in this *setch* since Ivan and Stephen buried the hatchet of war in each other's vitals." He laughed again, but with less humor. "And now we have a second historic meeting, between a simple priest and the most famous anarchist in Russia."

"Is that who I am?"

"My boy, you are entirely too modest. Here you betray a lifetime of training, destroy our best effort to infiltrate the government in twenty years, kill a priest, and claim not to know what you are. Very well, I shall tell you. You are an adulterer, a liar, a thief of our efforts, a betrayer of Holy Mother Church, and a murderer. Altogether, a superb product of the *Ratio Studiorum.*"

"You are a Jesuit."

"I have that honor."

"How did I come to be here?"

"I will tell you when it suits me. For now you will be kept in the *kurenny.*" He nodded at a huge man who was standing at the head of a group a foot back, a giant with the map of a Russian winter burned into his ugly face. "Stenka is my *hetman.* Do as he tells you."

"*Kurenny? Hetman?* What language is this?"

"The Kuban dialect." The priest studied my face for a moment, obviously amused by my surprise. Then he said, "Yes, Peter, these men are Cossacks."

The priest called himself Timo, a private joke, he said. Yermak Timofayitch was the legendary Cossack conqueror of Siberia. The priest, whose true name I never learned, hoped to conquer all of Russia for the Church. Those stories, he told me, could come later, after rest and food. But first rest.

I stayed at the village for nearly three months, gaining strength, wondering what the Jesuits planned to do with me, and coming to admire the Cossacks. Pushkin called their greatest leader, Razin, the only poetic figure in Russian history. Gogol recorded the glories of Taras Bulba. They produced Pugachev, leader of the most terrifying of all peasant revolts. They were not nomads, as many believed. On the contrary, each male child brought to his family a gift of land from the Tsar, land to be farmed as long as there was peace. But when there was war, the father went to the enlistment office and signed himself in, then each of his sons, from oldest to most youthful. Each village contained such a permanent office, and the fierce horsemen (that was no legend) formed in groups of village hundreds—*sotnyas*—and rode off to the war they so loved.

I had an opportunity to watch the men teach their boys the many acts of Cossack warfare: the construction of a camouflaged trench that could lure any enemy, the ability to maneuver a horse with the knees while the hands wielded saber and lance, how to use the steel in varying strokes against opponents of different heights and protected by different types of armor, and the talent of using the blade so effectively that they could leap on horseback over a stream, swing down from the saddle, and cleave the water with the saber without stirring a spray. When asked why they pushed themselves relentlessly, they replied only that they were fighting for their *volnitsa*—liberty.

The women were another matter. As big as many of the men, strong, full-bodied, they nevertheless seemed to somehow retain their femininity. As the summer approached, I went out to the *stanitsas* and saw the girls turn shyly and adjust the three corners of the white *kasinkas* which covered their hair. And then they smiled. They always smiled. Whether wrestling with pigs the size of ponies, carrying sacks of wheat, or sowing, they were more than contented; they were actually happy. Tolstoy had once written that Cossack women were "stronger, wiser, more cultivated and more attractive than Cossack men." I came to believe it. And for that reason I avoided them. I needed a woman for sex and for comfort. All that I had to do was ask—and the priest would have had me killed.

Father Timo left me alone for much of the time that I was recovering. I knew that he kept himself aware of my return to health; as a result, I assumed that the time had come for me to learn my fate when he at last had me brought to his quarters. After only the most perfunctory exchange of pleasantries, he said, "Father Arkady had doubts about you from the beginning. He was right, as we now know. You are today what you were then, a youth obsessed with violence. You have killed, perhaps out of love for your brother." He paused. "Perhaps because you enjoyed it. I have watched you these last few months. You have avoided me, which I can understand. You have also made no attempt to practice your talents as an artist, which I cannot forgive. Your only interests are the men and their swords, and the women and their bodies. There is no doubt that we should not have arranged to guarantee your brother's death; but we did, and we shall have to live with the consequences. And profit from them."

"What do you mean?"

"We will use you. Not indirectly, as we had planned to do when you were with Serov and later, we hoped, at court. Now we shall use you immediately and to our profit."

"And if I do not cooperate?"

"I am in no mood for games. You will do as we say or be tied to a stake for Kuban saber practice."

There was no doubt that the priest was serious. "Very well." I attempted to put the face of victory on my defeat. "I suppose I am in your debt."

"You owe us everything good which occurred before the arrest, and everything good which followed."

"Then tell me how you knew about the arrest. It was supposed to be a secret."

"It was, but Irene told Sonia of her plans, and Sonia told us."

"She works for you."

"No. We have been able to do her an occasional favor. You were kind to her. We were kind to her. Things equal to the same thing are equal to good information."

"The escape. How could you—?"

He held up his hand. "Once Sonia told us of the young artist who had tried to help her, the plan was simple. One of us wrote the letter for your mother to send to the Tsar. The visit was for her consolation, and the guards' diversion. They expected your mother to help you, a danger to which we would never expose her. When she did nothing, they assumed that any risk of a plot had passed. It was then up to our young friend in the guards to help you and advise us. Once you were shipped out, a group of my Cossacks followed the Death Box."

"How could they do that?"

"Think! Did you imagine that they would wear Bulba's red morocco boots and pleated pants? They wore a white *cherkuska* and woolen

Kubanka. And, even if your guards had not been warm with vodka, which they were, my Kubans could have crawled across Russia behind the wagon. They call their camouflaged crawl *po plastunski*. It brought them to you, and you to me."

"And if I had not escaped?"

"You would have been an evening's highlight at Tsarskoye Selo."

"A final question." The priest nodded. "I thought that Cossacks were all Orthodox, or *Rusalka*, not Catholics."

"Their battle cry is '*Za veru* [For the faith].' The Poles tried to change that faith. In a few pockets they succeeded. And we are not without friends in Poland!" He smiled. "You see, Peter, you must do as we tell you."

At that moment I hated Father Timo with a greater intensity, with a fiercer heart, than I have ever turned toward any man. The Jesuits had outsmarted me. Individually, many of them were the dullards and clods to be found in any collection of priests. As a group, however, they were superior to any other adversary. They operated in the world for a divine purpose. Arkady had caused me to revile that purpose, but I knew what it would have to do to those who accepted it. They could have been, like most priests, effeminate clerics recoiling from the affairs of men. The Jesuits were, instead, a most formidable assemblage of intellectuals who bent the world to what they saw as God's purpose. And now I was to fit into that purpose.

"What use will you make of me?" I asked.

"You are a linguist, which is a prerequisite. You are an artist, which is a cover. You are a womanizer, which may be helpful. And you enjoy violence, which is essential. As is the fact that you are not a priest. What you may have to do, obviously, we cannot do. We want you to accept because you are in our debt and we need you. We think that you will accept because of the adventure involved. And because if you do not, we will have you killed."

"Where am I going?"

"England."

The history of the Jesuits in England, according to Father Timo, had been every bit as adventuresome as their course in Russia. The Society had been founded at about the time of Henry's break with Rome, and the Jesuits had been heavily employed in the underground Church during the time of the Crown persecutions. Part of the reason for these repressive measures was the papacy's outspoken and somewhat undiplomatic refusal to deal with Elizabeth on the ground that she was illegitimate. The Society was ordered to deliver the message. The Queen did not agree and, accordingly, commissioned Sir Francis Walsingham to create an anti-Jesuit network. So obsessed with his work did Walsingham become that he almost bankrupted himself supporting it.

To be a Jesuit in England then was treason, a capital offense. Despite this unique and painful prohibition, dozens of members of the Society established a series of safe houses, disguises, and false identities which enabled them to say Mass and distribute the sacraments. Almost as soon as they arrived, they were hunted down, arrested, tortured, and publicly drawn, quartered, and hanged at Tyburn Gibbett. Undeterred, Jesuits went one step further: they not only supported Catholicism, they opposed the Crown. The Society worked to bring about the restoration of the Catholic Church, at times going beyond taking spiritual steps to end oppression. The most flagrant example of this was the Gunpowder Plot of 1605, which was known to at least two members of the Society, Fathers Greenway and Garnet.

There was a subsequent dropping off in the activities of both the Jesuits and the English police system until the reign of Queen Anne. One of her more interesting subjects was a man whose entire public career was of interest to the Jesuits: Daniel Defoe.

He was educated at what was then England's most famous school for Nonconformists, Charles Morton's of Stoke Newington. While it is unlikely that the Society ever infiltrated that school's faculty, Defoe did come into contact with Jesuits when he later became a merchant to Spain and Portugal. He eventually failed for 17,000 pounds, and his creditors accepted a plea of bankruptcy, which released him from his debts. A short time later, the Stuarts paid his notes, thereby restoring both his honor and his place in commerce.

Defoe was imprisoned on three occasions, each time obtaining his release through the intercession of a powerful, secretly pro-Stuart patron, such as Robert Harley or Charles Delafaye. Immediately before each term in jail Defoe had been active editing or writing political works: *Mist's Journal, Dormer's Letters*, and *Mercurius Politicus*. The first was rabidly Jacobite, and the others tainted. After each arrest he was released on the public condition of performing intelligence services for the Crown, and the secret pledge to his patrons of aiding the Stuarts. In 1724 he traveled the isles and published *A Tour Through the Whole Island of Great Britain.* The maps and appraisals which were used in the book were shipped to Rome and later used by Jesuits financed by the Stuarts.

All of this was secret until 1864, when a series of Defoe's letters to Delafaye were accidentally discovered. As it happened, the letters did not provoke a public outcry against the Jesuits. The principal reason for this was that John Henry Newman relied upon them in part for his *Apologia Pro Vita Sua,* published in the same year. Part of the financing for the book's publication came from the Jesuit-connected Lord Acton, whose thoughts on power are well known. A second reason for the benign reception given the Defoe correspondence was that Henry Stuart, Cardinal York, had become reconciled to the Crown shortly before his death, and the family had passed from politically troublesome pretenders to respected nobles.

When the Jesuits and British made use of one another in smuggling out of China the message that was to begin my mission, it was Cardinal Newman who served as intermediary between London and Rome. And when the Society insisted upon placing its own man in the mission, it was he who arranged for me to go aboard H.M.S. *Python* and be introduced to Sir Basil Hawkeland.

Simon placed the diary on a table, lit a cigarette, and walked to the window. Elspeth lay sprawled asleep on a couch across the room. He was glad that she was asleep; he would have been tempted to speak to her, and this was neither the time nor the place. His heart was still too full of anger, and his mind was too obsessed with the Jesuits.

One of the motivating forces behind McHenry's break with the Church had been his contempt for the Jesuits' belief that the end justifies the means. Hypocrisy and cant in an unlettered parish cleric bothered him not at all. It was expected, almost mandatory, if a priest was to survive a lifetime of fawning over insurance salesmen and building contractors. But in a Jesuit it was more than disturbing. They had woven a web of accomplishment and should not have wallowed in the intellectual dishonesty of doing whatever was necessary to achieve God's work.

He knew now that he had misread them. Peter had been correct: as individuals they might be every bit as contemptible as any other priest. As a group, however, they were very formidable indeed.

The Jesuits did operate on the principle that the end justifies the means. For them, however, it was not merely a slogan to make bearable the spiritual compromises of a successful priestly career. For the Jesuits, the principle was a driving force, enabling them to strive after their goal.

Peter's murder of Father Arkady was totally alien to what the Jesuits had taught him. But the Society forgave him. And used him again. They could not know what was in store for the Painter, or how he would react. The Jesuits knew only that he could serve some purpose of the Society. Father Timo had given Peter another chance. The Society would forgive anything, as Christ did, and try again to effect their belief in man. And if they failed, they simply began anew. Their commitment was personal, not institutional. They entered into unwritten contracts with people of promise in order to effect the greater glory of God.

One of their contracts, Simon knew, had been with him. He had been chosen while in the orphanage, chosen for his intelligence and aptitude for languages, and most of all for his epicanthic eyelids, the birth defect which set him apart, and which made him a beneficiary of their sense of obligation. He had also been chosen, he suspected, because the Jesuits believed that he would turn to them and offer them his life in service, a service meant to repay what they had given him. But they would never ask him for anything; to do so would have violated their promise. He had returned money over the years, kind words, advice on investments; but never what he suspected they wanted from him. And the contract remained personal. The Society, like its commitment, was personal, and on that level took what he offered to it. McHenry gave back only what he wanted. He had believed for years that they owed one another nothing. The Jesuits obviously would not agree.

He picked up the diary.

The Jesuit network had no difficulty transporting me to England. My destination on that island was Liverpool, from which the Hawkeland expedition would sail on the *Python*. I was met at the ship's gangway by an ordinary seaman named Robert Bellarmine. He took my seabag and led me up to the deck, where he deposited my gear and pointed me toward Sir Basil's cabin. Bellarmine passed me as we walked forward, knocked, and, when bidden enter, held the door for me. He announced my name and followed me in, but rather than leaving immediately, remained inside the cabin. My host slowly placed a silver page marker in a book, rose from his bunk, and placed the volume on a table littered with maps, books, and charts. He walked toward me, extended his hand, and pronounced his name.

General Sir Basil Hawkeland was a darkly handsome man of forty-three, young for his rank and reputation. He had distinguished himself as a subaltern by leading the remnants of an ambushed Indian army command to the safety of their fort on the Northwest Frontier. He went on to achieve an extraordinary reputation for military genius and personal courage in four later campaigns. Then, at the moment when he was about to be assigned to the Imperial Staff, he resigned his commission and entered Oxford as a thirty-year-old man. He took a First in Modern Greats and joined the Foreign Office. There too he was marked as a man of distinction. Refusing to believe that diplomatic victories could be bought for trinkets and few words of pidgin, he prepared for each assignment by immersing himself in the language and culture of the people with whom he was to deal. His public statement that it was easier to captivate than capture both infuriated and misled his superiors. One who did not misunderstand was Lord Salisbury, who made Hawkeland first his private, then official representative. When it became necessary to negotiate the oil question with the Vatican, it was understood that only Hawkeland could master a knowledge of Jesuit history, represent the Queen, and not offend the Pope. He did not disappoint. The Vatican asked George Curzon, the Under-Secretary for Foreign Affairs, to place Hawkeland at the head of the mission. Salisbury agreed and, recognizing the Chinese love of titles, quickly pushed through a knighthood and a brevet generalship for Hawkeland.

As I was later to learn, nothing could have pleased Sir Basil more than his appointment to the rank of general. He was not, let me state most emphatically, a glory hunter. His military reputation was that of a man who prized the safety of his men above all else. At the same time, he loved action. He still saw the world in terms of right and wrong, and so relished the quick resolution which combat afforded. At the same time, he recognized the preferability of diplomatic solutions. Like all great men, he was simple and puzzling. And I came to love him.

I shook Hawkeland's hand and gave him the name I had been assigned for the journey: Peter Leontov.

"Brandy, Mr. Leontov? Or would you prefer to share my bottle of small water?"

I must have smiled, because he immediately fetched a cloth-wrapped bag from beneath his bunk. He uncorked it and poured us both a large glass of vodka. Before I could sip mine, the ship heaved and began to back out of its slip. I said, "I thought that we were leaving tomorrow."

"We are. Any foreign agent wishing to watch as we depart can come down tomorrow and do so." He sipped his vodka and said, "Which is why you are here."

Bellarmine spoke. "I will be in my quarters, sir."

Hawkeland nodded. After the seaman had left, he said, "Peter, you will be of great value to me in military intelligence. You can paint, but it is a bulky device for using as a cover. And it does not fit in with the purposes of our mission. Something which is not clumsy to pack, however, is your facility with languages. I have spent weeks reading all that I could on the history, literature, art, and music of China. But I have not had time to learn the language. You speak Chinese. I am also advised that you are strong and daring, exactly the type of character flaw which appeals to a general unhappily on detached duty. And you are loyal. If you choose not to be loyal, I am told that there is enough to hang you many times. Or have I been ill advised by my Jesuit friends?"

"Like the ordinary seaman who just left?"

He slammed his hand on the table and fairly shouted, "By the head of the bloody fucking Christ Himself. The boy was sworn to secrecy."

"He said nothing." Hawkeland's head snapped back. I smiled and said, "No trained servant would announce that he was returning to his quarters. Particularly not one in military service. He would wait to be dismissed. And a member of your staff would wait for a discreet signal. Bellarmine simply announced that he was leaving. You would not grant social privileges to an underling. A priest would assume them."

Hawkeland smiled. "You don't miss much, do you?"

"I'm alive."

"Aye. So you are. And I venture the Jesuits know of at least one man who isn't."

"Let us say that the Society and I know something of each other's business."

"Fair enough. Let me tell you of the business. We sail for China, ostensibly to implement the findings of the latest Royal Opium Commission. A great many lords, at great expense, took a great deal of time to conclude that opium is bad."

"Why would the British government create a commission to study Chinese opium addiction?"

"Because there are now several hundred thousand British opium addicts. All supplied by British trading houses working in concert with the Chinese."

"How could such a thing happen?"

"As you may know, for a century only the East India Company could import tea into England. Every man, woman, and child on the island consumes nearly four pounds of it each year. The Company levied on each leaf. At its height, it supplied four million pounds a year to the Exchequer, half the cost of the Royal Navy. In exchange, fleets of lighters carried tin, rattans, coin, and a few musical snuffboxes. It came as quite a shock to the Company when the Chinese, who invented paper and gunpowder when my English forebears were living in huts, demanded more than trinkets for something England could not do without.

"Private companies sprang up to import opium from Benares, in India. Why the Chinese, of all people, would addict themselves to it is a mystery. As is why they smoke it rather than eating it in bulk as the Indians do. But smoke it they did, to the level of addiction. Millions upon millions of pounds were easily exchanged for tea. Because the Company was required to keep a year's supply of tea on hand at all times, it was forced to stock black leaf only: bohea and congou, mostly. Our addiction was never less severe than that of the Oriental. And so we fed one another's weakness.

"The spread of the drug through China became so great that the emperors fought to keep it out. Of course, we fought to get it in, and in the great Opium War of 1842 we won.

"But the Chinese are a patient people. They think in terms of centuries. We are not trained, or able, to do so. When the Company lost its charter, the Chinese government made it a part of letting tea contracts that opium also be exported to England. Over decades, the Chinese have spent millions in bribes to arrange the addiction of untold thousands of Englishmen.

"Her Majesty's government would like the trade to finally be ended. At least some right honorable members would. Many others sit in Westminster today because a trading house has delivered a rotten borough to an M.P. who speaks for that trading house.

"Of course, ours is not the only corrupt government. The mandarins also profit greatly, and many would hate to see the trade end."

"You say that this is all only a cover. Why spread it about that you are on a mission which invites the enmity of all parties?"

"Because, Peter, what we are after is far more valuable than all the tea and opium in the world. Our cover must reasonably explain our need to see the Emperor. Such an audience was suggested by the Royal Opium Commission of 1893, and we are to seek it. The Chinese are patient. We English merely tardy. If we are invited to meet the Emperor, we shall be allowed inside the Forbidden City as resident guests. Anyone allowed to be there after nightfall has the virtual run of the palace. We need that freedom to seek out a piece of paper."

"A map?"

"A formula. And if what the formula can do becomes public knowledge, there would be as brutal and total a war as the world has ever known."

I sat silently at the table. It seemed almost ludicrous to be discussing a world war when the sunlight was warming the tar of the ship, and the smells of the barque were mingling so gently with those of the sea. I allowed myself to say nothing. It was for Hawkeland to speak. At last he did so.

"Peter, that piece of paper can give us control of the world's oil supply."

"*Oil?* You're not serious. There's oil everywhere. In whales. In the ground. There's no shortage of oil."

He smiled, then stood and walked to the porthole. "For all your intelligence, you don't understand, do you? We are only now at the beginning of an oil age. No one knows how much of it there is, only that it is a finite resource. As more and more of it is used, more will be demanded. Man is insatiable. Ships, horseless carriages, factories, God knows what else. They all use it. And new machines will be invented because it exists. And one day it will run out. But even before that day, the present cost in money and lives to obtain it is incalculable. No one hunts whales anymore. They build derricks to harpoon the earth. That is right and just. It was put there for man to use. But it is no less an unforgiving enemy than the whale. With this piece of paper we can create, literally create, oil, out of dirt and vegetation, bypassing a million years of nature. Industrial and military power will be ours. And all we need is that one piece of paper."

"Who has it?"

He smiled for the first time. "Why, boy, a Jesuit priest, of course."

Hawkeland then told me the story of how the priest had come to possess this extraordinary document. In August of 1861, the Emperor Hsien Feng died of the accumulated illnesses brought on by a lifetime of debauchery. His son, T'ung Chih, then six, assumed the throne under a co-regency which consisted of competing empresses, Tzu Hsi and Tzu An. Tzu Hsi was to prove the more dominant of the two and, even as I write this, reigns as the Empress Dowager.

Tzu Hsi owned a body eunuch named Chou, whom she gave as a gift to the young Emperor. His instructions, which he executed most faithfully, were to induce his master to leave the Forbidden City and venture forth each evening to the brothels of the Ch'ien men quarter. In order to accomplish this clandestinely, the eunuch arranged to have a secret opening cut into the wall just outside the Western Gate of Perpetual Peace. Although their trips by mule cart were intended to be secret, it soon became common knowledge in the capital that the Son of Heaven was frequently engaged in drunken and disreputable conduct. He began to miss audiences, ignore his duties, and spend vast sums on the sensual carvings and paintings found in the shops of the Liu Li-ch'ang.

In the autumn of 1872, the young Emperor's marriage was arranged. Tzu Hsi, through her chief eunuch, An-Te-hai, sponsored a lady named Feng. The other co-regent, Tzu An, supported a young girl named A-Lu-te. The empresses could not agree, and Tzu Hsi suggested that the boy make his own decision. She was certain that he would listen to the advice of An-Te-hai, the powerful chief eunuch. She did not know that the Emperor had hated the chief eunuch from boyhood because of his stern tutoring. As a result, T'ung Chih chose A-Lu-te as his wife, with the rank of senior consort. Lady Feng was created Discerning Concubine and senior secondary consort.

Tzu Hsi constantly rebuked the youth for his choice, and ridiculed A-Lu-te. The co-regent instructed her night eunuch, Li Lien-Ying, to bring Lady Feng to the Emperor's bedchamber, in the hope that the discerning concubine would bear a son, and enable Tzu Hsi to kill the Emperor and continue the regency. As etiquette prescribes, Li would carry Lady Feng on his back, covering her only with a cloak. She would be left at the lower end of the dragon couch, from which position it was her duty to crawl to the level of the Imperial pillow. At that point, the uninterested Emperor would leave the chamber.

Although he had developed an affection for his wife, the Emperor rarely called her to his bed. He was so unprepared for the responsibilities of marriage, and so continually disturbed by Tzu Hsi's criticism, that he feared he could not function with anyone for whom he had true affection, anyone for whom he had not paid a few coins. Despite this, on rare occasions he would visit A-Lu-te at her quarters in the Palace of Heavenly Purity. But more often he would spend his evenings in drunken melancholy at the brothels.

One evening, A-Lu-te was called to the dragon couch. As she humbly inched her way forward, T'ung Chih lifted her into his arms and raised her face. When she looked upon her husband, she began to shriek, for his face was covered with syphilitic sores.

Tzu Hsi blamed A-Lu-te for the disease, but the young Empress did not take the time to defend herself at court. Instead, she had the Imperial physician brought to her. His name was Louis Fresnais, a Jesuit. It had been customary to maintain one Manchu, one Chinese, and one Jesuit physician since 1692. In that year, the Jesuit Jean Francois Gerbillon, a mathematician and mandarin of the third class, was asked to observe the Emperor, K'ang-hsi, who was dying of malaria. The priest knew of studies conducted by his brothers with a drug called "Jesuit bark," and now called quinine. He obtained a supply and used it to restore the Emperor's health. Although the privileges of both the Catholic Church and the Jesuits were often granted and withdrawn over the centuries, one of the three posts of Imperial physician was always thereafter filled by a Jesuit.

A-Lu-te commissioned Fresnais to seek a cure for her husband's disease. A short time later, the Emperor died, and A-Lu-te's own father, to please Tzu Hsi, induced his daughter to commit suicide. The Jesuit's work went on in secret.

For more than a dozen years, Tzu Hsi intrigued to retain her place at court. So enduring was she, so wise in the evils of statecraft, that she became known as the "Old Buddha." Although she was intelligent enough to divest herself of the powers of office during retirement, she retained an omniscient knowledge of the court through her army of eunuchs.

Later, another Imperial cipher became Emperor in name only. He was Kuang Hsu, and he ascended the throne in 1889. While he was not disposed to debauchery, or interested in endless trips to brothels, he was the master of a large harem. Tzu Hsi, through her eunuchs, arranged for the constant purchase of slave girls who were presented at court in the guise of gifts from the local nobility and those working to rise in the civil service. These men were more than willing to present gifts which cost them nothing, particularly when such acts earned them the appreciation of both the Emperor and the Old Buddha.

By then, the chief eunuch was Li Lien-Ying, he who had once carried the Discerning Concubine on his back. Kuang Hsu had heard all the stories that said that An-Te-hai had been no eunuch. To satisfy himself that Li was as described, the Emperor personally examined him and found that he had been fully deprived; that is, both his penis and testicles had been removed. Li would never forgive the humiliation. He returned on the night of the examination to Tzu Hsi and swore his eternal loyalty to her. He proved it by appearing never to communicate with her yet constantly collecting for his master new concubines, specially chosen by the Old Buddha, and advising her in secret of whatever the concubines learned from the Emperor.

Unlike the large chambers thought of when one discusses a Moorish harem, the Imperial concubinate was a series of gently shaped, connecting, low-slung units, each housing a slave girl and her eunuch. The houses opened onto rock gardens, still pools, and artificial waterfalls. Because the Emperor never ventured into the harem, it was a simple matter for the eunuchs to move the girls about, and remove any whose diseased state became too pronounced.

During all these years, Fresnais, the Jesuit physician, had been performing his regular duties at court as well as attempting to discover a cure for syphilis. A few coins to the eunuchs assured him of a steady stream of patients to examine. Their silence was guaranteed by their fear that the Emperor would torture them to death if he learned that they had sent Imperial slave girls to another man, whatever the reason.

At some point, quite recent to the beginning of our adventure, the priest had accidentally made his startling discovery. Fresnais sent word to the outside world, using the Jesuit code. He was, however, so aware of the extraordinary nature of his findings that he dared not commit them to writing, even within the linguistic lock box of the Jesuit code. He knew that the letter might be intercepted but would reveal nothing. He also knew that the science of torture in China was considered an exquisite art. And he was aware that he was a human being, a man, and therefore one who might succumb to the terrible beauties of such an art. The less on paper the better.

The formula, he advised Rome, would be given to the Society's personal emissary, who would also be told of a two-tiered code which would unlock the formula. Bellarmine was the Jesuit. We were to get him there. Our method of transportation was a barque which had been specially outfitted with coal-burning engines and armament, H.M.S. *Python*.

The *Python* was a whaler which had been rerigged as a barque. An ice house was constructed for mutton, the galley enlarged, the forecastle had been fitted with lockers and mess tables, and a lamp room, storerooms, instrument room, and chronometer room were added. The ship carried prefabricated huts in case we were shipwrecked, provisions and gear for two years, boatswain's stores, carpenter's stores, and a safe room. This last contained one thousand pieces of gold plate which we were bringing as a gift for the Emperor. The ship also carried five hundred tons of coal, but was rigged to sail under the full canvas of a barque. On the sides were two longboats, the *Asp* and the *Cobra*. Both had been fitted out with emergency non-perishable stores, and each could accommodate forty men.

Hawkeland made it clear to me that he only commanded the expedition; Captain Sir John de Brebeuf, an unprepossessing man of Norman lineage and good connections, commanded our ship. His power was clearly absolute. Even a decision which affected our mission could be made only by the captain if it also concerned the ship. I had not previously realized either the power or responsibility of a ship's commander. They were facts which were to be impressed on me again and again in the months to come. The executive officer was Lieutenant Peter Faber, as short and pudgy as de Brebeuf was long and lean. The torpedo lieutenant was named Robert Parsons, a quiet, almost shy young man much concerned with the military aspects of the ship. Technical duties were allotted to Lieutenant Regis, the engineering officer. He was generally not permitted to take part in officers' meetings, as engineering officers are considered of a lower caste. The other officer was Lieutenant Thomas Holland-Saunderson, Royal Marines.

Of this group, only the captain knew about Bellarmine. It was essential that the secret be kept in order to avoid the difficulties which would begin at our destination if the Chinese learned that we were smuggling in a Jesuit, particularly one who knew the location of the secret gate of

218

T'ung Chih. The Jesuits had done their part by providing us with a priest who had once shipped out as an ordinary seaman.

All of the officers knew that Sir Basil was most anxious that our vessel make its way under sail. To the limited extent necessary, the entire complement of officers were advised that we might have to fight our way out of China. Hawkeland wanted to be able to do so under steam. For that reason, he had de Brebeuf make it clear that the coal stores were to be used only on his direct orders.

Staying with sail was easy for the first two weeks. The crew remarked constantly on the kind face which the weather turned to us. I spent the time learning the names of the more than twenty sails which furled like darting gulls making for heaven, and coming to admire the men who spent their lives running before nature under billowing canvas shrouds. Hawkeland forbade me to work with the men, saying that it would be unseemly for me to do so. He did not, however, forbid my learning and loving all that I could about this ship. And hoping, with the men, that the weather would hold.

The end of the world came with the fifteenth dawn. An explosion to equal the firing of the ship's magazine resounded at first light. The entire vessel shuddered, rose out of the water, and seemed to fall back into the sea with a moan. I pulled on my boots and grabbed a slicker as I opened the door. A rush of rain and wind blew down the three steps and knocked me to the floor. I climbed up and hunched over, moving into the wind like a farmer forcing a plow ahead with strong spirit and spent muscle.

Once on deck, I heard Bellarmine yell. "Take hold." He was pointing behind me. I saw what he meant and grabbed a row of piping. It was good that I did so. The ship gave another scream, then hove down. This time the midship seemed to plummet directly downward, without regard for the stem or stern. A violent rush of black water covered me from both sides. Like a child strangling beneath an endlessly thick blanket, I felt my lungs give out. I began to suck for air and took in great mouthfuls of salt water through both my nose and mouth. I would have vomited, but there was no strength left to blow out the waste. I began to lose my grip on the pipe. I suddenly realized that someone was forcing my fingers off the hold, attempting to pry me away from life. With my right arm I reached up and broke water. I thrashed about, thinking only to kill the bastard who was forcing my fingers loose. I would not die alone.

Whoever my assailant was took my free arm and wrenched it upward. The water pressure made it seem that my arm had been pulled from its socket. Suddenly the water spilled off from my head and I was hauled, upside down and screaming for air, out of the pit. I was lifted up and felt a hand grasp my chest. "You'll be all right," a voice said. I looked around. It was Bellarmine. "Lucky for me you had the presence of mind to lift your arm up," he said with a smile. "Otherwise I might have gone down."

I nodded once. There needed to be nothing more for the bond between us to be forged.

"Keep a sharp eye," Bellarmine said. "Those killer waves are called 'washports,' and they give no warning." He smiled again and said, "Back to work. Hold tight."

He raced to the mainmast to begin his climb up into canvas. It was essential to trim the sails or they would be blown off, at best. At worst, a strong burst of wind would fill the mainsail and push it down, cracking all beneath it, until it turned the ship completely over and buried us forever.

The men were attempting desperately to get a footing and begin their ascent into the shrouds. They were to climb four stories into the air, then out along the halyards and unlash and furl the canvas. As each went up, it seemed that another slipped. At times it was impossible to say in which direction they were climbing, as the ship lunged so far forward that the masts seemed even with the water.

Hawkeland came up beside me and hailed de Brebeuf, who was attempting to inspire the men farther up into the rigging. When the captain turned to us, Hawkeland shouted, "The hell with the sails. Use the coal."

"Too late." Although I was next to de Brebeuf, I could hardly hear him as the rain covered his face and drowned his words. "The coal's too wet. We trim or we drown." He turned to run back to his men. Somehow they were inching their way up to the main topsail, main topgallant, and main royal sails. Bellarmine was in the lead, swinging his right arm and inching forward with his left, using his body both to crawl up into the sky and coax his shipmates forward. When he reached the main skysail and pulled himself up onto the moonsail, there was a cheer from below, and the men began to move more quickly. Too quickly. One reached to the port-side strut of the main royal as the ship hove down into a blast of water which separated his fingers from the wood and kept him from getting a grip. He began a slow, graceful turn out of the rigging, doubling over and over again; his pitiable farewell scream was ended by the splatter of his head on the deck and the spreading of his brains on wood. The storm washed away his remains and memory. There was no time to consider his death. Men were needed in the rigging. They slowly worked their way out to their positions and began to furl the sails. The water-soaked canvas was loosened slowly, hoisted free, furled, and knotted. An hour passed as the men worked to deflate the shrouds that could cover us all. A second man fell to his death, and we barely noticed. A third pitched backward into the mizzen topgallant, catching by his foot and being splayed against the sky, belly out, as the wind snapped his back and left him screaming for death. A brutal wash crushed his head against the mizzenmast, granting his wish.

At last a bosun's whistle sounded and the men began to inch their way to the center of the mainmast. Taking no chances and the greatest chance, each clung to the main rope and slid down, his flesh burning along the knotted hemp. The last man aloft began to move toward the center. A bolt of lightning caught him full in the head, and his body illuminated the sky with a profusion of colors and screams. His burning flesh was encircled by a spar line, which snapped across the sky from the center and coiled like a snake of jute, lashing his body to the wood. Once, twice, again, it cracked around him, until only one arm was free. The solitary limb swung steadily back and forth, giving the false signal: *I am alive.*

A dozen men volunteered to go aloft for him. De Brebeuf forbade it. Wisely, for a moment later that fragment of the mainmast snapped, and in a slow ballet of death the towering spike ripped free and the man pirouetted around and about the sky, then tumbled, actually completing one full revolution from top to bottom. All the while, the seaman's burning, crackling arm beseeched us to believe that he was alive.

"Damage report," de Brebeuf shouted. "Stokers prepare to go below and spread the wet coals. Steam crews stand by."

Hawkeland and I joined him as Lieutenant Faber, the executive officer, came forward and saluted. "Damage report, sir."

"Report."

"Sir, we've lost the propeller, sir. We can't repair the halyards in the storm, and it might not hold anyway. We can't use the coal because it's flooded. And we'll founder."

"Turn her head into the wind. Break out the sea anchor and hold her steady into the storm. Assemble the proper work groups to install the spare propeller." His voice was as matter-of-fact as if he had been ordering a pint.

"Aye, aye, sir."

As Faber turned to go, Hawkeland asked the captain, "What are your chances of installing the spare propeller?"

De Brebeuf smiled and said, "Two, sir. Slim and none at all."

With the sails trimmed, our only course of action was to wait for the buffeting winds to move us around as the captain wished. We did not have a great delay. The storm spun us about for several minutes, the entire craft lurching drunkenly, attempting only to stay afloat beneath the bombarding seas. When we buckled far around, de Brebeuf gave the order to stand by with the sea anchor. He sensed that another strong blow would force us about, and it did. The work gang quickly dropped the sea anchor, while the captain ordered the forward holds flooded to raise the stern.

As thousands of tons of sea water poured into the *Python*'s holds, I observed each man in his own ritual of prayer. If de Brebeuf had guessed wrong, the stern would rise up like a brawler unable to protect his middle; the next great shock wave would catch the powerless, exposed tail of the ship and force it down, ripping it amidships. If he had judged correctly, the stern would still loom up, unprotected, but the sea anchor would counterbalance the exposure, leaving us weak but taut.

De Brebeuf took the message that the forward holds were flooded, then gave the commands to close the flooding compartments and stand by. Hawkeland and I were with him on the bridge, and if ever I have seen controlled terror, the crew displayed it as they watched the next great wave come in two sections and take us exactly where nature had directed the water to destroy us.

The midships shuddered with an animal groan as the steel plating was seized upon by the rabid sea. The ship was pitched backward and on its side. The depression was just deep enough to allow a part of the next wave to pass overhead while the great mass of water caught the ship's underbelly. The *Python* gave one last gasp, then settled into the awkward angle which de Brebeuf had predicted.

Then, as suddenly as it had come, the storm departed, leaving us tied at both ends to an endless expanse of black and boiling water. De Brebeuf smiled at us and said, "Gentlemen, if you will excuse me." He stopped at the door of the bridge and turned. "Blow into the service pipe if you'd like coffee." He smiled and was gone.

The captain took a coiled sea rope, slung it over his shoulder, and

222

shouted, "Come on, lads. Carpenters first, then the rest of you." In an instant he was joined by three carpenters, each carrying his toolbox over his shoulder. At the tip of the mainmast he swung out and started for the splintered end from which the sailor had fallen only moments earlier. He looped the rope around both the mainmast and halyard, knotted a seat for himself, and let go. We all moaned as he dropped fifteen feet. He stopped short, then looped the rope around his shoulders and under his arms. Tugging on the shorter loop, he hoisted himself back up, grasped the halyard, and started out once again. He was then joined by the carpenters.

He first took a pole staff and laid it against the splintered arm, then passed it back with some instructions which we could not hear below. We could see one man sawing through the wood, using the halyard as workbench and support. De Brebeuf then dropped free of the rigging and swung over the water while waiting for the workman to hand back the pole. At length it was passed to him. The captain hoisted himself up, took a hand drill from the closest seaman, and began to bore holes from the bottom. He forced the wood against the beam, held out the drill, and felt it exchanged for a hammer and spikes. While one carpenter held the beam in place, de Brebeuf drove in two spikes, then pulled himself up and held the wood steady while the other men nailed in the top. The men made their way down, then stood back while the rigging crew went aloft. As Hawkeland, the officers, and I gathered around to congratulate him, de Brebeuf shook free. "That was not even a start," he said. "I'll be back when I find dry clothes."

Hawkeland turned to Faber, the executive officer, and asked, "What now?"

"General, I'll be goddamned if I know."

When de Brebeuf returned to the deck, he was clad in an old uniform with no insignia. He carried a mackintosh, knit cap, and woolen gloves.

"Holland-Saunderson," he shouted to the commander of the Royal Marine detachment.

"Aye, sir."

"Send half your men one-third of the way up into the rigging. Regis will issue them cables. Have the others stay below and take the cables when dropped."

"Aye, aye, sir."

"Mr. Regis."

"Aye, sir."

"Have a work gang tear back the deck over the storage area for the spare propeller. And rig a bosun's chair.'' The captain walked back to the crojack brace and watched as the officers and men set about their tasks.

Once the marines were aloft, they played down the cables, which were dropped into the cargo hold. Lieutenant Regis then took a party of men below deck to secure the lines to the spare propeller. He signaled when ready, and de Brebeuf climbed into the bosun's chair. The crew hoisted the chair and swung it out. De Brebeuf lifted the megaphone and gave the order to hoist. As one man, twenty-five Royal Marines began to strain at the cables. Suddenly, de Brebeuf swung across the sky, cutting over the deck. I was certain he would be impaled against a spar. Instead, he calmly turned in the chair as it swiveled across the ship. In an instant he was flung backward and down momentarily into the water. As the chair finished its tortuous journey, it locked into place above the rail. The captain, who had realized what the constantly pitching ship would do to his perch, shouted orders as if nothing had happened. "Hoist, I said,'' he called, and hoist the Royal Marines did.

For the next four hours, de Brebeuf continued his mad swings over the ship. He would lock in place long enough to shout orders, then sit calmly while the lurching, pounding ship carried him through the rigging, past spars and beams, then out again over the taffrail and into the water, all the while giving orders on placing and preparing the propeller. At the end of that time, relays of marines hoisted the spare propeller into place for the final maneuvers. Again de Brebeuf led the way, shouting orders from his perch on how to lock and hoist overboard the great winged screw. Everyone on the ship, including me, pulled at the great cables which slowly, literally by inches, moved the propeller up and out. A team of marines then looped lines over it and towed it to the stern. There the sailors resumed control of the propeller.

The captain came down to the deck only to allow further rigging, so that he could be suspended aft of the ship. Now the danger from the churning seas was greater. If the lines did not brake when controlled, his chair would not merely loop the deck, it would drive him into a beam, obliterating him in an instant. The danger did not deter him. He ordered torches set, for it was after nightfall. After these were in place, he shouted instructions to the crew to mount the propeller. As six men climbed onto the giant screw, I turned to Hawkeland and said, "I'm going.'' He nodded, and I clambered aboard next to Bellarmine.

On deck, forty men in groups of ten gently worked the ropes to lower us down behind the wheelbox and counter. When we were even with the point of insertion, we began to shift positions as commanded by de Brebeuf. As our weight was rearranged, he simultaneously ordered the deck crews to maneuver their lines. This constant motion slowly passed the propeller over the water and against the *Python*. Members of the deck crew scrambled down the netting and took hold of the giant screw. They guided it forward as we balanced on it, watching the *Python*'s tarred stern growing with each second as we seemed to hurtle into it. I turned my head as the screw bit into the wood. And held. Those of us on the propeller moved forward as the deck and rigging crews slid the screw firmly into the body of the ship. A huge locknut was passed down and the propeller was secured.

We returned to deck by climbing up the netting which had been put over for us. De Brebeuf was the last man to be brought aboard. When he touched the deck, the men broke into three screaming, lusty cheers, joined in heartily by the officers, Hawkeland, and myself.

The captain said, "You are all too kind," and went to bed.

Canton lies in the latitude of Calcutta, Mecca, and Havana, on the left bank of the Canton River seventy-five miles from the sea. My view from city to water disclosed what appeared to be a delta, but was in fact a partially filled-in bay. At its southeast corner is its one deep-water spot, a gulf forty miles on a side, with Hong Kong and Macao at its bottom ends. At its top is a cluster of low hills and ridged islands, through which runs a wide, deep channel. This is the Bogue, the entrance to China.

The Imperial navy believed that a ship that passed the Bogue had entered upon the waters of the Celestial Empire, the Middle Kingdom, suspended between heaven and earth. The first stop on the waterways of the Middle Kingdom was almost always Whampoa, thirty miles distant. It was here that merchantmen halted, with small vessels above the first bar, large ones below.

We made for the port, up water strewn with garbage, the most common of which was the corpses of unwanted children. We passed seagoing junks with huge single masts and painted saucer eyes, manned by families seeming hardly healthy enough to serve as passengers, let alone crew. We sailed by war junks the size of old frigates, each painted vivid red and black, some appearing to be deadly strong, and some so faulty that the rudder was a barn door. From both sides came shouts of promised joy available on the floating brothels, known as "flower boats." At the rails of each stood several girls, aged twelve to sixteen, each bare-breasted and waving. Small vessels called "duck boats" sat at anchor, carrying sloping planks for the ducks to waddle down to the water, there to feed on garbage, be rounded up and eventually slaughtered. And, by the thousands, houseboats with oval roofs, each packing below its decks the many generations of poverty which sustained life through reverence for the old. Finally, delicate as butterflies, the boats of the mandarins, the men with whom we would soon deal.

Hawkeland planned to land first at the factory settlement in Canton. It had undergone difficult times in the Opium War, and for a time seemed certain to strangle on the effects of the conflict, although some of the great commercial houses still maintained factories there. Hawkeland was convinced that we must, for security reasons, avoid Hong Kong, where the great traders were then, as now, headquartered.

The number of such houses remaining was substantially reduced from the thirteen which had thrived before the Opium War. Now there were only scattered rooms where the drug was processed and prepared for shipment and sale. The House of McNeely & Co. occupied the premises which had once served as the English factory, and were now home to this greatest of all merchant banking houses.

Once known as New English, the building was now nameless, but flew from its staff the flag of the particular branch of the McNeely family that owned the bank. On the ground floor was a cookhouse, a strongroom, servants' quarters, and two godowns. The second floor consisted of offices and a living room. Bedrooms were on the top floor. At a span of 120 feet, the house was more than double the size of any other on the street. At the river end of the building was a walled garden into which jutted a large veranda. From here one passed into the great hall, used as a dining room, library, billiard room, and chapel. Our host was Carroll Towson, an American assigned by his merchant bank to serve with McNeely & Co. for a period of five years before returning home to direct shipping business for his American employers. It was he who suggested that we dine on the veranda.

Two liveried servants brought in a portrait of Queen Victoria and sat it on an easel. I could see that everyone was pleased that Towson did not insist on a portrait of McKinley. We then took our seats, a servant assigned to each place, the table perfectly set, and the meal delayed.

"Forgive me, gentlemen, for this slight pause. I have taken the liberty of inviting my compradore, Hou Han Shu, to join us for dinner."

Faber shot to his feet. "Eat with a wog!" he shouted. "Their manners alone should preclude them from the table. Even if their color didn't."

"You will eat with whomever I say," Hawkeland announced quite evenly. "Jew or gentile, black, white, or Chinese. We are Mr. Towson's guests. As is this Shu fellow."

"Hou Han Shu," a voice said from the doorway to the great hall. A tall, ascetic-looking Chinese entered the room. His features were those of the pure Chinese, with eyes the color of evening, and a voice as cold as it was polite. As he walked toward us, he continued speaking. "As Mr. Towson may have told you, I am his compradore, or agent. It might be said that I serve to moderate the amount stolen by the Imperial hoppo, the lesser hoppos, the customs officers, and assorted lesser wogs." He had by this time reached Lieutenant Faber and held out his hand. Faber could not refuse it. After this cold amenity was concluded, Mr. Hou said, "I do not slurp." Faber blushed and looked down at his plate. Our general laughter was as much gratitude to Hou as amusement.

Towson made the other introductions, and the meal began while he explained why Hou had joined us. "Gentlemen, we have been advised that you will be visited shortly by the Tsung Tu, or Viceroy, of the province. A gentleman named Lui Pei. We assume that he is familiar with the recommendations of the 1893 Royal Commission, which mandated discussions with the Emperor. Lui Pei is probably here to determine whether or not you should be allowed to move on to Peking, and if the Emperor should see you when you arrive."

"What else would he do if we got there?" Faber asked.

"Let you cool your heels and send you home in humiliation."

"What cheek."

"Perhaps, but it is a reality of doing business in China. And it is because Mr. Hou understands those realities and subtleties that I want him to assist you. I hope that you will take no offense, Mr. Leontov."

"I welcome his aid and am honored by it." I nodded to Mr. Hou, whose smile indicated that he knew I was speaking the truth.

Faber said, "It seems to me that one linguist is enough. For purposes of space on board and purposes of trust."

Hou continued to smile as he said, "As Mr. Towson has told you, we are to be visited shortly by the Tsung Tu. This is indeed a singular occurrence. Normally visits are made only by the Hsun Fu, Fan T'ai, or Nieh T'ai. They would normally file reports with the Hu Pu, Ping Pu, Hsing Pu, Kung Pu or Li Pu, or Lu Pu, the last two being similarly named but deriving from different Chinese characters. However, Mr. Faber, you knew all of that.''

Hawkeland covered his smile with his glass and said, ''Your point is made, sir. We all welcome your help.''

''I am most grateful for your trust. My point was that Mr. Leontov knows the Kuan Hua, the official speech. Those who will test you will use it and the national speech, Kuo yu.''

''Test us?'' Parsons asked.

''Oh, yes. The Viceroy would not visit us were he not concerned with the loss of revenue which an end to the opium trade would mean. But he is not alone in his fear of penury. The six boards that I mentioned—Revenue, War, Punishments, Works, Civil Office, and Ceremonies—all derive great income from the opium trade. The money helps to hold the country together, as each board has two staffs of equal size and power, one Chinese and one Manchu. The theory is that the Chinese squeeze will filter down and keep a few restless souls still. The Manchu share is to filter upward to the Council of State and Inner Cabinet. It is more than a few customs agents and corrupt hoppos who live off the trade. The corruption goes all the way up and down the government.''

''How will there be a testing in language?'' I asked.

''You will not know that it is taking place. It will be merely a conversation, a gambit, an opening piece, as in chess. Once it is made, the Viceroy will hope to be able to cast your reply in evil terms. Then he can report it to the Tu Ch'a Yuan—the Censorate. This body is authorized—no, required—to keep watch on officials, including the Emperor. They may send him documents called 'memorials.' In these they may criticize any activity of any man, even the Son of Heaven. If the Censorate has grounds to criticize an English opium mission, it may criticize the Emperor for talking to the mission. And then His Imperial Majesty, the Lord of Ten Thousand Years, will have no choice but to crush you like an overripe kumquat. Your deaths, gentlemen, will be deeply regretted to Her Majesty by the Son of Heaven.''

''For which we shall be thankful,'' Hawkeland said. ''And you, sir, how precisely will you help?''

''It may be that I will not be able to do so at all. The Viceroy may object to the presence of a compradore. He may not.''

"I shall insist upon it," Hawkeland said.

"With all respect, sir, one does not insist in China. One works by indirection." Hawkeland nodded. "Even if I do stay, I may divine nothing. There may be nothing. If there is anything, it will be slight. But that should be enough. Whatever there is, sir, I will notice it and warn you."

When we adjourned the dinner, I stayed on the veranda. It was difficult to believe that the befouled river which housed so many of the dead, and those who envied the dead, should smell so fragrant. Towson joined me and said, "You're noticing the delicate scent of night."

"I am." He could tell that I was surprised. "Is it a common reaction?"

"Quite. The English were wise enough to place themselves at the most prominent point to catch the fumes of the pipes."

"Opium?"

"Yes. There are dens nearby. It serves you as it serves the Chinese, by blotting out death."

We said nothing while he filled a meerschaum with shag. He struck a match, drew the tobacco alive, and turned slightly. "That way," he said, "that is Macao. On the west slope of the Monte hill, just below the fort, is a beautiful ruin. The Jesuit Church of Saint Paul. Constructed simply, and beautifully, of sand, clay, lime, and molasses. But across the front are four of the most intricately carved granite columns I have ever seen."

"A ruin, you said."

"Yes. After one of the periodic dispersals of the Jesuits the building became a barracks for Goanese sepoys. Pigs all. They made it into a rubble which caught fire. Only the simple facade and elegant columns survived. I see a bit more than cheap symbolism there."

"Tell me."

"By rights, the Chinese should have conquered us, not the other way around. When Confucius taught ethics, Rome was only a village, and England did not exist. Two thousand years later, a united China prospered under the Ming. And Europe was a squabbling hotbed of principalities. During that time the Chinese produced paper, porcelain, printing, gunpowder, the compass, the wheelbarrow, and the fore-and-aft rig. Europe produced chocolate and the cuckoo clock. To salve our pride, we brought them God and opium."

"Which destroyed them?"

"Neither. They destroyed themselves. Like the ruined Saint Paul's, they built a facade of granitic strength and Imperial elegance. But the walls behind it were clay and molasses.''

"Is that symbolic of the Jesuits as well?"

"Oh, yes. But in quite another way. Do you know that both the Imperial court and the other missionaries, the Catholic missionaries, hate the Jesuits for the same reason? The Jesuits, you see, have become like the Chinese. The Protestants hand out learned, uplifting texts. In English. The other priests—the Lazarists and the Missions Etrangeres—strut about pulling down Chinese shrines in the name of Jesus. But the Jesuits speak Chinese. They dress Chinese. They win the friendship, if not the souls, of emperors, and then are free to preach everywhere. And when they do preach, they preserve all that is best in Chinese life. Honor one's ancestors. Respect Confucius or Buddha as you see fit. Burn joss sticks to Mary rather than candles. And worship Jesus.

"It's much like Saint Paul's. A true symbol of what is great and weak in China. And a symbol of the Jesuits' career here. No matter how many times they have been expelled or suppressed, a few of them remain at the peak, the court. Emperors become ill; Jesuit physicians minister. The Son of Heaven is commanded by law to keep the calendar; Jesuit astronomers help. And so it goes.''

"Then they survive because of their skills. And their pride brings them down."

"Perhaps pride brings them down. But I like to think that they survive because they believe that man must find his own way to God. And that there are as many ways as there are men."

"And your way?"

"I work at my job. And hope that I do it well enough."

"You must do it exceptionally well to have been retained by a British firm."

"They retained me so that I could be trained by them and offer something in return. After a time I will return to my American employer."

"A trading house?"

"A bank. Ingersoll and Constance."

230

At seven A.M. the next day we were visited by Lui Pei, Viceroy of the province. Hou's final warning to us had been that Lui Pei was a product of the vigorous system of examination which had produced China's elite. Those who rose through this system did so because of their knowledge of poetry and their ability to draft prose. When I ventured that this seemed scant background indeed for government service, Hou told me that as early as the third century, the Han Dynasty collapsed because of the intrigues between civil servants and court eunuchs. It was believed that a man who spoke and wrote well probably could think clearly and prevail in all intrigues, domestic and foreign. It was decided to leave the palace in the hands of the eunuchs and government service with the educated.

This decision did not curb the power of the eunuchs. Unlike any other country, the eunuchs were not kept only as harem attendants, but throughout the centuries they had dominated every aspect of Chinese government, rising even to become Lord Admiral of the Imperial Fleet and masters of armies. The power and luxury available to them actually prompted the young poor to castrate themselves and seek to enter government service.

Perhaps because they presented no sexual threat to either Emperor or Empress, their advice was solicited and heeded. They could make or destroy careers, choose both male and female concubines to whisper their messages, and influence every policy which emanated from the seat of government.

They rarely ventured from court, however, as the military governors and provincial civil servants did not view them as playthings but as warped and dangerous influences upon the nation. For that reason, the actual administration of the country was left to the educated elite, men like the Viceroy, Lui Pei.

The Viceroy was carried into the courtyard on a sedan chair borne by eight perfectly matched male slaves. Trotting behind the chair were his personal eunuch and a scribe. As he alighted and made his way into the building, Hawkeland entered the library and I saw why he had ordered me to wear my finest clothes. He was attired in full-dress uniform, with medals, badges, and sash indicating the order of his investiture, and a hat with plumed shako. He buckled on his golden saber and said, "Let's give the old boy a show." At that moment we were joined by Mr. Hou.

The Viceroy's eunuch entered the library first, bowed over to indicate his enslaved status. He turned back to the door and began a litany of titles and offices which continued as Lui Pei entered and took his place on a large rattan chair which had been set up for him. He was followed by the scribe, who seated himself on the carpet, legs crossed, stylus in one hand, inkwell in the other, tablet on his lap.

Hawkeland spoke first. "Most high sir,"

Before another word could be uttered, the eunuch jumped forward and said, "You will be silent. You are nothing. You are less than the feces of a rabid dog. You will stand and listen to my master's words. Those pronouncements, and your crow's cawing, will pass through me." He puffed himself up and said, "*I* am Yu Huang, chief eunuch to the Tsung Tu."

Hawkeland said, "A post achieved at no small sacrifice."

The Viceroy smiled, extended his hand, and the eunuch stepped back. "We will talk, Sir Basil," Lui Pei said in English.

Hawkeland stepped forward and, to my total amazement, performed the kowtow. On more than one occasion an entire mission had been abandoned when the Englishman in charge refused to kowtow to the Emperor. The British thought it more reasonable to send men and ships around the world and back, having accomplished nothing, rather than pay homage to the Emperor of the largest country on earth. Lesser officials usually received a ceremonial bow from Occidentals, with the kowtow being expected only from their underlings. Hawkeland's decision to offer such an extraordinary sign of respect could not help but assist the mission. The Viceroy knew at least that the man who wished to journey to Peking was not a prideful, wrongheaded Western barbarian.

"I am honored, high sir," Hawkeland said, then rose.

"We are pleased by your manners," the Viceroy said. "We will not talk, however, in the presence of this spawn of a whore." He extended one finger toward Mr. Hou. "The compradore is fit to treat with hoppos and their squeeze. He is unworthy to lick the sores of a dog if I am present."

"I agree. And I understand the high sir's view of one who would betray his own people for money. But would it not add to the Tsung Tu's pleasure to dictate the terms of this meeting while the compradore stands by, reminded by his enforced silence that he is the spawn of dogs."

The Viceroy smiled. "You are a clever man, Sir Basil. I shall pretend to be taken in by your humiliation of the compradore. He may remain." Lui Pei nodded to Hou, then said, "We are advised that you

232

wish to discuss the report of the Royal Opium Commission of 1893 with our Divine Master, the Lord of Ten Thousand Years."

"It would be our honor to kiss the feet of the Son of Heaven. If he heard our braying, our blessings would be ten times ten thousand times."

"Our master does not usually meet with Westerners. Those who enter his presence must have a reason beyond question."

"Tso ying tang chiu chung."

"Well, Sir Basil, you impress me."

"Even a dog can learn to bark in cadence."

The Viceroy said,

> "Shall I ask the willow trees on the dike
>   For whom do they wear their green spring dress?
>   In vain I saunter to the places of yesterday.
>   And I do not see yesterday's people."

Sir Basil replied:

> "Weaving through myriad courtyards and village squares,
>   Coming and going, the dust of carriages and horses—
>   Do not say I have met with no acquaintances
>   Only they are not those close to my heart."

Lui Pei nodded. "Very well. The old commissions spawned only new merchants for the trade. Perhaps it is meet and just to discuss an end to this business. But as a Westerner you must plan to dictate terms, to set a schedule. After all, it is England which now suffers from the drug."

"A wanderer in the Middle Kingdom is lost in time and awaits the bidding of his betters."

"If you are bidden to enter the presence of the Son of Heaven, it may avail you nothing. Or do you think to treat with him as an equal?"

"No man of Western station aspires to treat with the Son of Heaven as an equal."

"Perhaps, but we know that the thought is present in all Westerners. We teach our young of the Monkey Fairy, who aspired to be a god. He managed to eat the peaches of immortality, and it took all the wiles of Buddha to change the Fairy's fingers into the elements and the elements into the mountains of Wu Hsing Shan, which finally became the Monkey's prison. Before he was contained, however, he got loose in the land and caused great havoc."

"But Buddha was merciful, and did not unleash the wrath of No-cha upon him."

233

The Viceroy nodded. "You have prepared well. But too late. I prefer the earlier times, when there was no need for the awful powers of No-cha. Before horrible evils were set free upon the land, only the learned could prevail against the strong. A Taoist priest and no other."

"All is not lost," Hawkeland said. "Even in the newer legends, the Taoist's mouth can produce a white lotus and arrest the course of No-cha's spear."

"It is the lotus which brings you here."

"It is only you who can pluck it."

"This flower has deep roots, and the land which fosters its growth is black with the wings of the Pi Fong."

"Is there no route which is safe from the flutter of the land's Fire Bird?"

The Viceroy rose and said, "Your lips have said it." The eunuch knelt before the Viceroy and handed him a device with which he marked the paper. Lui Pei handed it to Sir Basil and said, "My *chop* is known in Peking." Then he rose and led his entourage out of the library.

Hawkeland turned to Mr. Hou and said, "Did I read him wrong?"

"No. I did. He wants you to succeed. He will send no unfavorable word about you to Peking. His *chop* validates the pass. You may travel to see the Emperor."

"Yes," Hawkeland said. "By sea."

We set sail at three P.M. Hawkeland had invited Mr. Hou to accompany us. His appearance at the ship was almost as dramatic as Hawkeland's had been at the House of McNeely. Clad in a red silk gown without design, he appeared taller than his six feet, which itself made him large for a Chinese. Yet, as always, he moved with an air of almost religious confidence. Behind him came three porters, each carrying a small suitcase. Captain de Brebeuf directed the porters to Hou's cabin with no apparent reluctance. The men soon reappeared and Hou tipped them lavishly. They bowed and scraped their way off the boat, and Hou walked to where the captain, Hawkeland, and I were standing.

234

"I will be in my cabin," he said. "I do not believe that you will need me for a while. When you do, simply give me a few moments notice, if you please."

Hawkeland nodded. Then he turned to me and said, "We'll have no pampered passenger on this part of the cruise, boy. I know you've had adventures. But with what? Guns? Knives? Bombs?"

"My hands. Almost exclusively."

"To kill?"

"To strangle."

Hawkeland seemed not in the least put off by my matter-of-fact tone. "Fair enough. Lieutenant Holland-Saunderson."

"Aye, sir." The marine ran to us.

"Our distinguished guest will change clothes. When he's back on deck, introduce him to the master-at-arms. His talents are limited, but his tolerance for death is apparently quite high."

"Aye, aye, sir." I followed Holland-Saunderson below deck as Hawkeland continued to move about, giving orders to the marines and a gang of sailors who had come up from below decks. While I was changing, we weighed anchor.

Evening soon arrived, a gentle and pastel guest. The only incisions in the sea's wall of silence came from the soft calls of heron and the insistent, pleasurable slicing of the air by flying fish. Hawkeland was on the bridge, smiling in anticipation of a combat which left me filled with dread. He nodded in the direction of his cabin, and I went below. Hou, de Brebeuf, and the other officers were already there. Sir Basil quickly joined us.

"Gentlemen. I will ask Mr. Hou to do the honors please."

"Thank you, Sir Basil. Although the Viceroy has given his approval to the journey, there are those who would still stop us. The Empress Dowager has spies everywhere, perhaps including even the Viceroy's household. For that reason we must be prepared for combat.

"There are two possible obstacles which we may face. The first is the Imperial navy. Frankly, I do not believe that it will be arrayed against us. There are two reasons for this opinion. First, the enemies of your mission are not yet persuaded that it will be more profitable to destroy you than to use you as negotiating ploys to make the Emperor look bad and his counselors look good to the Empress Dowager. Second, if the counselors were not certain of how to oppose you, they would almost certainly not have brought your presence to the attention of the Emperor. Theoretically, only he can order the fleet into action. In fact, the Admiralty could act and later justify its actions to the Emperor, but this rarely happens. So I do not believe that we will face the fleet. More likely, I suspect that we will be attacked by the pirate fleet of Madame Hsing.

"By way of background, Pai Chia Ching was the most successful river pirate of his age. The British thought to buy him off, and he was inclined to accept. His shareholders, however—"

"His *shareholders?*" Captain de Brebeuf shouted.

Hou smiled. "Of course, Captain. We may be a discreet people in some ways. In others we are more willing to acknowledge official conduct. You do sail under financing of the taxpayer, do you not?"

What might have been a difficult moment passed when Hawkeland began to laugh and de Brebeuf, seeing the truth of Hou's statements, joined in the amusement.

"His shareholders," Hou said, "poisoned him. His widow, Madame Hsing, rallied the crews by telling them that the shareholders would turn on them next. She led her band of brigands into combat, acquiring men and ships as she went and placing them at the service of high government officials. Today she commands six hundred war junks and approximately forty thousand pirates."

"That's impossible," Parsons, the torpedo lieutenant, said.

"You'll soon wish that it were. She has imposed a code of martial discipline which brings both order to her fleet and pride to her men, who look down on the ragtag swamp pirates that ply most of these waters. And she knows where to draw the line. Rape, for example, is forbidden. Unless permission is requested by the ship's purser, granted by the captain, and the act performed below deck. As I said, gentlemen, she has been able to combine piracy, military discipline, and human longing. A formidable opponent."

"More than that," I said. "We're mad if we attempt to take on forty thousand men."

"Agreed. We will not have to do so. I have been informed that much of the fleet is berthed at the Pescadores Islands. Three flotillas of three ships each have been ordered to join forces off Amoy. There is a recently formed sandbar there, bordered on the seaward by junks, intentionally scuttled. The debris will force us inward, where the pirates will have chained the river with bamboo links attached to their junks. It is there that we shall meet them."

"How do you know all of this?" de Brebeuf asked.

"The Jesuit mission in Taiwan has sent word."

"How? There is no telegraph."

"No, but there are windmills. When oil-soaked bales of hay are attached to the blades and set afire, they can be spun in sequence to form a code. And no one has reason to suspect that what they are seeing is not merely a natural disaster, or the manifestations of one of a hundred gods."

"What is the plan?" I inquired.

"Now," Hawkeland said, "it's my turn."

Combat, like the sea, is unforgiving of mistakes. For that reason, all was required to proceed precisely. At dawn Hawkeland ordered me to join a gun crew. I was to load cannon in a firing gang. Lieutenant Holland-Saunderson had assembled half his marines at the aft deck. The other half stood beneath the rigging. The group of sailors that Hawkeland had earlier addressed came on deck and ascended through the rigging. They were invisible from the stem of the ship, hidden entirely by the massive canvas sails.

Suddenly, from below, there was an anguished groaning. The engines were being fueled. At that moment, we moved hard astarboard, out to sea. The men aloft held their places as the great sails caught new pockets of wind. At the same time, the engines began to roar ever more loudly. I was afraid that de Brebeuf had lost his senses, that we were going to make a run for it. If we did so, with the steam blasting the engines, the *Python* would be propelled forward so quickly that the sails could not bear up under even moderate winds. Accelerating at that pace, the rigging would buckle, the canvas tear, and our entire complement be put at peril. Whatever we were doing, it made no sense to me.

The coal began to raise sulfurous vapors about the deck. We were soon choking. It took fifteen minutes for the soot to burn off before we were in clean air and making headway out of our own waste.

From the crow's nest came the hail "Enemy ahoy. Port bow. Not running."

De Brebeuf waved once and Sir Basil sprang from the deck and joined the second contingent of marines at the rigging.

"First platoon, port," Hawkeland yelled, and a third of the contingent picked up their ladders and ran to the far rail. "Second platoon, crouch." A second group moved to the starboard rail, hooked ladders over their shoulders, and squatted down. As they did so, the first platoon also crouched. Hawkeland was left at the rigging with the third platoon.

Hawkeland nodded to de Brebeuf, who gave the command to bring the *Python* hard to port. We were running now with the sun at our backs. The nine junks came more clearly into view. The shifting winds tore at the sails, which were not made to carry the elements at the speed of steam. At least, I thought, there was no soot.

And then I had it. It was only a matter of seconds. We were closing on the junks, with five to our starboard and four to port. Rapidly approaching was the sandbar, visible with the tide, and the scuttled junks which surrounded it. The semicircle of active junks was held together by a giant bamboo chain, visible at the water line.

"Strike sail," de Brebeuf shouted. Before his voice died away, the men hidden in the rigging were bringing down the canvas. In half a minute, we were charging the junks at twenty knots. The crew started down as random firing began. The marines stood ready to cover them, but it was unnecessary, as the junks were too far away to fire effectively. And too surprised at our loss of power to gauge our speed in time to react.

At the command of Lieutenant Faber, we swung our cannon out and opened fire on the starboard junks. The first ball must have hit a magazine, because the vessel quite simply disintegrated. The *Python* continued hard at the bamboo fence. I could see out the gunwale that it consisted of massive poles, burned and bent at the ends, covered with pitch and nailed together. There were at least twelve cables visible making the knot more than fifteen feet around. The *Python*'s angle was between the third and fourth junks. Pirates from the starboard junks were running forward to man the port vessels. Faber gave his commands and we fired grapeshot, small cannonballs held together by chains. One chain caught a pirate in the neck, lashed him once and carried him into the water. The debris of the volley caught other men in the face and chest and took them down.

The third platoon of marines set up two Gatling guns and began to spray the starboard junks. Dozens of men came pouring out of the holds, each bare-chested and bronzed, their hair held back by black scarves. As they emerged from the holds, the Gatling guns took them down. Their bodies jiggled once or twice, then fell most ungracefully into the sea.

"Stand by to ram," de Brebeuf screamed.

We braced ourselves and felt the *Python* shudder as it broached the bamboo chain. Another junk exploded. This time we were in the midst of it and parts of bodies were blown back over me. One pirate hit the deck behind us and moaned. A petty officer ran him through. As the pirates raced toward the fissure we had made, the ship came to a halt, half run up on the chain, half in the air.

Parsons waved his sword above his head, and he and his men went forward. Each platoon of marines dropped its ladder and scaled down the sides of the ship in groups of five, while the Gatling guns provided cover. On the starboard side, the first platoon went over the rail under the same protection.

Sir Basil ran forward and engaged the first pirate he saw. They clanged their sabers together, dipping them to the deck as their bodies pressed against one another. Hawkeland suddenly drew back his right hand, produced a knife, and sank it into the pirate, drawing it up from his navel to his chest in a ragged stripe that could be heard ripping. He ran ahead, hacking and slashing. He jumped to the deck of the enemy ship and came up behind a pirate taking aim on the *Python*. Hawkeland beheaded him. He caught two others running forward, challenged them, and, as they turned, slashed their necks.

At that moment, Lieutenant Regis led an engineering party forward, up over the sides, and down onto the twin ravines slit into the chain. He and his men set to work with axes and hatchets, using them no less efficiently than Sir Basil had wielded his saber.

"Full reverse," de Brebeuf screamed into the pipe. He set the twin telegraph arms, and we began to back off. Again he set the arms and we stopped. The engines continued to roar as the ship waited to lunge forward once again. The two platoons of Royal Marines had formed a square around the work party. One row firing, one row loading. Fire. Load. Fire. Load. Over and over the deadly chant was called as the pirates' bodies stacked up around Regis's work party. A rhythmic tone took hold, the whip of the axe, the burst of shot, the command to load, and the scrape of the hatchet. When the chant at last concluded, the chain was split.

Hawkeland, armed only with his saber and dagger, had stayed inside the square. As Regis finished the cutting, he waved once, and the work party ran for the ladders. Again Hawkeland took command of the marines, ordering the men back by groups, being certain that the square never seemed to be shrinking.

Fire and load. Fire and load. The stench of blood and vomit and the waste of men voiding as they died was rising now on the commands to kill. The work party was all back. The square was growing smaller. De Brebeuf set the telegraph arms, and the *Python* began to move quickly.

We could feel the massive metal plates cutting through the chain's underwater links. We threw netting over the side and the marines grabbed hold. One fell, twisting his foot and breaking his leg as he fell onto a junk, then down below its deck. Mr. Hou had seen it all from the aft deck. When the marine fell he leaped to the ship below. He picked up the man and ran forward, climbing into position to pass the sailor to us. Anxious arms reached out, and a rope was tossed. The marine grabbed it and was hoisted up the side of the ship. Hou ran forward, unable to catch the net. Another rope was tossed and he lunged for it. As he took hold, we began to pull him up. A stray shot rang from the deck and he fell. A hundred rounds from the Gatling gun shredded his assailant. But it was too late. Hou lay on the deck, the back of his head ripped and bleeding.

"All ahead," Hawkeland shouted.

"We go back," de Brebeuf said.

"Ahead, man. Ahead."

The captain realized that Hawkeland was right. He set the wheel. Its ringing chimed eerily as we pulled out of the carnage. Hou lifted his head once and raised his arm.

"Frater," Bellarmine screamed. *"Frater."*

But it was too late.

We made port without further incident. We disembarked and from there traveled overland to Peking. There were a number of benefits to be derived from this, not least among them the fact that the ship could take on provisions and repair armaments while the focus of attention was directed to those of us en route to Peking.

A second benefit was that this last leg of the journey enabled Sir Basil to enter the Imperial City as he wished. He had made it clear that he would not sit in the British legation house and send the Emperor pleading messages requesting an audience. (This apparently suited the diplomatic staff: we learned that they were furious over Sir Basil's decision to kowtow.) Hawkeland sent Lui Pei's pass to court, relying on the Viceroy's *chop* to gain us admission. The *chop,* and the curiosity which we believed had consumed the court since our victory over the river pirates.

Hawkeland's method of transportation was also to be somewhat different. It was traditional for Occidentals to travel by horseback, with ladies in carriages. We were borne on sedan chairs. Unlike those usually depicted, these were not open platforms in the Arabic style, but lacquered enclosures. Also contrary to custom, the curtains were kept open at all times. This generated sufficient interest in our journey to fill in any gaps in communication which might have attended our passage. Riding behind in an open wagon were several ordinary seamen from the *Python*. Along the way, one of them became lost in the crowd.

Our plan was for Bellarmine to accompany us to the outskirts of Peking. Not even Hawkeland's notoriety could gain admission for the sailors, but it did detract from any interest they might have otherwise aroused. Traveling alone, Bellarmine could hope only for death or, much more horrible, capture. With us, he could slip away at the appropriate time and begin his search for the secret door of the eunuch Chou, which we believed had never been sealed, and the location of which was approximately known to the Jesuits through the physician Fresnais. Once inside, Bellarmine was to find his fellow priest, obtain the formula, and return to the *Python*. Fresnais would be told to get word to us of Bellarmine's escape by sending his eunuch with the information. If the young priest did not get back, Fresnais was to risk sending his slave to Hawkeland with the formula. Then it would be up to Sir Basil and me to beat as diplomatic a retreat as possible.

The trip overland showed me only the cruel face of China. I did not see the mannered beauty of its social ceremonies, the ascetic discipline of its monks, or the flawless calligraphy which is so prized. I saw only a poverty and misery so all pervasive as to become almost tolerable through uniformity. There can be no other explanation for how the people bear up under the remorseless misery which life visits upon them so gleefully.

To Hawkeland, this was all exquisitely experiential. He did not view the tragedy of the people in a contented white man's way. He wanted to see it all, learn it all, and someday apply what he had learned to his duties. I had no such desire. Indeed, for most of the journey, made on the backs of the poor unfortunates pressed into our service, my only desire was to enter Peking. It mattered not whether we gained access to the Forbidden City. Its closer reaches, the Imperial City and Outer City, would have sufficed. Anything to escape the countryside and the unrelenting heat which was our constant companion.

One large marketplace we passed sold only manure. It was a bazaar where the poor gathered to purchase the bottled feces of the rich, to be possessed for the characteristics of the more favored. A protracted stop at the grisly place was made unendurable by the heat.

Safety prevented a lengthy stay at the next major settlement we passed. In caves below the roadway we could see portions of bodies reaching out to us. Sir Basil gave the signal to stop, and I saw him throw several handfuls of coins from the sedan chair window. As the change clattered against the rocks, ragged men and women appeared from the opposite side of the barren road, above us, and scrambled for the money. As they did so, the people in the caves came out, and I saw that they were lepers. What parts of the bodies were not covered with rags were covered with sores. These pustules festered purple, yellow, green, then stump black in the sun. The worms in their wounds were easily seen. The lepers crawled and hopped and dragged themselves up the incline. There they would remain until the beggars from the higher caves, who were not leprous, took the money and bought supplies. The lepers lived on tossed coins, and the beggars lived on what they took from the lepers. There was no objection to the taking. It was, in reality, a form of commission, because no one would deal directly with the lepers. When one of the beggars stole too much, however, the lepers would go to his cave at night and drag him, screaming and begging, back to their subterranean dwelling places. There they would cut open his armpits and loins and stuff in their own infected rags.

The roads were littered with beggars, people who would accept anything, even death when the struggle became too great. Those with something to offer would hold it in outstretched arms, begging anything in exchange for pitiful-looking crops, painted gourds, wretched chickens, daughters destined for waterfront brothels, and sons to be enslaved, with the parents to be paid only if the youth survived castration.

Perhaps the most intriguing of the sights was the wall literature on the barricades around each permanent collection of huts. From time immemorial, wall literature had served as the Chinese community newspaper. There were notices of lost property (including sometimes human beings), advertisements of the handbill type announcing new and startling remedies for various diseases and infallible cures for opium addiction. One wall was covered with an endless number of pages condemning the waste of writing paper, and another criticized the local magistrate for laxity. (The Chinese do not maintain a full-time, learned legal profession. In this they are at one with the world.) Most of the writing, however, is dedicated to lists of attendees at festivals and contributors to temple restorations. It is a form of communication I have not seen elsewhere in such volume or consistency. It breaks up the monotony of sterile boards, as public justice interrupts the tedium of the highway.

The justice took the form of prominently displayed criminals, or what was left of them. Some were lucky, and sentenced only to wear a wide wooden collar, the cangue, and steel manacles. They stood public punishment, with a placard to announce their crime, and humiliation a part of their penalty, along with the inability to feed or scratch or defecate without the assistance of another. Hands, ears, and tongues were commonplace fixtures on placard-bearing posts. One poor wretch suffered a punishment entirely expectable in a land where time is unimportant. For a serious theft he was chained hand and foot and placed on a pile of bricks. His placard announced that each day one of the bricks was to be removed. I counted thirty as we rode into Peking. Beneath the bricks was a vat of lye.

"The whole plan of the city," wrote Marco Polo of Peking, "was regularly laid out line by line; and the streets in general . . . so straight, that when a person ascends the wall over one of the gates, and looks right forward, he can see the gate opposite to him on the other side of the city. . . . All the allotments of ground on which the habitations throughout the city were constructed are square, and exactly on a line with each other, each allotment being sufficiently spacious for handsome buildings, with corresponding courts and gardens. . . . In this manner the whole interior of the city is disposed in squares, so as to resemble a chessboard, and planned out with a degree of precision and beauty impossible to describe."

It had changed little, if at all, in the intervening centuries. The city faced south, the direction of the vermilion king of summer and the source of fire and life. Its back was turned to the north, the direction of the tortoise and snake, the compass point of winter and death.

As we rode down Coal Hill, we had a panoramic view of the city. Peking was built low to the ground, its main path, an axial way, leading to the Emperor. A series of moats, gates, and courtyards combined to humble the visitor. We passed the Temple of Heaven, the Temple of Agriculture, the Front Gate, entered the Imperial City through the Gate of Heavenly Peace, passed through a short park and under another gate. There followed yet another moat, the great red Meridian Gate, and a long treeless courtyard leading to the Hall of Supreme Harmony. The Emperor and the Empress Dowager lived within that pleasure palace, as did the tradition of their predecessors.

More than two hundred years before the birth of Christ, the first Han Emperor began a palace at the site of the new capital of Imperial China, Ch'ang-an. Contemporary observers were overwhelmed by its magnificence. Once, a critic, seeing this extravagance, asked one of the Emperor's trusted generals how such an excessively grand palace could have been built when the nation had been beggared by years of war. The general replied, "Without great size and beauty, the Son of Heaven would lack the means of inspiring awe."

The passing centuries saw an almost unbroken series of emperors attempt to surpass their predecessors in creating palaces of opulence. Living quarters, audience halls, arsenals, shrines, harems, rotating pavilions to entertain guests, ponds, and statuary gardens, all were created without thought for the cost, in money or lives. Not surprisingly, the most beautiful of all the Imperial palaces, though not the most expensive, was that designed by the Jesuit Father Castiglione. Ironically, it was burned by the British in 1860 when the Chinese first attempted to cut back their opium consumption.

An exchange of runners at Coal Hill had confirmed that we were to be made welcome, if not greeted, at the palace and assigned private houses in one of the many opulent landscaped gardens that constituted so much of the Forbidden City. The runners had met at a famous landmark, an iron pillar bearing this odd inscription: "If any females with small feet dare to pass this gate, let them be summarily beheaded." This was apparently a legacy of the mother of Shun Chi, the first Manchu Emperor. It was her wish to preserve the purity of her line. She failed. An Emperor's mother who did not fail, however, was soon to take an active role in our mission. She was the Old Buddha, Tzu Hsi.

When Tzu Hsi was first admitted to the palace, she was not an Imperial concubine but only a handmaiden of low rank. She was assigned menial tasks in a portion of the Summer Palace called "the deep recesses of the plane trees." One of her tasks was to sing in her charming voice. The Emperor Hsien Feng chanced to pass by her one day while she was singing. Greatly charmed, the Emperor made her acquaintance and was delighted to find her humble enough to satisfy him in bed, but too strong-willed to be servile.

Many court astrologers warned against her advancement because of an ancient prophecy that the Manchu house would be overthrown by a warrior woman of the Yehonala clan, to which Tzu Hsi belonged. The Emperor ignored this advice, advanced her to the rank of Imperial concubine, and was poisoned by her.

As he lay dying, he realized his stupidity and in his own hand penned a valedictory decree: "After OUR death you are commanded to slay the Western Empress, so that she may attend OUR spirit in the next world. She must not be allowed to live and by her misdeeds overturn OUR dynasty." The order was hidden in the Imperial pillow, with instructions to carry it to Tzu An, the Senior Empress.

A eunuch named Li Lien-Ying had been commanded to massage the dying Emperor's limbs, which had been swollen by the poison. As he did so, he noticed the valedictory and read it. He arranged for its message to be carried to Tzu Hsi. She used this knowledge to persuade Tzu An, who knew of the valedictory, that the Emperor had relented and told Tzu Hsi of it. Tzu An trusted her co-regent and believed that the Emperor had decided not to slay Tzu Hsi. Tzu An burned the valedictory

When the Emperor died, the two empresses shared the regency. Tzu An lived quietly, and Tzu Hsi worked quietly, eventually causing her own son's death by syphilis. As I have recorded, she brought about the death of the beautiful A-Lu-te; poisoned her concubine and chief eunuch, An-Te-hai, when it was discovered by outsiders that he was no eunuch; brought about the death of the next Emperor; poisoned Tzu An; killed at least a dozen eunuchs while testing poisons and potions; and set up a government within the government. By the time we reached the Forbidden City, the Emperor sat at the head of the government, and the Empress Dowager retained all meaningful power. Her chief aide in these years of intrigue and slaughter had been Li Lien-Ying, who had risen to be her chief eunuch.

The strivings of the Old Buddha were not meant to restore her to the throne. That would have been both obvious and unworkable. She was content in the knowledge that Kuang Hsu was viewed as an incompetent, and so often bypassed. Both domestic and foreign leaders were as likely to treat with her as the Emperor. If official discussions were left to him, important ones were at least reviewed by her.

Anything as important as the opium trade was certain to hold her interest. While she did not use, or permit her courtiers to indulge in, the drug, there is no doubt that much of the wealth which enabled her to retain and exercise power came from her share of the squeeze. It was entirely likely, therefore, that we would be contacted by her before we saw the Emperor. What surprised us was the speed with which she made her approach.

Hawkeland and I were in the house which had been assigned to him when the presence of the chief eunuch was announced to us. As Sir Basil had just finished explaining how long a delay might precede any but the most curt acknowledgment of our presence, we were both greatly surprised by the sudden appearance of the Old Buddha's most trusted slave.

Bowing only enough to appear respectful, Li Lien-Ying advised us that Tzu Hsi would welcome our presence. Chancing that the eunuch spoke no English (I later learned that, in fact, he did not), I said to Sir Basil, "Is such a visit wise? The Emperor has tolerated our admission only because the Viceroy spoke for us. If we bypass him for the Empress Dowager, he may never see us. It's quite a chance."

"The Old Buddha is at least as powerful as the Emperor. It's not a chance; it's a calculated risk. Let's go."

The most powerful woman in the most populous nation on earth took our kowtows in course. We had no doubt that she knew all the particulars of Hawkeland's meeting with the Viceroy; but Tzu Hsi was too clever to give any indication of such knowledge. She pretended to be surprised and delighted by our humility. Looking at her, I first thought that it was just that cleverness which had enabled her to survive; she seemed too frail to have ever been able to count physical strength among her assets. Further thought, however, made me realize that no one could have survived as much and as long as she had without possessing physical abilities equal to her cunning.

Tzu Hsi raised a finger to her eunuch, who tapped his foot for us to rise. "Magnificence," Hawkeland began after he had risen, "may I first have the honor to present to the Empress Dowager a gift which symbolizes the inability of even China's greatest artists to create a tribute worthy of your divinity."

After I had translated, she raised one finger and the eunuch stepped forward to accept a box which Hawkeland had removed from his inside coat pocket. My admiration for the man continued to grow. He was intellectually, physically, and socially so secure that there was never a moment when he was not in complete command of all situations. He had already sent magnificent gifts to the Emperor, but I had not even known of the existence of this gift, which I later learned was a pair of golden Apsarases, the celestial water nymphs of Buddhist mythology. They had been pierced to provide for attachment to either costumes or headdresses.

It was clear that even the cunning old murderess who sat before us was impressed. After allowing herself a moment to take in the beauty of the gift, Tzu Hsi again raised a finger, and the eunuch turned to a small table. He removed a silken cover from the table, revealing a lotus-shaped bowl of brown lacquer lined with red. It seemed to date from the Sung dynasty, which made it as priceless as it was beautiful. There was an exchange of thanks and compliments, then the Old Buddha said, "We very much admire the first man to tap the lac tree for its sap. The tree, as you may know, is a poisonous sumac, indigenous to China."

"The artist is always to be admired," Hawkeland said.

"The artist, yes. To us, he is the one who places his calling before all else—family, home, self-advancement, even imagined loyalties to others."

"Such a course is dangerous."

"Such a course carries its own rewards. If the artist responds properly to his patroness, and reveals the secret of his work, there is no limit to what his rewards can be."

"We are only soldiers and emissaries, and so not prepared to comment on such lofty goals."

"We are."

"But then Your Divine Majesty has the benefit of history. Did the arts not reach a peak of brilliance during the reign of the Empress Wu Hou? And was she not the most vicious of all women ever to sit upon your throne?"

Tzu Hsi became as rigid as a corpse, a comparison which I instantly regretted contemplating. After what seemed too long a time, she smiled and said, "You asked two questions, Sir Basil. We can answer one. The arts achieved great prominence during the lady's reign."

Sir Basil bowed, and I followed his gesture that we should leave immediately. It was necessary, however, for the Empress Dowager to first shake her sleeve in token of dismissal. She did so only after saying, "We are not unforgiving, gentlemen."

We were left to remain in our quarters for two days contemplating

Tzu Hsi's words. There was no doubt that she was possessed of a long and vindictive memory. How she could achieve her ends without being unforgiving was something I could not anticipate. At the end of the second day of waiting, I heard people entering Hawkeland's quarters. There was no violence, so I was not alarmed when the sound of the group forming and walking began again, and ended at my door. It was Li Lien-Ying.

He was preceded by lesser eunuchs and entered leading a young girl. I sprang to my feet and waited, not knowing what to make of his appearance, particularly as the girl wore a small metal collar with a ring on the front; looped through the ring was a chain, which Li held in his hands. She knelt immediately, face in her hands, and was silent.

Li said, "I am here at the command of my Imperial mistress who owns me."

"Yes?" I was disturbed by his presence and that of the girl. Yet, as I should have expected, he was in no haste to conclude the matter.

"This slave is the trained concubine Plum Blossom. The cost of this slave to my Imperial mistress who owns me was one lac. In your money, that would be twenty-five thousand pounds sterling. She has been prepared to give you all manner of pleasure. My Imperial mistress who owns me commands that I present her to you and beg that you honor the Empress Dowager by accepting this small gift of her esteem."

"I am most honored. Please tell that to your mistress. However, it is against my personal philosophy to hold slaves. Please return the girl to the Empress Dowager with my most humble thanks and my prayer that I may serve her in the future."

"No?"

"No."

The girl gasped slightly and Li shuffled. "I must tell you," he said, "if she is not acceptable, my Imperial mistress who owns me will lose face and have no recourse but to whip the slave who has brought her to such a low estate. If the girl is marked, she will be fit only for the brothels."

I faced a most distasteful choice. If I accepted the girl, everything I espoused would be negated. If I did not, the best that she could hope for was to have one ankle chained to a pallet in a whorehouse by the docks. Her freedom would come when she was too ravaged by syphilis to be worth keeping. With the utmost regret, I nodded my acceptance. Li unchained the girl and snapped open the collar. With a quiet and uniform bow, the eunuchs were gone.

"Come here, child," I said. The girl barely lifted herself enough to move forward, and knelt gracefully at my feet. "Lift your head."

She did so and I almost gasped. She had the most exquisitely formed face I have ever seen. Her body was covered in the ceremonial dress in which slaves were presented, but I had no doubt how beautiful her figure would be. Rather than being covered in a traditional headgear, her hair, the color of a spring night, fell freely to below her shoulders. I stood and carried her up with me.

"You are Plum Blossom?"

"Yes, Master."

"How did you come to have such a lovely name?"

"It is the name given the concubine in the *Chin P'ing Mei*."

"What is that?"

"Master, said another way, *The Golden Lotus*. It is a book of great sexual deeds. Which I am trained to repeat, Master."

"I will not require that of you."

"I displease you, Master."

You know that you do not. But I will not force you."

"Then I owe you two debts, Master."

"You owe me nothing. You are welcome here." I truly felt this way, but I was also aware of the fact that the girl had come from Tzu Hsi, a suspect provenance at best.

"Master, may I tell you one story of the *Chin P'ing Mei?*"

"Yes."

"It is said that the author of these tales coated the corners of his manuscript with poison and sent it to an enemy, hoping that the reader would become aroused by his new possession and, licking his fingers to turn the pages, would soon die."

"I see. And did the enemy die because of his passion?"

"Yes, Master."

"Then there is no hope for one who receives such a gift."

"Master, the enemy of the author had no one to warn him. If he had had someone in his eternal debt, he would have known and been spared."

"But even if someone had been in his debt, she might have also been in the debt of another, more powerful, person as well."

"No one is more powerful than a slave's master."

"Then there are truly no debts between us."

"My master, what you take for your pleasure is a gift, to be shared in splendor."

She dropped her robe and stepped forward. Her skin was the color of burnished gold, broken only by the firm black points of her nipples and the spun ebony silk of her loins. And she was a truthful girl, because the night was one of splendor.

There had been only one other woman, of course, Irene, who had sought to exercise mastery from the beginning. Plum Blossom was different. She asked for nothing, either physically or emotionally. She had been spared drowning as an infant only because her father had been able to sell her. From the time she could comprehend, she had been trained to believe that serving her master was an honor, and whatever he allowed her by way of pleasure was a gift.

It was not an easy cast of mind to have her discard. Plum Blossom refused to call me by my name, saying only that she would lose face if the other women learned that her master could not command respect. At first she attempted to kiss my feet whenever I entered a room or she was called to my presence. I quickly put an end to that habit, although she would from time to time again attempt it. None of this, however, gave me the sense of mastery that I assume thousands of years of Chinese practice had worked to assure. I felt, rather, a sense of responsibility for the child. She was mine for as long as I was in China. If I freed her, she would quickly be enslaved again. If when we left I sold her or gave her away, there was little that I could do to guarantee the quality of her life. She sensed this fear on my part, and not only shared it but was grateful that it existed. I was her protector, and she made her dependence known. What she could not know, and I could not tell her, was that there was little strength left for me to offer her. I had spent much of my power in murder and flight. I was tired, and not at all reluctant to give myself up to her trusting embrace. But in some ways, I soon learned, she was wiser than I.

The most important way was in keeping our relationship at least somewhat formalized. She knew that our eventual, unavoidable separation would be easier if we left some measure of reserve between us. Another way was by being more willing than I to admit that the separation was in fact inevitable. Even in our most unguarded moments she was aware of this, and made me aware. It was a terrible but necessary way of developing the strength that would enable us to eventually yield the respite each offered the other.

This strength did not surprise me. Women have always occupied two conflicting roles in Chinese society. They are universally believed to be ineducable, trainable only as chattel slaves and concubines. Yet the first historian, the greatest rulers, and the strongest members of society are women. This last is proven every day when women hold the family together in the face of disease, drought, famine, and the sale or drowning of the young they have just borne. It was this strength which Plum Blossom brought to our relationship.

The clearest example of this came when we had been together about a month. The first frost had begun. She came to me on that morning and told me, "It is the ninth day of the ninth moon, Master, the Chung Tang festival. It comes with the frost. To avoid calamity, Master, it is traditional to seek out a high place—a hill or temple tower."

"You may go outside with the other women," I said. The informality of the harem structure had intrigued me from the start. It permitted the movement of women about the grounds. They gathered regularly for tea and gossip, going freely between the houses. I was not permitted near any of the concubines' quarters, of course, but had the freedom of the garden, just as my concubine, as the slave of the Emperor's guest, could mix freely with the women of the Emperor's harem. But I had not understood.

"Master, your slave begs that her master take her to a high place. It is traditional, Master, for long life."

I took her by the hand, and she led me out into the carbon night. We walked beside the interior stream which coursed through all of the Imperial gardens, up an incline, and over a pebble path to a wall of rocks. Behind the rocks was a covered stairway which led us up to the most beautiful garden I have ever seen. The Chinese call it *shon-shiri,* mountain-water painting. A series of waterfalls fed recirculating fountains which rose out of artificial lakes. Throughout the garden, water ran and poured and jumped from jade flowers, stone monoliths, and hollowed-out ginger trees. Each body of still water reflected not only the lemon of the moon but also a gay profusion of other colors. I turned, puzzled, to Plum Blossom, who nodded toward the sky.

The far night was peopled with dozens of giant kites, constructions which not only rose and dipped on the breeze but also displayed working parts as the wind caught and turned internal mechanisms. Dragons spilled scarlet paper from horned nostrils; the golden legs of centipedes rotated through the sky; and the white tongues of paper frogs rolled and curled endlessly.

I turned to Plum Blossom and said, "This is wonderful. Tell me about the feast."

She nodded. "Many years ago, Master, a scholar named Huan Ching was warned of a great calamity and told to flee to a high place as the frost came. He took his family and they survived, as did the wild animals you see above you. But all of his domestic animals had been slaughtered by the gods." She turned to me and held me very tightly. "In the household of a gentleman, Master, the slave girl is a dog. The frosts will come for you, Master, and your dog will die."

I held her as she cried, but I said nothing to soothe her. When at last I could attempt to do so, she covered my lips with her fingers. Neither of us, she knew, had the strength for lies.

I had read enough of Buddhism to know that Gautama's followers concerned themselves with the abstract: Did a falling tree make a noise in an empty forest? What is the sound of one hand clapping? Another type of Zen riddle obsessed us. Like the thief, the adulterer, or the spy, we constantly waited for the dropping of the second sandal. We were caught in the antechamber of the Empire. Nothing could be done except to wait.

When Hawkeland had met Lui Pei, the Viceroy, they spoke of opium; but they also spoke of the spiritual powers of the lotus. If the horrible spirit No-cha loosed his spear, a lotus could appear in the mouth of a Taoist priest and arrest the flight of the weapon. It is a flower of deep roots and pervasive power. A flower which hovered over the spirit of our mission.

We were in the land of the lotus, from which is derived the religious substance which frees men's minds and destroys their bodies. Our own minds had been set apart from our traditional concerns. I had Plum Blossom, and Hawkeland had his own woman. Whatever we desired was provided, and our intellects were left to be destroyed by the debilitating splendor of the Forbidden City.

252

Our bodies, of course, were merely waiting to be destroyed. We were in lotus land, but had not eaten of the plant. Rather than being ravaged by the flower, we were ravaged in another, more subtle fashion. While we became daily more distant from care, we were moving into a sphere of influence where our mission did not matter. We were left to wait, to consider the passing of time, the distance between ourselves and our ship.

There was an urgency to our mission, a sense of purpose which the court life was sapping from us. All depended upon quick access to the Emperor, quick resolution of our mission, and quick escape. We had only one purpose, and could not achieve it. Our greatest fear was that some act of ours, or some whim of the Emperor's, would force us to suddenly run and leave the one thing we had come to get. Our only realization was that when the other sandal fell it would strike with a crack.

In a land which measures time in centuries, a few weeks in the life of a barbarian mean nothing. The Emperor no doubt knew of our visit to Tzu Hsi and was content to let us wait—not as a punishment, but to save face for himself by appearing not to be concerned with what we had discussed with her. The Old Buddha herself, I am certain, expected that all information would eventually flow to her from the slave girls. She reasonably assumed that Plum Blossom and Hawkeland's concubine were terrified of her very name and would keep nothing from her. As a result, neither Kuang Hsu nor the Empress Dowager displayed any intention of hastening the next audience.

If we did not have an official audience with the Emperor, we could not plan our withdrawal from Peking. We would be forced to linger while not knowing if Bellarmine had successfully contacted Fresnais. If he had done so and returned safely to the ship, our continued presence at court could destroy the *Python*'s chances of making a safe withdrawal. If Bellarmine had failed, contacting Fresnais would be up to us. We could not do that unless we were prepared to leave immediately thereafter, and we could not depart until we established our bona fides by meeting the Emperor.

253

Then, when it was least expected, and so most expectably done, we were summoned to an audience with the Emperor and his closest adviser, Prince Yi. The place of our meeting was a sparsely furnished room on the ground level of the palace. As we entered and performed the kowtow, I remembered Hawkeland's description of the Emperor: cunning, an art lover, not unreasonable. Scant preparation for such an important meeting, but all that we had. I looked up as I rose from my bow and saw that the green audience tally had been hung, indicating that we were officially in the Imperial presence.

The Emperor moved slightly and Prince Yi spoke. "Sir Basil, I am so delighted to meet you. Your exploits, and your Christian concern for those you subjugate, are well known."

Hawkeland smiled broadly. If he returned the insult, the Emperor would be justified in ending the audience. If he showed weakness, our hope of future progress would be lost. He said politely, "Your Excellency, may I present Mr. Peter Leontov, my translator. Although his Chinese, like mine, can never approach the splendid statesmanship you display by so elegantly using, and thereby flattering, our barbaric tongue."

The Emperor raised his hand before Yi could speak. "What do you wish?" he asked.

"We beg to discuss with Your Imperial Majesty methods of implementing the recommendations of the Royal Opium Commission of 1893."

"I am delighted that China is about to have an opportunity to adopt again the wishes of another country. But why has it taken so many years to present us with this honor?"

"Your Imperial Majesty, it was, quite frankly, necessary to enlist the aid of some of the largest merchant houses, the very ones which profit from this poison. We believe, however, that now there is an acknowledgment of the evil, and that the trade can be ended."

"How sad for China. We had grown so fond of our semi-annual shipments of tortoiseshell combs and music boxes which play 'God Save the Queen.' "

"There are also Chinese who profit greatly from the opium trade, Your Imperial Majesty."

"But not nearly so many or so much as the English. At least not until recently, when your countrymen began to live only for the pleasures of opium. It is a pleasure, is it not, gentlemen? Or have some of your countrymen failed to be elevated like De Quincey and Coleridge? Have they, perhaps, become desiccated pieces of human refuse littering your cities? As thousands of my countrymen pockmark China's countryside."

"Your Imperial Majesty is too great a ruler not to suffer as his people suffer. My own Queen also feels the pain of her people. It is for that reason that we have been sent."

"Then for once it seems that there is something you want from the Middle Kingdom other than our gold and porcelain and teak and silk and tea. It seems that you want our cooperation."

"We beg Your Imperial Majesty's assistance."

"We cannot tell you how flattered we are, Sir Basil, that a country as new and small as England would deign to treat the largest Empire on earth as a fellow sovereign. Particularly after all the decades of opium abuse."

"My Queen and her nation are well rebuked, Your Imperial Majesty."

"Ahh! Your reputation as a diplomat is well deserved, Sir Basil. But perhaps your reputation as a leader of men is not as truly merited."

Knowing that a direct question could not be asked of the Emperor, Hawkeland said, "The Son of Heaven knows many things denied to his servants."

"You have a spy in your group, a Jesuit. Did you know that?"

"Your Imperial Majesty, I did know it."

"Your honesty is disarming."

"I knowingly transported the Jesuit, Lord of Ten Thousand Years. But not to spy; only to do the work of his Society."

"Things are not always what they seem, Sir Basil—a gift of a lacquered bowl, for example. The Westerner might attempt to place such a work in the development of Chinese culture. Yet the Chinese know that it is the individual work which is important, much more so than its place in a chain of development. Nonetheless, it is all of a part, and all deceiving if not viewed properly. One must always view things against the Chinese background. All figure painters, for example, live by reproducing the likenesses of the nobility. Yet the greatest of all, Liu Sung-nien, is best remembered for the less auspicious subject, 'Mending a Cassock.'

"And so what is expected is rarely present. As witness the Jesuit spy. He has already confessed to . . . Prince Yi?"

"Your Imperial Majesty, the dog has confessed to numerous lurid plots against the Lord of Ten Thousand Years."

255

"Yes. 'Numerous lurid plots.' Did you know of these, Sir Basil?"

"No."

It was lost to no one that the word hung alone. It was clear that Prince Yi was stunned; but, as I believe Hawkeland anticipated, the Emperor took this blunt comment as an insulted denial.

"We believe you." He held out his hand, and Yi handed him a scroll from which he began to read:

"Prince Yi and his colleagues have memorialized Us in regard to the case of the Jesuit spy, and submitted their proposals as to the penalties to be imposed. We have carefully perused and considered their report. It is clear that this Jesuit is guilty, because he has confessed, and, even though in the service of a false god, he is a holy man, and would not confess falsely. He has unburdened himself of his guilt in planning numerous lurid plots against the Son of Heaven and the tranquility of the Middle Kingdom.

"We have precedents to guide Our decision in the Dynastic law, and are by no means straining a point to serve the ends of justice.

"At this point, We pause and the tears flow down Our cheeks. In accordance with the advice of Our Princes and Ministers, We command that the Jesuit be summarily put to death. As a warning against further indiscretion, we order those responsible for his presence to witness his death.

"The amenity of decapitation is denied."

Whereupon the Emperor nodded to Prince Yi, and he in turn walked toward the window. Drawing back the golden curtains, he pointed to the yard, which was at our level. A gate opened and a figure in a long white robe of sackcloth was dragged forward, a rope around his neck. It was only Hawkeland's pressure on my arm which kept me from gasping when I saw that it was Mr. Hou.

He was taken to a stake in the middle of the yard and bound to it. The guards marched off and stood in three groups while slaves wheeled in barrows of stones.

"God," I screamed.

"Steady, boy," Sir Basil said.

"Do not close your eyes," Prince Yi said. "The Son of Heaven has commanded that you watch."

Hawkeland nodded.

The soldiers each took a rock. I could tell a moment later that they were almost pebbles. They began to throw them, laughing and chattering as they did so. The small stones were hurled about Hou, a few catching his lower body. As the soldiers found their mark, the tiny rocks began to cut his face and scalp. He drew himself up and closed his eyes, but there was no avoiding the missiles. After a few moments, they

256

took slightly larger stones and began running forward and hurling them like javelins. I could see small red circles forming beneath the white gown. There was a piercing scream and Hou's right side went limp as the leg was broken. More and more soldiers now were throwing stones. The tortured man's screams filled the courtyard as we heard bones being crushed beneath the robes. His torso slumped as the arms and shoulders were broken. The final onslaught began, dozens of rocks smashing down on Hou's face. The skin was torn away, the teeth knocked out, the eyes dislodged. From the mass of oozing flesh he called out, *"Eli, Eli . . ."* but before the prayer could be finished a guard came forward and brought an axe down on his skull.

The curtains were drawn.

Hawkeland held me up and forced me to turn around when the Emperor spoke.

"Gentlemen, We are interested in your country's desire to end the opium trade. Return to your quarters. You will want for nothing. And We shall think upon what is just and merciful."

We did not speak until we had returned to Sir Basil's quarters. He bolted the door, poured a drink, and said, "Mr. Hou was right."

"About what?" I wanted to cry and vomit and sleep, but I knew that it was necessary to listen to Hawkeland.

"After our meeting with Lui Pei, the Viceroy, I said that I had been wrong, and Hou took the error on himself. But he was right. The Viceroy was our enemy, but not because of the opium trade. The Chinese were wise enough to realize that if Her Majesty's government wished to do anything about the Opium Commission's report it wouldn't have waited until now. They knew all along we had another reason for being here. They just didn't know what."

"And so he passed us on to Peking."

"Yes, and told the pirates. They would have been as content to stop us, and the river pirates offered the best chance of that. The pass to Peking guaranteed that we'd sail into them. If we got through, the government would have to treat with us. Both halves of the government."

"I didn't miss the reference to Tzu Hsi's lacquered bowl."

"That's why he had to talk with us—to see if we'd made any sort of agreement with the old bitch."

"Hou would have told him that that was not our plan."

"Hou told him nothing. He allegedly confessed to 'numerous lurid plots.' If Yi's eunuchs had gotten anything out of him, the memorial

257

wouldn't have been so vague. And we'd have followed Hou to the courtyard."

"Why didn't we?"

"Don't you see? They're playing with us. The reference to each act standing alone, but being part of a continuum. Like the Viceroy appearing to be a friend, but setting all this in motion. And the great painter being remembered for mending a cassock. Kuang Hsu knows that the Jesuits are of a piece with our trip. He tore the cassock today, but he means to put it all together soon."

"Doesn't he think you'll realize what he's doing?"

"Perhaps, if he gives barbarians credit for such rational powers, which I doubt. But it doesn't matter. He still doesn't know why we're here, or who else may be involved. If we understand him, he expects we'll panic and lead him to what he wants to know. If we don't, we may become overconfident and lead him to it anyway."

"So what do we do?"

"We lead him to it."

We were trapped, literally, in a Chinese puzzle. We did not know if Yi had Bellarmine. If he did, the priest had not yet been broken, or we would not have continued to have our freedom. If Yi did not have Bellarmine, Father Fresnais would have found a way to tell us that the young priest had escaped—if Fresnais had been contacted by Bellarmine, and if he knew what had become of him. Certainly Fresnais would at least have heard of Hou's execution and made some attempt to reach us. But there had been nothing. We were required, therefore, to assume that Bellarmine was a prisoner and that Fresnais was watched too closely to send even a personal eunuch to us. And if our assumptions were correct, had Bellarmine been taken before or after obtaining the formula? Or were all of our thought processes false ones? Had Bellarmine perhaps failed to find the secret opening in the Western Gate of Perpetual Peace? The number of permutations offered by our problem was seemingly endless. Only Fresnais could solve the puzzle.

Hawkeland wanted a way to get to Fresnais, but could think of none. He knew that a messenger might turn on us or be captured. He was also aware that for us to attempt to pass through the harem would mean capture, castration, and death. He was afraid to be still, and equally concerned that any move might be the wrong one.

Perhaps his greatest fear was that I would reveal something of our mission to Plum Blossom. When I tried to explain how foolish he was being, he said, "I mean no criticism, Peter. Our friends in Rome have told me only a little about you; but I can guess and assume enough to know that you have killed, and run, for a long time now. You would be stronger than any man has a right to be if you weren't vulnerable to the charms and sexual accomplishments of a beautiful woman."

"I am weary. I do not deny it. But not weary enough to betray the mission. My respect for you, for Ballarmine and Hou—"

"You would not mean to hurt us. But you will not be surprised if I say that subtlety and indirection are everything here in China. Even a slave girl uses logic to stay alive.

"Peter, you are in an extraordinary sexual situation. You have actually been given a gift of another human being. You are in a land where beautiful women are chattel. She stays alive and out of a brothel by pleasing you, and the Old Buddha. You with her body. Tzu Hsi with information."

"It may have been her duty to inform on us," I said, "but she has not done so."

"You seem remarkably certain that an illiterate slave girl has gladly turned her back on the most powerful woman in China."

"I am."

"Come on, boy. The old bitch gave me a concubine too. My way of treating her is to say nothing."

"Then why did you accept the girl?"

"Because they're easier to watch when they're spread out beneath you."

I said, "Don't say that," and stepped forward.

Hawkeland saw this before I could stop my movement. He began to laugh. "Well, boy, we're supposed to get under their skins, not the reverse. Or is it reversed that you do it."

"Sir Basil! You are a son of a—"

He put his hand over my mouth. "Don't say it, boy. I'll have to kill you if you do." I nodded. He was right, of course; an insult against a man's mother was never tolerated, even from a close friend, even if unintentional. He lowered his hand and said, "You see what I've made you do, Peter. How irrational the girl's made you. Think her through.

259

Talk to her. If she has betrayed us, or will, tell me. We'll find a way around it. I won't make you hurt her. But don't be wrong, or the Old Buddha will fix us both to be harem attendants.''

I knew that there was only one way to learn what Hawkeland wanted to know, had a right to know. I could not torture or abuse the girl. I could only provoke a fight with her and attempt to obtain the truth in that way. Although it would cause me incalculable pain, I decided that the provocation would have to be immediate.

When I returned to my quarters, Plum Blossom moved to my couch, knelt, and bowed forward to kiss my feet. Angry with myself more than with her, I pulled her head back and snapped, "I've told you not to do that.''

"Master, how has this dog displeased you? It is only to show respect.''

"That is not the type of respect I want.''

"It is how I have been trained, Master. You do not let me wait on you, or bring you—''

"I do not keep you to wait on me.''

"I am pleased to do it, Master. It is my duty.''

"You have no duties to perform. We agreed the first night that there were no debts, no obligations. I will never hold you against your will. If you wish to go, I will arrange it.''

"Is my master sending me away?''

"I am telling you that you are free to go if you wish.''

"If I wish to be free of you, Master, I do not need your permission.''

"What do you mean?''

"Master, I have only to tell the Old Buddha of your desire to meet the Jesuit doctor.''

"You know of that?''

"I have heard you speak his name to the Lord Hawkeland, Master. His name is the same in either tongue. Fresnais.''

"What else do you know?''

"What everyone knows, Master. That no man, and particularly no white man, holds the power which he holds, and for as long as he has held it, if he is not a great man.''

"Do you know why we spoke of him?''

"He is a man of power, Master. You and Lord Hawkeland must wish to deal with him and use his power.''

"You know that we are here to discuss the opium trade with the Emperor. The priest's name was mentioned only because he may know something of the effects of the drug.''

"Opium has never been used at court, Master. He would not likely know of it."

"Then what would he know?"

"Every slave girl within the palace knows that he studies us to make special medicines, Master. Perhaps you wish to see him to discuss these medicines."

In China, even a slave girl uses logic to stay alive.

"To whom have you told this?"

"Who would listen to the howling of a dog, Master?"

"Do not play games of subtlety with me!" I shouted. In fear I grabbed her hair and twisted it back, forcing her down and around. "Name everyone who knows of your thoughts."

Through her tears she said, "Master, there is no one to tell but the Old Buddha. If I had told her, you and the Lord Hawkeland would now be on the rack."

"She could be biding her time."

"She does not know when the Son of Heaven will send for you again, Master. And if she tried to keep him from calling for you, he would do so to save face. No one knows, Master."

I released her and lifted her to a standing position. "I am sorry, Plum Blossom, if I hurt you."

For the first time since I had met her she raised her eyes to mine. "The owner of a slave never apologizes, Master. I am the one who must beg forgiveness."

"Why?"

"Because it is my time of month to be unclean. I cannot give you pleasure."

"After what I have done, you want to give me pleasure? Why? Because it is your duty?"

"We agreed, Master, I have no debt to you. I owe you no duty."

I put my arms around her and kissed her gently. The debt was mine.

Plum Blossom awakened me at dawn. I kissed her softly, but before I could act further she said, "My master wishes to see the Jesuit Fresnais."

"We will not speak of last night, Plum Blossom."

"But your need to see him remains, Master. Your need and that of the Lord Hawkeland."

"Only one of us needs to see him. But there is no way."

"My master has considered only the devious. You have thought to sneak through the palace or bribe a eunuch. Is this not so, Master?"

"Go on."

"There is only one way to reach the priest's quarters, Master. You must pass directly through the center of the Imperial harem."

"It cannot be done."

"It can be done, Master. That is how it must be done."

According to Plum Blossom, there was only one way for me to reach Fresnais's quarters: to pass directly through the center of the Imperial harem. She had a plan.

Centuries before, a slave girl had attempted to kill the Emperor when he came to take her from the harem. The investigation into the identity of the concubine dragged on, because of the Emperor's inability to speak and the fact that the stabbing had taken place outside the rooms of the women. The guilty concubine was eventually discovered and tortured to death. From that time forward, the Emperor ordered slaves brought from the concubinate by sending a note to the Empress. She then told two of the eunuchs to fetch the girl. In this way the concubine's identity was widely known before she was taken to the dragon couch. The assigned eunuch carried the girl on his back, naked except for a cloth thrown over her. This extraordinary sight was hardly noticed in the garden of the harem. Anything else would have been the cause of an instant alarm, because everyone but the Emperor, his slaves, and guests was required to leave the Forbidden City after sunset.

And so I came to be crossing the garden of the harem with the naked Plum Blossom on my back and a long cloth covering us both.

The soft night scents of jasmine and ginger eventually fell away as we turned onto a small path at the far end of the harem. The smell of medicines and chemicals became stronger as I followed Plum Blossom's whispered directions and found myself before a large detached house. I knocked gently and immediately heard a stir. In an instant the door was opened by an elderly white man in a simple black Chinese gown.

"I am a friend of Bellarmine's," I said.

He nodded and stepped back to allow us to enter. Once inside, I saw that almost all of the building was taken up with the apparatus of a laboratory. A small rack bed and foot locker were the only personal possessions in the room. These, and a crucifix over the bed.

I set Plum Blossom down and covered her with the cloth. She knelt at my back and I turned to the priest. "I am Peter Leontov," I said. "I sailed with—"

"I know who you are. What do you want?"

"First I must explain our rather unusual method of arrival."

"I am familiar with the protocols of the harem. What do you want?"

"To learn of Bellarmine."

"He came to me only a few days ago. Apparently he could not find the gate of the eunuch Chou. He foolishly bribed a merchant to transport him into the Forbidden City. The merchant reported him and he was discovered here yesterday. He had not had an opportunity to plan his escape any more efficiently than his entrance."

"How did they know to come for him?"

"I presume that Hou admitted to being a Jesuit."

"Bellarmine will not tell them even that much."

"What a good friend you are. And how naive. Bellarmine will break. He is white. He cannot endure as poor Hou must have done."

"And if he breaks he will reveal the formula."

"Ahh!" He raised his hand as if to both bless and dismiss me. "We come to that. No, he will not talk of the formula."

"Didn't you give it to him?"

"I told him all that I knew." The priest withdrew a sheet of paper from the folds of his robe. "He did not take the message. They were afraid to search, you see, because of my rank."

"Then you must give it to me."

"There is something that I must tell you."

"Something not on the paper?"

"No, it is there; but I must explain."

"You fool! All of you priests are the same. Only *you* can explain what any man can read. Only *you,* the most high, the *anointed,* can interpret what is plain. I can read."

He looked at me for a moment, then said, "I am certain of it. But it is in code."

"Good. If they take me I will reveal nothing."

"You are so brave." It was a taunt, not a compliment.

"No, only wise enough to know that if they do take me, I will be broken. If it is in code, I can tell them nothing."

"You may wish that you had something to tell them."

"I'll worry about that later. Is this in the Jesuit code?"

"No. That is vulnerable. It is a private code." Before I could again berate him, Fresnais held up his hand. "When I was last at home I had the pleasure of meeting a young man of the College of Mongre', our academy in Villefranche-sur-Saône. By now he has entered our novitiate in Aix-en-Provence, the Royal Bourbon College. He possesses a faith and love of God as strong and pure as Carrara marble. And his intellect dwarfs anything that our Society has yet known.

263

"We had a very long talk. I had doubts about my faith, and *he* comforted me. At the age of sixteen. Amazing!"

"The *code!* The *code!*"

The priest would not be hurried. "He expressed a philosophy to me. He will remember it and apply it."

"He is a schoolboy!"

"He has a great need to keep his thoughts secret. That is why he will need the code. He is a genius, you see."

"You're not talking sense. If he's a genius your Church will publish him."

"No. It will destroy him. That is why he will remember our conversation and apply what he told me to the formula."

"What is his name?"

"Pierre Teilhard de Chardin."

"I will reach him." I turned to go, then asked, "And you. What if Prince Yi decides that this is an appropriate time to take you as well?"

"I never expected to be the first man to live forever."

"We will go."

"One moment." He walked to the trunk, opened it, and removed a gold cross on a chain. "When Yi's men took Bellarmine, they ripped this from him. I gave them a few coins and they let me have it. As you may know, a priest's mother usually gives him her wedding ring to have placed in the base of his chalice. We take a solemn vow of poverty, and have no permanent chalice. So she gave him this to wear. He asked that I give it to you."

"He is my friend. I will not desecrate it."

"I know that."

We shook hands. I called to Plum Blossom and she rose and leaped onto my back. The priest draped her in the coverlet. We walked to the door, which he opened. As we stepped outside, he said, "Good luck to you, Painter."

I turned and looked at him.

"Are you still surprised at us?" He was amused.

"No. Not by anything you people do."

We returned to my quarters without mishap. I found that I was shuddering with fear and exhilaration, and knew from my earlier experiences that I would draw the strength from this mixture to go on indefinitely. I went to my belongings and removed the tube which Father Timo, the Cossack priest, had given me to hide my expense money for the trip to England. I commanded Plum Blossom to wait in her room. In this way she could not know what I had done and would be safe if questioned. Women were considered weak, and if they did not break quickly were often released.

Once the tube was in place, I entered her room. "I must go to see Hawkeland now. Gather whatever is precious to you—combs, jewelry, whatever. When I return, be prepared to flee in a moment."

When I finished telling Sir Basil what Fresnais had said, he crushed out his long black cigar and rose. "Will you help me dress, boy? My uniform is in the trunk."

"Uniform?"

"Aye. Yi has Bellarmine, and he'll break him. We're next. If I'm to be hanged, it will be as a soldier of the Queen, not as a ragtag diplomat clad in breeches and swallow-tailed coat."

"Very well, Sir Basil." I could not help but admire him. He was no imbecile who gloried in the slaughter. He was a decent man who meant to use his skills for good but enjoyed it much more if his skills put him in peril. Peril was at hand, and he wished to face it as a soldier.

We were talking quietly when Prince Yi's body eunuch came for us.

"Most honorable lords," he said, "the Lord Prince Yi, my master who owns me, commands that I request your distinguished presence in the cabinet room of the Emperor's apartment."

"Please take us there," Hawkeland said.

As we walked through the gardens, past the splashing pools and still shrubbery, Sir Basil gripped my hand and said only, "Be calm, boy. It will be all right."

He knew, of course, that I had killed and been at peril. He too had killed and been in danger far more often than I. But each of his experiences under fire had been face to face, against an enemy who expected to die or cause death. The nature of those battles had given Hawkeland an ability to control his fear and walk toward whatever Prince Yi had arranged. I, on the other hand, had killed only in rage. My victim was unprepared, and that was how I had conquered him. It was no preparation for what lay ahead. Hawkeland suspected this, and so offered me what strength he could.

The Emperor wasted no time on the protocols. "Sir Basil," he said, "you told us that you did not know that the Jesuit spy had come to do us harm."

"That is true, Your Imperial Majesty."

"It is a lie. We had earlier believed you because you were clever enough to admit to part of the truth. But you cannot expect further trust from us. Our noble brother Prince Yi has now brought before us a second member of your crew. We cannot be expected to believe that you unknowingly harbored two spies.''

"We do not know what the second spy has allegedly done, Your Imperial Majesty.'' Hawkeland was again required to speak in this way because a direct question could not be posed to Kuang Hsu.

"Prince Yi,'' the Emperor said.

"We have had the honor to memorialize His Imperial Majesty that the spy has attempted to foment plots against the tranquillity of His Most Imperial Majesty.''

Hawkeland said, "I would be honored if I could address the Son of Heaven in his role as the greatest of teachers.''

"Speak.''

"Your Imperial Majesty, I have no doubt that Prince Yi has a prisoner he can produce. Nor do I doubt that his eunuchs have tortured the prisoner with the utmost skill. But neither do I doubt that the Lord of Ten Thousand Years will find it extremely odd that two spies from one ship have suffered the most exquisite tortures and yet confessed to only the most general offenses. These men, or indeed any man, would have confessed to a specific crime to satisfy the torture eunuchs. If such a crime had been committed, and if Prince Yi knew of a particular offense, he would have questioned the spies and obtained information. Your Imperial Majesty is the greatest of teachers, and so must know that I speak the truth. I most respectfully suggest that either the Son of Heaven is being lied to by Prince Yi, or you need new torture masters.''

Yi said, "Let me torture Hawkeland, Your Imperial Majesty. I can—''

"Silence. How dare you bark like dogs in Our presence!'' Both men bowed deeply. "Yi. Have you cut out the spy's tongue?''

"No, Your Imperial Majesty.''

"Then bring him before us. He shall suffer the death of a thousand cuts.'' Kuang Hsu gestured, and Yi led us to a torture chamber, where a eunuch awaited us. Prince Yi nodded to the eunuch and he left. In a moment the eunuch returned at the head of a small group of guards who were bearing Bellarmine's weight. It was clear that he had been brutally tortured. Like Mr. Hou, he was clad in the long white sackcloth coat. He was going to die.

Yi nodded to the guards, who stripped Bellarmine and hoisted him above their heads. The eunuch clamped his hands in rings behind his shoulders and his legs in chains behind his buttocks, then bowed to his master. Yi turned to us and said, "If administered properly, as my eunuchs will, this punishment is equal to its name. It can take days for the victim to die. This dog will linger for at least that long. I assure you of this." He signaled for the eunuch to begin.

The Emperor raised his hand. The eunuch bowed deeply and stepped back. Kuang Hsu walked to Bellarmine and said, "Can you hear us?" The young priest nodded that he could. "You heard Prince Yi. This can take days, or, at our command, it can end in a moment. Whenever you tell us of Hawkeland's involvement, you will be given a merciful death." Kuang Hsu stepped back and signaled Yi, who nodded to his eunuch.

The slave took a slightly curved blade from its scabbard. He barely touched Bellarmine's forehead and twin cuts appeared, separated by only a fraction of an inch. He repeated the incision over the left nipple, and the priest screamed. The eunuch opened twin gashes on the inside of the right thigh, the left forearm, and the nose. Bellarmine was shrieking, twisting against the chains which held him in place. The slave cut again: on the tongue, the back of the right hip, and the tip of the penis. The young priest was screaming, "Kill me! Kill me!"

Oblivious to the sound, and obviously enjoying his work, the eunuch continued to slice, opening up dual cuts on the elbows and knees, the testicles, between the fingers, on the toenails, and along the rigidly extended penis. Then he turned, reached into a dish, and spun, tossing salt into the bleeding cuts.

"Peter!" Bellarmine screamed. *"Kill me!"*

I turned, shutting my eyes too late to avoid seeing the eunuch begin a new series of cuts between the buttocks. The savage slashing continued until Bellarmine's body was a mass of blood. Yet we all knew that it had only just begun.

"I beg you!" Bellarmine cried.

The eunuch began to quarter his penis.

"Peter!"

I reached over, pulled Hawkeland's saber from its scabbard, turned, shoved the eunuch away, and buried the sword in my friend's heart. Hawkeland reached forward and touched my hand. Both our arms were drenched in the seemingly endless flow of blood. Bellarmine shot upright, then collapsed in death.

"It's all right, Peter," Sir Basil said. Then Hawkeland pulled the saber out, and I heard it cutting backward through bone and muscle.

He turned from me and sheathed his sword. "Your Imperial Majesty," he said, "the Son of Heaven knows that there would have been no confession. There was nothing to confess. This torture defiles your throne. Prince Yi has shown nothing."

Kuang Hsu spoke very slowly. "Prince Yi has not failed in his proof. Such a thing would not be possible. The confession, however, was not forthcoming. The reasons do not concern us. We are concerned only that we cannot have Sir Basil as our guest any longer. You and your party are free to go."

We bowed and left quickly. Hawkeland grasped my left elbow firmly and moved me out of the death chamber and into the courtyard beyond. Now there was no exhilaration, no erection, no thought of the sensual nature of combat. Now there was only the struggle against nausea and the realization that at last I had done someone a kindness, and that I would always suffer for it. At last I was able to whisper, "The Emperor believed us."

"He did what he had to do. Do you expect to take the girl?"

"I insist upon it."

"There is no time to argue. Bring her. I think we'll get safely back to the ship."

"Truly?"

"We have the Emperor's word on it. But once at sea . . ." His voice trailed away.

"Surely the pirates would not be so foolish as to attack us again."

"The Emperor's system of communications is not the best. Prince Yi can arrange for something more effective than the pirate fleet."

"Yes?"

"The Imperial navy."

———————

Despite the danger, Hawkeland would not depart until noon. He was concerned that anything less than an ostentatious display of leavetaking would cause the English community to lose face. And he truly believed that Kuang Hsu's permission to leave would be honored. Once we were on the water, however, Yi could have us killed, blame the elements, and not appear to have been disobedient to the Emperor's wishes. If he did not do so, we would always be a danger to him, Englishmen who had won favor at court and subjected him to doubt before the Emperor. Whether or not he learned the purpose of our mission, he knew that we might return and threaten his position. For that reason alone, we had to die. My greatest fear, however, was for the safety of Plum Blossom.

I do not know when I had decided to ask Plum Blossom to marry me, only that I had firmly resolved to do so. I had not told Hawkeland, because there had never seemed to be an appropriate time. Nor had I told her, because of my fear that she might think it a command rather than a humble request. I decided that it would be best to put off the issue until we were safely at sea. Then we could both discuss it away from the unnatural setting of a master training a slave in the Imperial palace.

Once Hawkeland had made arrangements for us to leave the Forbidden City, I returned to Plum Blossom and found that she had everything in readiness. She begged permission to speak. I kissed her gently and reminded her again that she was not to conduct herself in this slavelike fashion. She nodded and said, "Forgive me, Master, but there is much in your slave's thoughts."

"Do not be afraid. We have the Emperor's assurance of a safe journey."

"It is not that, Master." She hesitated. "The other evening, Master, when I thought it my time to be unclean, nothing happened, Master. No blood passed. I am with child.

I held her tightly, feeling an elation I had not thought possible. When she moved her head slightly to kiss me, I kept her locked in my embrace, fearing that she would see my tears and think me unmanly. Looking back upon the memory of the child I have never seen, I am ashamed now only that I did not realize how fine such joyful tears truly were.

"Will I crush the baby?" I asked gently.

Plum Blossom knew what I meant and said, "No, Master. It is safe inside me, a part of you that I will keep no matter what may try to separate us."

"Nothing will separate us, Plum Blossom."

"As my master says." She lowered her head, and we both knew that it was time to go.

269

When we had first gone ashore, de Brebeuf had promised that a longboat would stand by at the docks twenty-four hours a day. I was not, therefore, surprised to see it when we arrived at the port. I was surprised, however, to see Towson in the bow of the boat smoking a pipeful of shag and attempting to read by the failing sun.

"Hello, Towson," Hawkeland called. "Do I ask permission to board a dinghy?"

"Granted, whether or not you choose to ask." He was on his feet smiling and waving us aboard. Sir Basil went first, courteously keeping half turned to the wall in order to help Plum Blossom down the steps. I paid the chair bearers, then scurried down to the longboat. Towson helped me aboard and, as I took my place, asked, "Who's the attractive young lady?"

I smiled and said, "My fiancée." In time, I thought. In time, I hoped.

"My congratulations." He gave the order to cast off, tamped out his pipe, put his book in his jacket, and repeated, "My congratulations."

"Thank you. But how did you get here?"

"In the hold. If all else failed, I was to attempt to make contact with Father Fresnais. If no one knew, no one could tell under torture."

But of course. I nodded and looked beyond him to the ship.

Captain de Brebeuf said nothing about a woman's presence aboard the *Python* until Plum Blossom was in my cabin and I was in conference with Hawkeland and the ship's officers. "Well, gentlemen," de Brebeuf began, "first I wish to offer my thanks to Mr. Leontov for bringing his lady aboard. She'll improve our trim tremendously." After polite laughter, he said, "I understand that the couple is affianced. I know that you all join with me in congratulating them." All the officers applauded, including Faber, who even ventured a "Here, here."

"Gentlemen," de Brebeuf resumed, "for reasons not relevant to our discussion, it appears that the Emperor has become displeased with us. We may expect to be attacked by the Imperial navy. None of you has ever fought a war junk. Neither have I. But I have studied them, and this is what you will need to know."

It was with surprise and fear that we listened to de Brebeuf. We learned that war junks carried crews of up to three hundred men, four or more masts, and strong hulls strengthened by double layers of planks. With their oddly shaped sails and quick-response long tillers, the junks could outmaneuver us. With armaments and training supplied by the British navy, they would have no reluctance to fight us.

I remembered an old legend, that the Chinese had been taught to build ships by the ancient Emperor Fu Hsi. He was the son of a nymph and a rainbow and so favored by his parents that he founded a race of magnificent sailors. Sailors who had, in fact, created the watertight compartment, the balanced rudder, and battened sails. The legend held that his ships had never lost an engagement. Listening to de Brebeuf paint a picture of the junks' power, I began to think that he knew and believed the legend.

Our path of escape would be down the Yellow Sea, between Formosa and the Riukiu Islands, and out into the Pacific. From there we would make for England. We dared not attempt to make any port in China, even one secured by the British. Our only hope of escape was to outrun the Imperial navy. It was a hope which lasted only through the night.

Dawn came darkly, with purple clouds descending to meet the rising sea. The first sound of the day was the lookout's call: "Men-o'-war. Hard astarboard, sir."

Coming through a cloud bank were three scarlet and ebony war junks of the Imperial navy. From the rear came three more. De Brebeuf ordered the ship hard to port and we made for the open sea. While we were still turning, Sir Basil told me to take a moment and go below to comfort Plum Blossom. He handed me a pistol and said, "If we are boarded, you are to see to the lady." I nodded and went below. Not surprisingly, Plum Blossom did not seek to keep me with her, or ask for comforting reassurance. She merely kissed me and told me to be well.

When I returned to the deck, I saw that we were racing for the open sea. Over the stern we could observe the six junks, now pursuing us in two parallel files of three each. At that moment the second in each file pulled out and quickly moved toward us. Although de Brebeuf had warned us, I was still shocked by the speed and precision of the maneuver. The captain watched the two ships for a moment, smiled, then gave the order for half speed. The junks began to gain on us, their prow paintings showing hideous teeth which snapped up and down in an ever narrowing ocean. They were less than a mile behind us and closing in a pincer formation. As they approached, I saw that the junks were propelled by a paddle wheel on each side. I raised my arm in the junks' direction, but de Brebeuf only smiled again.

"I saw," he said. "And I know what to do." He turned and called the order for hard about, then indicated that I should stand back. There was nothing for me to do but watch.

The *Python* shuddered as its engines were thrown into reverse at the same moment that the ship turned in a tight angle. I thought that we were going to face them from our port side and open fire. Instead we continued hard about, eventually completing a half-arc. At the moment we finished the turn, our nose was almost in the point of the pincer.

The captain moved the twin telegraph arms to full ahead, and the *Python,* massive between the junks, roared down the funnel which they created. We hit the two warships, splattering one paddle on each like a cannonball hurled at tenpins. As the widest part of the *Python,* the midship, made contact with the junks, they were gorged open and quickly flooded. From both sides the spray carried to us the agonized screams of doomed men, galley slaves chained to capstans now being pulled beneath the sea. As we cleared the funnel, I could see over the stern the twin halves of the foundering ships. There was a mammoth sucking sound, and the sea was suddenly empty behind us.

Two enemy ships were spread along our starboard line, and two were grouped at the port side. The *Python* made for the port targets. De Brebeuf hailed Lieutenant Parsons, shouting, "Fire at will. We are at twelve knots." Parsons saluted, then ordered the starboard gun crews to stand ready. He climbed onto the rail, looping an arm through the rigging. He relied on the twelve-knot engine, and his free hand ticked off the distance in seconds. He brought that hand up, and the *Python* executed a hard turn to port. At that instant Parsons screamed, *"Fire!"* Seconds later, one junk disappeared, having been caught in the magazine. The crew fell to wild cheering, which Parsons quickly silenced. He cocked his arm again, but this time pointed it at the second crew. Their volley rose smartly over the water but did not demolish the junk, which was turning. De Brebeuf knew to put the ship into a gentle turn which brought the aft crew again into line. Their shells crashed down onto the warship, splintering it into a burning hull. The *Python* continued its turn and came around to face the remaining junks, which had now closed to within hailing distance.

Lieutenant Holland-Saunderson ordered the Royal Marines into the rigging. Unlike our first engagement, where surprise had counted so heavily, here brute power alone was important. Every marine went aloft, including their leader. Gatling-gun emplacements were set up on rigged wooden platforms. Grenade teams took the next level position. At the top, riflemen hooked their bodies into the ropes and knelt at the ready.

As we completed our arc, the first junk sailed under our cannon and fired a full display of grapeshot into the rigging. I could actually see the cannonballs, chained together by iron links, as they slowly moved up into the sky. The ugly manacled balls ripped portions out of the mast, shredding the mainsail and toppling large sections of the rigging into the sea. A second round issued almost immediately but was aimed a bit lower. This time the target was the now exposed marines. Riflemen were wounded with chunks of flaming metal, while others pitched themselves into the sea to escape the burning canvas. Those who held their positions were caught in the next vicious round. Grenade teams were torn apart by their own burning charges, thereby adding to the destruction of the rigging. Men who attempted to maneuver about were fired on by sharpshooters on the deck of the second junk. Simultaneously fired rounds from the two junks pierced the mainmast, toppling it forward, its massive spire lancing the deck.

The main deck was covered with burning lines and flaming canvas. Sparks caught other sails and spread the torch throughout the rigging. One stream of flames brushed a powder trail, which quickly ran to the attached cannon, blowing the unsuspecting crew out through the deck. Holland-Saunderson was attempting to set up a fire party, but every team of marines which attempted to form a line to the sand buckets was picked off in formation.

Nor was Parsons able effectively to return fire. The junk had now come up under us. Our cannon were locked for firing against other men-o'-war, not low-slung junks. If we did not back off and turn, the Chinese ship would blow out our insides.

Holland-Saunderson alone knew how to save us. He had by now managed to collect about forty of his men on deck. He drew his saber and pointed at the junk closest to us, "Prepare to board!" he shouted.

De Brebeuf's voice sounded clearly through the megaphone, ordering him to stand fast. The marine officer turned, saluted with his saber, then disregarded orders by leading his men over the side onto the junk. The marines hit the deck running, opened fire, then fell into their classic square. As they gave one another cover for two rounds, the junk's crew was decimated. Forced to abandon their guns, the crewmen ceased firing on the ship and turned to face the marines. It was clear that the load-fire-load rhythm of the square could not be maintained. Holland-Saunderson gave the order to fix bayonets. Then, incredibly, he ordered an advance. As his men marched toward the enemy, they became lost in the close-quarters combat of doomed men determined to add to their company many of the enemy. Their extraordinary attack gave Parsons time enough to have a cannon unbolted and rolled backward. A second gun crew cut away the railing and the cannon was trained downward at the junk. An instant later the smaller boat was demolished.

De Brebeuf ordered full ahead, hoping to outrun the remaining junk. Ironically, it had already slipped behind us and allowed the *Python* to sail clear before opening fire. It loosed a single salvo which smashed through the rudder and stern post. The ripping away of our steering mechanism put us into a spin. Parsons took the occasion of a new angle to open a last salvo of bursts at the junk. After a moment, we were alone on the sea.

Rigging crews were sent aloft. The repair operation this time would not be as complicated or dangerous as what de Brebeuf had accomplished with the spare propeller. A jury-rigged rudder was put into place. The engines gave us steam, and the sails were maneuvered to give us direction. The heading was now south, toward Macao. Hawkeland planned to put Towson and Plum Blossom ashore at night in a longboat. If they reached land, they could rely on the Jesuit network to get them out on a safe ship. The rest of us would sail for England. There was no question of our going ashore. Our presence would lead only to another chase, and to destruction.

As we approached Macao, I prepared Plum Blossom for our separation. She accepted it with the passivity that I had both expected and hoped to see. Realizing that this calm was as much strength as training, I had hoped that she would have the courage to perform one final act to strengthen me. I asked that she legitimate the claim that I had made earlier, and become my wife. She agreed and, in the fashion of women everywhere, asked if there would be more to the wedding than our love.

"Mr. Towson," I said. "He is a man who sails with us. He can perform a ceremony of sorts."

"He is a *bonze* of your religion, my lord Peter?"

"He is a *bonze*. God will hear his words."

"He has already heard my prayers. But let us go."

We met Towson in de Brebeuf's cabin. Hawkeland was also there, as were Mr. Parsons, Faber, and Regis. For this social event, at least, the prejudice against engineers had been forgotten. Plum Blossom was frightened as we entered. Towson immediately put her at ease by lighting two candles and saying to her, "For joss." She smiled and I could feel her relax a bit in my arms. Towson smiled and put his hands on our shoulders. "Gautama Buddha has given us the San Pav, the Three Great Venerable Ones," he said. "Chang Tao-ling has given us the Son Ch'ing, the Three Pure Ones. And God the Father has given

Himself to us in the Blessed Trinity. Where more than one becomes one, there is mystery and understanding, God and man, husband and wife. There is no conflict, only love.''

Towson smiled again and said, "I don't suppose you own a ring."

I said, "No, but I have this." I removed from my pocket the cross which Father Fresnais had given me and placed it around Plum Blossom's neck.

"It is enough," Towson said. He asked, "Do you have something for me?"

"No. If you don't know, you can't tell them. And if you do not carry the formula, you will think only of my wife's safety."

"You are right. The formula has caused enough death already."

I took Plum Blossom on deck. The ship rocked gently at anchor. It was drizzling, and dawn would soon arrive. I was anxious for them to be gone, in part because I feared for Plum Blossom's safety, and in part because I feared that I would soon begin to cry.

"We are to be separated, my husband."

I could not help but grin foolishly at the sound of my new title. "Yes. At least for now."

She smiled and stroked my face. "For all your adventures and bravery you are still a European. We will not be together again. But you will not be alone. You will have the memory of me, and the knowledge that I will raise our son well."

"And you will not be alone. You will have the child. And for the rest of your life, you will own a slave."

The sky was beginning to turn to rose and purple. Over my wife's shoulder I saw Towson nod. I kissed Plum Blossom one last time, then bowed low and kissed the place where our child was resting. Towson took Plum Blossom by the arm and led her to the railing. As crewmen lifted her into the longboat, he turned to me and said, "I'll see to it that she reaches America safely. The Society will make the arrangements."

"I am grateful."

"No, Peter. It is we who are grateful. You betrayed us once. Perhaps it was deserved after the fact of your brother's death; I do not know. But we forgave you and asked you again to repay your debt to us by assisting in this mission. You have done much more. You gave to the members of our Society your service, your friendship, and your love. And you would have died for Mr. Bellarmine. That is more than we had any right to expect. Now we are in your debt. What you do with the formula is unimportant. How we repay you is essential.

"The Society will care for Plum Blossom. And her child. And the child's child, for as long as the line continues. There may be some that we cannot help directly, either because they reject us or because they will not have the talents that we can help to maturity. But for he who is possessed of these talents, we will do everything. Education, wealth, honors, whatever is desired, will be given freely. We will ask nothing in return. Not ever. And if he somehow comes to be of assistance to us, all of our resources will be turned to his protection.

"This I swear before Christ Jesus, the Founder of our Church, and the Inspiration of my Society."

Before I could even consider a reply, de Brebeuf quietly said, "All away."

Towson stepped into the boat. The winches and pulleys began to turn. As the longboat slid down below the deck, my wife turned to look at me one last time, her eyes filled, as mine were, with the finality of our parting. Then she was gone forever.

McHenry rose from his seat. This time he did not light a cigarette or fix a drink or think of Elspeth. He simply left the room, overcome by all that he had learned.

Every intelligent man wishes to escape from a difficult teacher. He needs to test himself against life using his own strengths, not the abilities of the teacher. Until now, McHenry knew, he had not been aware of what his teachers had been about. Even he, the most favored of partners, had not realized the depth and complexity of the Society's relationship with Ingersoll & Constance. Even he, who had fought with Chechoweo and profited from the Vatican, had been unaware of the unending, interconnecting strands of the Jesuit network.

Simon was a proud man. He did not like to admit that he was part of a combination. A combination more elusive than those created by corporations and governments, elusive because it was in this world and not of it.

It was a Society, an alliance, a combination capable of hard and brutal action, yet not able to be inhuman. Loyola was, after all, a victim of the Inquisition, not its agent.

The Jesuits did not seek only a consistency of power. They sought to use special people to effect their goal, their plan that all they did was for the greater glory of God.

McHenry was a banker. He had been trained to read the life of an alliance as being reflected only in its bottom line. The Jesuits had as their bottom line an ideal. When one idealizes a result, the intended end must be extraordinary.

He knew so much more now. He would have to pause awhile and think. Then he would finish the diary.

We made for Australia. I thought at first that de Brebeuf was mad, then realized how necessary his choice had been. If we took the natural course west, toward India, we would have crossed the patrol routes of the Imperial navy. Even if we had safely arrived in India, Yi would have many friends in the opium trade who could take steps to harm us. He could not be certain that we had not been sent to implement the Royal Opium Commission's recommendations, and so he could not let us live. Korea and Japan were hardly more hospitable. The British colony in Australia offered security, comfort, and shipyards in which to rebuild the damaged *Python*.

Disaster struck the day before we expected to make landfall. We were overtaken by a storm vomited out of Satan's mouth. A mass of clouds the color of scratched coal suddenly appeared and raced toward the *Python*. De Brebeuf ordered the men aloft to trim the sails and prepare for running before the wind. The vanguard of the attacking weather swirled over the water and was on us before the ship had been totally secured. Rain scalded the decks and drove us into our cabins. The rigging crew rode the spars up and down into the ocean. Two men were thrown from the canvas and disappeared into the sea. The remainder lashed the sails into place and made their way quickly below decks.

The storm continued throughout the day and night. There was hopeful talk of quick calm, to which Parsons chillingly replied that he had once sailed to Tasmania and been held in a similar storm for eleven days. Ours was to last for six. There was nothing to do but ride it out.

On the morning of the fifth day the engine room reported that the pumps had clogged. Not only was the *Python* drawing water, but the waves that washed below decks were gathering in pools. The combined flow was gaining despite all efforts to discharge it. I joined the men in the black gangway. Human chains were formed and buckets passed up and down twin ranks of men. The day passed with agonizing slowness. The hold pitched and rolled in the darkness, with the immense ocean running over and into the ship. We had no sail and no engines and, below decks, no sight of one another. Our hides and faces became black with oil and bilge water, our scalps were thick with the waste and sludge of the sea, and we smelled like Lazarus three days dead.

We passed buckets, two hours on and two hours off, for a day and a night. Each call to the line would have met with a groan if we had had the strength to complain. And whatever pain our voices wanted to pronounce, our shoulders and ripped palms carried silently.

After twenty-four hours, word was passed along the line that the hand pump had been reached and cleared. Eight hours later the main pump was manned. At that moment the sea itself seemed to realize that we would not quietly surrender and began to recede.

Our joy was short-lived. Once the holds were cleared, we were required to go below and get out everything which the bilge had besotted. Literally tons of meat had to be passed up to the deck and thrown overboard, each of us gagging at the stench of the rotted flesh. Dozens of wheels of cheese, many food tins, and hundreds of sacks of moldy flour, all were jettisoned. In the month to come, we would think often of those provisions.

On the next day, however, we thought only of the quiet sea we had purchased with our suffering. The water had taken on a cold and leaden tint, and the air was bitter. But all was calm. We were seven days out of Australia. Where, we did not know. We could not sight to our location because of instrument damage, and if we had known where we were we could not have corrected our position, because the rudder had been virtually destroyed.

The evening after the storm was the first one clear enough to allow Faber to attempt to take our position. He had once told me that the proper way to navigate was to correct one's compass and take two bearings on shore positions. But we did not know the precision of any of our damaged instruments, and there was no shoreline. As a result, Faber attempted to observe constellations. Once he had done so, he roused a sleeping Parsons and had him report to the bridge.

"Mr. Parsons, I have one celestial arm as the straight vertex of an equilateral triangle. Please identify the other two verticals."

"Aye, sir." Parsons took sightings, then whispered, "Good God."

"Magellanic Clouds, Mr. Parsons?"

"Magellanic Clouds, sir."

"Thank you, Mr. Parsons. I merely wanted confirmation. Please call the captain."

It was left to de Brebeuf to call us together and explain that the two officers had fixed our position as south of Australia, south of Tasmania, and beneath the Southern Cross. We were drifting toward Antarctica.

"Take care of your men, gentlemen," the captain said. "Explain the situation, guard against panic, and rely on the strength of these sailors. They are an excellent crew, and they will take what comes with professionalism and courage. Let us do the same."

It was almost beyond comprehension, but in a matter of days we were on the Southern Continent, towed ashore by our longboats, the *Asp* and the *Cobra*. A quick reckoning revealed sufficient stores and equipment for us to survive for only a matter of weeks. Within that time we hoped we would either have made jury-rigged repairs to the *Python* or been found by a whaler.

Spirits were remarkably high. Perhaps it was the exhilaration of being off the ship, which had become dank and fetid. Or perhaps it was the excitement of new adventure. I know only that de Brebeuf knew his men well. They turned quickly to their new tasks with enthusiasm.

I knew better. I knew that we were at the bottom of the world, presumed lost by all who had known of our expedition, totally lacking in the stores, equipment, and clothing necessary to survive. We could rely on improvisation and high spirits for a time. Food could be rationed, ice boiled into water, and extra layers of clothing taken from the dead. But in the end we were lost and alone. We were truly at the bottom of the world. I had an image of the earth spinning above, observed by the crew as it stood to one side, removed from the world and beneath it. On maps our journeys might appear to be over water and across land. They were not. Our trek would be upward from the bowels of the universe. I knew, as I am certain the others did, that it would require a true miracle for us to survive. And I did not believe in miracles.

Lieutenant Regis led a team of ship's carpenters in building a hut ashore, although hut is hardly a fair description. The structure was fifty by twenty, with walls packed with quilted seaweed for insulation. A larder was tunneled out and bunks made from the ship's fittings. The supplies in the longboats were replaced with fresh stores. Crews were assigned to not only repair but also clean the stench of sweat from the *Python.*

The greatest hardship, ironically, was to be water. The ocean, of course, was too salty to be potable. The ice could not be sucked, for fear that it would rip off warm flesh. As a result, it became necessary to hack huge chunks from the land and melt it, then allow it to cool.

When de Brebeuf called the officers together to assign repair details and the building of signal fires, I made the first real use of my civilian status to absent myself and walk along the ice fields. I intended to explore some of the bergs which lay just off our camp area. As I approached the water's edge I saw a school of Orca, killer whales, heading toward the ice shelf, blowing loudly. They dove beneath the ice, and I ran to the edge in order to be able to watch their magnificent power when they next ascended through the water. The ice, which was about four feet thick, suddenly exploded all about me. Great shards of frozen water shot upward, then fell in a storm around my head. At that instant, the six whales, lined up smartly, surfaced and blew.

The head of one was within five feet, and the explosion of hot air from its snout covered me with a warm briny vapor. I fell backward, and at precisely that moment the whales did too. Their snouts and backs slashed into the ice shelf, split it open, and caused a reverberation which forced the floe on which I was now isolated to tremble. I leaped to my feet and began to pick my way to safety. I could not run, because the huge killers constantly broke the surface, then dove, snout first, splitting open the frozen sea. Each arcing attack brought them closer and closer. With each movement, they rose six to eight feet in the air and leaped forward nearly twice that distance. Their massive forms caused the ice to splinter and fall away from beneath me. I was now separated from the mass of the shoreline by about five feet.

The whales behind me were making a horrible sound, signaling and blowing water and air. I glanced over my shoulder and saw their horrid teeth snap in preparation. The sight froze me. I could hear shouts of *"Jump! Jump!"* but I was immobilized with fear.

The floe on which I stood twisted away from the impact of a surfacing killer. I fell forward and hit my head. Rather than being dazed by the blow, however, the collision with the ice jolted me into action. I began to crawl toward the edge of the small floe, toward land, where a group of men had already formed a rescue party. The whales began to thud against the bottom of the ice, hoping to scent my position, then cut through. I heard a crash and felt the ice behind me shudder. Suddenly around my waist I felt arms. It was Parsons.

"You're still close enough to jump," he said. The whales cracked against the bottom once again. "It's your only chance."

I nodded, stood, looked once at Parsons, then leaped for the shore. I fell short, as he must have known I would. In an instant he was in the water behind me and again holding me. In another moment we were encircled by a rope and pulled the last few feet to shore. At that moment I could hear the killer pack turn and blow. Too late! We were ashore.

I awoke in my cabin. Sir Basil was seated beside me reading. When I stirred he spoke. "Well, boy, you're quite a lot of work. We had to chip you and Parsons out of your clothing."

"Then he's all right?"

"Oh, yes. He knew enough to get you off that floe. Thawing you out was up to the rest of us."

"I am grateful. Is Parsons here?"

"Ashore, with a work party. Seems the British still turn out an occasional hardy soul."

"It would seem."

Before we said another word, there was a deafening roar. We heard wood splitting and the screams unique to dying men. Hawkeland told me to stay in my bunk, but I grabbed my blankets and followed him. As I came out onto the deck, there was a second crunching sound and the *Python* heaved. On shore, men began to stream out of the hut, pulling on clothes, attempting to carry supplies. The entire ice pack buckled beneath us and the ship rose. As suddenly as we had been lifted, we were thrown down, stem first, and a great sheet of ice closed over the aft section. We began to be pulled away, the men running from the hut seeming to recede into the vast and barbarous cold.

De Brebeuf called for his megaphone and, once it was in hand, gave a series of rapid commands. The men ashore were ordered to drop all stores and sprint for the *Python*. Deckhands were mobilized; rope ladders and hawsers were tossed over the side. Torches were lighted on deck. Those not working erupted into spontaneous cheers of encouragement. We were being bound and carried off in an ice floe, and if the men ashore did not reach us they would be doomed to die in the Antarctic night. Five men reached the side of the vessel. As they scrambled up, two more leaped and fell into the fissure between ship and ice pack. The *Python*'s natural movement crushed them. Seamen were hoisted overboard by their feet, extending their arms to their comrades. Three more reached safety by grabbing onto their shipmates.

The pack ice split apart with the ugly and unforgiving thunder of artillery. The men ashore watched hopelessly as we were wrenched back into the sea and turned away from them. A ravine opened beneath the hut, and it was carried off in two sections, then split and fell into the water. Nine men were left on the ice, without supplies, without shelter, without transport. A group of Orca trumpeted in the night. I looked ashore, and one of the men raised his hand to us in mute acceptance and farewell. It was the last I saw of Parsons.

The *Python* was gripped firmly by the ice. For three months we drifted in a mostly southerly direction. There was no way to put a boat over the side, as the floe ran for endless miles on either side of the ship. We were, however, able to let men down onto the ice pack. We would go out in parties looking for breathing holes. It was in these that Weddell seals often surfaced for rest and oxygen. As cruel as it seemed at first, it was necessary to harpoon them. Their blubber gave us heat and light, their meat was delicious, and the remainder provided renderings for jelly and paste.

The loyalty and intelligence of the Weddells was stunning. On one occasion we saw a cow Weddell shoot out of the water and hit the ice immediately before a pack of killer whales broke water. Rather than waddling to safety, the cow turned and, bellowing loudly, stuck its head into the water. We had all learned from my near disaster to respect the killers' intelligence and ability to conduct a group action. Obviously, the Weddell did not share this respect. The killers leaped toward the cow, which lunged backward. Then, incredibly, it returned to the water's edge and provoked the pack again. And then we saw why. One of its helpless pups was attempting desperately to force itself up on the far side of the break. The pup paddled furiously as high dorsal fins circled, casting grisly shadows from heights of five and six feet. Suddenly the mother appeared and sprang into the approaching pack. As one, the dorsals cut and swirled in the water, turning the surface into a foaming pool. The seal disappeared, and the fins then wheeled and made for the pup; but again the cow leaped out of the water and distracted one killer. The Orca pack, however, closed on the baby. The mother sprang upward, caught the pup in its teeth, and hauled it away. The killers turned again on the mother, who apparently led them back down into the icy ocean. The pup, meanwhile, had reappeared on the surface and was attempting again to climb out. Bleating piteously, straining to move upward onto the pack ice, it was unexpectedly propelled upward as the mother's snout appeared in the air. She had forced the baby Weddell to safety. The killers were now behind her. Two advanced while three dived. In a moment the water went red. Then an Orca broke through the ice, its jaws opening as it came down. It caught the crying pup and cut it in half. The death scream echoed across the ice. A second killer devoured the remains, and we looked away.

At the beginning of the fourth month adrift, when it seemed that we could no longer endure one another, or the *Python,* nature intervened to distract us. The pack ice split more violently than ever before and began to heave. Great chunks of frozen sea were lifted up out of suddenly formed fissures and jammed against the ship. Entire sections of the hull were ripped through as the jagged spears of ice were hurled against the *Python.* One forward sleeping section was pierced, with ice and water trapping seventeen of the crew.

Those men who were able to get to the deck went immediately to their stations.

Boat parties boarded while launching crews worked the ropes and pulleys. But the fear of the ice proved greater than even the discipline of the Royal Navy. One of the launching crews worked too quickly, and the *Asp* was jerked inward, hurling the chief bosun and thirteen of the crew into the sea, where they froze before lines could even be brought to the rail.

De Brebeuf immediately ordered all hands into their respective boats and indicated that only he and Regis would work the pulleys. As the sailors ran forward, the ice accelerated its drive against the ship. We were caught from both sides with such force that the *Python* rose into the air and hung there. A second impact forced the stem higher and we were left tilting at a precarious angle. The captain and Regis never hesitated. They successfully lowered the *Cobra,* commanded by Faber, then hoisted the *Asp* back to deck level, supervised the boarding, and lowered it into the small lake that was forming around the ship. Lieutenant Regis started down the pulley wire, rappeling smoothly. As he was about to step off for the final descent, a shard of ice was forced up by the tide created by the sinking *Python.* He was spun wildly about, his legs crashing into the hull with great force. He reached out and pushed himself away, then fell into our waiting arms. We later determined that his legs were badly bruised but not broken. By then, de Brebeuf had started down into the boat and was quickly taken on board.

We had now only to sail in open boats across the Antarctic waters, which had never been charted, to reach a land which had never been crossed.

The two longboats steered together for several days. We were generally able to beach at night on a floeberg. These massive sheets of ice provided space enough for men and boats, as well as possessing sufficient thickness for a camp and fire. The boats provided a little shelter, and for food we existed on our stores and an occasional fresh-killed seal and its blubber.

We eventually weakened to the point where we could not row against the current but had to content ourselves with floating, and poling away from the floebergs when they came toward us. When we camped at night, we were so weary that we actually sweated in our sleep, melting the ice beneath us. The residue ran into our sleeping bags, and we awoke each morning in pools of ice water. As our meager stores of food and water were consumed, we prepared to die.

Ironically, a deterioration in the weather saved our lives. On the thirty-second morning in the boats, the sun fairly burned the ice to slush. By noon, however, a violent wind froze the slush into ice pancakes. Lying about on the suddenly hard surfaces were thousands of trapped fish. De Brebeuf ordered a massive catch. We were all delighted to be occupied with something other than poling. We were even happier that night as we stuffed ourselves with the blood and salt of the fish, rather than the paste of seal blubber. No Tsar ever dined more royally.

Five days later we made a landfall. We were carried by a violent current onto a deserted beach. The weather was the worst of our journey, with winds which could easily sail a man fifty yards, and snow which cut like steel. But we were delighted. It was land.

And just in time. De Brebeuf and several of the men were too badly frostbitten to go on. We discovered this only after setting up a small cabin, building a fire, and finally stripping off our foul garments. The captain's toes had taken on a scaly discoloration which caused them to resemble the stubs of a mutant's paw. The others were in no better condition. It was agreed that nothing could be done except amputate.

None of us possessed any medical training. Without such skills, however, it was certain that gangrene would kill de Brebeuf and the others. While we sat about thinking of our sad state, Regis said, "I'll do it." And he did.

I have already alluded to the strange treatment accorded engineers in the Royal Navy. They entered the service through a different route than line officers, were not part of the executive branch, and except on special missions such as ours, could not mess with the other officers. Despite these indignities, Regis never complained: neither about the humiliation, nor about his bruised legs, nor about being the only one with the courage to perform surgery. He fashioned instruments by paring down knives and straightening hooks, sterilized them in a blubber fire, and administered morphine to the patients. Acting alone, he went through the running putrefaction of de Brebeuf's rotted toes and the other men's limbs. The severed joints which he carried away fouled the entire beach where he buried them. The blood and vomit of the sick destroyed what clothing he had left. Yet his only comment was a polite acknowledgment two days later when it became clear that all would live.

Sir Basil led a party in scouting the island. They found a penguin rookery but no human life or sign of prior visits. Nonetheless, they brought back enough of the birds for us to vary our diet from seal meat and blubber. Cleanliness returned to our lives, and order to our existence. When, after eight days, we were again somewhat fit, it was decided that we would send a party back to sea in an attempt to reach a whaling station. Faber stayed on the island with de Brebeuf and the sick, as well as most of those in reasonably good health. They would be needed to make the camp work. Hawkeland, Regis, three seamen, and I returned to the ocean.

Regis and the sailors spent a day modifying the *Asp* before we sailed. He and the three seamen, a pair of Welshmen known as Parry One and Two, and a Yorkshireman named Healy who had once sailed these waters, bolted the *Cobra*'s masts inside the *Asp*'s keel to prevent her breaking her back in heavy seas. They cut down the other boat's mast and sail to make a mizzenmast and sail for us, giving us a jib, standing lug, and a small mizzen. In this strengthened longboat we were to cross the Antarctic waters and return with help. For a few days it seemed that we might succeed.

After a week the ocean came suddenly to life. It did so in the shape of the highest, broadest swells any man will ever suffer. These water dervishes rose from the surface and rolled across the sea. Fifty feet in height and three hundred yards long, these walls seemed to come at us, then they suddenly collapsed of their own weight and fell from sight.

Healy smiled knowingly and shouted, "Southern ocean rolls. And at that height, approaching a maximum, they're coming off a shallows."

"Couldn't the shallows be beneath the sea?" Sir Basil asked.

"Aye, sir. But with all due respect to your lordship, it ain't." Healy pointed to the sky. Above us a solitary bird soared and dipped. "A skay," the rating said. "And they don't never come more'n fi'teen mile out from land."

Heavy seas and our own weariness forced us to take three days to make that last leg. The first man to see land was Parry Two, who leaped to his feet shouting and waving wildly. We all moved about for a better view. Whether it was his sudden movement or our own, I do not know, but he unexpectedly pitched forward and was enveloped in the black sea. He had not even had time to scream.

Our second casualty was suffered when the *Asp* foundered on the rocks. She had been stronger than any of us. We were beyond omens and hope, but we all agreed silently that the destruction of our sturdy little home could only be an evil portent.

Once ashore, we took shelter in a cave, built a fire on our stove, ate, and slept. In the morning we set out to walk across Antarctica. After traveling only a mile, we came upon the turf and tussock nests of a flock of albatross. While Healy and I ran through the nests shouting and waving our hands, the others stole eggs, each of which yielded a twelve-pound chick. On the far side of the nests was a small beach where piles of driftwood were collected. These were spars washed ashore, remnants of earlier victims of the ice. We returned to our cave with the eggs and fuel. After gorging ourselves, we roasted enough meat for a ten-day journey and bundled the rest of the firewood. At last it seemed that nature had chosen to favor us.

I was wrong.

The weather became increasingly bad. It was not only the cold but also the wind on which it rode. The unrelenting wind found a way down my throat and into my belly, grasping my heart and testicles with icy fingers. The cold changed to mist within me, and scalded as it made its way through my extremities. Each step was an undeserved torture of the flesh. Our eyebrows froze solid, our tongues could not suck, and it was a Calvary to blink. Whatever we had done to offend man, or God if He existed, was being well repaid on this awful journey into a waste so cold that the heart breaks at its recollection.

We frequently took temporary shelter under random outcroppings of ice. These curvatures of snow and water extended like silver tongues and drooped over us. It seemed that they had been laid out to provide us only with a semblance of shelter, as we were always in the path of a vicious wind. But they were some refuge, however slight, and we thanked a provident nature when they appeared out of the mists.

When we awoke in the morning, Healy was dead, frozen in place. We silently agreed to leave him there. Parry One, who had been close to the other rating, rose and walked outside. We allowed him a few moments of solitude, then prepared to join him. At that moment we heard the wind rip loose several shards of ice. I ran to the mouth of the cave, and saw Parry a few feet from the entrance.

"Parry!" I screamed. As he turned, he saw me gesture toward the falling debris. A massive spear of ice slid off the side of the cave and sloped out toward him. He was too terror-stricken to run. I watched helplessly as the ice traveled completely through his body and impaled him. I was at his side in an instant, but it was too late. He looked at me quizzically, shuddered, and died.

Sir Basil and Lieutenant Regis joined me on the ice. "We should get him inside," Hawkeland said. Regis went into the cave for his axe and returned. I noticed for the first time that he was hobbling. Before I could speak, he began to swing at the ice spear which had gouged out Parry's body. When the ice was removed, Hawkeland and I lifted him and carried him inside. At that moment I asked Regis, "Are your feet all right?"

He smiled. "There was a bit of frostbite. It didn't hurt until I felt the comparative warmth of the cave. I'll be fine."

"Let's see your feet," Sir Basil said.

"They'll be fine, sir."

"Do as I tell you."

Regis sat down and, with great effort, pulled off his boots and what was left of his socks. Neither Sir Basil nor I would have offended him by offering to help. One look at his feet revealed that we could not have done so.

"Gangrene," Hawkeland said.

"Is it that bad?" Regis asked.

"At best. The left foot certainly, the right perhaps not yet."

"Then we must get on with it," I said. "The sooner we find a camp the better."

Regis shook his head. "I'll stay here." He looked to me. "But I am grateful."

Sir Basil said, "We'll have no schoolboy heroics. You can still stump

287

along, and I shall expect you to do so. If you die, you die. But there shall be no more about it."

Both Regis and I knew that further argument would be pointless. We nodded our agreement and the engineer tugged on his footgear. We began again.

We marched on for the rest of the day. Near evening we decided to make camp in the shadow of a berg which resembled the Matterhorn. Far beyond it was a mountain and at the top of that mountain the smoke of a camp. I recall that its effect on us was as ordinary as the words "a camp." We simply stood there for several minutes, not believing. Then we all broke down and cried.

There was no question of pressing on that afternoon. First we rested, although our encampment was not a quiet one that night. Instead we laughed and talked and planned. It was now only a matter of time. And distance.

For days we trudged. Regis fell farther and farther behind. Sir Basil and I began to take turns carrying him. This so wearied us that by the end of the fifth day, when we at last found another outcropping, we merely collapsed inside it.

For dinner we had some dry oatmeal and three cubes of sugar each. In celebration of the shelter's discovery, Sir Basil distributed strips of jerky that he had been saving for a special occasion. Outside the wind tore across the ice in a frenzy, having no purpose or direction other than to bring terror to our hearts.

Regis looked at his jerky a moment, then put it down. "I don't need this," he said with a smile. "The beggars on the mountain must have seen us. I'd best tell them where we are. I shall be outside a little while."

Before I could rise, Sir Basil extended his hand and I remained still. Regis rose slowly and walked to the tent flap. "Hallo," he called as the curtain fell behind him.

In a moment we were all asleep.

In one of the ironies of our travail, the climb, which should have been cruel, was a form of surcease. The angle of ascent was harsh, but contained enough outcroppings for us to find shelter at will. We rested and climbed. We would not die until we reached the top. Then we would have won.

We dragged ourselves on. What was left of our gloves shredded on the side of the mountain. Our faces were cut and our clothing slashed. Yet we pulled and shinnied and inched our way up the ice.

Until we smelled the fire. Hawkeland and I looked at one another, then literally scrambled the last hundred yards. We drew on that unknowable reservoir which each man possesses, and found it sufficient to propel us to the top. Sir Basil was first to the peak. He stood erect for an instant, then turned to greet me with a maniacal laugh. Hawkeland was still laughing wildly as he extended his hand and pulled me up. Then I too began to laugh. As we shrieked, the mountain roared its derision back at us. Sir Basil turned back to the fire, hooked his hands on his hips, listened to the echoing scorn, then doubled over with laughter. Suddenly he pitched backward down the mountainside. He should have fallen only a few feet, but, in another of the Antarctic's ironies, he hit a slight outcropping of ice. It should have broken his fall. Instead, he slid across it and plummeted down onto a boulder.

I scampered to him, stumbling and falling, finally reaching the place where he lay mortally wounded.

"We'll be all right," I said, cradling his head in my arms. "You'll see."

"No. You will see. But I will soon die." He coughed once, violently, blowing a wad of phlegm and blood over me. "Go back to the fire and wait," he said. "It will save you."

"You're coming with me."

He smiled faintly. "I've already forbidden schoolboy heroics. It doesn't matter a whit to me whether I die here or at the heat." He smiled again, more broadly now. "I may soon wish for the cold."

"I think not."

"You know, Peter, it's not the dying I mind. It's the giving up of life. God bless you." Then he was gone.

I listened to the horrible wind building to gale force. I knew that I lacked the strength to go back up the mountainside to the fire, so I used Sir Basil's body for warmth. He kept me alive that night, as he had so many other times. In the morning, I took the formula out of my coat (where I had carried it since abandoning the *Python*) and placed it inside Sir Basil's tunic. If anyone wanted it, let them come for it themselves. Then I buried him beneath stones and snow, and crawled back up the mountainside to sit by the fire and wait to die.

Chapter Fifteen

When I finished the diary, I invited Campion to read it. He was as downhearted as I that the formula was not given. I asked if he had any further information.

"A bit. Peter was picked up a day or two later by a field party from the Klausmundt expedition. They heard a strange sound and went to investigate, apparently thinking that it might be some new species of wildlife. As they approached, however, they realized that it was echoing laughter. They searched, found Peter, and took him back to their base."

"Wasn't it their campfire which he had found?"

"No one knows. He never discussed the ordeal, at least not to our knowledge. And as you know, except for a few sent back on a hospital ship in the summer of 'ninety-eight, the entire Klausmundt expedition was lost in the winter of 1900. Peter was on the ship, but I doubt that we could trace the others."

"I must reluctantly agree. You said the Painter made contact with a priest in Cairo."

"Teilhard de Chardin. I have spoken with him. He told me, under obedience, that he had no clue as to the location of the campfire or, even more troubling, why Fresnais, the Emperor's physician, would have mentioned him."

"They *had* met."

"Oh, yes. Just as Fresnais told Peter. Pierre Teilhard was flattered but bewildered. Whatever Fresnais saw in his fellow Jesuit, Peter did too. He kept in touch with de Chardin over the years, in one of those

290

taunting anti-clerical friendships which are all we allow our most intellectual youths.''

"You believe that the priest knows nothing? Do not be offended. It is
a fair question.''

"I agree. I told you that he responded in obedience.''

"I am familiar with your concept of the virtue. Well! The diary is interesting, but worth little. However, I must be fair. The capture itself
has been of great assistance to me. When you make your request, it will
be honored.''

I did not see Campion again until late in the World War. By then my
career had enjoyed, or suffered through, a number of violent fluctua-
tions, most caused by the leadership's inability to appreciate the inherent wisdom of Gallipoli. When he came to see me, he was a man
aged beyond his years. I knew, of course, that the Vatican had served as
a conduit for intelligence from all parties. And I knew that his Society
was the one group uniquely qualified to transmit and use this material.
I had no doubt that much of his weariness stemmed from such duties.

Campion was pleased that I remembered his fondness for cognac.
We shared a few quiet moments discussing the war, then I confessed,
"You have chosen a bad time to seek me out for a favor, if that is why
you are here.''

"It is.''

"Gallipoli, you see . . .''

"You can still be of assistance.''

"I have given my word.''

"We do not view the Hun as the ultimate evil. We believe that after
the war is over the Germans can be put on the proper track.''

"They can be crushed militarily, and then economically. Theirs is a
disease of the blood, a disease which makes them cry out for war.''

"That may be. But the Church does not view the Boche as the
greatest threat to its existence.''

"What is?''

"Communism.''

"I'll crush them next.''

"No doubt. But the danger is imminent.''

"I have no way to get any of your people out of Russia. That simple
bastard Nicholas has made too much of a mess for that.''

"We want to send someone in.''

"Perhaps. Perhaps not. May I ask why?''

"You have already said it. Nicholas has brought Russia to the brink. The communists will push the country over soon enough. Then there will be no place at all for the Church. Unless one among them, a man who has come to us for help, achieves power."

"One of your products?"

"No. That was one of our mistakes with Peter. We were too close to him to be objective. Except for Father Arkady, who made his own mistakes. No, this man approached us some time ago on a strictly business basis. Get him into Russia and he will help us. He knows of the Polish network, but that will not do. We need your help."

"You would deal with a communist?"

"I will deal with any dog who can help me."

"We are most flattered. But I must ask what this would do to England, the war effort."

"We are assured that a reorganized government would stand firm *and* have the people's backing. We believe that to be so."

I could not help but admire the priest. With one stroke he offered me the chance to repay my debt and reassert my claim to national leadership. He knew how closely the two were tied. And he was right about the war. The Russian people had no love for the Kaiser. A new regime could strengthen the Eastern front and assure our victory in the West. And the credit would be mine.

"Very well. How can I help?"

"The Germans have him. We can arrange his release through the Vatican, if you will give back the Boche two of their imprisoned spies."

"Done. But a question."

"Yes?"

"You mentioned one mistake with Peter? What was the other?"

"Not following his temperament. He was an artist. We thought choosing someone whose brother had been hanged by the Tsar was a wise idea. It was. And is. But not when the survivor is an emotional artist."

"This new man is detached?"

"When the Tsar hanged his brother, he merely continued studying for his university examinations."

"Detached indeed. What is his name?"

"Lenin."

ON THE ICE

Chapter Sixteen

The Concorde banked over New York Harbor before beginning its approach. McHenry could see the towers of Manhattan in the distance—not the romantic skyline of the movies, but the naked streets of the financial district where he had first survived, then prevailed. At that moment he recalled an event which occurred shortly after the announcement that he had become a partner of Ingersoll & Constance. A hospital had asked McHenry to join its board. Suspecting the hospital's reasons, he asked George Ingersoll's advice. "Yes," Ingersoll agreed, "they do want you because of your new-found wealth. But you will overcome that and be useful for other reasons. You have good blood." McHenry had always assumed that Ingersoll referred to his strength in rising through the firm. Now he knew.

There were, of course, other strengths as well. He had worked to retain the physical powers acquired in Special Forces. And there was the power of his mind. He needed that strength to maintain the realization of self which would enable him once again to prevail. He had been lost for days in the ground fog of the diary. Peter and Plum Blossom had obsessed his thoughts as the formula had fanned his desire for action. McHenry knew that he had to put everyone and everything but the formula out of his mind in order to prepare himself for the bitter struggle which would soon take place on the ice.

A tradition of Ingersoll & Constance was observed as McHenry came through the gate into customs. George Ingersoll's chauffeur, always dispatched to meet partners returning from overseas, greeted McHenry, took his baggage checks, and directed him to the illegally parked, undisturbed limousine. The return to his home would be equally traditional: George Ingersoll always left the same three gifts for returning partners.

During the ride into the city, McHenry's extraordinary mind made connections between all that the diary had taught him and all that he had experienced. The Jesuits would send a man for the formula, probably to hold it as ransom for a return to some standard of higher moral conduct. The Chinese would go after it, if only to salvage their faltering petroleum industry. And the British, sitting over the rapidly depleting North Sea reserves, would use McHenry to obtain the formula, then attempt to kill him.

His own reason for seeking the formula was much more personal. That he would find it, decode it, and return safely he did not doubt. Only *his* mind could make the connections necessary to do all three. From the diary, he alone had learned what to do to break the Jesuit code. Not even the Society could do that. Once the key was obtained, he would learn how to relate it to Chinese petroleum, which undoubtedly formed the basis for the formula. Peking could not do that. And Sharp, McHenry knew, would follow them to the ice. For that reason, he had already begun to formulate the plan that would enable him to kill Dole's butcher. Only he could do it all. And he would.

Simon entered his condominium apartment and walked to the table in the living room overlooking the East River. True to tradition, George had sent the Office Book, a summary of all important developments which had occurred during the returning partner's absence; a bottle of George's favorite champagne, Charles Taittinger; and a dozen of his favorite flowers, the camellia, named for the man who had discovered the flower in the Philippines and later perfected the strain. The botanist, George Kamel, was, of course, a Jesuit.

Chapter Seventeen

Simon McHenry was seated in Vultan's study. Elspeth sat in a Queen Anne chair facing him, flanked by Cartier and Bresnau. Vultan stood by a three-dimensional map of Antarctica. Whatever McHenry had read about the famous study, it was not what he had expected. After a moment he realized why. There were no pictures, no reminders at all of Katherine Bates Vultan. McHenry immediately understood why. He had been terribly hurt by a loss suffered at the outset of a love affair; how much more painful it must have been for Vultan to be deserted, even because of death, after a splendid marriage.

Vultan waited by the map. When the initial formalities were concluded, he would listen to McHenry, then give the plan of action. He knew that it would be important to determine how McHenry took direction. Vultan had been told, and a quick introduction had confirmed, that Simon McHenry was a man who moved easily in the civilized world but was at heart a loner, capable of great cruelty. He was, Vultan thought, much like himself. That would make it more difficult, when the time came, to kill him. More difficult, not painful.

McHenry began slowly. He knew that Vultan and his men had been vetted by both Dole and Langley. They had been shown the part of the diary dealing with Antarctica and had been given an outline of the problem. McHenry would tell them their specific mission.

"As you are aware," he said, "we are going after a cache left by Sir Basil Hawkeland's ill-fated expedition to the South Pole. Somewhere between their landing place in Antarctica—and we don't know where that was—and the place where the Painter was rescued—and we don't know where that was—a decision was made to leave on Hawkeland's corpse a small metal tube. Sir Basil died nearly a century ago. We must find his body and return with the tube.

"There are some references to position and direction in the diary. Unfortunately, the references were not original with the writer, who could not handle navigational instruments, but were derived from the comments of others. Those others had just endured a fierce naval battle, drifted thousands of miles in a battered ship, been trapped in an ice pack, rowed through a frozen sea, and trekked overland in Antarctica to the place where they died. Add to their wretched state the probable unreliability of their much-abused instruments, and we are left with the conclusion that we have no accurate knowledge of any position at any time."

"If I may," Vultan said. McHenry nodded. The explorer pointed to the map. "I suggest we take what little we do know and work backward. I can make a good guess as to the original landing site but would rather not. We know that Hawkeland died near or on a mountain, at the top of which was a fire. We also know from their laughter that the discovery of the fire was the final irony of their expedition. That means that it was an abandoned campsite, or a mirage, or I know where they were.

"If it was an abandoned campsite, the fire would not have been alive. In any event, it would have been a sign of human life in the area. There would have been no call for laughter.

"If it had been a mirage, it is unlikely that Hawkeland would have talked about the fire saving Peter. It is possible, of course. Both men were weak, perhaps delirious, and certainly longing for both rescue and the rapture of freezing to death.

"But I believe that neither of these theories is correct. I believe that they reached Mount Erebus, a massive and still active volcano."

"Then we start at Erebus?" Elspeth asked. It was the first time that she had spoken since Cartier and Bresnau had met her plane from London. She had not even looked at McHenry.

"You have actually raised two questions," Vultan said. "First, no, we do not start at Erebus. The Antarctic is not a continent like any other. It was once part of the great southern mass called Gondwanaland, as our hemisphere was then part of Laurasia. Before that, one continent, Pangaea, embraced the earth. All of the continents but one have, to a large extent, solidified themselves. The Antarctic shifts noticeably.

"Assuming that they did scale Erebus, remember that it is an active volcano. Hawkeland may have since been covered with material from inside. A tremor may have dropped *him* inside. Or the burial site may have slid down off the mountain. So we will start at another place."

"You said that I raised two issues, Mr. Vultan."

"Yes. Well, ahh, if I may be indelicate, nothing will kill you more quickly than copulating on the ice."

Elspeth began to rise, but McHenry moved her back into her seat. "The lady is coming," he said, "because the security of the mission requires it. There is nothing physical between us."

Vultan said, "When two people are as attractive as you, and you tell me that there is nothing physical between you, I can only assume that you are homosexuals, which is unlikely, or that there has been a great deal between you. Because that is undoubtedly the case—as sufficiently evidenced by Mr. McHenry's tone—I am required to believe that you hate one another. I will not bore you with a lecture on the difficulties of what we are about to attempt. Hatred in a small tent is much more intolerable than poor sanitation or a split canvas. Hatred cannot be remedied except by leaving it behind."

Elspeth said, "I have no hatred for Mr. McHenry."

"Perhaps not. But Mr. McHenry has said nothing, and he seems very much like a man capable of raging hatreds."

"I am indeed," McHenry said. "But Elspeth is coming for security reasons."

Everyone realized that he had not said that he did not hate Elspeth.

Vultan nodded and said, "Very well. And with regard to the tube, can you decode its contents?"

In an instant McHenry had some realization of why Vultan was so highly regarded. There was nothing in the section of the diary given to Vultan which would have revealed the existence of a code. Nor would Langley have told him. Vultan had merely assumed that the only thing small enough to fit in the tube that could be valuable enough to launch the mission would be a coded message. And he had phrased his question to elicit the greatest amount of information from McHenry.

"No," Simon said. "I can't decode it now. But I will discover how."

Chapter Eighteen

Sullivan & Cromwell is one of the most respected law firms on Wall Street. Its first great success was achieved when William Nelson Cromwell, an oddly shaped man with crossed and protruding eyeballs, helped Theodore Roosevelt secure Panama's allegiance to America.

After World War I, the firm came under the direction of John Foster Dulles and, later, his brother Allen. The latter became a highly placed intelligence agent who masterminded the surrender of Italy through the Vatican. He subsequently became director of the Central Intelligence Agency. Foster, of course, became Secretary of State. He was a dedicated anti-communist and devout Presbyterian. His son Avery is a Jesuit.

McHenry had frequently come into contact with the firm through his work with Ingersoll & Constance. He used that connection to arrange a meeting with a member of Sullivan & Cromwell's estates department. McHenry knew that Teilhard de Chardin had been exiled by the Church to New York, forbidden to speak or publish. He had died while in residence at Manhattan's Saint Ignatius Church. It was McHenry's belief that the law firm had handled matters for de Chardin's estate. He needed some source, some clue, to lead him to the key to the code.

The partner in the estates department did not provide it. He knew only that the priest's papers had been boxed and shipped, decades before, to the Jesuit retreat house, Saint Francis Borgia on the Hudson.

McHenry thanked the lawyer, left the office, and began the drive north to Westchester County. While he was en route, the attorney, as a courtesy, called the superior of the retreat house. The priest, just as courteously, thanked him. He did not bother to mention that he had already received a coded telex from Rome telling him to expect McHenry. Rome did not know what McHenry wanted, but it did know from Father Campion's yellowed files that the diary referred to de Chardin.

Pierre Teilhard de Chardin occupies a unique place among modern Jesuits. After his ordination as a priest, he refused a chaplain's commission and served during World War I as a stretcher bearer in the French army. At the request of his regiment he was made Chevalier of the Légion d'Honneur. The Society criticized him for not accepting the officer's post. His work as a geologist and paleontologist led to his election to the Académie des Sciences. The Jesuits forbade him to publish his works. Leopold Senghor said that "Teilhard's thought has enabled us to dispense with Marxism . . ." The Society reviled him as a communist. He loved France almost as much as he loved God. The Vatican condemned him to die in exile.

In some ways his case was reminiscent of Galileo's. Contrary to legend, the Church did not condemn Galileo for teaching that the earth revolved around the sun. Indeed, years before, the Church had honored Copernicus for establishing the existence of the heliocentric universe. Galileo was condemned for saying that where scripture and science disagreed, scripture was wrong. The churchmen who condemned him had not read him. The Jesuit cardinal who prosecuted him said that there could be no conflict between scripture and science; there could only be priests who read scripture incorrectly.

Centuries later, priests who had read de Chardin condemned him erroneously after deciding that his work and scripture conflicted. His volumes cannot be condensed here. One of his thoughts can be—that there is a unity of God and man and nature. That was enough to terrify the curialists. To them, de Chardin was preaching the long-condemned heresy of pantheism, a doctrine which lowered God to the level of man.

In fact, the Jesuit was arguing that man could reach toward God if he loved.

The priest was condemned. After decades of renowned study, he was ordered to go to New York to live out his days. He was forbidden to print or discuss his work. Publishers and academies offered him access to the world. A Jesuit, a man of obedience, he remained silent. Pierre Teilhard de Chardin died alone, thousands of miles from his home and work, on April 10, 1955. It was Easter Sunday, the Day of Resurrection. The final entry in his diary was from Bernanos: "Every spiritual adventure is a Calvary."

The man who most influenced his choice of paleontology was a long-dead Jesuit named Athanasius Kircher. Kircher invented the magic lantern, wrote the first treatise on hypnotic phenomena, invented the first alphabet for the deaf and dumb, and wrote the first cartographic representation of ocean currents. His legend so influenced de Chardin that the Frenchman sought to emulate him.

During his years of study, de Chardin had worked in Tibet, Egypt, and China. He frequently found it necessary to write in code. The Society had its own systems, as might have been expected. One of the first modern codes—that is, one based on letter groupings and frequency—was devised centuries ago by the same Jesuit, Athanasius Kircher. Variations on this type of code were employed by the Society as part of its efforts to protect intelligence gathered for the papacy and other Catholic sovereigns.

During World War II, very few men knew of even the existence of the German code Ultra and the Japanese code Purple. Fewer still could decipher them. One such man was Colonel William Freedman, a leading American cryptanalyst. The Vatican caused him to be visited frequently by Father William Hoffman, a priest with close ties to the Jesuits. Hoffman was also a cousin of Franklin Delano Roosevelt, one of Roosevelt's few Catholic relatives. Colonel Freedman became so concerned over the possibility of Hoffman obtaining information for the Jesuits that he was forced to ask the President to end his cousin's visits.

In the centuries between Athanasius Kircher and Ultra, the sophistication of codes had grown greatly, as had the abilities of cryptanalysts to break those codes. As a result, by the end of the nineteenth century, Jesuit codes were no longer based on letter groupings but on intellectual conceits. The language key was frequently simple. Before it could be broken, however, it was necessary to know the private theoretical construct on which a priest had built his code. Simon McHenry's problem was compounded by the fact that Fresnais, the physician, had based his secret writing on the thought processes of de Chardin. But de Chardin had not known that he was creating the basis for a code.

The principal business of a retreat house is set out in its name. It functions as a place into which one can retreat from the distractions of a materialistic society. Such a facility was the house of Saint Francis Borgia. Named for the third Superior General of the Jesuits, a man whose family did much to introduce the Society to the pleasures of power, it was situated on a mountainside overlooking the Hudson River. The four buildings and thirty-two acres had been a gift to the Society from Donald von Franz, the first Catholic Morgan partner. The entrance was a mile-long avenue set between giant fir trees. The trees slanted and came imperceptibly closer as the drive turned gently toward the main house. In the days before air conditioning, this ground plan guaranteed that whatever breeze there was would be carried along the trees to the main house. McHenry knew that the superior's quarters would be at the exact end of the approach.

The main house had been renamed Sherman Hall. McHenry was not surprised. Nor was it unexpected that the reception area would display a fine oil of William Tecumseh Sherman, soldier and atheist. At the time that he became Chief of Staff of the United States Army, his son was ordained a Jesuit priest. From that day forward, all Jesuit outposts in lands administered by the territorial departments of the army received special protection.

The lay brother who served as porter admitted McHenry and showed him into a small parlor. McHenry knew the procedure. He would be allowed to wait until he became nervous and *then* would be admitted to the superior's presence. He smiled his thanks and closed his eyes quickly, so that the brother would notice. The porter advised the superior of the guest's attitude, and the priest sent him back for McHenry. As the two men walked down the freshly waxed corridor, McHenry took in the universal smells of the rectory: lemon polish, candle wax, old books, and soap. Always missing were fresh air and flowers. Except in the superior's office.

"Mr. McHenry, I am Father Shildkraut." The Jesuit's voice was slightly accented. He remained seated, gesturing the visitor into a facing chair. McHenry was pleased with the priest's stiffness. He resented the false bonhomie of the younger clergy. Priests, regardless of their demeanor, considered themselves a breed apart. McHenry was content to leave them there.

He felt a soft wind from an open window. "A lovely breeze," he said.

"Yes. It always seems to be cool in this part of the house."

"How lucky for you." He looked away from the window. "You're from Germany?"

"A long time ago. But still the accent." He smiled. "Do you know the country?"

"Not as much as I would like."

"Westphalia?"

"Yes. Your home?"

"Paderborn, to be precise. Best known for a castle which achieved an unfortunate renown during World War Two. Webelsburg, it was. Each year the highest officers of the SS, the so-called Chapter of the Order, met for a ritual of spiritual exercises."

"Like the Jesuits."

"Regrettably, yes. Himmler was, for whatever reason, a great admirer of the Society."

"And how did the Society feel about him?"

"We were condemned by Hitler. An honor unique among all the orders of the Church. And we tried to show our appreciation. One young Jesuit, among many who served secretly, was infiltrated into the SS unit at Webelsburg. He sent the Allies enough facts and the Germans enough misinformation to save thousands of Jews marked for extermination."

"Pius must not have liked that."

"Even the Pope cannot order a Jesuit to hate."

"Was he killed—your friend?"

"The Nazis learned who he was and what he was doing. They chained him up in a dungeon and began to whittle away at his body. The Germans cut off a toe, hacked out a chunk of leg, stripped off some skin. A little bit each day. A doctor kept him alive, and the soldiers made bets on how long he would last. They had cut off up to the stumps of his thighs when the Americans shelled the castle. The Nazis left him there to bleed to death. . . . But you did not come here to be reminded of how little we work at being God's children."

"Do you know why I am here?"

"The lawyer called. It has something to do with Father de Chardin."

303

McHenry assumed that the Jesuit would know even more of the reason for his visit. He dared not do otherwise. As a result, he followed the agent's rule of basing his lie in the truth. "Indirectly. I am an investment banker with Ingersoll and Constance."

"Our old friends."

"I thought that you would know of them. Through them I have a client with an interest in an offshore Chinese property. We are, quite frankly, concerned that certain minerals allegedly present in great quantities may have been recently salted onto the property. There are only scattered reports dating from before World War II. Teilhard de Chardin conducted many paleontological and geological studies near the site of the asset. We hope that his reports might indicate whether or not we are looking at a valuable claim."

"Father de Chardin's diaries are here, of course. The Church, as you know, forbade their publication during his life."

"Surely everything has since been published. I believe that it's been decades since he died on Easter."

The priest smiled at the irony. "Yes, years. His death resurrected everything but the diaries. He began them at the Jesuit house in Peking, Chabanel Hall. We have them. But they are really of a spiritual nature."

"I assure you, Father, I am much too thoroughly backslid to be corrupted by the pyrotechnics of de Chardin's mind."

"Of course. I will have Brother Santino arrange an office for you. If there is anything you wish—coffee, notepaper, cigarettes—Brother Santino will get it for you."

"You're very kind." McHenry stood and asked, "Will I see you again before I leave?"

"I doubt it. This promises to be a hectic afternoon."

McHenry patiently sifted through the papers. As the priest had warned, many of the entries were of a purely spiritual nature, most in French and a few in Latin. He had no difficulty in translating any of them but found nothing of value. Near the bottom of the second box he discovered a letter in English postmarked Hartford, Connecticut. It read as follows:

Dear Father de Chardin:

On behalf of the Hartford Accident & Indemnity, I express our thanks that you have chosen us to write the insurance for your expedition. I must

304

say that I am more in sympathy with your American colleagues who seek our underwriting than with your disregard of our coverage. Perhaps it is that you rely upon other forms of protection.

I do envy you your return to China. The Orient has always held a special fascination for me. One of my most prized possessions is a set of five carved Chinese figures. The most engaging of these is an old man—Hsan-hsing, a benevolent old god, I assure you. May he be with you on your journey.

Now that I am inching my way up in the company, I shall have time to study the letters you have promised. This too is in keeping with my admiration for Chinese thought; they insist (quite rightly) that two or three days without study and life loses its savor.

The same result follows, I suppose, from doing the wrong work. I once told a friend that with a family my job was "to keep the fireplace burning and the music box churning and the wheels of the baby's chariot turning and that sort of thing."

Not that this is bad work at all. I could have gone another way, but did not. There are times when what I do is stimulating and rewarding, both intellectually and materially. And there are other times. I will save your letters for those other times.

I had a friend, Ronald Lane Latimer, who disappeared into the Orient some time ago. You may encounter him, although I doubt it. I told him that the real world as seen by an imaginative man may very well seem like an imaginative construction. You, as a paleontologist, must be careful to remember this. Do not be too quick to create intellectual constructs out of the earth.

> Children picking up our bones
> Will never know that these were once
> As quick as foxes on the hill. . . .

And here I am, sermonizing you. After all, I truly

Here the page was torn. The next sheet was evidently the Jesuit's reply.

Dearest Friend:

Thank you for both the quickly issued policy (without which our American backers would never have let us leave), and the sermonizing. You were right throughout.

The intellectual constructs *are* the greatest danger. My only hope is to unite man to God. My only fear is that the Church will not understand and suppress my works. If such is to be the case, *ita:* so be it.

I too look forward to the exchange of letters. They are, for me, in deserts and on mountainsides, a favorite form of relaxation. I must confess, however, that my superiors have not always agreed. As long ago as my days as a novice, my letters were scrutinized and sometimes sent back by my superiors. But I did not complain. I am sworn to obedience, as one must be in God's service. When a missive was rejected, I wrote another, or rethought the first. Nothing was lost by obedience.

You, of course, cannot live by such strictures. You are, after all, a poet, and therefore

The next page was missing.

McHenry went through the remaining papers. He did not change his schedule, nor did he make any notes. He finished at six, thanked Brother Santino, then left for the city.

"Do you think he learned anything?" Father Shildkraut asked Santino.

"He was a difficult man to read."

"Then what do we know? That he must have derived some clues from the Painter's diary. That de Chardin figured in the book. That he knew enough to trace Father Teilhard here. And he is very bright." The priest breathed deeply. "I must let Father Halloran know. Would you be so kind, Brother?"

"Of course, Father." Brother Santino walked across the floor, opened the door to the radio room, and crossed back to where Father Shildkraut was seated. Then Santino picked up the priest's legless body.

Chapter Nineteen

Xavier was seated by the window of his bedroom when Father Halloran entered. The Superior General of the Society of Jesus crossed to the Pope's chair, knelt, and kissed the Pontiff's ring. Xavier embraced the priest and bade him be seated. He handed a sheet of paper to Halloran and asked, "Do you know their names?"

He looked down the list and said, "Yes. These are some of the most influential Catholic laymen in America. Politicians, contractors, insurance salesmen. All powerful."

"I know. Each year we receive a list of America's most generous Irish and are asked to name them Knights of Malta."

"I wonder what the poor Maltese ever did to be so besmirched."

"My point exactly." Xavier reached for the list, signed it, and dropped it onto his night stand. A pigeon settled on the window ledge and began to coo. The Pope raised a finger, and Halloran stood and closed the window. "You know, Charles, each evening the pigeons come and sit on the ledge. When we hear the cooing, we remember Saint Francis walking in the woods delivering his sermon to the birds. At such moments we are haunted by the beauty of the least of God's creatures. Then we think, What filthy birds!"

"Not only in faith and morals is Your Holiness infallible."

"And what of your plan, Charles? Is it without error?"

"The fault is not in the plan."

"Then there is a flaw."

"A leak."

"Your man in China has been exposed."

"No. The fault is here at home."

"Robustelli?"

"Yes."

"You are a hard man, Charles. I've told you that. You do not say perhaps, or that you suspect, or that you fear. Is there no room for error in your calculations?"

"No. I tapped the cardinal's phone."

"How *dare* you? Charles, the man is a prince of the Church."

"Your Holiness is too forgiving. Cardinal Robustelli would destroy you, drive you from the papacy, and turn the Church back a thousand years. I will do whatever needs to be done to stop him."

"*Whatever?*"

"Your Holiness has set limits. They will not be exceeded by those operating directly under me."

"We commend you, Charles. You have parsed moral liability into the smallest possible sections."

"If Your Holiness wishes to know what my field priests must do to stay alive—"

"We do *not* wish any harm to come to any man."

"Robustelli and his people will be watched. When we know the entirety of the plan, we will act."

"No, Charles, you will do nothing. *We* will act. You will tell me what you learn and what you plan. The final decision will be ours. And the guilt."

"There will be no guilt."

"*We will decide.*"

"*Ita!*"

* * *

307

Father Agnelli left Rome's Leonardo da Vinci airport for Paris. He was dressed in the simple black soutane which is the acceptable travel garb for priests in Italy. He carried only an inexpensive overnight bag and his breviary. The fact that he was hatless was not the occasion for conversation that it might once have been. He arrived unnoticed at Orly and went to a men's room. Once inside he entered a stall, locked it, and changed into a cheap black suit, white shirt, and black clip-on tie. His instructions had been to make himself as inconspicuous as possible, and he believed, correctly, that nothing would be less noticeable than another American seminarian. He stuffed his cassock into the bag and put the breviary on top of it. There would be no opportunity to say the prayers of the Divine Office. He did not consider it a matter for confession.

In Paris, Agnelli went to a pension on the Rue Brey. He was certain that he had not been followed.

Luigi Mancini followed Father Agnelli to his pension, then walked to the small flat which he kept two blocks away. An intensely devout but not terribly bright former soldier in the Swiss Guards, Mancini knew where Agnelli would go next, and when. He would follow him. It was the most important assignment of his life, and it caused him to laugh out loud in anticipation. Standing at attention, holding a halberd to impress visitors, that had not been the glorious service to God that the youthful Mancini had dreamed of performing. This assignment, and the secrets that had been entrusted to him, these were the actions of which sainthood was made. And he wanted to be a saint. He lived a good life, honored the Pope, loved the Church, and possessed precisely the spirit of obedience that would have made him dear to Charles Halloran.

The Superior General of the Jesuits had suspected from the beginning that there would be a leak in the Chinese operation. He had to assume that it would originate in the Pope's household and flow to Robustelli. To trace the leak, Halloran turned to an alumnus of the worker-priest movement.

Father Ignazio Terone had first been attracted to the Church in the 1950s. Those were the halcyon days of the worker-priest movement, a concept which sent hundreds of clergymen among the ranks of laborers. The Church had taught for centuries that work was noble, *but* . . . It was no sin to work in an office on Sunday, but *servile* work on the Sabbath was mortally sinful. Christ loved the poor, but the Pope heaped honors and titles on the wealthy. The duality of standards worked into every aspect of life and was threatening to destroy the Church's grip on the European poor. The worker-priest movement was launched and at the moment of its greatest success was suppressed by Pius XII. By then Ignazio Terone was a Jesuit seminarian, a youth learning to be both a priest and a telephone lineman. The Society had continued his dual training despite the papal ban on the movement. The intention was not to go against the Pope's wishes but to give the youth a skill he could pass on to the poor in rapidly developing mission lands. The mission to which he was assigned was a leper colony in Jakarta. There he met Father Charles Halloran. The younger priest so impressed Halloran that when he became Superior General of the Society, Terone was one of two men he immediately chose to be his secretaries.

Placing the tap had been simplicity itself. Halloran had Terone climb the pole outside Robustelli's residence, split two wires in the relay box, and disappear. When the static became intolerable, one of the cardinal's secretaries telephoned for a repairman. No one was expected to, or did, pay any attention to a slightly overweight middle-aged uniformed technician. In the basement Terone pulled a screwdriver from his utility belt; he also palmed a bugging device known as a Universal, a plastic bit with five bitch receptacles. He slipped it onto the appropriate switching device, connected each of the housing's five male lines, then tightened the Universal. It appeared to be merely a plastic connecting device.

Terone shut the box, went upstairs, and asked to be taken to the garden. There he saw the utility pole which housed Robustelli's phone box. The young priest let Terone out into the alley, where he climbed the pole, opened the box, replaced the frayed wires, and attached a relay for the Universal. Once again it would appear that the box contained only normal equipment.

Father Halloran continued to hope that there would be no leak; but he had known in his heart that there would be. He had also hoped that if there was a leak, it would be one of the ancient housekeeping nuns, a devout unlearned woman who could have her head turned by a few moments in Robustelli's august presence. He knew the words the cardinal would use: "Dearest sister in Christ. The catechism is gone. Rabbis speak from our pulpits. All discipline has been removed from the schools. Ecumenism is a code word for communism. Even the habit of your order has been shortened. The Holy Father's own staff betrays him. For the sake of the Church we both love so much . . ."

Halloran could hear the words and see the nun being recruited. That was the leak his heart said was there. But intellectually he knew that it would be someone higher up. He had been disappointed to learn that it was Agnelli. Disappointed, but not surprised. He was too old for that.

The tap had told him how Agnelli would travel, when he would leave, and where he would go. Halloran's man would be waiting.

Luigi Mancini stood in a doorway on the Rue Brey. Above him the street emptied out onto a major avenue where the constant crowds would give him cover. He preferred to follow Agnelli; it was safer. He could have waited at the priest's destination, but there was always the chance of a last-minute change in plans. This way he would be certain and follow the priest on foot through the streets of Paris to the Louvre.

Achille Marchant, like Ignazio Terone, had entered the seminary during the height of the worker-priest movement. Unlike Terone, he thought the movement, and the people it was meant to serve, quite bothersome. He had been chosen by the archbishop of Paris to study in Rome, where he came to the attention of Monsignor Robustelli, then a rising professor of theology. The seminarian possessed all the qualities which would have endeared him to Robustelli. He was brilliant, but parochial; devout, but disenchanted with mankind; and he viewed the Church as a vehicle for his personal salvation, a vehicle which he cared to share with as few as possible.

After Marchant was ordained, Robustelli arranged for him to be sent back to France to work as a museum guard, in a union which was heavily communist. The monsignor did not approve of the worker-priest movement, but was already planting people throughout the Church in preparation for the moment when his strange view of Catholicism would be unleashed on mankind.

The assignment fitted Marchant perfectly. It allowed him a lifetime of reading and enjoying the works of beauty honored in the Louvre. He was freed of the necessity of baptizing squalling children born to illiterates, excused from fawning over parishioners in the hope of shaking them loose from their cash, set free from having to sit endlessly in the confessional while the weak coughed out their failings.

When the worker-priest movement was abolished, Achille Marchant resigned from the Archdiocese of Paris and stayed on at the museum. Robustelli had assured him that such a step was necessary, and that he remained in the state of grace. Freed of the intellectual and social constraints of the movement, Marchant rose through the museum's ranks.

It was not at all difficult for him to arrange to make a special tape for Father Agnelli.

The Pope's secretary had been told to go to Marchant's office. There he would pick up a cassette which was ostensibly one of the recorded lectures on the "Mona Lisa." Hundreds of tourists rented them each day. It would attract no attention. And it would be safer than communicating by telephone. Cardinal Robustelli had become concerned that his phones were being tapped. It was inevitable. Rome itself was becoming unsafe. They were too near the final steps of their mission to take chances. And it was certainly a risk to allow the Pope's secretary any contact with Robustelli's staff. A few days of vacation were in order.

Agnelli took the cassette to the gallery where the "Mona Lisa" was displayed. He walked around the painting for the prearranged time, absorbed the message, then inconspicuously made his way back to Marchant's office and surrendered the tape. Then he left.

Luigi Mancini knew the passwords that would cause Marchant to give him the tape. He loitered in the halls until Agnelli had returned the cassette, then walked toward the priest's office. Once admitted, he said, " 'I am the shepherd.' "

" 'My flock knows me,' " said Marchant.

" 'And I know my flock.' "

The tape was handed over and Mancini left. Once outside, he flagged a taxi and gave directions to his pension. He could not have been happier.

Father Agnelli did not know that he had been observed throughout his visit to the Louvre by a German-Swiss named Hans Schiller. That was how Schiller had planned it. He was an experienced counterintelligence agent, and too knowledgeable about his craft to allow himself to be spotted by either the priest or Mancini. He allowed Agnelli to return to his pension and followed Mancini, certain that he had the tape.

Hans Schiller was the epitome of a European security agent. As a youth he had served in the Wehrmacht and been awarded the Iron Cross Second Class, the same decoration which Hitler had worn throughout his career. Discharged in Germany, Schiller had stayed on and worked throughout the period of initial recovery. In 1956 he returned to Switzerland and entered a university. It took five years and seven hearings before he was officially found to be free of Nazi taint and forgiven for the youthful exuberance which had led him to enlist. Armed with his degree and citizenship, he entered intelligence work.

A brilliant agent, competent administrator, and ruthless executioner, he had been assigned to follow Mancini. It was to be Schiller's option whether he picked up the tape himself or allowed the former Swiss Guard to do it. He had left the task to Mancini, allowed him time to return to his pension, and then went up the stairs. In his right hand he carried a small trunk. His left hand was in his pocket. He placed the trunk on the landing, knocked gently, then stepped to one side. Schiller was facing away, to the right, when the door opened. Mancini never saw the hypodermic needle which Schiller plunged into his arm.

Father Halloran took the package and weighed it in his hand as he sat down. "Thank you," he said to Hans Schiller.

"Of course."

"What about Mancini?"

"Safely stored; I carried him away in a small trunk."

"He was not harmed?"

"Your directions were followed scrupulously, Charles. He is unconscious but easily revived. Although from what I'm told of his intelligence, no one could tell the difference." He lit a cigarette and said, "You should have let me kill him."

"It was not necessary."

"He betrayed the Pope."

"He is a slow-witted youth, easily subverted by Robustelli."

"Who will wonder where he is. A cover could have been set up if you had let me kill him."

"A cover has already been established. A bad cold which will keep Mancini in his flat for a few days. By then we should be finished."

"If the tape is helpful. What is on it, Charles?"

"If I knew, I wouldn't need you."

"Do not revile me, Charles. The things that I do to—what?—earn my daily bread, such things are necessary in the real world. A world which you successfully avoid here."

"For your sake, Hans, I hope you never learn just how barbaric my real world is."

That night Halloran played the tape again and again. And for the first time in his adult life he cried himself to sleep.

Chapter Twenty

Marshal Kiying was seated in the rear of the room. He wished to do nothing, say nothing that would detract from Colonel Feng's excellent presentation. Lung and Feng had gone over it many times before, but this was the final, most detailed review. And, as had happened at each previous meeting, Kiying was able to study the differences between the two men. Feng, the rationalist, explaining weather patterns, supply coordination, communication techniques. Lung, the emotional soldier, wanting only to cut through details and jump into action. As he opened his second pack of cigarettes that morning, Kiying thought again that he had formulated the only possible plan. Vultan would obtain the formula and kill Lung. If there had been any doubt of the plan's desirability, it was being dispelled by the dialogue he heard that morning.

"After leaving the People's Republic," Feng said, "you will fly an evasive path to Antarctica. Because we are going to drop you in, it is important that the plane not be spotted. We will, therefore, route it beyond the Ross Sea, which would normally be the best turning point. A non-evasive drop would turn inland over McMurdo Sound, then over Ross Island to Mount Erebus. Instead, remaining above spotting altitude, the transport will fly farther south to the Great Ice Barrier, then northwest to Mount Erebus. The plane will continually occupy a center air lane between various national scientific camps and areas where outlying stations are established.

"As you know, there are no military installations in Antarctica. What radar is present is purely scientific. It is neither capable of nor programmed for searching out high-flying military transports. You will be in no danger until the plane descends for your jump.

"Although we know that the Vultan party is making for Mount Erebus, we see no reason for you to destroy yourself or your men on a similar trek. Why Vultan himself is undertaking the march is beyond me. But he is. You will be waiting at the shadowed side of the volcano.

When Vultan obtains the formula, *and comes down from the mountain,* you will take it from him."

"Why not attack him on the mountain?"

"*Because,* Major, he is a dedicated anti-communist. He would throw the formula, and himself, into the volcano before he would allow you to take it from him."

"But surely a surprise attack—"

"There can be no guarantee of *any* attack succeeding. Vultan has spent decades surviving as both an explorer *and* an agent. His aides are little more than trained killers. And McHenry has shown himself to be capable of studied savagery. You *will* take the formula when the Vultan party *descends* from the mountain."

"Yes, sir. You said there was no danger until the drop."

"We will put you and your supplies down as close to Erebus as possible. In those conditions, however, there can be no certainty that you will not drop into an ice chasm, a water pocket, or some other hazard which we can neither scout for nor anticipate. The two men we are putting down with you have shown themselves to be excellent. Their experience in Tibet has readied them. Hopefully, our training has prepared you."

"It has, sir."

"Then nothing remains but to wish you luck."

Walking down the corridors of their headquarters building, Feng realized that Kiying was thinking, and so he said nothing. It was just as well, he thought, that his chief's mood precluded conversation. Feng was convinced that they were sending the buffoon to his death. He was also convinced that Kiying could not have undertaken such a plan without a full awareness of its inevitable conclusion. That meant that the marshal either believed the mission to be a fool's errand or he had an alternative means of obtaining the information. Feng did not know which of the possibilities was correct.

Kiying was pleased that his aide was silent as they walked to his office. He knew that now that the plan was operational, Feng would narrow his concerns and look for a chance to express them. Until this moment, it had all been a projection, a possibility, and Feng knew enough not to question Kiying's plans. But at the end of that day's briefing they were moving into the field, and the colonel could not help but wonder why Kiying was sending the moronic Lung to his death without an alternate source of information. All of which meant that Feng might ask about Vultan.

Viator Vultan was the marshal's greatest achievement. Kiying had been the first Chinese commissar assigned to Albania, and his message of a system of communism even purer than Moscow's had won the boy to him forever. Kiying knew that an intellectual fire lighted in youth was almost impossible to extinguish. And he knew that he alone could handle Vultan. If he died without ever using the Albanian, Kiying would still be content. He would have placed him in the highest circles of the Central Intelligence Agency. That alone was the greatest coup. To secretly use him now would be the supreme victory. To share the information would lead to too many inquiries as to other, similar agents. Entire networks could be destroyed in the joy of discovering secret assets. No, he would not reveal anything to anyone, not even Feng.

It was not an easy decision. There was his genuine respect for Feng's intellect. More important, however, was his true affection for the young colonel. Both were lonely men in a lonely profession. They shared a love for Chinese poetry and philosophy. Both were students in a country which only periodically valued intellectual achievement. Kiying often thought that if he had married he would have wanted Feng for a son. The two men had reached a rare passage in human feelings: they could divine one another's thoughts and each anticipate the other's intellectual needs. They had gone from superior and subordinate to co-workers to dear friends to men with a deep relationship, a sharing born out of their loneliness, elevated by their respect, and totally free of sexuality.

For these reasons it would hurt deeply not to be able to share the news of Vultan with Feng. It would hurt even more to reveal the information, however, because, as Kiying had known from the first, Feng was a Jesuit.

Feng operated alone. Other Jesuits knew at least the name of their bishop, but Feng's position was too vulnerable to permit even that limited knowledge. He was entirely isolated, without the spiritual or emotional support of any other priest. He could not say Mass, receive the sacraments, or recite the Divine Office. This total religious solitude had helped to foster his extraordinary relationship with Kiying. Despite the differences between them, Feng reciprocated all of Kiying's warmth toward him. And, he believed, that warmth insulated him from suspicion, permitting him to survive.

Kiying had, in fact, permitted Feng to survive because it suited his purpose to do so. There was often information which he wished to make known through non-Chinese sources. He would discuss it with

Feng, secure in the knowledge that the younger officer would eventually pass it on to the Vatican. Some of that information, through the simple process of betrayal, reached people Kiying could not reach directly. Their response was sometimes action, communicated through the press. More often the response was further information, filtered back through the Vatican, then to the Black Pope, and then to Feng. The Kaiser and Wilson, Hitler and Roosevelt, Stalin and Eisenhower, all had communicated through the Vatican, although not always knowingly. Feng was Kiying's unknowing line of inquiry and channel of response.

There were others. These told him that his plan for Lung's removal was a good one. Its only flaw was the almost certain inquiry which would follow. Feng, if present, might be disposed to point out that he had originally cautioned against retaining Lung on the staff. If he chose not to harm Kiying, his very loyalty might be the cause of further inquiry; and torture might impel Feng to reveal that he was a Jesuit. That revelation would surely kill Kiying. Feng's continued presence was itself a danger. He would have to die. And he would have to bring it on himself.

As they entered Kiying's office, the marshal said, "Does it occur to you, Colonel, that Lung may do everything wrong?"

"I am afraid that it does, sir."

"As am I, Colonel. As am I. And even if he succeeds, Lung will be nothing but a nuisance in years to come."

"If I may, sir"—Feng watched as Kiying signaled him to proceed—"a closely controlled operation is necessary. No one outside this office. I am flight qualified. His severance can be arranged, and the formula retrieved."

"Yes, but you should not be alone. Lung is a good soldier; he could kill you."

"Your presence increases your options, sir."

"In what way?"

"It provides a second man while preserving utmost secrecy. If there is an inquiry, your willingness to expose yourself to such danger in the service of China will remove any advantage which an enemy might seek. You can go to his assistance and report his gallant death, or you can go to end his treachery and bring about his death."

"It is not pleasant to kill one of our own. But you are correct. Only my presence guarantees our absolute control over what is eventually learned. We will need a helicopter, Colonel. A carrier transfer and a

316

plane. Please arrange it. And execute all code messages by hand. You are right that there can be no knowledge outside this room."

When the younger officer left, Kiying thought that it would all work out very well. He would control the facts and circumstances of both men's deaths. In that way he would be assured survival. It was not merely an old man's greedy desire to stay alive which drove him, nor was it ego. It was simply that it was necessary for him to prevail. He had guided every operation of importance from the beginning. The continuity of his power was essential. Despite all of that, however, it would not be easy for him to kill Colonel Feng. But he would not be the first Jesuit that Kiying had executed to save himself. He would not be the last.

Chapter Twenty-one

Charles Halloran had personally recruited Feng Yao. And despite the tape's evidence of Feng's betrayal, the Superior General of the Jesuits was convinced of his ability to choose men. Feng Yao possessed the eagerness to serve Christ, even unto death, which the Jesuits knew was the sine qua non of a Chinese assignment. Halloran had sensed it during long walks along the Potomac when he had been on the Georgetown faculty and Feng was at the School of Foreign Service. The seminarian had been Halloran's first selection for the program. He remained convinced that it had been a good one.

Several days before Feng was to leave, Halloran had driven him to the Jesuit retreat house, Manresa on the Severn, not far from Annapolis. There were no other retreatants on the grounds. The two men had prayed, tossed a football, and walked by the water. When there was only one night remaining, Halloran told Feng that he could change his mind and still be ordained, still be of great value to God, the Church, the Society. "If you go," Halloran said, "you will surely die there."

Feng Yao seemed almost amused. "If I stay," he asked, "will I live forever?"

No, Halloran thought, it could not have been Feng Yao who had betrayed them. Yet the tape proved that Robustelli had a man in China. The tape had been processed and transcribed by Father Tomas Krause, Halloran's second secretary. When he expressed surprise at the brevity of the transcription, Father Krause told him, "It is complete, Father. We immersed the tape in a chemical solution, causing the voice imprint to be raised approximately two-thousandths of a millimeter. That put the impression high enough on the erased tape to be picked up by the special recorders. We magnified the raised sounds and transcribed them phonetically. Then we inserted likely missing sounds based upon a computerized probability of what those sounds would be. The blanks are indicated by asterisks."

"Forgive me, Father. It just seemed so short."

But when Halloran read it, he knew why Robustelli had insisted on the indirect transmission. And he knew that they had been betrayed.

Marsh[al] [Ki]ying is prepa[red] to use *** [an]. It is imperati[ve] that [y]ou continue to keep us inf[or]med of Juda[s's] plans so [tha]t we may [a]dvise our ma[n] [in] Kiying's office. All further [commu]nications must be through the pic[tures].

Halloran looked up from the report and shook his head. He lit a cigarette, then said, "Tomas, have you any idea as to what pictures he could mean?"

"No, Father. There are a number of possibilities, of course. It could refer to microfilm or microdots. But they require equipment to enlarge. Or he could mean a notation on a film frame. The spool, though, would have to be passed. They may have planted a code in a newspaper or magazine photo, but that would be impossible to spot."

"So we are nowhere. Which leads me to ask for an opinion that has nothing to do with computers. What hunches do you have, my friend?"

"Only a fear, Father. What if we are too logical? What if the process of ratiocination has broken down? What if we are looking too hard? Or in the wrong place? Or are proceeding from the wrong premise?"

"Those are interesting problems, Tomas. Now please give me the solutions."

"Ahh. If only I had answers."

"If only you did."

After Father Krause had left, Halloran allowed himself to admit how disturbed he was. He had assumed that Kiying would field a party. He had never suspected a second Chinese force. Feng should have known of it; it was not logical that he would not know. The only excuse was that he had not had an opportunity to get the information out. That would have been a first, a totally illogical first, because it would have meant that Feng had been captured. And Halloran would have known of that, because Halloran, and not Feng, knew the identity of all the Jesuits in China. Reason dictated that Feng had betrayed them. Perhaps out of fear or loneliness, or after torture. Any other conclusion strained reason.

What if the process of ratiocination has broken down?

For once in his life, Charles Halloran decided to be emotional. He would rely on the love which he and Feng Yao both had for God. Which left only one logical conclusion: Robustelli had his own man in China.

Halloran locked himself in his office with the file of every priest who had ever been involved with the China program.

He consumed three quarts of Perrier and an equal number of packs of cigarettes. By dawn, there were only four likely suspects.

The priest knew, of course, that he might be completely wrong. Robustelli's man might not be a Jesuit. He might not even exist. But such considerations were not logical. He lived by logic, and the process of ratiocination had left him with these four files.

Wang Ch'ung. Born in Canton to a professional couple who fled in the late 1950s. They had gone to Hong Kong, then London. The youth entered the Society from its preparatory school at Reading. He had been recruited for the China program, passed all training requirements, and sent to Hong Kong. From there he was to have been flown to the mainland and dropped. Unfortunately, his commercial flight to Hong Kong had crashed at sea.

It was possible, of course, that he had never boarded the plane. But that was not reasonable. A switch would have taken place at the other end, once the priest was logically within reach of his goal.

Pai-ien Chiao. Educated by the Jesuits at Peking. Fled to Hong Kong with his sister in 1945. Eventually came to America, entered the novitiate in Wernersville, Pennsylvania, in 1950. Recruited for the program and dropped into China in 1964. A series of entries in his folder indicated that many of the network handlers believed it foolish to send back someone who had not left until adolescence, leaving behind too many contemporaries who could recognize him.

Their fears had proven well founded. He had been picked up shortly after landing and executed. It was possible that he was alive and turned,

319

but not logical. In 1964 Robustelli had been a monsignor. Even after factoring in the man's vanity, Halloran could not credit him with having, as a monsignor, established in China a network capable of turning agents.

Fa T'ang. Born Hankow, 1948. Evacuated with mother three years later. Completed his studies for the priesthood in Rome in 1979. Recruited for the program, trained, and sent to Hong Kong in 1981, the year that Robustelli was created a cardinal.

During his stopover in Hong Kong, Fa T'ang took up with a woman, refused several orders to return to the Society, and disappeared five months later.

It was possible, Halloran thought, that Fa T'ang had used the woman as an excuse to disappear and go underground. But that was not logical. He would have no value to the Chinese as their Jesuit contact. More importantly, as bad as he was, Robustelli had too great a respect for the priesthood to disgrace it with even sham fornication.

Which left Lung Ch'ien. Born in Hong Kong, 1952, and sent to Rome by the archbishop for seminary training. Transferred to the Jesuits after completing the minor seminary at age seventeen. Finished his studies in Rome two years after Robustelli became a cardinal. Killed in an automobile accident five weeks before he was to leave for China. Father Halloran remembered. He had said the funeral mass.

"This is a filthy job, Tomas," Father Halloran said. "In more than the obvious way. If you don't want to do this, you have only to say so."

Father Krause smiled and placed his massive hand on Halloran's shoulder. "Charles, let us do this ugly business together and be done with it."

The years had hardened the grass into a sheet of steel over the gravesite. The two men clawed at the earth with shovels and pickaxes for three hours, working by the light of two small arc lamps. It was well past midnight when the earth began to yield to the regular motion of their shovels. An hour later Father Krause said, "There's no need to raise it. Give me that claw hammer."

Halloran handed over the tool, then knelt on the edge of the gravesite, leaning forward with an arc lamp in each hand. Krause sank the hammer into the side of the wooden casket and pulled hard. The rotting wood gave way. In a moment, four more strokes had removed the entire upper half of the coffin.

Krause said, "I hope I rest as still as these rocks."

320

Chapter Twenty-two

Father Halloran pulled the ankle-length white alb over his head and tugged the vestment, symbolic of purity, until it was smooth. He knotted it at the waist with a cincture, as a warrior of old girding his loins. Next he lifted the square lace amice, symbolic of a helmet, touched it to the back of his head, lowered it, and tied it into place. He kissed the cross on the stole of office and put it around his neck, then clothed himself in the square white chasuble of the day. With each addition he had said a prayer. Now he began the greatest prayer of all.

"In the name of the Father, and of the Son, and of the Holy Spirit. Amen.

"The grace of our Lord Jesus Christ and the love of God and the fellowship of the Holy Spirit be with you all.

"And also with you."

Halloran stepped up on the side altar in the Jesuit mother house chapel and began the substantive prayers of the Mass.

"I confess to almighty God, and to you, my brothers and sisters, that I have sinned through my own fault . . ."

Halloran had no idea what the pictures were. Every one of Robustelli's men was being watched, but none had attempted to contact Agnelli, nor had the young priest taken any steps to reach them.

"A reading from the book of Revelation."

He read the words, but he did not hear them. His men had carefully searched Agnelli's room and found nothing. They had even obtained a roll of film which he had left for developing after his return from the so-called vacation. Again nothing.

"The Responsorial Psalm."

Nor had the tap on Agnelli's phone yielded anything.

"A reading from the first letter of Paul to the Ephesians."

If it was a microdot, he did not know how it had been sent. If it was a photograph in a predesignated magazine or newspaper, he did not know how to discover the issue or copy. He had considered every logical method of conveying messages on film. And he knew nothing.

"A reading from the Holy Gospel according to Matthew."

"Glory to you, Lord."

"Jesus said to his disciples: 'When the Son of Man comes in his glory, escorted by all the angels of heaven, he will sit upon his royal throne, and all the nations will be assembled before him. Then he will separate them into two groups, as a shepherd separates sheep from goats. The sheep he will place on his right hand, the goats on his left. The king will say to those on his right: 'Come. You have my Father's blessing! Inherit the kingdom prepared for you from the creation of the world. For I was hungry and you gave me food, I was thirsty and you gave me drink. I was a stranger and you welcomed me, naked and you clothed me. I was ill and you comforted me, in prison and you came to visit me." Then the just will ask him: "Lord, when did we see you hungry and feed you or see you thirsty and give you drink? When did we welcome you away from home or clothe you in your nakedness? When did we visit you when you were ill or in prison?" ' "

As he finished the Gospel, Halloran saw Father Krause walk out to the main altar, genuflect, go up the stairs to the tabernacle, unlock it, genuflect again, and remove the sick-call kit. He locked the tabernacle, reversed his steps, and was gone. The sight pleased Halloran. As a Jesuit, he had always known that he would do little if any parish work, but what there was he eagerly sought out. Like Pope Xavier, he had kept as close to the people as his many offices had allowed. And like the Pope, he encouraged his staff to do so as well.

Halloran concentrated his mind on the Mass and the awesome power which priests possessed, and the terrible danger it carried within itself. A priest could learn to live without a woman. He could even struggle with the awful loneliness of his office and survive. But at this moment in the Mass he risked the deadliest sin of all, pride.

A man could go only so far on logic, even a Jesuit. There then came the decision to make a quantum leap of faith, or deny the chasm. If one went forward, there came the knowledge that the priest alone could change bread and wine into the body and blood of Christ.

"The day before he suffered he took bread in his sacred hands and looking up to heaven, to you, his almighty Father, he gave you thanks and praise. He broke the bread, gave it to his disciples, and said: 'Take

322

this, all of you, and eat it: this is my body which will be given up for you.''

"When supper was ended, he took the cup. Again he gave you thanks and praise, gave the cup to his disciples, and said: 'Take this, all of you, and drink from it: This is the cup of my blood, the blood of the new and everlasting covenant. It will be shed for you and for all men so that sins may be forgiven. Do this in memory of me.' ''

It was pride that a priest had to fear the most, and which eventually destroyed more of them than any other weakness. It allowed them to justify the distance they put between themselves and the people they were meant to serve. That was Robustelli's greatest sin: the prideful forgetting of the fact that he had been placed on earth to serve, and the arrogant belief that he alone knew the path to God.

It had always been the teaching, if not the pronouncement, of the Church that salvation is a subjective thing. A man must follow an erroneous conscience. If a cannibal in an undiscovered tribe thinks it a precondition to salvation that he eat a certain food for his salvation, that precondition exists.

"This is the Lamb of God who takes away the sins of the world. Happy are those who are called to his supper.''

"Lord, I am not worthy to receive you, but only say the word and I will be healed.''

Halloran believed that the Roman Catholic Church was the one true Church of God; that Jesus Christ, God and the Son of God, had been sent to earth to found the Church, to die for men's sins, and to rise again to heaven to sit in judgment with the Father. In judgment of people who had made their own choices. Damnation followed from rejecting God, not from choosing another means of accepting Him.

When the Church had grown too wealthy, too powerful, too incestuously mated to the monarchs of Europe, the poor and forgotten had deserted Rome gladly. In reaction, the Church drew in upon itself and became, in the worst sense, parochial. The concept of freedom of religious choice had been hidden from view by theologians who feared that liberty would become license. But the right to choose, the liberty, had always remained. The Catholic Church recognized a catholic salvation. Robustelli did not. That was why he would have to be stopped.

"Go in the peace of Christ.''

"Thanks be to God.''

Father Halloran walked toward the main altar, bowed in the direction of the tabernacle, and, as he turned to go into the sacristy, he remembered the words of the gospel. *When did we visit you when you were ill or in prison?*

And then he had it.

Chapter Twenty-three

"Extraordinary," Pope Xavier said. "How did you come to suspect?"

"I didn't. At least not at first. My secretary, Father Krause, gave me the clue, but I failed to understand it at first: ratiocination is not always the proper course. It seems, Your Holiness, I was too logical."

"Well, Charles, that is a confession I never expected to hear. How did logic fail you?"

"I was looking for what the word fragment *pic* logically suggested: a microdot, a film, some photograph. As a priest, I should have seen the obvious but did not. Until after Mass this morning. Father Krause went to the altar to get the sick-call kit. Agnelli knew that Your Holiness always insisted upon doing some of the work of a curate, no matter how high your office. That guaranteed that you would honor his request that he be allowed to do the same.

"Agnelli took down whatever he learned of our conversations, encoded the message, then went out on sick calls. He carried his messages in the repository of the host, the golden pyx. The message would be left in a sick room, bathroom stall, wherever."

"You are certain of your facts, Charles?"

"Father Agnelli has been questioned by Hans Schiller." He quickly raised his hand. "I know your desires, Holiness. Agnelli was questioned under Sodium Pentothal."

The two black limousines drew quietly to a stop. Robustelli's residence, like that of most cardinals in the Curia, was lavish, maintained with an endless flow of gifts designed to advance careers, arrange mixed marriages, and speed annulments. A two-story wrought-iron fence surrounded the mansion. The main gate was secured by a padlock wrapped in a heavy chain. One of the Swiss Guards, in civilian clothes, stepped from the lead car, walked to the lock, and snapped it with a heavy cutter. He pushed open the gates, walked up the drive, and waited for the others.

The eight guards jumped from the cars and lined up at the door. There was no sound other than their heavy breathing in the cold night air. The group's commander handed the lock cutter to a subordinate and rang the bell. A young priest opened the door and jumped back as the Swiss Guards ran into the house and took up positions by telephones, garden doors, and stairways. Robustelli entered the room, his violin and bow in one hand, a glass of champagne in the other.

"What is going on here?" he screamed. His voice trailed away as Pope Xavier entered. "Your Holiness." Robustelli walked forward to kiss the Pope's ring but, seeing Halloran, bolted upright. He nodded and said, "Most Reverend Father."

"Your Eminence." Halloran did not bow, and Robustelli noticed.

"I will dismiss my staff," the cardinal said.

"Everyone will be still," Xavier announced quietly. "You know why we are here."

"Ahh. Yes. *I* know. You are here to insure the mongrelization of the Church. What has taken two thousand years to build up—"

Xavier raised his hand, but Robustelli shouted him down. "I will *not* be still. What has taken two thousand years to build up, you would destroy in an instant. You and the rest of the swine. Jews exonerated of the murder of our Saviour. Protestants yapping from our pulpits. Prayers in the vernacular so that any dog can bark in time to the priest's commands. This is not my church."

"No. I know that. Yours is the church which burns heretics, tortures dissenters, and condemns freethinkers. The church which made war on the Jews."

"So, you know of that. Very well, Giancarlo, yes, that is my church. A church which has sanctioned all that you find so reprehensible."

"Sanctioned, perhaps, but then regretted. Every one of those offenses—every body racked and mind tortured—has been committed because we made stupid, stupid mistakes. God sails in vessels of clay. And we who are His vessels easily founder on the shoals of human weakness. But we are not the Church. We are only its servants. The Church is love for all men."

"*Love!*" Robustelli spat at the Pope's feet. "*Basta!* Your love is weakness. It is the timidity of a church which thinks it belongs to the heathen, and that Christ died for scum."

325

"You are no theologian, Pietro. Are you a historian?" Xavier watched Robustelli's eyes narrow. "I have a simple question for you: Do you know the only person to whom Christ promised salvation?"

"His Blessed Mother."

"No, Pietro. On the day that Christ was crucified he hung between two thieves. One reviled Him. The other, a man named Dismas, having no reason to believe that Christ could help him, told his evil companion, 'Leave him alone. He has done nothing.' And Christ, seeing the thief's love and devotion, said to him, 'This day you shall be with me in paradise.'

"Heaven was not promised to the Virgin, or the Apostles, or later to any of the saints. No, Pietro, in all the history of all the world, of all the men and women who ever lived, Christ promised heaven only to a thief. You are right, Pietro. Christ died for scum. Christ died for me."

Xavier nodded to two guards, who walked forward and braced Robustelli. "As your Pope and Bishop, we strip from you the power of the priesthood. We strip from you the power of your bishopric. We strip from you the honors and privileges of the rank of cardinal. And we give you the opportunity to think on your sins and repent of them. You will be taken to a Carthusian monastery in the Alps. There you will be kept in a hermit's cell from the day of your confinement to the day of your death. You will never again see another human being. Those whom you have infected will be similarly detained, each in a separate monastery.

"And finally, because we are filled with love for all men, we grant to you absolution of all your sins, and a plenary indulgence remitting all spiritual punishment. It is effective at the moment of your death, if you humbly ask God's forgiveness."

"You do not speak for any God that *I* know, Giancarlo. You speak for the forces that would destroy my church."

"No, Pietro. I would give my life before I would harm our Holy Mother the Church. But I would forfeit my immortal soul if I ever stood in another man's path to God.

"Take him away."

After the residence had been cleared, Pope Xavier said to Charles Halloran, "We must find some way to stop Father Lung."

"A message can be sent to China. Then it will be in their hands."

"It must appear that the information comes from another source."

"I can arrange it."

"One thing, Charles. The boy, Lung, he must not suffer, either physically or spiritually."

326

"Yes, Your Holiness."

"You know, Charles, if you cannot alert your priest in Peking, the entire mission rests in the hands of a man whose masters are Wall Street and the petroleum industry. I wonder if that should alarm us."

Chapter Twenty-four

Simon McHenry was not afraid of oil, or the men who produced it. He was an investment banker, a man who managed money, and a student of business. In each of those roles he had learned that the face of greed painted on the petroleum industry by its enemies was a false one.

As a student of business, McHenry knew that the public's discontent with its most important industrial unit could be traced to one man's mistake. The man was John D. Rockefeller. The mistake, in his own words, occurred the first time that reporters asked him a question. "I should have said, 'What do you want to know, boys?' Instead, I shut the door and pulled down the curtains." In what became a sad and senseless cycle, the public viewed oil men as secretive; and the men in petroleum, resenting this image, became secretive. The industry took almost a century to realize that it had to sell not only gasoline but itself as well. The lesson was learned in the early 1970s, when much of America was manipulated into believing that the industry was responsible for the Arab oil embargo and its aftermath.

McHenry the investment banker knew better. He realized that while the price of oil quintupled in the years after the embargo, profits accounted for a smaller share of gross revenue than before the squeeze. It was true that the rewards were great, but the risks were greater still. The investor's return on an oil dollar was lower than the yield from money placed in automobiles or pharmaceuticals, and no higher than the return from any of the Fortune 500. And as a money manager, McHenry knew that one-third of all after tax profits went into exploration and research.

Everyone spoke of barrels, but few knew, as McHenry did, that each barrel was a forty-two-gallon unit of measurement; and that each produced gasoline, jet fuel, ethane, liquefied gases, kerosene, heating oil, petrochemical fieldstocks, naphtha, lubricants, wax, coke, asphalt, and road oil. Its all pervasive reach, its rewards and challenges, made the petroleum industry what Santayana called the "ideal essence" of American business. All of this McHenry knew.

What he did not know was what the code's letter groupings would be, or what technical information it would contain. He needed the former, of course, to translate the message into plaintext. The latter was necessary so that he could tell from the beginning of the translation if his premises were correct. If the technical data did not begin to appear in the plaintext, he would have to make corrections in what he perceived the basis of the code to be, in order to reach the scientific conclusion of the message. And, if there was not time to memorize the entire text, he wanted to know what was of the essence.

McHenry was certain that his assumptions concerning the intellectual conceit underlying the code were correct. To obtain the letter groupings he went to the library of Fordham University, a Jesuit school. A quick review of the card catalogue told him where to find the book he wanted. The list that would provide the plaintext was in Latin, but he had no difficulty memorizing it. The problem he encountered was that the list contained only twenty-four entries, two short of a sufficient number to convert to an alphabet. It was a barrier which McHenry would have to overcome himself. The technical data he would be given by a man from Langley.

"Listen carefully," Dole had told McHenry before he left London. "If you think you are onto the code, Langley will give you a man to tell you what to look for. He's supposed to be a strange chap, at best. One of those corporate-lawyer types who shuttle back and forth between the industry and government. I suppose they thought you could talk to one another. He's not a scientist at all, but rather someone with a 'Q' clearance who happened to fall in love with the oil business. Mordant, I think is how they described him. He cares only about his family, his country, his books, and his industry." Dole lit a Sweet Afton and said, "I'm always uncomfortable around the stable."

They were to meet in a sitting room of the Metropolitan Club, overlooking Fifth Avenue. A sign on the door of the room announced that it was closed for cleaning. The room, McHenry knew, would have been swept for bugs. It was nearly two hundred feet long, with no service doors near where they would be standing. If someone did inter-

328

rupt, they would appear to be merely two businessmen who had stepped into a private area to discuss a deal.

As McHenry came through the door, the man from Langley turned and nodded slightly. Simon could see that beneath his open suit coat he wore suspenders. It reminded him of the way many of the partners dressed at Ingersoll & Constance. He suddenly felt a great longing to be done with the mission.

A parade was making its way down Fifth Avenue. Bands and drill teams passed in review, each preceded by a banner proclaiming it the representative of an Hispanic church or civic group. Next came a silk flag bearing the image of the Virgin. Then the color guard and marchers. McHenry had no idea what holiday or feast day it could be.

The man from Langley studied the parade for several minutes. McHenry watched his face each time a new group marched into view, flanked on all sides by parish priests who called cadence for the children. Simon studied the man's face, and knew that they shared at least one unhappy memory. "I was once a Catholic," he said.

The man from Langley said, "There aren't many on active duty these days."

"It was the priests for me. What was it for you—the theology?"

"No, theologically I'm quite sound. I couldn't tolerate all those priests telling people how important it was to fail in this life in order to succeed in heaven."

"Priests have always been unintelligible to me."

"That is precisely when you should listen to them."

"Yes," McHenry said, knowing that this was why he had come.

"When they start to drone on that things are never what they seem to be, that only the unexpected is expectable, that is when they're onto something."

The man from Langley looked at McHenry. "There is a great deal of misinformation about the product, and its sources. Colonel Drake's first well, for example, was drilled between a creek and a bluff. For generations, people believed that oil would be found only under those conditions. Even into this century many scientists thought that petroleum came only from marine matter. It doesn't, and the discovery that it does not was one of the great breakthroughs in the industry. Yet the first dozen people to make the discovery paid no attention to their own findings. They either thought that they were wrong or that the information meant nothing because of the limited drilling technology available then."

"Was there a great deal that people didn't know they knew?"

"The reverse really. The resource as we know it is finite. That has always been known, and it has always been disregarded. Which is why people waste it, then complain when it is not available."

"The complaints may be about profits."

"You profit from me, Mr. McHenry. As do most other industries. And the media. And the politicians. As do the Americans, who pay less for fuel than all but a handful of countries in the world.

"And, there are expenses. We could extract it from tar sands, shale or coal, but the government gives virtually no help to industry, which cannot finance the research alone. So we need you. And what I gather is a code that you are seeking.

"Tell me what you can about your source. Geologist? Engineer? Explorer?"

"Priest."

The man from Langley smiled. "I appreciate the irony. You would not be going to this trouble if the code could be broken by a computer, which means that you will be working under difficult conditions, probably in what was once quaintly called a mission land. And, I must assume, with limited time.

"Any man who could create such an intriguing code would have had some scientific knowledge, and would have left at least rudimentary clues. Once you make your conversion to plaintext, if you can't commit it all, memorize anything having to do with wax content, the part of the country discussed, weight of the oil, rock formations, soil composition and residual elements. You should also learn what you can about the nature and direction of any fault, and the specifics of any rock formations."

"I understand."

Simon turned to go, then said, "Helping me may be a matter of some danger."

"So I understand."

"Then you have not only my thanks, but also my respect."

All that he said was, "I am not ungrateful."

Chapter Twenty-five

Dole leaned back in his chair and turned slightly. He had an unobstructed view of the gravestone which served as his signal post. It occurred to him that he had used it for too long. Security was not endangered, but the humor was gone. He would have to think of something new. As would Sharp if he truly expected to carry out the plan he was presenting to Dole.

Sir Fraser looked back at Sharp. The assassin's form was at parade rest. He only reverted to a military stance when he wanted to convey the impression of being the logical originator of action, not merely the thug. Dole was amused by Sharp's inability to recognize how wrongheaded an approach he had conceived.

"So, Sharp, you want to kill McHenry?"

"Sir." He had never lost the barracks habit of using the single word when responding in the affirmative.

"Will you be more effective than you were that day in the man's hotel?"

Sharp bristled but said nothing.

"We can only hope." Dole lit a Sweet Afton. "Not only don't you take care of *me,* Sharp, your liege, your lord, your patron and benefactor. Your *friend,* Sharp. You couldn't even take care of poor Caroline what's-her-name." Dole went to a chatting tone. "I've told you, haven't I, Sharp, that McHenry plans to kill you for that?"

"Sir."

"Strange fellow, McHenry, he kills your agent and blames you. Well, that will teach you to run your own string. Are you taking anyone in-house to the Pole, Sharp?"

"No, sir."

"Ahh, aren't you the courageous, polysyllabic devil. I gather that you propose to wait for McHenry at Mount Erebus and shoot him up. Is that it?"

"No, sir. I propose to follow him."

"This isn't a tail on the Strand, Sharp. This is the Antarctic wasteland. What do you propose as a disguise—a snowman suit?"

"There is camouflage clothing, sir."

"Go on."

"Sir, if I wait at Erebus, it may accomplish nothing. Hawkeland may not have been dead; he may have crawled down off the mountain. There may be—"

"I'm well aware of all the reasons to start at the beach, Sharp."

"Sir. I can go airborne, sir, a day after them. Barring truly bad weather, they'll leave tracks. In the event of a storm, I'll follow by compass. If they turn back early, I'll know it's because they have the formula. If not, I'll follow them to Erebus. Either way, I have them."

"Mmmmm. Well"—he tapped his teeth—"there's no doubt that we have to get rid of McHenry. What about the girl?"

"She loves him."

"I'm afraid you're right. I had hoped the usual post-assignment fog would lift; however, she is deeply in love with him. I can see it all: guilt, protectiveness, every straw." He lowered his voice. "Strange, isn't it, Sharp, that we who've never been loved can spot the emotion so clearly in others. But, the girl must return. And McHenry must live long enough to give her the formula." He glared at Sharp and knew that he would be obeyed.

"And Vultan?"

"He's an American asset. I don't think they'd be overly thrilled with our disposing of him. But he has been crackers round the bend since his wife died. I'll talk to his control. For now, do nothing about him."

"Sir."

"And, Sharp."

"Sir."

"All sorts of people go to the South Pole these days: teachers, scientists, vacationers. Do mop up when you're through. Take some Indians. Put it on expense."

"Sir."

In the closing days of the nineteenth century, thousands of Indians of the Ona and Yamana tribes roamed the Patagonian grasslands. They trekked over the brutally cold wilderness in search of clusters of wild sheep and, in an ocean of nearly freezing water, hunted for king crabs and seals. They carried their few possessions on their wives' backs and walked proudly naked in even the worst storms.

Then came the Protestant Patagonia Missionary Society and Catholic priests who brought the love of God and engaged in gunfights for the right to preach it. Civilization did away with nudity and brought chastity and syphilis, as well as tuberculosis, smallpox, and yellow fever. The number of unconverted, uncivilized Indians was brought to safely less than ten thousand.

The only thing that did not change was the Indians' resistance to cold. Vultan had learned of it years before, and had taken Onas with him on his expeditions and arranged for them to man the base camp after his solitary trek. For the assault on Mount Erebus, he had contracted for four Onas. As had Sharp.

Chapter Twenty-six

McHenry saw Antarctica as an endless white abyss. After tumbling hopelessly into the void, after the initial fear of death, the snow invited one to the easy surrender of the enveloping wastes. The landscape was startling in its intensity. Except for a few primitive lichen and splotches of moss near the coast, there were no plants at all. Nor were there mammals; the largest land animal was a tiny wingless fly.

And there was the cold. Vultan warned McHenry at the outset: "You do not become accustomed to the cold; you learn how to endure it. Once you believe you have conquered it, the cold will kill you. The Indians are the only exception."

There were four of them, all but one of whom were veterans of one of Vultan's earlier expeditions. Their tribal names were almost unpronounceable, so Vultan had christened them Matthew, Mark, Luke, and John. Such high-handed treatment was offensive to Elspeth, but the Indians knew why he had done it; on the ice, speed and cooperation were essential. If anyone unfamiliar with the Ona dialect was unable to quickly and effectively attract one of the Indians, death could result. Anyone brought to the Pole by Vultan could master the four writers' names, and the Indians had used them long enough to know how to respond promptly.

Matthew, the leader, was in his mid-forties, small and wiry like the others, sharing also the Oriental features of their tribe.

Mark was apparently Matthew's kinsman, although McHenry could not learn if he was a brother or cousin. Shorter and broader, he was more outgoing than his leader, always cadging smokes and smiling as he worked. Luke was a relative, as they all seemed to be, but much quieter than the others. Finally, there was John, taller, leaner than the others, more Spanish-looking, commanding in his presence but mute, the result, Matthew told them, of a childhood accident. What John's voice did not convey, his eyes did. He missed nothing. He alone was new to Vultan.

McHenry saw little enough of Elspeth's eyes, or any other part of her face. She wore a reinforced nylon shield to protect her delicate skin from the wind. He assumed that it was best that he could not see her, as he had some idea of the hatred which she felt toward him. McHenry knew that he had gone too far in his attempts to hurt her. She had probably expected to be struck and called a whore. It went with the assignment. Elspeth could not have expected that he would challenge her womanhood and attribute her motives to lesbianism. Both of them were too intelligent to care what another person's sexual preferences were. Elspeth was, however, proud of her womanhood and her femininity. His false accusation hurt terribly. The fact that both knew that it was false made it hurt no less.

McHenry could not bring himself to apologize. He had never before allowed himself to love, and so had no defenses for the hurt that burned within. Major Gordon, Colonel Sharp, Caroline, all had been the victims of his cool, studied, carefully considered rage. His fine intellect had never prepared him to contend with the effects of love. He was angry with Elspeth for deceiving him, and furious with himself for allowing it to happen.

He did not have the leisure to think about her when they first arrived. It took an entire day to unload the landing craft in the cold. The temperature had dropped to minus forty degrees Fahrenheit, and, with winds of fourteen knots, the temperature was the equivalent eighty-five degrees below zero; flesh could freeze after less than one minute of exposure.

The supplies were loaded on six motorized sledges, with Vultan driving the lead craft. McHenry and Cartier shared one, Elspeth and

Bresnau followed, Mark and John each drove a transport sledge, and Matthew and Luke came last in a two-man vehicle. They carried provisions for one month on the ice, were prepared for temperatures as low as a hundred degrees below zero Fahrenheit, were equipped to descend into chasms and to climb Mount Erebus, and were armed to kill one another.

Their trek across the ice was based on Vultan's theory that Peter might have made a mistake. The explorer knew that the artist had been weak, hungry, half mad, and less skilled than a novice in matters of navigation. Vultan believed that Hawkeland had probably been buried on the side of Erebus, but could not be certain. The unusual atmosphere of Antarctica enabled a man to see three hundred miles; but the strange infraction of the light also played tricks. It was an accepted scientific fact that objects out of sight on the Southern Continent would suddenly appear quite clearly, occasionally upside down, then disappear as quickly.

Peter might have buried Hawkeland on Erebus. And he might have buried him a hundred miles away and, dazed and hopeless, later have seen the cairn reflected in the clouds. An out party of Scott's first expedition had been saved when, leagues from camp, they had seen the Union Jack upside down in the sky, hovering over a base which could not have been seen by the lost men.

Vultan knew that during the almost one hundred years since Hawkeland's death, Antarctica had been moving, melting, and sinking into the sea. To find a burial site along the way was almost impossible. To ignore the possibility of its being there was to doom the mission before it began. They would go over the ice.

On the first morning it began to rain.

"How can that be?" McHenry asked Vultan. "Why doesn't the rain freeze?"

"At this temperature, Mr. McHenry, forty below, snowflakes are less than one millimeter in size. Not until the mercury reaches five below will the mist appear as snowflakes."

"Will it impede our travel?"

"Oh, no, Mr. McHenry. But it will make you feel perfectly dreadful. The snow-mist will get inside your parka, making everything from your groin down and navel up absolutely drenched. As we pick up speed, the insulation and your body heat will combine to turn that drenched feeling into one of sticky dampness. You'll pick at every inch of your body, but the conditions will be such that you will have no relief. Tonight when we camp, you will be able to towel off and change, but for the next twelve hours you will be in agony."

"You don't seem to mind."

"Your agony, Mr. McHenry, is no concern of mine."

"I meant your agony."

"Of course I mind, Mr. McHenry. The secret of strength lies in not allowing anyone to know that you mind."

Three days later they were at the foot of the Beardmore Glacier. Vultan left two of the Indians, Mark and Luke, at the lower glacier depot with a week's supplies and all but one sledge. In the event that the main party was caught on, or in, the deadly ice fields and chasms of the glacier, there would be some hope of refuge at the base camp which could be reached by two-way radio.

McHenry and Cartier led the way up the glacier, stringing wires in pitons as they went. When they reached a plateau, they let down nylon ladders and hoisting wires. The supplies were lashed to the ropes and lifted by Vultan and Elspeth while Matthew and John guided the bundles from the ladders.

All went well until they reached the soft snow. The six men shared the burden of carrying the supplies, as four divided the packed gear, while the two Indians trudged behind, pulling the sledge itself. Elspeth marched between the two groups of men. McHenry was constantly aware of her presence, her eyes looking through specially treated glasses, trained always on his back. He never looked at her; he knew what the eyes would show.

Every step in the soft snow consisted of several parts. Their heavily booted feet had to be drawn up out of three-foot-deep powder, the hips and knees had to force the legs out and down, the other side of the body had to catch up, and the torturous process was then repeated. Within an hour they were perspiring freely; by noon they were gasping for air, and Vultan called a halt. He ordered an oxygen bottle passed, and everyone breathed according to his instructions, including the Indians. He allowed a brief meal of tinned rations, then ordered the party to continue the climb.

"You look lovely," he said to Elspeth as they started up.

"You are too gallant." She shook her head, but her once lovely golden hair stuck to her sopping forehead. "I never thought one could complain about the heat of Antarctica. I am simply drenched with sweat."

"My wife often said that horses sweat, men perspire, and women glisten. You are glistening."

"I'm grateful, but I'm also stinking with sweat." Elspeth adjusted her radio. She would send the first transmission that evening.

They camped that night at the foot of a field of pressure waves, hard ridges of ice which sharply bottomed out into valleys. The descent would be simple, the climb on the far side a torture. The greatest danger was found in unexpected soft spots, iced-over holes in the pressure waves. A man could step onto the apparently firm surface of a wave and disappear forever into a tunnel of swirling, suffocating snow. Vultan estimated that the trek across the ridges would take two days, at which point they would have to cross the crevasses, then make a forced march to the foot of Mount Erebus and begin the ascent.

The party lived in large yellow fiberglass tents. In one corner of his tent Vultan hung a blanket separating Elspeth's sleeping area. A separate enclosure had been set up for cooking. After the evening meal, Vultan called Simon and Elspeth out onto the ice and pointed at the sky.

"God's fireworks," he said. "The aurora australis."

They watched in silence as endless sheets of silver were snapped out above them, changing to yellow, green, and red. The sheets contracted then, splitting and falling in silver bars which were overshot by thousands of glittering rays. Streaks of crimson arced over the horizon, then vanished, leaving the sky suddenly barren.

"Stay here," Vultan said. "It takes many forms and many colors. Stay here until you are physically weary from watching. But if your weariness is ever of their glory, be prepared to die."

In the morning, Cartier did just that. They were moving carefully down a pressure wave, proceeding in their usual columnar formation. The party advanced slowly down one side, the Indians controlling the descent of the sledge with ropes, one fore and one aft. As they started up the incline side, Cartier stepped into a soft spot and screamed once. His cry was made all the more horrible because it was the moan of a man who knew that he was about to be plunged into a pit of frozen quicksand. He spun madly about, and then was gone.

"Halt!" Vultan shouted. He looked around and repeated his command. "Come around this way"—he pointed—"and give no thought to rescue." He moved his hand again, then said, "Mr. McHenry, please be so kind as to surrender your pack." Simon did as he had been told, leaving the gear in the snow. "Thank you. Now, on your hands and knees, please, probe with your knife. And go gently."

McHenry crawled forward, unsheathing his bayonet. As Vultan had

337

commanded, he inserted the blade every few feet, each time cutting into solid ridges of ice. Once across the floor of the ravine, he started up, probing gently. He inched his way to the top, hooked one hand over the ledge, and turned to look back. The crest broke and he fell forward, realizing as he plunged downward that this pressure wave did not end in a flat but in an abyss.

He turned over once and began to slide, revolving as he went, trapped on his back as surely as a mortally wounded terrapin. His head spun around beneath his shoulders. He was now plummeting blindly toward the abyss. He raised his arm and brought it down sharply into the ice. The blade caught, then broke and dragged, screeching like a finger on exposed bone. He could feel the spray of loose ice being gouged out and thrown up as he pulled the knife along the ridge. Desperate now, he began to hack up and down with the knife handle. Each chopping motion slowed him slightly, but not enough. He attempted to right himself, hoping that he would have an instant as he went over the side to twist around and clutch at the ledge.

His desperate grasp twisted him over and left him on his belly as his descent continued. He closed his eyes and waited to die. His mask and goggles blocked out all sound but the crunching of soft snow beneath his body. It took a moment for his fearful mind to realize that he was on wet, soft snow. The porous surface would slow his fall, if he could act. One last time he raised his battered arm and drove the knife down. The moss beneath had softened under the moist overlay, softened just enough to allow the blade to bite the ground. He wearily drew his legs up, then drove them down into the snow. He stuck in the soft powder.

Chapter Twenty-seven

Colonel Sharp watched McHenry's slide. His infrared glasses provided a rose scrim for the drama, their special power-sight permitting him to remain almost a day's march distant from the others. As long as he stayed to the rear, Sharp knew that the Antarctic's strange atmosphere would not project him and his Indian guides above the Vultan party.

He was pleased with the conclusion of McHenry's fall. He did not want him dead. Not yet. He believed, with Dole, that McHenry had discovered the key to the code. The British computers could not break it, he knew; so it would be essential to have McHenry do it for them. Sharp was content to wait. The expectation of killing the American, and how it was to be done, only served to heighten his enjoyment.

In the morning, Sharp saw the party break camp and move toward the crevasse, a series of jagged apertures extending over the remaining area of the glacier. Once past these chasms, Vultan's group would have an open field to the foot of Erebus.

Most of the openings could be easily traversed by simply handing packs and tools back and forth between individuals. Particularly wide openings could either be descended or crossed by swinging hand to hand over a nylon rope carried over by a man brave enough to jump. The rope was then tossed back and nailed into place. The most dangerous openings were at the end. It was there that the sledge, which could usually be pushed and pulled over the canyons, would be abandoned, the supply load redistributed, and the march over clear snow made to the base of Mount Erebus.

The morning went well. In midafternoon, however, as they were pushing the sledge across a ravine, Matthew suddenly looked up and stared. His sight had been caught by parhelia, mock suns created by the refraction of light from thousands of tiny many-faceted ice crystals suspended in the dry atmosphere.

He allowed himself to be distracted for a moment too long. When he turned back to the sledge, Matthew's eyesight was impaired. He saw dozens of yellow globes where he should have seen the tied-down sledge. Reaching forward to steady himself, he hit the starter. The sledge shot out over its guide wire, its tether catching Matthew's leg and dragging him to the abyss. He became tangled in the rope, clawed desperately as the sledge moved toward the descent, then felt his body go over the side of the cliff. The nylon wire played out as the sledge twisted backward. This final turn secured Andrew's leg in the guide wire. He hung there, his face and hands only inches from the sledge's whirling steel tracks and constantly spinning drive shaft.

Vultan ordered Bresnau and John to bring the packs to the ledge. Then he turned to McHenry and said, "Ready?" Simon nodded.

They drove clamps into the edge of the cliff which looked down on a two-thousand-foot drop. Bresnau handed them bolts, which they twisted into the rope. They crossed these through a series of hooks which they nailed into the ice. McHenry stepped back across the ravine with John and repeated the procedure. He threw the rope back to Vultan, who secured it. There was now a double rope over the chasm, enough to hold two men and serve as a pulley for the sledge's wires.

McHenry crossed back to Vultan, placed several coils of rope over his shoulder, took a packet of pitons and a hammer, then stepped forward. Vultan looped a rappeling line around Simon's waist and leg, attached the clips, then helped McHenry down over the ledge. Vultan would serve as the land anchor.

Simon dropped ten feet and stopped. He hammered in a piton and hooked a bolt over it, then ran the coil through the bolt, tied it in a bowline, then dropped another ten feet. He repeated the process nine more times. By dropping below the sledge, he allowed himself room to maneuver if the machine could not be righted and started to fall when it should have risen.

McHenry knew that he could not free Matthew from the sledge. The heavy clanking chains and massive thrusting screw of the drive shaft precluded lifting the Indian out. A wrong move would catch one man in the treads and impale the other in the blade.

Simon inched his way along the chasm wall, moving slowly against the sheer surface, holding close to avoid the freezing wind. He knew that he could not move far enough over in this fashion, so he leaped back and out. He bumped along the canyon wall, smashing his face, shoulders, and chest across the granitic ice. The pull of the rope moved him back to his original position. He leaped again, and could hear Vultan, John, and Bresnau working the ropes to move him to the far side. McHenry sailed backward into the wall, felt Vultan tug twice, and knew that the ropes had cleared the sledge. He began the climb up out of the pit.

At intervals matching those of his descent, McHenry drove in pitons and hooks, looped rope, and drew the side wall of rope along the face of the canyon. When he reached the edge of the cliff, he held up an arm, and Vultan looped another coil of rope over his shoulder. McHenry rappeled back down, stood on the bottom line of rope, and worked his way out. Vultan traced his movements from above, then pulled gently when McHenry was directly below the sledge. The three men above slowly hoisted Simon toward the cliff. They stopped when he was just beneath the sledge. He reached up and looped ropes around the machine's runners.

McHenry slowly positioned himself against the wall of ice, with the sledge's treads constantly rotating before him. Each link was sharpened

340

to a razor's edge to guarantee traction. Each minute, hundreds of blades clanked around the machine which hung inches from his face. Matthew's weight acted as a counterbalance to the sledge, and as long as he remained motionless his body and the machine would be slightly separated. Simon gently worked his hand up between Matthew's legs and the spinning screw of the drive shaft. He began to loop a line around the Indian's waist. The thick rope was only a fraction of an inch from the power-driven shaft. As McHenry maneuvered it up into place, the rope's edge was caught in the screw. It began to shred, but the shaft moved so quickly that the rope looped the steel arrow. In an instant, the line was caught and pulling McHenry into the path of the blade. If he pulled free, he might wrench apart the delicate balance of the two hanging weights. If he did nothing, he would lose his arm.

As the blade pulled him into its path, McHenry let go of his support line and looped his free arm around Matthew's waist. He wrenched his arm loose, and the sledge started down. The spinning screw split his parka's sleeve and leg, then cut the side of his boot and first pair of socks. The dead weight of the two men held fast, and the sledge jolted to a stop just below McHenry's boot.

Simon saw another descent line fall beside him. He moved his head a fraction and observed one of the party moving down the ice face. The rescuer stopped at his side, then rappeled back and out over the chasm, maneuvering along the rope walk built by McHenry, and working up to a position on the far side and just above the two men.

The rescuer saw that McHenry was supported only by his rappeling line. If Matthew were cut free and McHenry caught him, the two would be totally dependent on that one line. Not only might the line snap, those above might not be able to hold the rope with its suddenly increased weight. But there was no alternative. The rescuer reached over and began to slice away at Matthew's line. McHenry realized what was planned and moved slightly so that he would be prepared to catch Matthew. He and the Indian were directly over the sledge, its powerful shaft spinning rapidly beneath Simon's bowels. If the sudden change in load proved too great, he and Matthew would be impaled on the giant screw and would ride it into the abyss.

Their rescuer cut into the line several more times, finally separating Matthew from the sledge. At that instant the pull on the lifeline was doubled and the sledge began to fall free. The sudden increase in weight dropped the lifeline toward the shaft. The men above realized what was happening and worked frantically to lift McHenry and Matthew. The two men slid rapidly down the wall and began to pass the screw. As they twisted in the air, Matthew's legs came into contact with the blade. It ripped through his flesh, cutting open his legs, his groin, his belly. He twisted violently, and McHenry lost him. The Indian fell forward, bounced off the sledge, and floated gracefully out of view.

It took several minutes to lift McHenry to the top, while his rescuer stayed below to watch for possible fouling of the lines. When he had safely reached the top, McHenry waited to lift his rescuer to safety and offer him thanks. But before he could speak, Elspeth took off her mask and said, "I didn't do it for you. I did it for Matthew. Now let us attempt to console John."

Simon followed her to the tent, where Vultan was pouring everyone a whisky. Elspeth looked toward John. The Indian simply nodded at her and McHenry, then turned away.

"We will remain here for twenty-four hours," Vultan said. "We must redistribute the load and forget that we ever had such a malign convenience as the sledge." He turned to Elspeth. "If your schedule allows it, I suggest that you make your next transmission now. I do not know when we will again have the luxury of a tent."

Colonel Sharp had observed the rescue. He found it satisfying to observe that McHenry's courage was not restricted to sneak attacks in hotel rooms. Sharp had learned long before that it was no weakness to respect an enemy. It made it more pleasurable to butcher him. And what he had planned for McHenry could only be described as butchering.

He was pleased that he had not encountered the difficulties endured by Vultan's party. He knew that it was because he was following the other group's lead, taking advantage of their having broken open the territory; but it was still pleasant to proceed without problems. It allowed him to save his strength for the slopes of Erebus. It was a clear trek now to the volcano. He wanted only his enemies and himself at the final confrontation. So he killed his Indians.

Chapter Twenty-eight

Major Lung's difficulties had begun right after going out the door of the airplane. He had jumped first and felt the relief of all paratroopers when the chute opens. Lung expected a smooth drop, but almost immediately he heard a scream. He moved slightly in his harness and saw one of his men streak into view in Roman-candle form. The Roman candle is so called because the extended white stream of the firecracker so closely resembles the awful spectacle of a paratrooper plummeting to earth at the end of a long, straight unopened silk column. The soldier's defective chute deployed one hundred feet from the ground, just in time to jolt him from his shocked condition and allow him to feel his body shatter and his leg bone being driven up into his heart.

The third man's parachute opened properly, and he fell in formation behind Lung, just the correct distance down the jump line. He wore eyeglasses, which had not been securely taped to his temples. They blew away; but he was unconcerned, as he always carried two additional pairs, as required by regulations. He watched the earth coming up and shifted slightly to catch the wind and move himself down the line toward the dead man. He knew that Lung would want to bury him and gather up his equipment.

The third man was an experienced paratrooper, and if he had seen the water coming up he would have followed procedure. A drop which comes down over water requires the soldier to punch the round harness lock on his chest, thereby opening the straps which lead to the shroud lines. The paratrooper begins to inch his way out of the harness until he is fifty feet above the water. He then drops free and swims away. If he does not, he will be covered by the canopy, which absorbs water quickly, immediately burying the soldier in the equivalent of a thousand pounds of shroud. The third man would have followed procedure if he had seen that he was coming down on an ice sheet which obviously covered a small body of water. But his glasses had blown away, so he crashed through the ice and drowned.

Lung had landed safely and seen the third man die. There was nothing that he could do to help him. He could, however, make use of what the second man left behind. He went to the crushed body, stripped off the gear and radio, and built a small mound of snow over the corpse. He covered this with a few rocks, shouldered the equipment, and left for his hiding place.

For all his tempestuousness, Lung had known enough to prepare for this moment. He would be in the most inhospitable region in the world, waiting for experienced agents to come down from Erebus with the greatest discovery in the history of science. He knew enough to be ready.

Lung set up camp in a ravine off the main climbing path, well hidden but close enough to hear any movement. Vultan's party would pass him and return without suspecting his presence. When the descent began, Lung would be doing the listening, and Vultan would be making the noise. Machine guns, the traditional weapon of ambush, would be set up and camouflaged, then hooked to automatic devices which would activate the weapons on the far side of the path once the first round was fired. They were staggered to provide for coverage up and down the trail while allowing room for Lung to remain hidden.

He went into his tent and reported his coordinates to the aircraft carrier which would dispatch the helicopter that would take him to safety once the formula was obtained. But despite his overcoming the loss of his men, and the ease with which he had set up camp, Major Lung could not avoid the feeling that he was in trouble.

Chapter Twenty-nine

Above the Bluff Range, west of Mount Terror and beyond the Matterhorn Berg and Clissold, rises the source of the most fierce warmth on the Southern Continent, the volcano Erebus. McHenry could understand how Peter and Hawkeland had been cruelly deceived. Moving hopelessly across the worst region on earth, in the cruelest weather known to man, they had had to believe that what beckoned them was the warmth of another man's fire, not the sputum of a volcano.

Simon studied the cone through his glasses, then remarked to Vultan that the mountain seemed clear of snow and ice. "Is that because of the heat?"

"No, Mr. McHenry, because of the wind. When the wind shifts at that altitude, it takes only hours to cover even Erebus in three feet of snow. Don't be disappointed; the footing will be cruel enough when we assault the top."

"When will that be?"

"In about three days. Tomorrow is the easy part."

The initial ascent was reminiscent of the field passage which begins any major climb in Europe; but in place of weeds and wildflowers, the four passed through fresh snow. It had fallen and frozen firmly. The passage was not difficult. At the end of a long day's climb they were nearly two-fifths of the way to the top. Bresnau and Elspeth made camp while the other men cached a supply of food and distilled water in a small cairn which they marked with a phosphorescent orange flag. When they entered the tent, Bresnau had prepared a meal of tinned beef, vitamin cookies, strong tea, and sugar. Like every other meal they had eaten on the ice, it had been planned and packaged before the expedition began. That was Vultan's way. Each pack was equally loaded and properly arranged; each member had a task and could replace at least one other marcher; each step was planned. They knew that they would need that organization when they began the ascent of the volcano's face.

Vultan led the way, followed by Elspeth, Bresnau, John, and McHenry. There were still some paths, and support could be found in an occasional outcropping of rock. The difficulty came from the exceedingly strong winds which threatened to lift them from the wall of ice and throw them down onto the snow fields below. They once again encountered the problem of perspiration at the South Pole as the climb depleted their strength and coated their bodies with a hot, sweaty itching which could not be relieved. By four o'clock they had scaled another one-third of the mountain. Vultan called a rest.

After the death of Matthew and the loss of the last sledge, Vultan had divided the necessary supplies and equipment among the five remaining members of the party. One concession to their limited strength was the decision to carry only one tent. Their one concession to Elspeth was that they waited outside while she changed out of her marching clothes before the evening meal. None of the men made any attempt to look into the tent, nor was any comment made until she said that she was ready.

"*Dea incessu patuit,*'" McHenry said before they entered.

"What's that?" asked Bresnau.

"Something the Jesuits taught me, something I'd thought I'd forgotten. 'And she revealed herself to be a goddess.'"

Vultan said nothing, but thought of his love for Katherine. He decided to do something in Katherine's name for Simon and Elspeth. There was, he knew, sufficient reason.

Vultan led the way to the top of the volcano. He crawled up the frozen face of Erebus until he could wedge his body against the stone and ice. He drove in a piton, attached a clamp, and passed through the rope. Elspeth followed quickly and efficiently. McHenry, John, and Bresnau concluded the line. After a short break at eleven, Simon replaced Vultan in the lead. He worked the mountain smoothly and quickly for two hours, then he saw the first properly positioned outcropping. He signaled to Vultan, who responded that he too had seen it and to go ahead. McHenry removed a coiled rope from his shoulder and hurled it toward the outcropping. The line held, and Simon began to work it down and back to the wall of the mountain. When he was certain that it would hold, he quickly scaled the stone face of Erebus until he reached the outcropping. Once in position, he lowered a nylon bucket seat to Elspeth and attached the necessary lines and pulleys. Their expert use of the chair brought them to their final stopping place that night.

"In the morning," Vultan said, "we will begin the final assault. We must all rest as well as possible." He nodded to John and Bresnau, who stepped outside the tent. "Did you know," Vultan said, "that during the course of our marriage my wife and I had many, many violent quarrels. Oh, yes. We did. It was the natural, the inevitable consequence of confining two such independent spirits in a marriage. But our marriage survived. In part because we had a habit: no matter how strained things were between us, we always said good night. It often led to the, ahh, well, the resolution of things."

Vultan remained seated, saying nothing more. After a moment McHenry said, "Good night, Elspeth." It was followed instantly by her "Good night, Simon." They went to their separate bedrolls and turned down the lamps. Vultan was pleased. He knew that he had not effected a reconciliation, but he had forced two people who were in love to recognize the inevitability and desirability of that love. It was one of the rare moments since Katherine's death in which he had been able to recapture some of the feeling she had given him. And he was happy to share it with Simon and Elspeth. He did not want them filled with hate for one another. It was much more desirable that they admit and cherish their feelings. Vultan wanted them to have at least that much when he killed them.

There were no more outcroppings, no other footpaths, no easy toeholds. Now they made their way by inches. McHenry went first, literally dragging his body up the jagged face of Erebus. He clawed with his fingers, hugged with his knees, pushed with his shoulders until he gouged out a slit. Once he had torn that fraction of an inch from the mountain, he worked on the incision until a piton could be placed against it, then driven into the volcano. His balance was precarious, his strength ebbing, his blows weak. He needed the portable oxygen bottle, but there was no way to hold it and work the mountain. The temperature was eighty-seven degrees below zero Fahrenheit, with a wind of twenty-eight knots. If his flesh became exposed, it would freeze in thirty seconds.

When he could work no longer, he signaled Bresnau to come ahead. The other man replaced him on point and continued to fill the face of the wall with pitons. Elspeth carried the pack of the man working the mountain. At the bottom of the line, Vultan and John added pitons to ease their descent. No one looked down, or spoke, or really thought. They did exactly what Vultan had told them to do. By late afternoon they reached a plateau, a table set naturally beneath a curved opening in the mountain, and established their final camp.

They were two hundred feet from the top. Each of them knew that Erebus was active, but did not think about it. The volcano posed no threat to their camp, which was set almost inside the natural curvature of the mountain. The constant stream of smoke emitted by Erebus did not warn of an impending lava flow. The noxious odors of the volcano were overcome by the oxygen they carried.

After they had eaten, McHenry stood by the tent flap which they had lowered over the face of their camp. He was thinking vaguely of an overture to be made to Elspeth. Vaguely, because the antic pattern of the mists held him so. The snow and steam and cold combined to cause odd shapes to appear and vanish in the haze. Even the land moss seemed to be shifting, with each new burst of wind appearing to re-arrange the mountainside. It took several minutes before he allowed himself to believe that one shape was impervious to the weather. He first thought that it was a rock formation, then thought that it might be an optical illusion, and only reluctantly admitted that it was a cairn. When he called the others to his side, they were silent, except for Vultan, who said, "Sometimes a man is allowed to be lucky."

The cairn was across a short chasm and above them, near the top of the volcano. Because the chasm ran from the lip of Erebus down to their camp, it would be necessary to work across the opening, then climb to the gravesite. Despite the excitement which they felt at McHenry's discovery, they knew that it was too late in the day for them to attempt the climb. They would wait for morning.

The first step was to rig a lifeline across the abyss. It was nailed into rock formations on the camp side, and McHenry carried it to the other side by inching his way out, nailing in a length of rope and attaching a pulley. As each short section was secured, he moved farther, pressing himself against the mountain wall, hanging from the line, and chiseling out a toehold. He stepped into the new footing, strung more rope, mounted pulleys, and looped connecting lines through them. When he reached the far side, he nailed in a second lifeline and set up a turnaround wheel so that they could hoist one another across the chasm.

The greatest danger, Vultan told him, was not the climb. That was hazardous enough, but it would be nothing new for McHenry. The true danger, he said, was digging into the cairn. All of Antarctica was constantly shifting. Erebus, because of its extraordinary internal heat, was melting from within while new layers were always being added on the surface. The base of the cairn could be practically nonexistent, with only the volcano beneath. If they lost their footing and fell into the volcano, the only hope for survival was if they landed on one of the lava rock ledges which ringed the upper interior of the mountain. These ledges ran at angles, like mine shafts, throughout the upper portions of the volcano. Directly beneath these ledges was the molten center of the volcano. Because of the semi-liquid consistency of the burning lava, and a man's natural buoyancy, it was possible that a man could fall into the volcano and thrash madly about for several minutes before the white-hot stones eventually seared off his flesh.

As Vultan had predicted, the climb was no more dangerous than the rest of the ascent. Pulling back the rocks would prove more difficult. The constant shifting of the winds had prevented a permanent covering of the cairn, but the incessant cold had crystallized the stones into a unit. McHenry signaled for Bresnau, and once he was across the two men began to remove the cover of the gravesite.

Several hours later they were finished. Bresnau nodded, and McHenry reached down to remove the rocks around Hawkeland's face. They gasped, looked away, then back at the excavation. The cold had mummified the body. Sir Basil Hawkeland looked exactly as he had at the moment of death.

They reached down for the body. But it moved away from them. The landfill beneath the snow quickly shifted and the corpse and rocks dropped more rapidly. McHenry and Bresnau felt a painful pulling at their waists; the lifelines were holding them up and preventing them from reaching the body. Their weight had disturbed the balance of the cairn on the plateau. They were suspended in mid-air, and Sir Basil Hawkeland was inside Mount Erebus.

Chapter Thirty

McHenry and Bresnau rigged a descent bar, securing its base to a rock plateau beneath the lip of the mountain. In this way they could climb Erebus and descend into the volcano without fearing that the volcanic rock would break under their weight, sending them down into the lava. Elspeth worked the rigging, playing the twin lines for a proper descent. Vultan waited at the mouth of Erebus, prepared to raise them quickly if they began to fall. The two men wore oxygen tanks and gas masks to combat the poisonous fumes of the volcano.

Bresnau insisted on making the first descent. He scaled the short distance to the summit, then stopped and studied the interior. When McHenry joined him, he pointed to an ash ledge on their far left. Hawkeland had fallen onto it, his legs beneath a few of the loose stones of the cairn. It was approximately one hundred feet down to the ledge. They would have to descend in a straight line, then swing over to the outcropping. Any other plan would have required them to re-rig the descent bar, and they did not know how long it would be before Erebus claimed the remains of Sir Basil Hawkeland, and his secret.

Jumping out, Bresnau rappeled down into the volcano. He hit the interior wall, bounded out, and rappeled again. He continued to descend toward the level of the plateau where Hawkeland's body rested. Once at that point, he pumped his legs to move himself toward the shelf, where he would await McHenry. As he touched the rock ledge, it fell away beneath him. Off balance, he took his right hand from the rope and clutched frantically at the disappearing ledge, then plummeted down, twisting in his rope. He hung upside down over the fiery lava pit as McHenry came down the rope.

Simon stopped several feet above Bresnau's body, looped the hanging portion of his rope between his legs, and cautiously began to lower himself toward the other man. When he was completely bent over at the waist, he was able to reach out. Bresnau pulled himself up enough to reach between his legs for McHenry's outstretched hand. They strained toward one another, touched, then meshed their fingers into one another's palms. Bresnau nodded vigorously, and Simon knew that he was ready to be pulled up. McHenry looked over his shoulder and could see the half-hidden form of Vultan prepared to drag them both to the surface.

Simon grasped Bresnau's hand firmly. He felt Vultan begin to lift them. Bresnau turned slowly, gracefully twisting until his body was erect. As they started up, Bresnau thought only of the incredible fire below, and the heat which his own body was already generating. Heat which caused his palms to sweat, and his glove to come off in McHenry's hand.

Bresnau somersaulted down into the lava, landing on his back. His legs fell away beneath him, and he twisted violently, attempting to will himself up into McHenry's hands. His clothing burned away, then his hair and skin. Thrashing in the boiling, bubbling sea of burning rock, he cocked his head back, trying to buy every second, no matter how tortured. The steaming lava burned away his face mask, entered his breathing hose, and was sucked into his mask. The sparks flashed down his tube and ignited the oxygen which entered his mouth and throat as a stream of fire. His body was ignited from within. Flames ate out through his flesh and disintegrated him.

McHenry looked away at the end. He knew what would happen to Bresnau and that the sight would sicken him. And he knew that the slightest inhalation of the stench of body waste would cause him to vomit, and then strangle on the oxygen line. When he finally opened his eyes, it was to look up. He raised his arm and pointed it toward the ledge. He would try to reach Hawkeland. Vultan understood.

Simon pumped his legs back and forth, gently increasing his arc until he was moving in ever-widening swings toward the ledge. As he came close, he hooked the rope through one arm and around his back, using his free hand to take a pick from his utility belt. On his last swing, he threw out the arm with the pick, driving it into the plateau and simultaneously hooking his free elbow onto the ledge. The rock beneath his arm began to crumble immediately, but the pick remained inside the harder inner surface area. He pulled himself up, feeling the outer area crumble away as he scrambled to where Hawkeland's body lay.

McHenry knew that he should search the corpse for the formula and make his escape. But he had read too much about Sir Basil Hawkeland and come to know him too well to leave him inside the inferno Erebus. Like another, earlier heathen, he was determined to properly bury the man. He quickly looped a rope around the body, secured it, and tied it to his own line. Looking up, he could see Vultan signaling him to go ahead. He hooked his rope into place, raised his arm, and placed his free hand around Hawkeland's corpse. As he rose into the air, he began to lose consciousness. He realized that the poisonous fumes of the volcano had become too potent for the purifying charcoal in his gas mask. He realized that he would soon lose consciousness.

Vultan hoisted desperately, knowing that two dead weights could not be lifted. He saw McHenry twist the line around his waist, giving him a tighter grip on Hawkeland's corpse. Vultan knew that McHenry was fighting to stay awake long enough to break the surface. He did not think that Simon realized that the lines had fouled. McHenry was trapped only a few feet from the surface.

Simon felt himself rise, then stop as the rope knotted. He moved slowly, barely able to suck in enough air to stay even semi-conscious. He realized he was near the mouth of Erebus. Vultan was moving frantically above him, apparently attempting to unfoul a line. As he hung motionless, Simon took out his pick and reached up to the mouth. He wanted to cleave it into the stone, giving himself the support needed to stay in place while Vultan worked the ropes.

All he remembered was feebly waving the pick in mid-air. It left his hand. He began to slip.

351

Chapter Thirty-one

Feng landed the two-seat jet fighter on the deck of the aircraft carrier and sat still while Kiying climbed out of the plane. He joined him on the deck, and they walked with the flight crew to the helipad. The ship had originally taken up its position to receive word from Lung when he was ready to be retrieved from the ice. It had often served on secret missions. As a result, the officers were not surprised when ordered to land a fighter and arrange the transfer to a jet helicopter. The entire crew knew enough to carry out its assignment without question. The two intelligence officers were cleared for take-off from the helipad five minutes after landing.

"I'll take the controls," Kiying said as they buckled themselves into their seats. "Unless there's something I don't know about this craft."

"No, sir. You are certified for this type. The only modification is the heat strut assembly. We can stand on the ice for thirty minutes with the heat struts operating. After that, the ice melted by the struts will form too deep a pool and freeze around the blades."

"I understand." Kiying lifted them expertly from the helipad, guided the craft smoothly out over the water, and made for Erebus. "The deck crew had Lung's position?"

"Yes, sir." Feng took out an envelope which had been handed to him on the flight deck. He opened it and read Lung's location.

"I'll put down about a thousand yards away. I don't think he'll hear us." Kiying turned his head. "Or is that too far to walk in these conditions?"

"No, sir. The weather is supposed to close in, but we should be in and out before then."

"Good."

"Sir?"

"Yes?"

"If Lung does not yet have the formula . . ."

352

"He almost certainly does not. He'd have radioed for a helicopter if he had it."

"Then we are to go after the Vultan party? Once I attend to Lung?"

"No."

"But the formula . . ."

"I have another source."

"And if it is not successful?"

"Then it is not."

Feng nodded. He knew that his pride should have been wounded because he did not know of the other source; but he realized that Kiying always prepared for every contingency, and that the second agent was also probably unaware of yet a third man. Or woman.

Chapter Thirty-two

Elspeth nodded to Vultan when she heard Simon moan.

"Ahh, Mr. McHenry," Vultan said as he walked to Simon's sleeping bag. He sat down, placed one hand beneath McHenry's head, and raised him. A mug of tea was in the other hand. McHenry took it and sipped gently. "You don't seem to be dead."

"It's much too cold for that."

"So, you not only know of my destiny, you expect to share it."

"What happened?"

"The volcanic fumes were too powerful for your gas mask. You started to go under, if you'll forgive the expression. You did, however, have sufficient presence of mind to make a last thrashing attempt to pull yourself up by thrusting your pick into the air. Elspeth grabbed it, giving me enough time to take your wrist."

Simon looked across the shelter floor at Elspeth. Neither one needed to speak. He finally nodded and asked, "Were you cut?"

"No. Thank you for worrying. I took the underside of the blade." She nodded at her utility belt. He saw the pick. "I think I'll keep it."

"Of course." He turned to Vultan. "And Hawkeland?"

"A noble gesture indeed." Vultan extended his arm to the rear of the shelter. Hawkeland's body sat erect against the stone wall. Simon stood, waited a moment to be certain of his balance, then walked to Sir Basil's corpse. John stood mute guard beside it. Simon was still stunned by the perfect composition of the body. He put his fingers to the dead soldier's lips and said, "I know you."

"Mr. McHenry," Vultan said, "you know the poor fellow because you've read the diary. So you also know more than I do about the code. These papers"—McHenry turned and saw several sheets spread on a folding table placed beside a lamp—"were in a tube in Hawkeland's coat. Does that comport with what you know?"

"It does." Simon walked to Vultan.

"Then will you explain the code to me?"

"No."

"I am the commander of this mission."

"You are also Langley's asset. Too many people don't like me. If I give you the key, you may kill me. Under orders, of course. I know that it would appall you to do so. But I would be just as dead."

"So you will decode the message, destroy the original, and require me to take you home."

"Safely."

"Safely. Of course. Although you may not want to destroy the original. Whatever you may think of Langley, its computers are quite good at this sort of thing."

"So am I."

"But not as good as I, Mr. McHenry. I know enough about letter frequency to realize that certain letters which are almost necessary to a transmission are virtually nonexistent in this sequence."

"Yes. Challenging, isn't it?"

"Then you do know the key."

"I think so."

Vultan stepped back and turned up the light beside the small folding table. McHenry put down his mug of tea, seated himself, looked at the first four letters, and smiled. He knew the code.

LFMC
GT EPA TLFA RV RSQ DRQM CQAAEGTC G PLM KAAT BPLQCAM
ZGEP EPA RKDGCLEGRT RV BSQGTC EPA EAQQGKDA GTVABEGRT
ZPGBP LVVDGBEAM EPA AFUAQRQ LT GTVABEGRT KQRSCPE
LKRSE EPQRSCP FRQLD DGBATBA PA MGAM KAVRQA G BRSDM
DALQT ATRSCD ER PADU PGF KSE EPA LFRQLD TLESQA RV

BRSQE DGVA MGBELEAM EPLE G BRTEGTSA EPA ZRQO

G PLM LEEAFUEAM ER BQALEA L URSDEGBA ER MQLZ EPA
GTVABEGRT VQRF EPA KDRRM G EQGAM
GTTPFAQLKDA VRQFSDLA MQLZGTC SURT EPA VRDODRQA ZPGBP
PLM RVEAT UQSMSBAM UQLBEGBLD FAMGBGTA CATAQLD FAMGBLD
OTRZDAMCA LTM EPA PRUA RV BRFKGTGTC EPA EZR

LVEAQ MABLMA SURT MABLMA RV ZRQO G OTAZ EPLE G PLM DALQTAM
L EQSEP CQALEAQ EPLT EPLE ZPGBP PLM KAAT EPA RQGCGTLD
CRLD G PLM VRSTM L FAEPRM RV BPLTCGTC
BRFFRT FLEEAQ GTER RGD G BRFFSTGBLEAM ZPLE G OTAZ ER QRFA
QAESQT ZRQM ERDM FA EPLE L BRTELBE ZRSDM KA FLMA GT
EPA GTEAQGF G BRTEGTSAM ER ZRQO

EPA RQGCGTLD VGQA UQRMSBGTC ZRQO PLM KAAT MRTA LE EPA
QALQALE TALQ EPA CSDV RV UR PLG LT LQAL RV QGBP DLTM
LTM LKSTMLTE FLQGTA UDLTE DGVA G OTRZ TRZ EPLE TAGEPAQ
KQRSCPE LKRSE EPA GTGEGLD CRRM VRQESTA L QRBO VRQFLEGRT
MGM GE

EPA GTEAQGGRQ RV EPA CSDV ZGDD KA VRSTM GT EPA FLGT
ER KA RV L DLQCA GTEAQFRTELTA MAAY ZGEP QRBO RV EPA
UAQFGLT LCA LTM RV KRSTMAM LTM VRDMAM QRBO EPA FLQO RV
LT A Z VLSDE

G MGM LCLGT LE BRSQE EPA ZRQO ZPGBP PLM
KAAT VQSGEVSD LE UR PLG EPA FLEAQGLD GTBDSMAM
TREPGTC FLQGTA KSE GE BRSDM KSQT EPA STGURQF
ADAFATE PLM FR KA EPA QRBO VQRF ZPGBP KREP PLM
KAAT ELOAT. ZPLE G PLM EPRSCPE L VRQFSDL URQ
QATMAQGTC RGD VQRF MGQE PLM KAAT QLEPAQ UQRRU
EPLE RGD BRSDM KA VRSTM GT REPAQ EPLT FLQGTA
FLEAQGLD

G MGM TRE BRTBOSMA ZGEP EPLE G BRSDM
TRE G TRZ DALQTAM EPLE EPA BQSMA RGD VQRF ELBPGTC
ZPLE KSQTAM MRZN UQRMSBAM LT LQFRA DGOA QSKKAQ
CSQTGTI KSE EPA BQSMA KQRSCPE ER FA VQRF ELQOF
LTM DLQLFLG KSQTAM MGBPE EPA MGVVAQATBA BRSDM
KA VRSTM GT EPA ZAGCPE RV
EPA RGD EPA DGCPE BRSDM
KA KSQTAM ZGEPRSE KLM AVVABE EPA REPAQ BRSDM TRE.

LVEAQ L FRTEP RV VSQEPAQ ZRQD G
VRSTM EPLE EPA GTEQRQMSBEGRT RV L BPAFGBLD PLM
VRQBAM EPA MLQD BQSMA ER KSQT MRZT DGCPE GE

PLYYATAM LE TGCPE ZPAT G VADE VLEGCSAM G MGM TRE
TREA ZPGBP BPAFGBLD G PAM GTEQRMSBAM RQ EPA LFRSTE
G ZRQDAM VQRF EPLE FRFATE ER MSUDGBLEA EPA BRSU
ZGEPRSE DSBO

G BRTEGTSA ER ZRQO LTM PRUA ER ATM EPA
QGMMDE RV EPA QAMSBEGRT RV MCQO BQSMA ER DGCPE
KAVRQA EPA BRTELBE VQRP QRFA G RZA BRTEGTSAM
ZRAK ER EPA BPSQBP LTM ER EPA FLTBPS
ZPR

McHenry asked for a cigarette and more tea.

"Well," Vultan said, "do you understand it?"

"Of course. As would any student of the Jesuits."

The Society of Jesus was founded in 1541 as the personal spiritual army of Pope Paul III. Created to counteract what the Church perceived as the excesses of the Reformation, it was meant, like any army, to be deployed quickly, to adapt to local conditions, and to create successful tactics for winning the world back to Catholicism. Like any army, it served under a general.

At the time that Father Fresnais had written the message which had been cached in Hawkeland's grave, the Society had served under twenty-four superiors general. There were far too many characters in Chinese for the number of priests to be the key. English consisted of a twenty-six-letter alphabet. Allowing for the slight variation between the number of generals and the number of letters in the alphabet, the key fit. Latin, of course, was the obvious choice for a Jesuit, so McHenry discarded it. French was the shared tongue of Fresnais and de Chardin, but the former had reason to believe that the latter would soon switch to English. The Jesuits were sending more and more of their French seminarians from the house at Laval to a facility in the Channel Islands, at Jersey. Fresnais had been home in time to see the growing anti-clericalism in France, and correctly anticipated that de Chardin would soon acquire, and use greatly, a knowledge of English. McHenry decided to break the code into English plaintext.

De Chardin's superiors had feared him from his earliest days in the Society. Afraid to release him, hoping to channel his brilliance into the work of the Jesuits (which was all that he desired), his superiors did not turn him out. Instead, they restricted him to as great an extent as they believed he would tolerate. One of the ways in which they did this was to censor his correspondence, thereby thwarting his use of letters. He had told this to Fresnais, and had also informed him that he would be obedient. But he would not stop. He would go forward to the next letter. Or he would realize an error and go back to the preceding letter. His correspondence had explained it all.

The code was simplicity itself. To a Jesuit.

The letter A became L, because that letter was the initial of the last name of the first Superior General of the Jesuits, Saint Ignatius Loyola. B became K. The second superior was Jacob Lainez, but L had been used, so Fresnais went back one letter. C became B, for Saint Francis Borgia. D converted to M, for Edward Mercurian. E was A, for Claudio Aquaviva. F became V, for Mutius Vitelleschi. G was C, for Vincent Carrafa. Francis Piccolomini gave his initial for H. The initial of Alexander Gottifredi substituted for I. The J converted to the N of Goswinus Nickel. Then K from Paul Oliva and L from Charles de Noyelle.

The next Superior General was Thyrsus Gonzalez. The G had been converted from Gottifredi, the ninth superior; so Fresnais took the preceding letter, F. Michael Tamburini gave his initial for the N, and O was represented by the R of Francis Retz. The sixteenth superior was Ignatius Visconti; the V, however, had been represented by Father Vittelleschi. Fresnais, therefore, moved to the letter U.

The English letter Q did not convert to code. The numerically analogous superior was Aloysius Centurione. C, however, had been used; as had the preceding B and the succeeding D. Any other choice would have broken the integrity of the code.

The letter R took the Q in code. The corresponding priest was Laurence Ricci, but Retz had been used for the R. Fresnais had gone backward for his substitute.

The next priest was Thaddeus Brzozowski. His initial, like the letters on either side of it, had been used. McHenry was forced to conclude that the S had been omitted from the plaintext. That would make for a more stilted message, one more difficult to translate; but he was certain that Fresnais would not break the structure of the code.

The letter T converted to E. The appropriate priest was Aloysius Fortis. F had been used (as a substitute for the G in Gonzalez). By moving forward, Fresnais chose E.

U became S. The priest's name which matched was I. P. Roothaan. R had been used for Retz, and Ricci had been given the preceding alternative, Q. The subsequent choice was S.

The letter V did not translate. The appropriate priest was Peter Beckx; but B had been used, as had A and C.

Z was used for W. The priest's name was Anthony Anderledy. A had been used, as had B. But knowledge, the Jesuits teach, is a continuum. A slight sophistic turn put Z before A.

The last priest was Ludovicus Martin. M, however, had been used, as had the letters which bracketed it. Therefore, his corresponding letter, X, could not be used.

There were two more letters than superiors, and, as logic dictated, they were the last letters, Y and Z, and so not used.

In the code, all letters were available as symbols except for H, I, J, W, and X. In plaintext, all letters were available but S, Q, V, X, Y, and Z.

McHenry knew that he was correct when he saw the heading of the message. Every piece of Jesuit correspondence begins with the letters A.M.D.G. They represent the Society's motto: *Ad majorem Dei gloriam*—to the greater glory of God. Fresnais had trained himself to think in his code. He had headed the letter with the legend L.F.M.C. After that, the code fell quickly into place.

> In the name of our Lord, Greeting.
> I had been charged with the obligation of curing the terrible infection which afflicted the Emperor, an infection brought about through moral license. He died before I could learn enough to help him. But the amoral nature of court life dictated that I continue the work.
> I had attempted to create a poultice to draw the infection from the blood. I tried innumerable formulae, drawing upon the folklore which had often produced practical medicine, general medical knowledge, and the hope of combining the two.
> After decade upon decade of work, I knew that I had learned a truth greater than that which had been the original goal. I had found a method of changing common matter into oil. I communicated what I knew to Rome. Return word told me that a contact would be made. In the interim, I continued to work.
> The original fire-producing work had been done at the retreat near the Gulf of Po Hai, an area of rich land and abundant marine plant life. I know now that neither brought about the initial good fortune. A rock formation did it.
> The interior of the Gulf will be found, in the main, to be of a large intermontane deep, with rock of the Permian age; and of bounded and folded rock, the mark of an E-W fault.
> I did again at court the work which had been fruitful at Po Hai. The material included nothing marine. But it could burn. The uniform element had to be the rock from which both had been taken. What I had thought a formula for rendering oil from dirt had been rather proof that oil could be found in other than marine material.

I did not conclude with that. I could not. I now learned that the crude oil from Taching, when burned down, produced an aroma like rubber burning. But the crude brought to me from Tarim and Karamai burned light. The difference could be found in the weight of the oil. The light could be burned without bad effect. The other could not.

After a month of further work I found that the introduction of a chemical had forced the dark crude to burn down light. It happened at night, when I felt fatigued. I did not note which chemical I had introduced or the amount. I worked from that moment to duplicate the coup. Without luck.

I continue to work and hope to end the riddle of the reduction of dark crude to light before the contact from Rome. I owe continued work to the Church and to the Manchu who

McHenry lit another cigarette, inhaled, and reflected on the message, all the while keeping his eyes on the papers before him. He did not want Vultan to know that he was done with the conversion into plaintext. But not done with the message. He thought back to Peter's diary and remembered part of his meeting with Fresnais.

"Then you must give it to me," Peter had said of the formula.

"There is something that I must tell you."

"Something not on the paper?"

"No, it is there; but I must explain."

Peter, of course, had not let him explain; and McHenry, like the Painter, had failed to realize that the priest was about to say that his work was not finished. Not then. McHenry, however, was certain that Fresnais had continued his experiments. A man who could discover that petroleum was available from non-marine sources when no one else in the world knew it, and considered it merely a step forward, such a man would not have stopped because in a moment of weakness he had failed to record one element. The essential element, to be sure, but only one. That the priest had gone on, McHenry did not doubt.

What troubled him was the reference to the Manchu. Certainly no priest could have admired the Old Buddha or court life; although a Jesuit would recognize the debt his Society owed to the dynasty for the honors and concessions it had heaped on the order. And a Jesuit, knowing that the diary might be captured, and that the code might be extracted, could have put the reference in to assure the Manchu that experimentation would continue as long as they ruled. That rule ended fifteen years after Fresnais passed the diary to Peter. One step remaining, and more than a decade to recreate it. Yes, there was a formula.

359

McHenry knew it. A formula for converting ten billion barrels of heavy, waxy crude oil from the northeastern fields of China, converting it to the light crude so desperately needed by the West. And, McHenry knew, to make that conversion by laboratory procedure rather than by catalytic cracking could assure a supply of industrially usable oil such as the world had never known.

But the priest did know that there would be a formula. McHenry could only assume that it was still inside China—and certainly unknown to the Chinese, with their limited petroleum industry. Simon would take what he knew back to Langley. The missing information would keep him alive. Only he knew the code, and someday it would be used to convert the formula. When it was at last discovered.

Vultan asked, "Are you finished?"

"Yes."

"Have you broken the code?"

"I have."

"Then what does it say? Tell us, man! Tell us!"

There was a rush of wind as the shelter flap blew open. "Yes, Mr. McHenry," Sharp said. "Do tell us."

Simon froze in place. Vultan thought of moving, then recalled all that he had been told about Sharp in briefing. He too remained still. Elspeth moved slightly, more from fear than a desire to come forward. John had not moved from beside Hawkeland's corpse. Sharp motioned for them both to walk to the side of the shelter. McHenry was isolated, but there was no chance yet at even a desperate effort.

Sharp fired once, blowing off the top of the Indian's head. Elspeth screamed.

"Be silent." Sharp waved the rifle slightly toward her, but did nothing else. He was certain that she was unarmed.

"You have no need to hurt her," McHenry said.

"How loyal. How touching. But you needn't worry. I won't hurt her. All the things I'd planned to do, I won't. It wouldn't be any fun, you see, if you weren't here to witness my raping and torturing her. And I can't have you alive while I'm at my sport. I remember you as being very quick."

"And me?" Vultan asked. "I am an American asset."

"Yes," Sharp said. "You were. And they regret how you've come apart." The first round hit Vultan with such force that it lifted him from the ground and slammed him against the ice wall. The body had risen so quickly that the second bullet, also aimed at stomach level, entered the right kneecap, severing it in two. Vultan twisted once against the wall, slid to the floor, and died.

"I did him a favor," Sharp announced. "He can go back to his missus now."

McHenry said, "Nothing that quick for me, I suppose."

"No, Mr. McHenry, nothing that quick. One shell in the right arm. The elbow if I can angle it right. One in the left. Then the right kneecap, followed by the left. Then I put down the rifle and use the pistol for a belly shot. A strong man like you ought to last four, five minutes." He smiled. "Slow minutes."

"By all means make it last. When's the next time you'll have an erection?"

Sharp lifted the rifle and aimed, then stopped, thought for a moment, and lowered the weapon. "No, Mr. McHenry. You don't do that; you don't trick me into letting you die quickly. And no requests for a cigarette, or a moment of prayer, or a kiss from the girl. Nothing that gives you any chance at all. Just me and the rifle."

"Do you expect me to beg?"

"No, Mr. McHenry," Sharp said. "I expect you to die." He raised the rifle. Elspeth screamed as the bullet shattered McHenry's right arm, sending him down against the wall of the cave. She screamed again. "Shut up!" Sharp said, and turned back to McHenry.

Sharp looked briefly at Elspeth and laughed. The occasion was comfortable now. He was at leisure to destroy McHenry. There was Dole, of course, and his insistence on the formula; but that was later. There were always acceptable reasons for incomplete success. Not failure at all, but incomplete success. The Indian was disposed of, preventing any later testimony. Vultan was dead, which would delight the Americans. And Sharp would return the girl, who was now hysterical and no threat. He turned back to Simon and aimed at his left elbow.

Elspeth calmly drove the mountaineering pick deep into Sharp's skull. The butcher turned and began to stumble forward, one hand reaching for the rapidly falling rifle stock and one hand grasping the steel nail which was imbedded in the top of his head. He jerked both hands up, pulling desperately at the steel axe. His efforts succeeded only in ripping out his scalp and ear. Blood poured down in an endless gush, covering what was left of his face. He drew the axe around into his line of sight, then fell forward, driving his nose down onto the deadly blade.

Elspeth ran to Simon and embraced him. In seconds she would stop his bleeding, dress his wound, and radio for the Indians to come for them. At that moment, however, nothing needed to be said.

Chapter Thirty-three

Marshal Kiying brought the helicopter down within a thousand yards of Lung's reported position. Feng leaped out and secured the hatch. The weather had not yet degenerated into the horrible anvil of wind and ice it would soon become. As a result, Feng took only minutes to cross the powdery field to Lung's shelter. When Lung saw him pull back the flaps, he was first speechless, then terrified. Feng would not come to help, or to lead reinforcements. Colonel Feng could have only one mission.

The Jesuit leveled his pistol at Lung, and said, "The Holy Father knows who you are, and why you are here."

Lung nodded his head. He was no longer afraid. To die for failing Kiying was to waste his life. To die for his divine mission was to gain all.

"Our Holy Father," Feng said, "has commanded me to tell you that he knows you acted out of an erroneous conscience. As a result, there is no sin. He commands that I impart to you his benediction and a plenary indulgence remitting all spiritual punishment for the transgressions of your past life. He commands that I ask you to pray for him this day when you are in Paradise. And, finally, our Holy Father commands that I kill you."

Which he did.

The Jesuit walked to the young priest's body, knelt, and, as he had done all too often in his life, traced the Sign of the Cross on a victim's forehead, kissed the place that he had touched, and whispered, *"Requiescat in pace. Benedicat tu, in nomine Patri, et Filii, et Spiritui Sancti. Amen."*

"I am sorry," Kiying said.

Feng started, then rose slowly, his pistol at his side. "May I turn around?"

"I would not shoot you in the back."

As he turned, he saw Kiying's pistol in his hand. They would be firing from equal positions, Feng thought, but he would have forty years on his side. "How long have you known?"

"I have known."

"If you kill me, you will never be able to retrieve the formula alone."

"There is no formula here." Kiying studied Feng's face while watching his gun hand. "I developed a prize asset. His placement was the crowning achievement of my intelligence career. Regrettably, the death of his wife caused him to become unbalanced. There was no way to arrange for his assassination without risking the entire overseas Chinese network. As a result, I put out word of the formula, used agents to place people in motion, and guaranteed that my asset would be sent here. His death by other hands was inevitable."

"All of this to kill that man?"

"No, my friend. All of this to kill you. The faltering asset and Major Lung were merely background. Because of them, you asked for this mission to Antarctica and, in your own handwriting, made all of the necessary arrangements. Tragically, the mission was your last. As you said, my presence gives me unique control over the final story."

"Why now?"

"Because I have allowed you to become too close. You must believe that to be true. In time, you would have slipped. Or you would have incurred an enemy's anger, and revealed the fact of your priesthood under torture. To have had a Jesuit on my staff would mean my execution as well."

"So, in the end, you are only an agent who kills to stay alive."

"Oh, no, my friend. I am much more. From the first day that I joined Mao, every success enjoyed by my superiors has been due to me. Every scrap of information, every operation, has been because I am the supreme agent. I am the beginning of all that our effort has been. I am the continuum. What I do is justified by what I am."

"And there was never a formula."

"I said that there was no formula here. What everyone seeks is safely hidden in Peking."

"How could you . . . ?" Feng's voice trailed away. The enormity of his opponent's power made inquiry futile.

"You offend me, Colonel. Am I not as learned a student of China's history as you? The formula was discovered by a Jesuit. Of course you know that. Everything that he said and did was recorded in the Manchu archives. When the dynasty fell, other Jesuits said and wrote things.

The archives, and the anguished confessions of tortured priests, enabled me over the decades to learn what was in the diary. And what was not.''

"But you have done nothing with the formula."

"Now is not the time. I know that your masters in the Vatican are not evil men, but in the world of realpolitik, the world in which I make my way, they are children. They would use the money to end abortions, a practice which I admit is obnoxious to me. But do they think that they can succeed in America? The country will use all of the new oil, believing it, through some magic, to be an infinite resource. And the abortions will continue anyway. The Americans are too concerned with pleasure. More foolishly, they insist on morality which hobbles their public conduct, yet forbid the very morality which could strengthen their private lives.

"And does my country deserve the knowledge? The government would quickly bargain it away for a few Western industrial tricks. They too are children.

"I have been the guardian of the secret for fifty years. My perspective, my realization of man's needs and wants, these combine to make the disposition of the formula something which can be allowed only to me, no matter how compelling a motive another man may have. The world is not ready to be freed from responsibility. What our masters, yours and mine, might hope to achieve is as nothing compared to the power of the formula. I shall decide when to reveal it. Unless I choose to die with it."

"We have been friends, my enemy," Feng said.

"No man could have asked for a better son."

Both men raised their weapons and quickly fired one round. They were experienced agents, so each moved as he fired, hoping to turn the other's shot into a miss or a light wound. But one was quicker than the other, possessed of better reflexes. That one escaped harm. He stood sadly as the mortally wounded soldier fell forward, inhaled once, and felt his heart freeze forever.

The Jesuit walked to the other man's body, knelt, and, as he had done all too often in his life, traced the Sign of the Cross on a victim's forehead, kissed the place that he had touched, and whispered, *"Requiescat in pace. Benedicat tu, in nomine Patri, et Filii, et Spiritui Sancti. Amen."*

And then, his heart ravaged by all that the years had seen him do, but his intellect calmed by the knowledge that all that had been done had

364

been done for the greater glory of God, his eminence Chi Rho Cardinal Kiying, Prince of the Church, servant of the servants of Christ, archbishop of Peking, and, most importantly, Superior General of the China Province of the Society of Jesus, rose and turned, and walked into the mists.

ABOUT THE AUTHOR

Eugene FitzMaurice is uniquely qualified to write *The Hawkeland Cache.* He attended both a preparatory school and law school administered by Jesuits; practiced law on Wall Street; was a state counsel to President Ford in 1976; and now specializes in petroleum law.

A former reporter for both Metromedia Radio and the Philadelphia *Inquirer,* Mr. FitzMaurice drew on these experiences, as well as his career as a trial lawyer, for his first novel, *Circumstantial Evidence.*

He is married and the father of two children.